Witness Protection 3
Alpha Mike Foxtrot

Holly Copella

In loving memory of
Zack Kinsley

ACKNOWLEDGMENTS

Copella Books: First Paperback Edition 2016
Printed by CreateSpace, An Amazon.com Company
Cover Artist: DXPO

PUBLISHER'S NOTE

Chapter One

<u>*Chapter One*</u>

The mansion ballroom was filled with men and women dressed in expensive formal wear and designer evening gowns. Some of the guests socialized at the bar while others waltzed to the live orchestra. The happy bride and groom danced in the center of the crowded dance floor, unable to take their eyes off each other. The wedding reception resembled something straight out of a fairy tale. Dozens of neatly dressed waiters and waitresses carried trays of hors d'oeuvres through the crowd while others sought out the massive buffet surrounding a large ice sculpture of a bride and groom. The impressive four-foot-tall wedding cake adorned with edible pearls sat on a table near the back for all to envy.

An attractive woman in her mid-twenties danced with a handsome, distinguished gentleman in his early fifties. Jackie Falcone wore a stunning, teal evening dress, which held her curves. The thin-strapped dress allowed for maximum cleavage and a daringly high slit rode halfway up her right leg. Her long, dark hair was worn elegantly in a French twist with a sprig of baby's breath for an added touch of class. Her gentleman friend, Ross Madrid, wore a conservative black tuxedo with a gray vest and matching tie, which further accented his moderately graying full head of hair. The couple seemed comfortable dancing with each other at a respectable distance while gazing into each other's eyes. Their gaze was loving, although far from romantic.

"When you asked me to attend this wedding with you, I was a little apprehensive. You know, having to wear a dress and all," Jackie announced while grinning at her handsome date. "I'm glad I came along."

"You were my first choice of dates, my dear," Ross replied then lifted her hand and suavely kissed it.

Jackie blushed slightly at the romantic gesture and held back her grin. "Oh, Ross," she announced with a dreamy sigh. "You can certainly lay it on thick when you want something."

He chuckled softly at her honesty. "Would you believe me if I said I just want to enjoy our dance at this moment?"

She considered the question then smiled more naturally. "Actually, I would."

"You know, if I had a daughter, she'd be just like you," he announced charmingly then sank into his own fantasy. "Beautiful, smart, and a major pain in the ass."

Jackie grinned at the comment, taking it as a compliment from her fatherly friend. "Without a doubt." She casually glanced around the room, although she was looking for something in particular. "What sort of trouble do you suppose the guys are getting themselves into?"

He groaned softly. "You had to go ahead and ruin my perfect evening." Ross gently tapped his ear, containing a micro ear transmitter, and then returned his hand to Jackie's hand on his shoulder. "Guys, mother hen wants to know what sort of trouble her boys are getting into tonight."

Several grunts and groans were heard through Ross's well-hidden, ear transmitter. Ross made a face and eyed Jackie, who gently touched her own ear transmitter to listen as well.

"I'm guessing the *usual* sort of trouble," he casually replied.

†

*T*he handsome, well-built man in his late twenties suddenly grinned right before a fist struck him in the face. Bogart took the hit better than his pretty boy face suggested he would. Bogart, dressed in black combat attire, was a 'hunky' handsome man with flowing golden-brown hair and sideburns nearly a shade darker. Despite the hard hit and his bloodied lip, Bogart looked back at his assailant and offered a dimpled smirk.

"Is that the best you've got?" he demanded with a hint of arrogance.

Another fist found his face and he stumbled back a step this time. He honestly didn't know when to keep his comments to himself. To his left within the basement storage room, his partner was taking a beating alongside him. Monroe, who was also dressed in black combat attire, took a moment to glare at Bogart.

"Wisecracks only work if you have the brass balls to back them up," Monroe lashed out at Bogart.

Monroe ducked as another fist nearly found his face. He punched the estate security guard in the abdomen then, as he doubled over, Monroe followed through with an elbow to the back of the guard's neck. Monroe straightened, turned to Bogart, and arrogantly indicated the fallen man.

"See? Brass balls," Monroe announced firmly.

"You might want to--" Bogart began.

As Monroe turned, another man punched him in the groin. He clutched himself and doubled over in agony.

"--watch those brass balls," Bogart muttered while grimacing, almost feeling his pain.

Another estate security guard came at Bogart. He instinctively blocked the man's fist and punched him in the abdomen. He regained some of his earlier cockiness and attempted to flip the guard over his hip. The guard was reluctant to be thrown off his feet, surprising Bogart. Bogart cried out as the guard grabbed him by the shoulder and the thigh, picked him up in the air, and power-drove him to the floor. Bogart groaned as he writhed around on the floor then let out a slight chuckle.

"You're so going to pay for that," he gasped at the man then muttered more to himself, "How the hell does that little shit do that kung fu crap?"

Two of the four guards descended upon Monroe, who was still on his knees recovering from his groin shot. As the men stood over him, Monroe suddenly came to life and gave an uppercut shot to the first man's groin. Intensity and angle both worked simultaneously with the hard hit. The man was launched into the air and barely had time to clutch himself as he fell to the floor. Monroe bolted upward, leading with his shoulder, and rammed the second guard in the chest, casting him across the floor with his powerful hit. Monroe straightened proudly, adjusted his combat jacket, and turned to Bogart, who was now fending off his own two guards.

"It's all about angles and impact," Monroe casually informed his friend.

Monroe Dallas was a tall, lanky man in his mid-thirties, who sought a stylish flare to his wardrobe. Despite not being overly muscular, he was more powerful than most suspected. Monroe's light brown hair was neatly trimmed, although not nearly short enough to constitute a buzz cut, deeply contrasting in looks of his less than appearance conscious counterpart. Bogart was a country boy and his lack of refinement was easily noticed. Monroe looked around then down, as if suddenly realizing his counterpart was missing.

Bogart was now on the floor, taking a beating from both guards. He finally found his moment and, from his position on the floor, kicked the first man in the knee, dropping him. Bogart then pulled a hunting knife from his boot and stabbed the second man in the foot through his leather work boot. The man cried out in agony. Bogart pulled the bloodied knife free, sprang to his feet, and punched the man across the face. As the injured guard fell to the floor, Bogart turned to Monroe and grinned charmingly.

"I'm better at fighting dirty," Bogart replied.

Monroe shook his head with disapproval. "Ross specifically said no lethal force," he casually reminded.

Bogart tilted his head and grinned charmingly. "Hence 'fighting dirty'." He then frowned and turned defensive. "Besides," he announced and pointed demandingly at the guard with the bloodied knife. "Does he look dead to you?"

Monroe groaned giving up. "Let's just get these four tied up before something else goes wrong."

†

*W*ithin one of the mansion's elegant upstairs bedrooms, a man and woman collapsed to the large bed together while kissing and groping each other. The woman was in her late forties and, judging by her elegant gown, she was possibly the mother-of-the-bride. Her visit to the hairdresser that morning was ruined nearly two seconds after the couple hit the bed. Stray locks of her excessively auburn tinted hair fell from their place despite all the hairspray and bobby pins. The muscular man on top of her, at least ten years her junior, was an imposing 6'4" with broad shoulders and biceps the size of tree trunks barely hidden beneath his black waiter's uniform. His buzz cut and thick facial stubble made him look moderately intimidating, which possibly explained the woman's attraction. Kirk Mandel broke off the kiss and looked at the woman beneath him with concern while both panted.

"We're liable to ruin that dress," he insisted then grinned. "You can't return to the party looking bedraggled. Your husband and guests will be suspicious."

Before she could protest, Kirk moved off her and easily pulled her to her feet. She was slightly surprised by the concern over her dress then grinned her approval.

"Good idea," she announced then playfully pushed the hired waiter back onto the bed. "You make yourself comfortable while I slip into something more durable."

She pulled him partway up by his tie, surprising him, and kissed him aggressively on the mouth. He barely had time to return the kiss when she broke it off, pushed him back down to the bed, and headed into the bathroom. Once the door shut, Kirk sprang up from the bed and touched his mostly invisible ear transmitter.

"Guys, how much longer?" Kirk demanded in a hushed voice so his conquest wouldn't hear him. "This isn't exactly my field of expertise."

"Come now, Kirk," came a calm, reassuring voice over his ear transmitter. "Don't sell yourself short. You've been known to leave a woman satisfied every now and again."

Kirk suddenly sneered and allowed his hostility to surface. Obviously, his intimidating appearance wasn't just for show. "Don't piss me off, Gil," he snarled softly. "I'm not in the mood."

"Well, you better get in the mood," came another male voice through his ear transmitter. "You need to keep *mother* occupied another ten to twenty minutes."

Kirk threw his broad shoulders back and straightened. "Oh, so now the pretty boy needs to weigh in, huh, Beck?" Kirk demanded, losing his sense of humor. "Maybe it's time for one of you to start playing the boy toy to cougar trophy wives."

The bathroom door opened, catching his attention. Kirk tapped his ear transmitter and turned to face the mother-of-the-bride where she stood in the bathroom doorway. She had changed into a leather bodice and held a soft, sex toy whip.

"I think this is more durable," she announced then slapped the whip against her palm.

Kirk stared at her with surprise, whimpered softly, and then muttered under his breath, "Where the hell is Zack when you need him?"

Chapter Two

*T*wo men wearing black waiter uniforms stood in the dimly lit mansion study with a small penlight aimed at the wall safe behind a framed portrait. The faint sounds of the orchestra could be heard through the closed door. Beck Larue lined the right and left edges of the safe with explosives. His casual attitude regarding the explosive material gave more of an impression of a child playing with Play-Doh. Beck was in his mid-thirties, stood over six feet tall, and maintained an impressive athletic build. His light brown hair was moderately rumpled and his rugged good looks and sturdy gaze lent a perfect balance between intimidating and cuddly.

"Can you believe those two whining about their assignments? Civilian life has made Monroe and Kirk soft," Beck casually announced while shaking his head with moderate disgust for his teammates. "I remember when they used to enjoy this cloak-and-dagger bullshit."

The second man casually shrugged and showed little emotion while holding the penlight for Beck to see the edges of the safe. "They're too uptight," Gil casually remarked in his usual, unruffled tone. Gil Rafferty was a ruggedly handsome, tall, well-built man in his late thirties or possibly his early forties. His short dark hair, peppered with gray, gave him a slightly distinguished look. "Those guys don't know how to relax and go with the flow. They lack a certain maturity."

Beck stopped working and performed his best damsel in distress impersonation. He squealed and shirked defensively while holding the explosives in his hand. "Oh, a bad guy's hitting me," he cried out softly in a high-pitched voice. "Someone get my balls out of Jackie's purse."

Gil could barely hold back his laughter and nearly dropped the light. "That's a good one."

"You know we can hear you," came Jackie's stern voice through their ear transmitters.

Both men jumped with surprise and exchanged looks as well as defensive gestures. Beck forced a smile and returned to his explosives.

"Oh, good evening, Jackie," Beck announced cheerfully, resuming his polite demeanor. "Is Ross light on your feet?"

"Save it," Jackie snarled through his earpiece. "The whole team knows you two are whipped by your girlfriends, so you don't really have much room to talk."

Both men exchanged puzzled looks, shook their heads, and shrugged. Gil mouthed the word 'whipped'. Gil casually waved him off as if indicating Jackie didn't know what she was talking about. Beck finished applying the explosives and took a step back.

"We're just about ready here," Beck announced while gently clearing his throat.

Both moved away from the safe and stood behind the large, heavy wooden desk. Gil ran his hand along the expensive, elegantly carved desk, which was possibly an antique.

"Pity to ruin such a beautiful desk," Gil muttered.

Beck raised the remote in his hand and grinned. "Fire in the hole--"

Gil casually placed his hands to his ears and ducked behind the desk with Beck as he pushed the button on the remote.

✝

*W*ithin the crowded ballroom, the wealthy men and women continued to dance and socialize. Still on the dance floor, Ross suavely dipped Jackie, held her there a moment, and smiled charmingly.

"Get ready," he announced.

The explosion wasn't very loud to those within the ballroom, more like a low rumble. Although not loud, it was forceful enough to vibrate the mansion, causing the chandeliers to clatter and ceiling dust to fall to the floor. The lights suddenly went out, leaving the room mostly dark, causing everyone to cry out with alarm. Those working security within the ballroom quickly directed everyone to the nearest exit, although it was hard to see where they were going through the dim moonlight shining in from the wall of windows. Ross held Jackie back from the pushing, chattering crowd of refined people now reduced to panic induced creatures slipping into survival mode.

"Go outside and wait with the car," he announced to Jackie. "I'll make sure the guys get out."

"Maybe I should come along," she announced with concern.

"No, Jackie," he commanded in an authoritative tone, revealing his true personality. "If something happened to you, Holden would never forgive me. Just wait with the car."

She reluctantly nodded, although it was against her better judgement, and followed the herd of guests pushing and shoving their way outside. As she glanced back, she saw Ross disappear through one of the nearby side doorways into the darkened mansion.

✝

Meanwhile, within the master bedroom, a woman's loud cries of delight filled the dimly lit room. Kirk, obviously naked beneath the covers, was securely tied to the posts of the large bed while the lady of the house, dressed in her leather bodice, wildly bounced on top of him. She firmly caressed his bare, massively muscular chest. The headboard slapped the wall with a loud banging that almost matched her cries of ecstasy. Kirk pulled against his restraints in an attempt to free himself. His expression was a cross between delight and agony from the rough ride. When the house rumbled, he looked around, knowing all too well what was happening, and then looked at the woman on top of him.

"That sounded like an explosion," he gasped, although he was barely heard over her sudden desire to scream out profanities.

The bodice clad, mother-of-the bride didn't let the rumbling or his words interfere with her good time. "It's fine," she gasped nearly out of breath.

He groaned softly and allowed his head to hit the pillow beneath him. "They're going to leave me here, I know it," he muttered softly beneath her loud cries.

✝

$\mathcal{M}$onroe and Bogart stood before the fuse box within the mansion basement, which was now in complete darkness except for the small penlight between them. Bogart grinned and gave Monroe a thumbs up.

"Our mission is complete," Monroe announced giving a general nod to the fuse box. "Let's meet the others at the rendezvous."

"Before something else goes wrong," Bogart muttered while rubbing his sore jaw.

Both men hurried through the dark basement.

†

$\mathcal{A}$t the same time within the mansion study, the smoke continued to waft across the large room. Gil and Beck stood before the safe with the door torn off its hinges. They tossed large wades of cash and jewelry aside and grabbed a lone manila envelope. Beck glanced inside the envelope while Gil aimed the penlight to reveal the contents.

"Got it," Beck announced while shutting the envelope and signaled for Gil to go.

Both men hurried past the severely damaged desk with the safe door impaled through the heavy wood and headed for the study door. Beck stuffed the envelope into the inner pocket of his jacket for safekeeping. As they stepped into the dimly lit hallway, several guards saw them and pointed while shouting something neither man could hear. Gil and Beck exchanged frowns. As the guards ran toward them, both men turned and ran down the nearly dark hall. Gil touched his ear transmitter as they ran from the guards almost fifty yards behind them.

"We have the package, but we've got some company hot on our ass," Gil announced without slowing his pace in order to keep up with Beck. "We're heading for the kitchen now."

"I'm on my way," came Ross's response.

†

11

*J*ackie stood outside the mansion not far from the kitchen entrance. The rest of the guests had gathered on the front lawn as instructed. Although she couldn't see them, she could hear them ranting about the rumbling they'd heard prior to the lights going out. Jackie insecurely rubbed her bare arms while pacing in front of the rented black Mercedes. Some of the kitchen staff and caterers were now collecting on the back patio. If they had seen her on their way from the kitchen entrance to the patio, they didn't give her presence much consideration. Jackie watched several caterers on the back patio sneaking cigarettes while waiting for the announcement that they could return inside. She glanced at her watch while listening to the guys talking to one another over her hidden ear transmitter. She glanced from the kitchen door to the nearby basement door. The basement door was only fifty yards away, being almost hidden by some shrubs. She groaned softly and pulled her long hair free from the French twist.

"Come on," she muttered softly.

†

*G*il and Beck ran into the empty, dark kitchen. The caterers and wait staff had evacuated upon security's orders, leaving behind trays filled with tasty pastries. Ross waited for them to pass through the door. Gil had his small tool bag slung over his shoulder while Beck now brought up the rear. Beck scooped up a handful of puffy pastries as they passed the loaded island counter.

"Three guards right behind us," Gil announced to Ross as they ran across the kitchen.

As the first two guards came through the kitchen door, Ross raised the fire extinguisher and sprayed the white foam into the men's faces. They were startled and temporarily blinded by the white substance hitting them. The third man tripped over the first two men in the darkness. Ross grinned, tossed the extinguisher aside, and ran after his men toward the outer kitchen door. Ross slowed near the sideboard, snatched a bottle of champagne, and ran out the door.

†

*B*ogart and Monroe ran along the dimly lit basement corridor, heading in the direction of the outer basement door. Monroe reported their location to Ross through his transmitter, since they were no longer alone. Although from a distance, four guards pursued them through the darkened corridor. They reached the outer basement door and attempted to open it. It was locked!

"What the hell--?" Monroe launched while fumbling with his lock pick.

"I thought this door was unlocked," Bogart bellowed out with surprise.

"So did I."

Bogart watched the approaching men in the corridor behind them. "Here we go again," he muttered then smirked as he blocked the first fist that came at him.

The four men ganged up on Monroe and Bogart, foiling Monroe's attempt to pick the door lock. Monroe and Bogart attempted to fight the men, but they had nowhere to move to avoid all four of the mansion guards. Monroe and Bogart were punched multiple times then cast to the floor. Both sat up against the wall while bleeding and breathing heavily. Bogart glanced at Monroe as the four men stood over them.

"Well, do you have any brilliant plans?" Bogart asked almost demandingly. "If you do, by all means, share them."

"This is usually the part where Zack comes in and takes some guy's nuts off," Monroe muttered.

"Well, Zack ain't here," Bogart suddenly scoffed with irritation.

"Excuse me," came the familiar female voice.

All four guards glanced a few feet down the basement corridor to the attractive young woman in the teal evening dress. They appeared bewildered by her presence.

Jackie smiled sweetly while posing seductively near the outer basement door. "Could you gentlemen tell me where the ladies' room is?"

Two of the guards approached Jackie with little emotion and no patience while removing their guns from hidden shoulder holsters. Jackie suddenly sneered and kicked off her high heels.

"No imagination," she scoffed lowly.

As they reached her, Jackie suddenly spun into a high, roundhouse kick, the slit in her dress allowing for the fast fierce kick. She struck the first man in the chest with her bare foot. Before the second man could react, she was already in the return kick and nailed him in the abdomen. Bogart and Monroe took their cue and tackled the men hovering over them, who were now paying attention to what was happening down the hall. One-on-one, the guards didn't stand a chance against the two, highly skilled men. Once they had the guards on the ground, Bogart grabbed one of their discarded guns.

Monroe gave him a disapproving look. "No gunplay, Bogart," he reminded.

"I ain't shooting no one," Bogart snapped back at him.

Jackie took out the last man, slamming him into the stone wall, and then casually reclaimed her shoes. She looked at Bogart and Monroe while offering a sly grin.

"Our ride should be waiting outside," she informed them and nodded to the outer door.

All three hurried for the basement entrance. Jackie had successfully picked the lock to gain access to the basement when she heard the men being attacked from her position outside the door. Once Bogart and Monroe passed through the door, Jackie stopped by the closed door to jam the lock. Gil, Beck, and Ross were waiting by the luxury rental car. Ross had his arms folded across his chest and glared disapprovingly at Jackie by the door.

"Stubborn girl," Ross scoffed. "She never listens."

As Monroe and Bogart approached the vehicle, they looked around with surprise and possible concern.

"Where's Kirk?" Monroe asked.

"He's a little tied up," Ross replied casually while hiding his grin. "He'll be fine. No one's looking for him. Well, except maybe an irate father-of-the-bride."

The basement door was violently shoved open, throwing Jackie away from the door. Before she could recover, one of the guards stepped through the opening and grabbed her around the neck. He pulled her against him from behind and aimed his gun at her head.

"All of you," the guard fiercely cried out. "If you value this woman's life, you'll drop your weapons and put your hands on your heads!"

Without hesitation, Jackie rammed her elbow into the man's ribs then spun into a roundhouse kick for his face. A gunshot rang out followed by Jackie's scream. The guys reacted with alarm. As Jackie fell to the ground, Ross's expression shattered.

"Jackie!"

Chapter Three

One month later.   Somewhere west of Colorado Springs.

The open plains were picturesque in the early morning.   Without a cloud in the sky, it would be another warm, dry day.   The peaceful morning was interrupted by a faint rumbling that grew louder.   The sound of thundering hooves increased as a cloud of dust closed in.   A herd of nearly one hundred horses ran across the wide-open fields as if being chased by a predator.   Not far behind the herd were three men on four wheelers.   They muffled shouts through their bandannas as they chased the horses, herding them with a purpose.   The loud crack of a whip caught the herd's attention.   Two fifteen-year-old girls on horseback galloped toward the herd from the side not far in front of them.   The first girl wearing a black cowboy hate rode a large black horse and cracked a bullwhip.   The second girl rode a brown and white paint horse and intentionally trailed behind.

The dark haired girl with the bullwhip in her hand cut across the herd's path, cracking her whip the entire way.   The sound prompted the horses to veer from their current path.   She rode after the lead mare, allowing the rest of the herd to follow, swiftly changing direction like a flock of birds.   The men on the four wheelers screamed at one another, although they were almost too far apart to hear what the other had said.   They drove after the second teenager, a blond girl wearing a brown cowboy hat, as she rode on the paint horse now chasing behind the last of the herd.   The blond girl swiftly removed a rifle from her saddle holster, dropped the reins across the horn, and spun nearly sideways on the saddle.   As her horse continued to gallop after the herd, the girl fired the rifle at the men on the four wheelers behind her.   The ground exploded just before one of the vehicles, startling the men, but not stopping their pursuit. She aimed carefully despite her sideways position on the horse and fired several rounds. One bullet struck the first four wheeler in the front tire. The ATV swerved and tumbled, tossing its rider. The second ATV took a shell in the front and immediately expelled steam. It sputtered and lost momentum. The third ATV with its determined rider continued its pursuit.

The blond girl spun around, facing forward on her horse, and sat back deep in the saddle, clinging to her rifle with both hands. The horse sank onto his haunches, digging his back hooves into the ground, and skidded to a stop without use of reins. The horse pivoted around in time with the girl as she turned her shoulders and leveled the rifle. She now faced the approaching ATV with her rifle aimed directly at the rider. The man cried out and swerved at the sight of the girl with the high-powered rifle aimed at him. She redirected her aim and squeezed the trigger. The back tire of the ATV exploded and the vehicle floundered to a stop. The girl grinned, replaced her rifle to the saddle holster, and sent the horse back into a gallop without ever kicking him. All three men watched the blond teenage girl ride after the herd.

†

*T*he herd of wild horses trotted back across the invisible line into the game lands with the two girls on horseback bringing up the rear. The wild horses were no longer fearful of those herding them. It had been a long, exhausting journey for the herd. Monique and Colleen were the ultimate tomboys in their blue jeans, cowboy boots, and plaid shirts. The only thing girly about either was their shoulder length hair, and even that they wore in ponytails beneath their cowboy hats. Somewhere beneath the hats and dirt were two attractive, teenage girls, but they didn't have boys on their minds-- only horses. The two girls stopped their horses and watched the herd return to their sanctuary. Both smiled proudly but it didn't last long. They frowned and exchanged concerned looks.

"We can't keep this up, Monique," the brunette on the black horse informed her friend as she removed her black cowboy hat and wiped the sweat from her forehead onto her sleeve. "That's their third attempt this month."

"We just need to buy a little more time," Monique replied then straightened in the saddle and gingerly rubbed her sore butt. "The park rangers will investigate. My father promised."

"I'm worried they're going to slip past us and send them off to slaughter," Colleen remarked while frowning. "Your father and the rangers aren't working fast enough."

"I know," Monique muttered.

Both girls watched the herd and sank into their own worries about the fate of the wild horses. Their survival from the poachers depended upon the two girls, but they were alone and exhausted. They wouldn't be able to keep up the pace much longer and the herd would fall into the hands of men who just wanted to slaughter the beautiful creatures.

Monique finally looked at her young friend, who wore a defeated expression on her face. "We need to be proactive," she announced firmly.

Colleen gave her a puzzled look. "What do you mean? What can we do that we haven't already been doing?"

"We know what direction they were herding them," Monique replied. "They'd have to be moving them closer to their pick-up destination. They'll have some sort of corral set up to contain them, and there will be trucks to transport them." Monique's face lit up with enthusiasm. "We just need to go back out there and scout out the area they were heading. When we find the corral and the trucks, we'll have them. I can tell my father, and the rangers can do their job."

Colleen appeared equally enthusiastic for the first time. "That's a good plan."

"I know," Monique announced and grinned slyly. "I'm a genius."

Her friend frowned at the comment. "Yeah, in your own mind."

They turned their horses and rode in the direction they'd come at a leisurely gait.

†

After nearly an hour of riding, the two girls reached an old ghost town in the middle of nowhere. Neither was familiar with the dilapidated old town. It consisted of the main street and two side streets, though most of the buildings on the side streets were reduced to piles of rubble. The buildings along the main thoroughfare appeared almost structurally sound, having survived hundreds of years in the dry conditions. As they rode through the main street of the old ghost town, both paid particular attention to the ground and the fresh ATV tracks. They finally stopped their horses and looked around, seeming puzzled.

"This can't be right," Monique groaned with frustration. "There isn't a corral of any kind to contain the horses."

"I don't see any tractor-trailer tracks either," Colleen remarked.

"The guys came through here, but this can't be the pick-up location," Monique finally announced then sighed as she looked around with defeat. "What now?"

Colleen shrugged, not seeming overly concerned. "We have plenty of time before we have to return home," she remarked simply. "We can ride onward for another hour before we have to turn around."

"Okay then," Monique sighed and pointed onward. "Wagon's ho."

They rode out of town, continuing their journey. Monique and Colleen rode at a leisurely gait for another hour or longer, stopping once at a stream for everyone to fill up on water. They passed a mildly rocky area on a slight hill, before reaching the top of the small peak, which again turned into lush pasture down the hill. Their perch on top of the hill offered a bird's eye view of a strange sight in the valley below. Monique and Colleen exchanged bewildered looks.

"Am I seeing correctly?" Colleen almost gasped.

Monique slowly nodded and stared with the same speechless expression. In the valley below lie the overgrown remains of an old, abandoned amusement park, which covered nearly thirty acres of flatland. Despite the vegetation growth, they could easily make out nearly two dozen rides beyond the chain link fence, overgrown with plant life. From their overhead vantage point, they could see the main entrance with the dilapidated gates standing open. Toward the back of the park on the opposite end, a portion of the fence just behind the wooden roller coaster was down as well. What remained of the macadam parking lot was mostly covered in grass, although small portions of blacktop were exposed, giving a general layout of the original parking lot from years past.

Toward the left of the park was what they could only assume to be a haunted house, which looked very much like a mansion. There was an old sky ride high above the park with one or two carts smashed on the ground below. Swampy areas, particularly surrounding the dilapidated flume ride, were all that remained of the water rides. In the greenish water, they could see boats partially submerged from years of neglect. Vegetation has grown rampant particularly around the wet areas.

"I've never seen anything so cool and creepy at the same time," Monique muttered aloud.

Colleen suddenly tapped her friend on the arm and pointed. "Look, over there."

Although difficult to make out beyond one of the larger buildings from their vantage point, a large tractor-trailer was parked on the other side of the park. It was parked alongside a tall, chain link fence surrounding the massive generator building. The area was large enough to contain the wild horses prior to transport.

"This is it," Colleen boldly announced with enthusiasm. "This is where they were driving the herd."

"A long trek, don't you think?" Monique remarked, expressing some apprehension.

"I doubt those bastards cared what condition the horses arrived in," Colleen informed her friend. "What do you think? Should we report this place to your dad?"

"I don't know," Monique replied while remaining concerned. "Maybe we should nose around and make sure. If my father reports this place to the rangers and they come up empty-handed, they'll never listen to us again."

"Okay," Colleen agreed with little persuasion. "We'll take a quick look around. We'll let the horses graze at the bottom near that roller coaster. A section of the fence is down back there. We can be more stealth on foot."

"Sounds like a plan," Monique replied.

Chapter Four

While the horses grazed safely out of sight beneath the roller coaster, the girls crept around the abandoned amusement park. Colleen carried her bullwhip over her shoulder, much like a young Indiana Jones, and Monique kept her high-powered rifle slung over her shoulder. As Monique had described, the amusement park was both cool and creepy. The carousel was overgrown with vegetation, yet the fading chipped horses seemingly rose out of the weeds. Rusted bumper cars were nestled in their grassy graves. Obviously the floor beneath was metal, but it was so overgrown it couldn't be seen. The Ferris wheel stood tall and high above them. One of the covered cars had broken free years ago and lay broken at the bottom. It, too, was covered in plant life. The fun house looked more like a death trap beckoning them to enter, but neither were brave enough. They passed several rotting concession stands and a few game booths, most of which were falling apart. Another ride with spinning carts attached to long arms looked like a sea monster reaching out of its grassy ocean. Ironically, something resembling a Viking ship held in place by a large pendulum showed little wear over the years. Off to the side, there was an entire section of kiddie rides in a secluded area by themselves. Colleen eyed the Viking ship and noted its oddly immaculate condition.

"I got sick on one of those," Colleen casually reported to her friend.

"I know," Monique replied while glaring at her. "You threw up on me, remember?"

Now that they were actually in the old park, they could see there were two larger buildings closer to the front of the park. One was near the main entrance and the other was close to the fenced generator building a little further away. The one near the park entrance was undoubtedly the old gift shop and possibly a sit-down style restaurant. The girls were more interested in the building near the generator and the parked tractor-trailer. They kept low and quiet while creeping around the building and approached the parked truck. Monique touched the mammoth machine and glanced at her friend.

"Engine's cool," she softly reported.

Colleen gave a slight nod to the back entrance of the building. The door was open, possibly to allow air inside. Someone had to be within the building. The grass beneath the tractor-trailer was still alive and the blades that had been driven over were still flattened, indicating the truck hadn't been parked in the grassy area for too long. They gathered their courage and approached the building. As they got closer, they could hear voices inside. Monique grabbed Colleen's arm and slung her to the side of the doorway. They listened to the men's voices but couldn't make out what they were saying. They crouched down and crept along the side of the building toward a nearby window. Monique darted beneath it to the opposite side and both girls peered in through the severely grimy glass. There were three men dressed in dark suits within the room and their voices were louder now. It seemed odd that poachers would be wearing suits. Despite that there were three men, they didn't recognize any as those on the four wheelers, and logically so. The poachers chasing the horses weren't wearing suits. They dressed more like backwoods hunters. One man stood facing the other two with his hands held up defensively in front of him.

"I swear to you," the man announced in a tense tone. "I'll make this right."

It was at that moment both girls saw the other two men had guns aimed at the first man. Their eyes then strayed to another man in a suit lying face down in a pool of fresh blood. The dead man was only a few feet from the nervous man holding his hands in the air. Before either girl could process what might have happened to the dead man on the floor, a gunshot rang out. The frightened man's head snapped back as blood and chunky matter exploded out the back of his skull, spattering on the wall behind him. Both girls gasped as the man fell to the floor not far from the other dead man. In the tense moment, Monique's rifle slipped from her shoulder and bumped the side of the building, creating a distinctive metallic clatter. Both men turned and saw the girls peering in through the dirty windows. In that brief moment, the men's faces were burned into the girls' minds. Both men were in their late thirties or early forties. The dark haired man, Hoffman, had a scar on his temple that unnaturally left a bald spot through his right eyebrow. The other man,

Tremaine, had light brown hair with wisps of silver on his temples. His unusually large nose gave the impression of an old-time television detective. It seemed as if an eternity had passed that they stared at one another, but it was actually only a second.

"Run!" Monique cried out in a shrill voice.

Both girls ran past the tractor-trailer and through the amusement park. They only had a few seconds head start before the men appeared behind them. Knowing the men were armed, the girls veered to the right, running through the dilapidated vendor stands. A gunshot rang out. Wood splintered near Colleen's head. She let out a scream but didn't slow, remaining on her blond friend's booted heels. Colleen removed her bullwhip as they ran, let it trail behind her, and then cracked it in the air. It seemed odd and appeared to serve no purpose. Both girls spun around the corner near the carousel, giving their pursing friends little chance to line up a shot. The two men rounded the carousel and stopped. Both girls were gone! Tremaine and Hoffman looked around the overgrown area with bewildered stares. There was so much tall vegetation, they could be almost anywhere within the tall grass.

The sound of a whip cracking alerted them to their location, but it was already too late. The whip coiled around the Tremaine's neck and he was pulled off his feet toward the jungle infested carousel. Monique partially appeared over the back of one of the carousel horses with her rifle aimed. As she squeezed the trigger, Hoffman saw her, cried out, and threw himself to the ground. She nearly clipped him, the bullet striking the stand just behind where he had stood. Tremaine gasped and struggled against the taunt bullwhip around his neck while thrashing around on the ground. The whip suddenly let loose. Tremaine scrambled to his feet just in time to avoid the rifle shot that exploded the ground in front of him. He ran across what would have been the walkway and joined Hoffman safely behind a vendor stand. Tremaine looked around for his gun. It was on the ground a foot from the jungle infested carousel. He made a motion for the gun. A girl's hand appeared from the jungle and snatched the gun, disappearing as quickly as it had appeared.

"Christ," Hoffman snarled. "Now they're both armed."

"We'll wait them out," Tremaine replied. "They have nowhere to run."

The bullwhip cracked again. Both men exchanged bewildered looks. The sound of the bullwhip made no sense to either, and they actually seemed quite humored by it.

"Is that supposed to intimidate us?" Tremaine announced with a soft laugh.

Both men heard a strange rumbling sound. They turned and saw both the black horse and the paint horse galloping straight for them. There was a whistle from the carousel. The horses nearly plowed down the men while galloping for the carousel. The semiautomatic fired rapidly at both men, forcing them to take cover. Monique jumped onto her horse during the gunfire. Once she was seated on her horse, she fired her rifle at the small vendor stand, exploding pieces of wood, allowing Colleen time to leap onto her horse's back. She swung up onto the horse without use of stirrups. Both horses were sent into a gallop without either girl touching the reins or kicking them. Monique continued to fire her rifle as they galloped away. Both girls reclaimed their reins as they galloped down the main thoroughfare of the amusement park, heading for the entrance and the safety of the hillside.

Two men on ATVs suddenly appeared at the entrance and fired at them. Colleen's horse suddenly reared up with a loud squeal, causing Colleen to topple off the back. It was only a short drop, and she managed to roll with the fall. Monique spun her horse, circled Collen and reached down. As if practiced, Collen was half pulled and half leaped onto the back of Monique's horse. Monique sent her horse into a gallop and chased after the running black horse. Two more men on four wheelers cut off their path just up the road. Colleen cried out while clinging to Monique from behind as the riderless black horse slowed at the sight of the men. Colleen only hesitated a moment before taking a chance and cracked the whip from her position on the paint horse behind Monique. The black horse picked up speed and jumped the men on the four wheelers. Both men leaped from their ATVs to avoid the horse jumping over their heads.

Monique veered her horse to the side, knowing the two of them together couldn't make the same jump on her horse. Colleen would almost certainly fall off the back. The time it took to round the four wheelers slowed their escape. Two more men suddenly appeared just ahead on the main road and aimed their guns at the girls on the paint horse. Monique's horse skidded to a stop on her command, digging up turf covering the macadam beneath. She spun the horse in a tight circle. The men from both sets of ATVs were now surrounding them with their guns aimed. Monique and Colleen stared helplessly. There was nowhere left to go. In the distance, they could see the black horse racing up the hillside and disappearing over top to safety.

✝

$\mathcal{T}$he small farm was quiet in the early evening hours. The little, two-story farmhouse was surrounded by gorgeous flowerbeds and a massive garden. Not far from the house was a small barn and a fenced pasture. A dark-haired woman in her early thirties paced the porch of the house while rubbing her shoulders. Marie Cooper gazed along the open land toward the woods and waited. Although a country girl much like her daughter, Marie attempted to cling to her feminine side with the way she dressed country casual. Being a single mother had taken its toll on the woman, and days like today just added to her stress. A newer jeep with the top down drove along the dirt driveway and approached her house. The speed the jeep maintained on the old dirt road indicated the driver was feeling aggressive. Marie exhaled, somehow feeling better, and hurried to greet the jeep. An attractive blond woman also in her early thirties approached Marie. Donna dressed slightly upscale compared with Marie, and it was obvious her life was less stressed--though not today. Donna stared at Marie with concern as she slowed her approach.

"They're not here?" Donna almost gasped, sharing the same expression as her friend.

Marie shook her head as she looked toward the woods and continued to subconsciously rub her arms. "This isn't like them," she announced, her voice trembling. "It's nearly dark. They know the rules."

"Back for dinner and no wandering off the property in the evening," Donna replied then looked around as well. "I should call my husband." She looked back at Marie while wrenching her fingers together. "Should I call my husband?"

"My brother took his truck along the trails," Marie informed her timidly. "Hopefully, he'll find them."

The sound of thundering hooves alerted both women. They looked toward the woods with enthusiastic anticipation. The black riderless horse ran along the pasture, passed the barn, and skidded to a halt before the women. Both women's expressions revealed their worst fears.

"Oh, my God," Marie gasped while placing her hand to her mouth. "Thunder came back alone!" She frantically looked around. "Where's Colleen?"

Donna caught the excited, sweated horse and attempted to calm him as he pranced around. Marie took two quick steps past the horse and stared at the woods' edge, waiting for the second horse to appear with both their daughters. The second horse didn't come.

Donna ran her hand along the sweated horse's hindquarters then suddenly pulled her hand back with a gasp. Marie looked at Donna and saw the blood on her hand. Although the horse's injury was minor, it didn't settle well with either woman. They exchanged horrified looks. Where were the girls?

Chapter Five

$\mathcal{T}$wo days later.   The rural residential development just outside Colorado Springs was peaceful in the early morning hour. Average middle class homes lined the clean empty streets.   Most of the homes were dark, although most would come to life in a few hours as the workday began.   A quaint, modern two-story home sat nestled on a corner lot with a realtor sign out front.   Sold was boldly posted across the sign.   Within the home, boxes were stacked in every room.   Within the master bedroom were more boxes.   The furniture was mostly in place and the curtains were hung and closed. A ruggedly handsome man in his mid-thirties slept peacefully beneath the covers.   He wasn't built excessively muscular, but he had broad shoulders and a toned chest lightly covered with just enough hair to run fingers through.   His nearly black hair was neatly trimmed, and the dark stubble on his face suggested he shaved daily.

The sound of handcuffs snapping shut woke him out of his sleep.   He jerked and looked at his wrist now cuffed to the bedpost near him.   He partially turned over and looked at the woman hovering over him in the bed alongside him.   Jackie smiled boldly and caressed his shoulder.

"Guess what today is," she cooed softly and warmly kissed his chest.

Holden Falcone shut his eyes and grinned with pleasure. "Happy birthday, Jackie."

She swiftly pulled him onto his back and jumped on top of him.   He let out a startled gasp then looked up at her as she straddled his hips and smiled.   Her hair was wild and mussed and her lacy nightgown was nearly see through.   She ran her hands along his bare chest and shoulders while maintaining her lustful smile.

"I'm ready for my birthday present now," she announced seductively.

Holden groaned and pulled her down on top him with his free hand. He kissed her warmly but with aggression, to which she eagerly responded with the same. Holden ran his free hand along her hip and thigh, gently pulling her lacy nightgown upward. A recent scar from a bullet wound was clearly visible on her outer thigh. His hand subconsciously ran along the scar, almost as if feeling it out. Jackie caught his traveling hand and pinned it to the bed alongside his head. He groaned softly and let her have her way with him.

†

*L*ater that morning, Agent Holden Falcone entered the Federal Bureau Building in Colorado Springs. He wore one of his nicer suits that Jackie had picked out for him. Although he would never admit it, Jackie knew Holden liked Monroe's flare when it came to fashion. Holden probably wouldn't be extremely happy if he knew Monroe had personally picked out all the clothing Jackie had bought for her husband. The guys didn't want him reeking of 'fed' in what they often teased to be 'cheap suits and expensive sunglasses'. Holden carried three cups of coffee in a cardboard carrier. He entered the elevator and received a look from two fellow agents occupying the elevator with him.

"Still kissing the boss's ass, eh, Holden?" Agent Metzger teased.

Agent Metzger was easily ten years older than Holden. Despite his years serving with the Bureau, it was evident the man was jealous of Holden's outstanding performance as a federal agent. Metzger had let himself go the last few years, indicated by his soft mid-section and unshaven face. His grooming habits were subpar as well. Rumor had it he spent his evenings at a local bar, although there were no traces of alcohol detected on the man. At one time, he was probably considered attractive, but his lifestyle rapidly aged him. He had more wrinkles than most middle-aged men and his dark hair was thinning, so he seemed to compensate by allowing it to grow longer in the back, giving it a stringy appearance.

Holden cast a glance at the disgruntled agent and smirked. "Just a nice guy, Metzger."

As the doors closed, they rode the first few floors in silence. The second man, Agent Dodson, glanced at Holden and seemed to have a mission in mind regarding the new man.

"Who exactly did you know to get this job anyway?" Agent Dodson finally asked.

Agent Dodson was almost the complete opposite of Agent Metzger. He was a no-nonsense, by the book kind of guy. He dressed neat, keeping his light brown hair in a military buzz cut to conceal his male pattern baldness, and he was in great physical shape for a man in his late thirties. His personality left something to be desired though.

Holden glared sideways at his fellow agents. His look was almost threatening. "Excuse me?"

"Well, it seems to me there were a lot of excellent candidates right here in Colorado kissing ass for that promotion," Metzger casually remarked. "And then you just came in and swooped it up with your charm and good looks?"

Holden faced the door and refused to look at the arrogant men. "I'm a good agent, Metzger," he scoffed. "My record speaks for itself. I don't have to kiss ass--just bring coffee."

"Seriously--?" Dodson snapped a little louder, clearly annoyed, and turned to face Holden, who still refused to look at him. "Who do you know?"

The elevator doors opened, allowing Holden to make his hasty departure before he struck a fellow agent.

"Have a nice day, gentlemen," Holden remarked with a slight growl as he stepped out of the elevator.

Both men went their own direction while muttering to each other. Holden held his temper and shook his head with disgust. He approached the last office at the end of the hallway and knocked on the open door. Blake Harris lounged slightly reclined in his chair with his feet propped on the desk and his eyes closed. He opened his eyes then motioned Holden in while placing his feet on the floor. Blake was a distinguished looking man in his forties, but the last few days had given him the appearance of a much older man. Even his light brown hair seemed to have turned gray in the last day or two. He wore dark circles under his eyes and remained unshaven for the second day in a row. Holden studied his boss as he entered the office. He took one coffee and handed the tray with the remaining two to Blake.

"Still not getting any sleep?" Holden asked with concern for his new boss.

Blake waved him off and attempted a smile as he removed both cups of coffee. "Just going through some stuff with my daughter," he gently replied then hesitated. "She's, uh, fifteen."

Holden smiled and nodded while taking a seat across the desk from his boss. "I understand," he replied. "Boys, huh?"

Blake snorted a laugh and rubbed his tired eyes. "I wish," he muttered.

He seemed to realize Holden was staring at him. Blake forced a smile and indicated the picture on his desk. Holden glanced at the framed photo of the blond girl on her pinto horse. Holden hid his smile and nodded.

"Well, it had to be one of the two," Holden replied.

Blake held his head a moment then straightened as he exhaled. He looked around his slightly messy desk and removed a folder. He met Holden's gaze with a slight grimace.

"I hate to do this to you, being you just started last week and all," Blake began then hesitated.

"No, it's fine," Holden replied and extended his hand. "What's the assignment? I'm willing to take shit assignments if it gets certain people off your back."

Blake stared at him with a strange look, but it was almost as if the comment didn't register. "What? No, it's nothing like that," he announced and handed him the folder. "You're the unknown face around here, so you were my best option. Well, even if you weren't an unknown face you'd be my best option." He fumbled slightly. "I know it's tough since you're still getting settled into your new home, and I'm sure your wife is going to absolutely hate me." He gently scratched his two-day old stubble. "I need to send you undercover for a week maybe two."

Holden stared at Blake as he opened the folder. "Oh," he remarked softly with a note of disappointment in his tone.

"I'm really sorry," Blake informed him with some sympathy. "I wouldn't do it if it wasn't important."

"No, I understand," Holden reluctantly replied and offered a smile to reassure him. "When do I start?"

"Today," Blake replied.

Holden looked at his boss with surprise. "Today?"

"It's really important, Holden," his boss announced while studying him. His eyes conveyed the importance, or perhaps just his exhaustion.

"No, it's--I'm sure Jackie will understand," Holden remarked then groaned softly while fidgeting. "Today's her birthday. I made a big deal about taking her out; you know, just the two of us--" He attempted to hide his emotions while putting his nose into the folder and muttered, "--without her friends."

"I'm really sorry about this, Holden," he replied with a soft groan. "What if I sent her flowers and apologized for you? Maybe she can still make plans to go out with her friends."

Holden looked up with horror. "No," he announced a little too quickly then fumbled. "I, uh, would rather she took a break from them. They're, uh, a *bad* influence on her. The last time she went out with them, she ended up in the hospital."

"Oh, that's terrible," Blake proclaimed, suddenly coming to life.

Holden eyed him suspiciously. Blake sank back in his chair and gently folded his hands together over his abdomen. His fingers fidgeted slightly, strumming his tie. Holden's boss was definitely tense.

"I'll tell you what," Blake announced and shot forward in his chair, a sly grin on his face. "Take the afternoon off and spend it with your wife. You don't have to report to your undercover assignment until this evening."

"That's generous of you," Holden replied and studied his boss, trying to read him.

"You'll be working undercover at Marble Crest Manor in Denver," Blake informed him. "Your employer will provide your, uh, uniform, and you'll be living on property in the servants' quarters."

"Servants' quarters?" Holden remarked with surprise.

"Yes," Blake replied. "You're going undercover as Milton Crosby's butler. We have reason to believe the old man is running a child slavery operation. We need you to search his house and computer for any information that will give us proof one way or the other. His personal chef came to us with this information, so you'll have his assistance. He'll groom you to play the part as well as fill you in on what he's learned."

"Child slavery," Holden scoffed with disgust. "If I find out he's guilty and call for backup, send someone right away. The old guy's life may depend on it."

"I hear you," Blake muttered and sank back in his chair. "Go on. Go home. Tell your wife I'm sorry for ruining her birthday." As Holden stood and was about to leave, Blake stopped him. "Oh, and Holden--"

Holden turned and looked back at his boss. Blake's look was stern and serious.

"You report only to me on this assignment," Blake announced firmly. "I don't want your findings or your assignment reported to anyone but me. My eyes and ears only. You got that?"

Holden nodded. "Yes, sir."

†

*L*ater that evening, after Jackie had sent Holden off with a farewell quickie, she turned the kettle on for a cup of tea. While she waited for the water to boil, she looked around at the stacks of boxes and suddenly felt defeated. Had she actually thought she'd get more done with Holden out of town for a week or two? She suddenly felt overwhelmed with her task of unpacking. How did she manage to accumulate so much stuff in such a short period of time? It wasn't as if the boxes were filled with her childhood memories. All that stuff was still in her old bedroom at her father's house. Well, technically it was her house since her father had passed away, but she couldn't bring herself to sell the house or part with any of his belongings. Now the house was basically a pit stop for the guys going to and from missions.

Jackie groaned with disgust at the enormous task before her. She turned off the kettle and opened a bottle of wine instead. It was, after all, her birthday, and she didn't have to unpack everything tonight. Actually, she was thinking horror movie marathon. First, a hot bubble bath. She collected her glass of wine and headed for the kitchen doorway. Jackie then hesitated, reconsidered, and went back for the bottle on the counter. She took both the bottle and her glass from the kitchen with her.

Chapter Six

*J*ackie slept peacefully beneath the covers on her bed in her tank top and sleep shorts while the movie continued to play. The empty bottle of wine sat on the nightstand alongside the empty glass. The television shut off, leaving the room in near darkness and blissful silence. Jackie stirred and looked around the dimly lit room. She wasn't sure what had woken her from her sleep. She glanced at the television. In her disorientation, she didn't remember the movie ending or turning off the television. She returned her head to the pillow, nuzzled it, and drifted back to sleep. Her dreams were all over the place as events of her life played out on an endless loop. Not all were good memories, considering she'd seen more than her share of bloody killings in her short life. She whimpered softly in her sleep then felt Holden's arms holding her, comforting her, and the world was again as it should be. Jackie woke for some unknown reason and looked at the clock. It was two in the morning. She was glad she didn't need to work a regular job anymore. Being a self-employed pilot for hire brought in enough money without the worries of working for an employer.

She felt Holden cuddling against her from behind while holding her in his sleep. She enjoyed his strong arms around her. Perhaps, more so, she enjoyed his early morning enthusiasm when he'd hold her. She enjoyed the way his hard body felt pressed against her. Jackie caressed the arm firmly holding her and smiled to herself. Her eyes suddenly opened with horror. Holden wasn't home! Jackie screamed as she rammed her elbow backward into the man behind her. She grabbed the revolver tucked away in its holster strapped alongside the mattress. Jackie leaped up from the bed so fast, she knocked the empty wine bottle to the floor. It struck the hard floor with a firm clunk. Despite the dim lighting, Jackie aimed the gun at the man in her bed. He was now sitting up with his hands in the air, allowing her the opportunity to release her breath and reach for the bedside light. When the light came on, she stared at the man sitting up in her bed as he innocently stared back. Her expression suddenly dropped.

"Zack?" she suddenly cried out with surprise.

The man in his early fifties, Zack Kinsley, was shorter than average, being lucky if he made 5'8" with a moderately average physique. Non-impressive by most standards, he appeared almost innocent at first glance. He wore a black tee shirt covering his amazingly athletic build, which would easily go unnoticed beneath his clothes. His brown hair was kept short and neat, although moderately spikey on top. It was uncertain if the hairstyle made him look slightly intimidating or more like a cuddly toy.

"Sorry," Zack announced gently while offering a tiny smile as he slowly lowered his hands. "I tend to wander in my sleep. I didn't mean to cuddle."

His words were almost disorientating to her. What the hell was he even rambling about? She wanted to shoot him on principle alone!

"What the hell are you doing in my house?" she finally cried out, her rage returning.

Her bedroom door was suddenly thrown open and four men in only their boxer shorts rushed into the room in standard two-by-two formation with their weapons drawn. Jackie gasped and aimed her revolver at them. Ross, Monroe, Beck, and Kirk looked like a group of middle-aged strippers wearing nothing but their boxer shorts with their bare, excessively toned chests proudly on display. There were times Jackie enjoyed an eyeful of the guys strutting around in nothing but boxer shorts, but this wasn't one of those times. She wanted to shoot someone. The guys looked from Jackie to Zack and uncertainly lowered their handguns.

"Christ," Kirk snarled then groaned with hostility. "It's fucking Zack."

Kirk and Beck shook their heads with disgust and left the room. Monroe offered a tiny, weary smile while scratching his mussed hair.

"Happy birthday, Jackie."

She sneered at him. Some birthday. "Thanks, Monroe," Jackie scoffed.

Monroe filed in behind the others and left her room. Ross glared at Zack in Jackie's bed and shook his head.

"What the hell are you doing here?" Ross demanded of the man. "And please take that to mean, 'what the fuck are you doing in Jackie's bed?'"

Zack stared at Ross with surprise, his mouth partially hanging open, and maintained his innocent look. "Language, Ross," he scolded and indicated Jackie. "There are ladies present."

Both men paused and looked back at Jackie. She still held the gun on them with her finger firm on the trigger.

"Do you intend to put that away or shoot one of us?" Ross asked as he folded his arms across his bare chest, his gun casually draped in his hand.

Jackie felt as if she was having some bizarre nightmare. All the guys running around her house, half-naked, and Zack in her bed. It just didn't seem real.

"I don't know," she snapped in anger. "I'm still debating it." Jackie finally lowered the gun then held her head, cursing herself to wake up.

Ross looked back at Zack demandingly. "I thought you were in Russia or Asia or Bora Bora."

"I was," Zack replied and casually leaned back on Jackie's bed, crossing his ankles and placing his hands behind his head, "but I got bored."

"You mean she tried to kill you again," Ross scoffed while raising a demanding brow.

Jackie glared at Zack where he had made himself comfortable on her bed. She again debated shooting him.

"Do you mind?" she demanded and indicated him spread out on her bed.

Zack glanced at the bed, gave her an innocent look, and then appeared embarrassed. "Oh, sorry."

He jumped off her bed and stood on the other side not far from Ross. At least he had been wearing shorts when he cuddled against her in his sleep. Unfortunately, the incident was already burned into her mind. Jackie replaced her gun to the hidden holster alongside the bed and eyed both men.

"What are you guys doing here?" she finally demanded. "Why didn't you call or at least knock on the door?"

"It was late," Ross replied matter-of-fact. "We didn't want to wake you, so we just showed ourselves in."

"I just got into town," Zack remarked innocently. "The sofas and spare bed were already occupied." He then folded his arms across his chest and gave her a scolding look. "Let's be reasonable, Jackie. It's not as if you were using the *whole* bed."

Jackie groaned, shook her head, and looked at them with limited patience. "I meant, why are you here at this hour in the first place?" she demanded.

"Just visiting, darling," Ross replied warmly then smiled. "Look, it's late. Why don't you go back to bed, and we'll talk in the morning."

"Fine," Jackie grumbled and approached the bed from her side.

Zack approached the bed from his side and started to climb in as well. Jackie glared at him with a venomous look. Ross grabbed Zack's arm and pulled him from the room. Bogart appeared in the doorway looking rumpled and exhausted while scratching his mussed hair.

"What's going on?" Bogart muttered.

Ross gave him a disappointed frown. "Nice of you to join us, Bogart," he remarked. "Had this been a real crisis, you'd be dead."

Bogart appeared puzzled. Ross shooed him away from Jackie's bedroom, offered Jackie a polite smile, and then shut the door behind him. She stared at the closed door after they were gone and shook her head with disbelief. Jackie suspected they were up to something or they wouldn't have shown up unannounced in the middle of the night. She could hardly wait to hear their explanation. She collapsed on the bed and held her head.

"This isn't going to be good," she muttered then turned off the light, although she doubted she'd get much sleep after her Zack attack.

✝

The following morning, Jackie shuffled toward the kitchen nearly colliding with the same box she'd been stumbling into every morning for the past three mornings. She wore a light robe hanging open overtop her sleep shorts and tank top, being aware that she had unexpected overnight houseguests. She hadn't bothered showering yet, since she felt she was owed an explanation for the guys crashing at her house in the middle of the night. Jackie stopped in the doorway to the kitchen and stared at the island counter littered with her father's former Navy SEAL buddies. All were dressed in their finest casual attire, which included blue jeans or cargo pants for most. The more stylish ones wore button shirts, while those who preferred not to worry about bloodstains wore basic black cotton tees. However, all were in agreement regarding footwear. Each wore their standard black combat boots, which were perfect for stomping on heads. The guys were talking and laughing with one another over coffee and a box of ill-gotten pastries. For a moment, it seemed almost like old times. Rather than become nostalgic, Jackie had to remind herself that she was mad at them.

She noticed Gil was suspiciously missing, although Bogart seemed glad to take his place. Somehow, the conman had managed to weasel his way into their lives. Better theirs than hers. The last time Bogart followed her home, she and Holden were unable to get rid of him for almost three months. She withheld her groan. She'd always been happy to see them, but that was until last month when she'd been shot. Holden held her father's team accountable for her injury, and he'd be unhappy to discover them collecting in their kitchen drinking all his coffee. Jackie put on a smile and entered the kitchen. The six men acted as if they had just noticed her, but she knew damned well they probably heard her coming down the stairs. They were obviously up to something and it wasn't to wish her a happy belated birthday.

"Morning," she announced in her best faux cheerful tone as she crossed the kitchen.

"Good morning," came the round of responses.

She could feel six pairs of eyes upon her as she approached the stove and turned on the kettle for her tea. Surprisingly, the kettle whistled almost immediately. Someone had already prepared the hot water for her arrival. She was aware that her favorite cup was missing from the dish rack. As she turned to see who had taken her mug, Zack handed her the mug with tea already prepared the way she liked it. Now she was really concerned by their visit. They were being *too* nice. She accepted her tea, turned her back to the counter while leaning against it, and stared at the men, who suddenly seemed to mind their own business. Ross was the only one who met her gaze and offered a charming smile. She could see through his charm from years of experience. The more soulful his blue eyes, the bigger the favor.

"Again, we're sorry for showing up unannounced in the middle of the night," Ross announced gently.

She stared back at him with little emotion. "No, you're not," she replied and sipped her tea.

Beck and Monroe cast glances at Ross, having felt the tension in the room. Kirk, Bogart, and Zack remained quiet and pretended they weren't in the room. Actually, to her surprise, Zack no longer was in the room. He had a tendency to disappear and reappear like a magician.

"Okay," Ross gently replied. "We deserved that."

"Whatever it is, the answer's no," she firmly announced while setting her mug on the counter. "Do you have any idea the trouble you've caused on our last 'play date'? Do you even know how pissed Holden is at you--all of you? He didn't even want to accept his new promotion because it practically put me in your backyard."

Beck and Kirk were now mysteriously missing from the kitchen, having slipped out unnoticed as well. Even Bogart seemed surprised to their hasty, silent departure. He was just too new to the team to see the perfect storm brewing. Hurricane Jackie was a force of nature to be reckoned with and none wanted to be present when she made landfall.

"I understand that Holden was upset," Ross gently replied, "as were all of us. No one wanted to see you shot, Jackie." He inhaled deeply and seemed to consider his words carefully. "I did, however, tell you to wait by the car."

"Sure," she scoffed while gesturing across the kitchen at Monroe and Bogart. "I was just supposed to stand there and listen to frick and frack get their asses kicked on the other side of the basement door."

Monroe and Bogart exchanged surprised looks to her newly found hostility directed at them. Ross took two steps closer to her and searched her eyes, attempting to lay on the charm. Unfortunately, that didn't work with her. At least, not today it wouldn't. She folded her arms across her chest and glared impatiently at him.

"The last thing we want to do is cause problems between you and Holden," he gently informed her.

She turned her head to avoid looking into his eyes, because she wasn't going to let him smooth talk her. She then realized that 'frick and frack' had now left the kitchen as well, leaving her alone with Ross. It was so typical of them. Big, tough Navy SEALs. They could take down a small army of men with slingshots and Popsicle sticks, but they wanted no part of Jackie in a foul mood. She was starting to wonder if she really was their mother hen.

"Can we just stop playing games?" she demanded then groaned softly and finally looked at him. "Just tell me what you want, so I can say no. I have a lot of work to do while Holden's gone."

"Fine," he replied with a sigh. "We need a little aerial recon, that's all."

She raised her brow skeptically. "Aerial recon?" She smiled insincerely and shook her head. "Gil can do that. You don't need me."

"Gil's away on *vacation*," he gently replied.

Jackie stared at him with a strange look that quickly turned to concern. "Oh, no, not again," she groaned.

"Gil's a big boy," Ross informed her as he sighed softly. "If he wants to remarry his ex-wife, that's his decision."

"Yeah, third times a charm," she muttered then glared at him. "You should've stopped him."

"They didn't run off to get married," Ross replied. "They're just seeing how the honeymoon goes first. Cut the guy some slack. He desperately needs to get laid." Ross fidgeted and appeared embarrassed. "Sorry, that was crude."

"I've heard worse," she remarked under her breath. "What sort of aerial recon?"

Ross smiled more naturally, obviously believing he'd hooked her into playing his game. "Simple assignment. Couple of days. No danger involved, I promise. We just need eyes in the sky," he announced. "There are two missing girls--"

Jackie's arms fell to her sides as she straightened. "Missing girls?"

"We're going to meet both their mothers," he replied. "They're going to give us maps and possible locations to scout out. Supposedly, there's a search party looking for the kids, but it needs to be kept quiet. The father doesn't want it out that his daughter is missing. Foul play has not been ruled out."

Jackie groaned softly and ran her fingers through her hair. "So you want to leave today?"

"Within the next hour or two would be ideal," he replied.

She glanced at the stacks of boxes, sighed softly, and then looked back at Ross. "Fine," she announced gently. "Let me shower, throw a few things in a bag, and we can leave."

Ross smiled warmly, placed his hands on her shoulders, and kissed her cheek. "You're the best, Jackie."

"Yeah, yeah," she muttered and left the kitchen.

✝

*J*ackie took nearly thirty minutes to shower, dress, and throw some things in an overnight bag. Since she was uncertain of the amount of time she'd spend in the air, she dressed casually comfortable for a long flight. She wore her black yoga pants tucked neatly into her calf high, black boots and a white tank top with her leather shoulder holster over top. She carried her leather bomber jacket, which she took on all her flights. She preferred her bomber jacket, since it contained plenty of pockets to carry all her womanly necessities, which consisted of sunglasses, duct tape, her cute little .22 semiautomatic, and a couple dozen rounds of ammunition. Her yoga pants were special tactical wear for women, designed with a built in gun holster in the back, which was perfect for a standard Glock semiautomatic pistol. She left her room with her overnight bag filled with only the basic necessities; her travel kit, a change of clothes, her double hip holster containing slightly heavier firepower, and additional ammunition.

Jackie headed downstairs to meet with the guys. When she reached the bottom of the steps, she noticed a stack of dismantled packing boxes on the floor near the door. Jackie dropped her bag at the bottom of the stairs and entered the living room. The entire room had been unpacked and set up to look exactly as she'd had it at their home in Chicago. She crossed into the kitchen and found everything put away, including the dirty dishes. Jackie snorted a soft laugh then walked down the hallway. She entered the study and found Monroe and Bogart softly arguing while setting up the desktop computer.

"Stop handing me the power cord," Monroe huffed. "I want the printer cable."

Bogart tossed the cord aside and glared at Monroe. "What the hell is a printer cable?" he demanded.

"Don't you know anything about computers?" Monroe asked with annoyance.

"I know I don't like them," he replied. "Do you know anything about a Chevy Big-Block engine?"

It was too early in the morning for Jackie to sit through another city boy versus country boy debate.

"Did you guys unpack the entire house?" Jackie asked, alerting them to her presence and putting an end to the debate.

Both men straightened, looked at her in the doorway, and put on their best smiles.

"Kirk and Beck are setting up the guest bedroom, and Ross was scrubbing down the guest bath," Monroe announced cheerfully. "Apart from your bedroom, I think that's everything."

"I'm impressed," Jackie announced while hiding her smile. She was about to leave the study when something occurred to her. "Oh, by the way, Bogart."

He groaned with defeat, straightened, and rolled his eyes. "What did I do now?"

Jackie ignored his comment and approached the desk. She opened the side drawer and removed an old black and white photo of an attractive woman taken more than twenty years ago.

"When I was packing the guestroom at the old house, I found this photo." She handed the slightly wrinkled photo to him. "Is it yours?"

Bogart accepted the photo, stared at it a moment in silence, and then smiled with relief. "Yeah," he announced cheerfully. "Wow, I thought I'd lost this forever. I didn't know what happened to it. Thanks."

Monroe glanced over his shoulder at the old photo of the woman. "Who is she?" he asked.

"That's my mother," Bogart replied proudly. "She died when I was only a few years old. The woman was a saint."

Bogart managed a smile and placed the photo into his back pocket, undoubtedly explaining the wrinkles in the picture. To Jackie's knowledge, Bogart didn't even own a wallet. It was unclear whether he even had a driver's license or photo identification. As a matter of fact, Jackie wasn't even sure if Bogart had a last name. There was an awkward silence, which was unusual with Bogart. Jackie felt the tension and slipped out of the study. She headed down the hallway toward the stairs. Ross, Beck, and Kirk were heading down the stairs at the same time. She waited for them to reach the bottom and grinned her approval.

"Thank you for doing the unpacking for me," she said almost timidly, feeling bad for the way she'd treated them earlier in the kitchen. "I couldn't have asked for a nicer birthday present."

She hugged each of the three men, who were quick to accept her affection. Ross placed his arm around her shoulder and grinned.

"This isn't your birthday present," he informed her while chuckling softly. "This is just a down payment on your piloting services. We're just about finished."

"I'll fill a few thermoses with coffee for the trip then," she announced cheerfully. "Let me know when you're ready."

"You've got it," Ross replied.

Jackie entered the kitchen and found two large thermoses. She filled each with the fresh coffee that had been warming in the carafe. She grabbed a few packets of sugar and added creamer to one of the thermos. She leaned against the counter a moment, sank into thought, and then grabbed a box of cookies. She stuffed them into a backpack with the thermoses. A few of the guys tended to get cranky when they were hungry. Dread swept over her. She *was* their mother hen! Ross entered the kitchen with a strange smile on his face and held up the picture of Bogart's mother.

"I found this on the floor in the hallway," Ross announced while grinning.

Jackie groaned softly and shook her head. She couldn't believe Bogart lost the photo in such a short period of time. Jackie accepted the photo from him. Before she could explain, Ross chuckled softly while hiding his grin.

"Did you find that in your father's stored junk?" Ross asked while tilting his head.

Jackie gave him a bewildered look. Before she could comment, he must have read her look and continued.

"That was one of the best shore leaves of my life," Ross informed her while grinning slyly. "Natalie from South Carolina. She had the sweetest Southern accent." Ross sighed while leaning against the counter. "It seems like a lifetime ago."

Jackie stared at him with astonishment, uncertain how to respond. She wasn't sure she wanted to respond. "How long ago was that?" she finally asked, feeling slightly tense.

"Oh," he groaned softly while thinking. "Close to thirty years ago."

Jackie felt her entire body stiffen. "You were, uh, sweet on her?" she asked while attempting a smile, but her mind was already reeling with the information.

Ross suddenly grinned. "She had a Southern accent to die for, and I was a twenty-something on shore leave. You do the math," he teased.

They heard a car horn honk just outside the house. Ross was suddenly enthusiastic.

"Oh, that must be Zack," he announced. "He was meeting an acquaintance."

Jackie gave him a curious look. Ross hurried from the kitchen. Jackie followed him while slipping the photo into her back pocket. Bogart and Monroe hurried into the hallway from the study and joined them.

"Is that Zack?" Monroe asked Ross while beaming with excitement.

Ross nodded. Jackie felt slightly suspicious as she followed the guys to the front door and stepped outside. They stopped on the sidewalk. Ross placed his arm around Jackie's shoulders and pointed to the driveway.

"*That's* your birthday present," he announced boldly.

Jackie stared with surprise at her father's black Mustang parked in the driveway. A heavy-set man with wild, curly black hair, wearing an excessively large Hawaiian shirt, casually leaned against the car and smirked. He gave her a playful wave. Sometime ago, although not all that long, Jackie had traded her father's car to Othello for a fake passport to get her out of a life-threatening situation. She never thought she'd see the car again. Jackie felt the tears welling up in her eyes. She hugged each of the guys while fighting her tears. Once she had thanked each of them, Othello approached her with the car keys.

"I took real good care of her for you," Othello announced as he handed her the keys.

She accepted the car keys and hugged Othello. "Thank you, Othello." Jackie then pulled away and gave him a surprised look. "Did you drive all the way here from the east coast?"

"Nah, the car and I took the train most of the way," he replied cheerfully. "Monroe said I could crash at your place a few days, since you wouldn't be here."

Jackie cast a look at Monroe while raising her brows in silent question. Monroe slipped behind Kirk, to avoid being seen.

"He said you could use a state-of-the-art security system at your new house," Othello announced. "I'm the man for the job. It should only take me a couple of days. I'll be gone before you get back."

Jackie again smiled warmly at the reclusive man she barely knew. "Make yourself at home," she replied. "And thanks again for my father's car. You didn't have to return it. I did owe you for all your help."

He casually shrugged then grinned. "If you can't help out a pretty woman in distress, what's the point of getting out of bed in the morning?"

Chapter Seven

*T*he panoramic, aerial view of the Cooper farm could be seen below as the Bell 412EPI helicopter passed overhead. The commercial 14-passenger helicopter contained a spacious, 220-foot cabin with aft-sliding side doors and adjustable seating for the team's needs. At the farm below, the black horse stood by the gate and watched with interest and obvious tension as the helicopter descended into the open land over one hundred yards away. Marie and Donna hurried out of the house onto the front porch and watched the helicopter land. The six men filed out of the helicopter as the rotors slowed. Jackie removed her headset and joined the men. Marie and Donna hurried from the porch, half jogging to meet the unfamiliar men, the desperation clearly on the women's faces. A man in his mid-forties appeared from the garage and joined the women in their approach. They met the team and Jackie not far from the barn.

"Are you them?" Donna gasped with urgency. Her eyes were red and swollen from days of crying. "Are you the men my husband hired?"

Ross politely extended his hand to the grieving woman. She uncertainly accepted it. "Yes, ma'am," he announced. "I'm Ross." He then introduced the rest of the guys and Jackie.

"I'm Donna, Monique's mother," she gently informed them with a slight quiver in her voice. "And this is Marie Cooper, Colleen's mother. Uh, that's Dave, Colleen's uncle."

Uncle Dave was a simple sort of guy dressed the role of a gentleman farmer. He had sandy brown hair and a thick goatee a shade darker than his actual hair. Had he been wearing American Civil War attire, he could almost pass for General Custer. He wasn't much of a talker, and neither was his sister. Marie was in no condition to even speak. She covered her eyes and sobbed softly.

Her brother placed his arms around her and led her away from the men to pull herself together. Jackie could feel every nerve in her body twitch to the women's anguish. It tore her up every time her father was deployed, but she at least knew where he would be. She couldn't imagine what these women were going through not knowing where their daughters were and if they were even alive. Donna led them to the porch. The men sat on the porch railing and, for the next twenty minutes, listened to Donna retell as much of the story as she could while the guys looked at pictures of the two girls and their horses.

"Of course, I immediately called my husband to Marie's house after Colleen's horse had returned," Donna continued. "He confirmed my fears. The injury to the horse was likely from a bullet." She trembled slightly while clutching her tissue. "Monique carries a rifle, but he ruled that out. He fears their disappearance may have something to do with his profession and felt it best to keep what happened out of the media. Some of his most trusted men have been scouting the area since Colleen's horse returned. We've also involved the park rangers we felt we could trust and one or two local police officers."

"But you haven't received any ransom note yet?" Ross asked with a curious look.

"No," she replied. "That's what has me worried the most." Donna attempted to hold back her tears. "Someone has my daughter and her friend. They've been gone three days now. I don't even want to think--" She could no longer hold back the tears.

The men fidgeted, uncertain how to react to the emotional woman. Monroe immediately joined Donna on the bench and placed his arm around her. She sobbed uncontrollably on his shoulder. Monroe was probably the most openly compassionate man on the team and had little reservations when it came to comforting women. The rest of the team seemed better equipped to break things and kill people. Being a man of action, Ross sprang to his feet, causing the others to do the same. Monroe remained seated and continued to console the sobbing woman.

"We have two missing girls gone three days," Ross bellowed out to his team. "Time is of the essence on this one. Beck and I will go through Colleen's bedroom, and Monroe will take Bogart and go back to Donna's house to search Monique's bedroom. I want to know everything these girls were into."

Donna sniffed and lifted her head from Monroe's shoulder. "They weren't into anything," she replied gently while dabbing her eyes with the tissue. "They had horses on their brains. Everything from riding to saving the wild herd on the game land."

"Wild herd?" Ross asked.

"Monique told us about some poachers trying to steal the herd from the game land," Donna replied while clinging to her damp tissue. "My husband and the park rangers have been scouring the area in shifts. The herd is still there, but they haven't found any trace of poachers or the girls. That's where he's been concentrating his efforts."

Ross turned to Jackie. "I want you to fly Zack and Kirk over the game land and seek out this herd of wild horses. I want to know about any buildings or campsites within a few miles of that herd. If you see anyone, find out who they are."

Jackie nodded and headed from the porch with Kirk and Zack on her heels. Beck was already joining Marie and Uncle Dave, explaining his need to search Colleen's bedroom. Marie joined him and led him into the house. Donna took Monroe and Bogart to her jeep, although she allowed Monroe to drive, since she was still shaking from her emotional breakdown.

†

*T*he security office holding cell was located in the basement of the building opposite the fenced generator. Colleen paced the cell, which contained three walls of stone block and one wall of bars. There were two bunks built into the wall, although neither had mattresses, and a toilet near the back. Colleen kept her eyes on the door to the security office beyond the solid metal cell door and watched for their captors. Monique stood on the two thin, folded rotting mattresses, allowing her to peer out the small, barred window just above ground level. She held a metal hoof pick in her hand and chiseled at the cement holding the bars in place. It would seem in three days' time, they had put a deep divot beneath the bars. Monique groaned and flexed her sore shoulder. Colleen glanced at her.

"My turn?"

"Another few minutes," Monique replied then took a moment to lean on the window ledge.

Just outside the building, Monique's horse, Storm Cloud, grazed within the fenced generator area. Her horse remained saddled and carefully stepped around his reins while grazing.

Monique frowned and sighed. "He's right there," she muttered. "We just need to get out of this damned cell."

"Your father will come for us," Colleen assured her friend. "Thunder went home, I know he did. Your father probably has half the Bureau searching for us."

"I know," Monique sighed, although she appeared defeated.

Colleen suddenly perked up and looked at her friend. "Someone's coming," she shouted in a whisper.

Monique jumped off the mattresses. Colleen grabbed the mattress on top and threw it onto the first bunk. Monique grabbed the second mattress and tossed it onto the other bunk. Monique replaced the hoof pick to its holder inside her boot and both girls jumped on the first bunk together, placing their backs to the wall. The outer door opened and Tremaine, the man with the excessively large nose, entered. He placed a paper bag through the small opening in the bars on the floor along with two bottles of water. He straightened and glared at them.

"The boss said to feed you," Tremaine muttered. "If it were up to me, I'd let you rot in here."

They waited until he left before jumping up from the bunk and hurrying for the bag and bottled water. Colleen eagerly opened the water and drank several swallows. Monique opened the bag and peered inside. They exchanged looks.

"Think we can trust eating it?" Colleen asked.

Monique removed the professionally wrapped sandwiches and two bags of chips. "I don't think they've been tampered with," she replied and handed her friend a sandwich.

They returned to the bunk and tore the wrapping off the sandwiches. Both attempted to eat slow but had a difficult time controlling themselves. They only had a bag of pretzels and an apple each over the last two days. Thankfully, the faucet in their cell worked. After letting the brown water run a few minutes, it eventually cleared and seemed drinkable.

"What do you think they intend to do with us?" Colleen asked between mouthfuls of sandwich.

"I'm guessing they don't know what to do with us," Monique replied. "That's probably why they locked us down here."

Colleen groaned and shook her head. "I hope your father finds us soon."

The girls had just finished eating their sandwiches when they heard a commotion within the security office. Both girls sprang to their feet and stood near the bars, hoping to hear the intense argument. The outer door was unlocked. Both girls returned to the first bunk and sat close together. They were fearful after hearing the loud, angry voices. Tremaine and Hoffman entered the holding area and paused before the bars. They could hear someone else within the security office. Monique and Colleen looked at the two men. The girls attempted a calm appearance, but both were now shaking.

"Hats off," Hoffman ordered from the cell door.

Monique and Colleen exchanged bewildered looks then removed their cowboy hats. When they looked back at the two men, Tremaine took their picture with his cell phone. Just as quickly as they had entered, they had left, slamming the outer door. Both girls slowly moved off the bunk and approached the cell door.

They heard low male voices in the security office followed by a loud, "Son-of-a-bitch!" The unfamiliar male voice then started shouting softly. "Do you know who that kid is?" he demanded. "Her father is a fucking fed!"

The voices continued to shout as the men left the security office. Their voices could be heard into the hallway. Monique and Colleen exchanged looks.

"That's either good or bad," Monique announced nervously. "They'll either abandon us here and hightail it to the Mexican border or dispose of us as fast as possible."

"Dispose?" Colleen suddenly gasped. "You mean--?"

Monique frowned and nodded. "If they intend to kill us, they won't wait long."

She removed the hoof pick from her boot. Both girls grabbed the mattresses and piled them in front of the window. Monique began chiseling at the bars with a sense of urgency.

Chapter Eight

$\mathcal{T}$he Cooper farm was fairly quiet in the late morning hour. Ross paced the length of the porch with his nose in Monique's journal. He read in virtual silence, although his brows knitted periodically, suggesting something caught his attention. Donna and Marie sat on the bench together and watched him read from the journal, possibly wondering what he found interesting. Beck and Monroe talked with Uncle Dave out by the garage while Bogart sat on the porch railing across from the women and flipped through a photo album.

"You weren't kidding," Bogart finally remarked. "These girls love their horses."

"They had Storm Cloud and Thunder since they were colts," Marie replied gently. "The girls were--?" She glanced at Donna for confirmation.

"Eight years old," Donna replied.

Marie nodded. "They spent every waking hour training those horses. Sometimes, I actually believe the horses know them just as well."

"Huh," Bogart snorted then grinned. "Maybe we should let the horse find them."

All three looked at Bogart.

"What?" he remarked defensively while catching their looks. "You said the horse came back to the farm. The animal is obviously smarter than he's being given credit." Bogart shrugged and returned to the photo album. "Sort of like me."

"Trust me," Marie replied with little hope. "If you set that horse free, the only place he might go is to Donna's house. It wouldn't be the first time either horse has gotten out of his fence and took a walk. That's usually where they end up."

Ross lowered the journal and looked toward the paddock where the black horse stood by the gate staring toward the woods. Every so often he'd let out a whinny.

"Does he always do that?" Ross asked.

"What?" Marie questioned.

"Stare at the woods and neigh."

"Sometimes at night, after Colleen puts him away, he calls to Storm Cloud," she replied. "On a quiet night, you can hear Storm Cloud calling back to him."

"He looks tense," Ross remarked.

"I'm sure he is," Marie replied. "He's been locked up for three days without Colleen or Storm Cloud. Dave would disagree with me, but I think those horses miss each other and the girls when they're gone."

The helicopter was heard in the distance, catching the horse's attention as well as those at the farm. Ross shut Monique's journal and set it aside. As he walked off the porch, Bogart set the photo album down and hurried after him. Ross approached Beck and Monroe at the garage with Uncle Dave.

"I need a tracker," Ross informed Beck.

"Yeah, sure," Beck replied. "What am I attaching it to?"

Ross pointed to the paddock and the anxious horse that now watched the approaching helicopter. "I want you to attach it to that horse."

"Damn!" Bogart cried out excitedly while grinning. "I knew I was right."

"You aren't right yet," Ross reminded. "It may be a waste of time, but I'm willing to put a little faith in the horse."

Beck nodded with conviction. "Yeah, sure. You've got it." He hurried for his duffel bag near the porch.

As the helicopter landed, Ross headed away from the farm to greet Jackie and his men. Monroe and Bogart remained behind him. Zack and Kirk got out of the helicopter. Jackie was only a minute behind them.

"Anything?" Ross asked.

"We found the herd," Kirk informed him with little emotion. "It's like the lady said, the rangers are searching that area for the girls. We spoke with two of them. They haven't found anything. No girls; no poachers."

"Okay," Ross replied while nodding. "I'm going to need Jackie in the air. Monroe and Bogart will go with her this time. Kirk and Zack, you're with Beck and me. We're going to commandeer Donna's jeep."

"What's the plan?" Kirk asked.

"I'm hoping a certain horse can give us some answers," Ross replied.

†

$\mathcal{I}$t only took Beck a few minutes to attach the tiny transmitter to the horse's leather halter. The horse seemed unusually excited and danced around by the gate. Marie and Donna stood near the fence and watched with anticipation. They exchanged soft whispers about the horse's rising excitement. It almost seemed as if the horse knew they intended to set him free. Jackie, Monroe, and Bogart returned to the helicopter and lifted off a few minutes earlier to keep from swaying the horse's interest. Once the men were outside the fence, they stared at the horse with strange looks. The horse snorted and started trotting along the fence line near the gate. He'd then spin wildly on his hindquarters and trot in the opposite direction.

"It's like he knows something is up," Beck remarked and eyed Ross. "Maybe we should wait in the jeep."

Ross nodded. As the three men headed for the jeep, Ross looked back at Donna and Marie.

"Once we're in the jeep, open the gate," Ross informed them.

Both women nodded. Ross hurried to join the others in the jeep. Thunder snorted loudly and bolted along the fence line, spinning wildly. Donna and Marie exchanged nervous looks. Marie took a deep breath and headed for the gate. Thunder charged the gate and nearly crashed into it. Marie cried out with surprise. The horse suddenly squealed and reared up. He wanted out! Marie took a deep breath, unlatched the gate, and hid behind it as she pulled it open. The black horse galloped through the open gate and ran down the driveway. Kirk put the jeep into gear and drove after the horse, maintaining enough distance so as not to chase it. Beck fiddled with his tracker while the helicopter flew above at a safe distance, also following the horse. It only took Thunder five minutes to reach the Harris farm next door. The running horse was neighing excitedly the entire way, his head held high and his tail flumed behind him. The jeep pulled down the driveway and stopped at a distance. All four men groaned softly.

50

"Marie was right," Ross muttered. "He just came back to Donna's farm."

The black horse pranced around outside the barn while snorting. He then trotted into the barn while neighing excitedly. When he didn't find what he was looking for, he trotted out of the barn, stopped, and neighed loudly with his head high in the air. He snorted and sniffed the air. The only sound was the faint sound of the helicopter overhead in the distance.

"So much for that," Beck remarked. "At least we didn't waste more than half an hour on that."

The horse suddenly took off down the driveway and headed for the woods. All four turned in the jeep and watched with surprise.

"That's not the way to the Cooper farm," Zack informed them.

"Track him," Ross ordered then looked at Kirk behind the wheel. "Go, go, go!"

Chapter Nine

The helicopter flew high above the trees over the game land.

Jackie piloted the helicopter with Monroe in the passenger seat alongside her. Bogart rode in the back and kept watch with binoculars. The black horse ran through the path in the woods and crossed a clearing, startling the herd of wild horses. The horses jumped around and watched the running horse. A few attempted to follow, but they soon gave up chase.

"Echo one, do you have eyes on jackrabbit?" Ross's voice came over Jackie's headset.

"Echo one?" Monroe muttered and glanced at Jackie. "Who's echo one?"

"Who's jackrabbit?" Bogart asked, equally confused.

"Copy that, gold leader," Jackie replied into her headset.

Monroe and Bogart exchanged dumbfounded looks then shook their heads in unison.

"He's holding his current course and speed," Jackie informed Ross.

They followed the horse for nearly half an hour. He was starting to slow his pace, growing tired. All three suddenly straightened in their seats and looked ahead in the distance.

"Ross, we have an old ghost town up ahead," she announced into her headset. "The horse is heading straight for the town."

They could see the jeep closing in on the horse then drop back, so not to frighten him. Thunder trotted into the ghost town and neighed loudly. There was no response. He stopped in the middle of town with his tail flumed and his head high. Thunder snorted loudly and listened. An unkempt man, looking a bit like a hillbilly, walked out of one of the more sound buildings, startling the horse. He smiled at the horse and talked softly to him while approaching.

Jackie kept her distance from the air. "Ross, there's someone in the town. He's approaching jackrabbit."

The man caught the horse by the halter. Thunder suddenly squealed and reared up in the air. He immediately leaped forward, bowling the man over. The horse took off through town.

"He ran from the man," Jackie informed Ross. "I think he scared jackrabbit."

"Keep eyes on the horse," Ross replied. "We're going to talk to the guy and search the town."

"Roger, gold leader."

The man now covered in dirt straightened and brushed off his pants. He looked to the sky and saw the helicopter passing overhead. The jeep drove through town and skidded to a stop almost behind him, startling the man. When he saw the four intimidating men get out of the jeep with their handguns drawn, he smiled almost nervously.

"Oh, hey," he announced, "you guys must be lost."

Zack and Kirk took flanking positions on either side of the street, causing the man to look nervously around.

"I didn't do anything wrong," the man announced defensively. "I'm just passing through myself."

"Glad to hear," Ross remarked while grinning. "That means you have no problem with us looking around."

"Uh, problem?" the man fumbled. "Uh, no, of course not. Have a look around. Take your time."

Kirk and Zack were already entering the buildings on either side of the street. Beck walked past Ross and the stranger, heading for the next building up ahead. Ross paused by the man and grinned almost sadistically.

"So how did you get here?" Ross asked.

The man stared at him a moment then pointed down the road. "I have a four wheeler. Some friends and I are taking the day to explore the valley."

"Oh?" Ross announced cheerfully. "Let's meet these friends."

The man uncertainly led him to the next building. Ross glanced down an alley, hesitated, and turned. He walked along the alley with the man now following him.

"The guys are this way," the man announced.

Ross ignored him and stopped at the end of the alley. A large panel truck was parked behind the larger building. Within the truck was stock fencing.

Ross indicated the truck while studying the man. "You always take a truck full of stock fence with you on your rides?"

"That?" he questioned. "That's not ours. That was here when we got here. Come, I'll introduce you to my friends."

Ross followed him through the back door. They walked along a rickety old hallway and approached the front room of the building. The man spoke to Ross as he passed through the doorway. Ross drew his weapon from his concealed shoulder holster.

"Here," he announced. "These are my friends."

Ross passed through the doorway and immediately kicked the man hidden to the right of the door and aimed his gun at the man hiding on the left. None of them were armed, but it was an ambush all the same. The man he was following raised his hands in the air and appeared alarmed.

"They didn't mean any harm," he quickly announced. "They're just a little untrusting."

"Yeah?" Ross demanded then grinned. "Me too."

He motioned with his gun, waving the three men to the nearby table. They were the same men who had been herding the horses three days earlier. The men took their seats and stared at Ross.

"We're looking for two missing teenage girls," Ross announced. "A blond and a brunette. Have you seen either of them in the last three days?"

"Teenage girls? Out here?" the first man suddenly asked. "No, there haven't been any girls out here. Why would teenage girls be out here?"

Ross nodded. "Assuming you're telling the truth, you have nothing to worry about," he announced casually. "Of course, if I find any trace of those girls in this town, we're going to have ourselves a good old-fashioned western lynching."

"I swear," the first man announced more quickly. "We haven't seen any girls out here."

†

*B*lake Harris entered his office with little enthusiasm while sipping his coffee. He collapsed behind his desk and allowed his head to fall into his hands. He refrained from groaning. The events of the last few days had clearly taken their toll on him. It was possible he hadn't slept since his daughter's disappearance. He finally straightened, took another large swallow of coffee, and attempted to get on with his day. Blake sorted through the mail on his desk then hesitated when he saw a letter sized envelope with bold typing on the front and the Bureau's address as the return address. Blake stared at the envelope a moment longer then carefully took it by the edges and sliced it open with the letter opener. He dumped the letter and a photo onto the desk. When he saw a crude printer copy of his daughter and her friend in a photo on plain paper, he nearly grabbed the letter without thinking. He hesitated and quickly removed a pair of latex gloves from the drawer. He carefully opened the letter with a tweezers and his pen. Blake's expression shattered as he stared at the crudely typed letter in all caps.

It simply read: *If you ever want to see your daughter and her friend again, all evidence in the Roderick files must never see a courtroom. When Justin Roderick goes free, so will the girls.*

Blake stared at the letter for several minutes or longer before he jumped to his feet. Without hesitation, he placed the letter, the photo, and the envelope into a plastic evidence bag, removed his gloves, and hurried from his office. Blake rushed from his office and nearly collided with two agents. Both men were startled by his hasty entrance into the hallway.

"Something happening?" the agent suddenly asked.

Blake looked at Agents Hoffman and Tremaine then held up the letter. "This needs to go to forensics immediately," he announced. "If it's legit, Justin Roderick's people have my daughter and her friend."

"Justin Roderick?" Agent Tremaine gasped then looked at his partner. He looked back at Blake and shook his head. "He was just booked last week on human trafficking."

"His men have your daughter?" Agent Hoffman asked with concern clearly on his face. "We need to do whatever it takes to get her back."

"What do you need us to do?" Agent Tremaine asked, springing into action.

"Get this to forensics and then dig up everything you can on Justin Roderick's case," Blake announced then vigorously ran his fingers through his hair. "I need to, uh, talk to my wife. I'll be back in an hour or two."

Both men nodded and watched Blake hurry along the hallway and head into the elevator. Hoffman and Tremaine exchanged looks but didn't comment. Hoffman held back his tiny grin.

"We should probably get right on this," Tremaine announced while indicating the bag containing the ransom note.

"Yes," Hoffman replied. "We have a lot of work to do."

†

*T*he helicopter hovered overhead in the distance as the horse rested beneath a shade tree, seemingly in the middle of nowhere. Jackie groaned and looked at Monroe seated alongside her.

"If he's going to nap, I may as well set her down," Jackie remarked. "My arms are getting sore."

"Wait," Monroe announced and pointed out the front. "He's moving."

The horse looked around, let out a neigh, and listened. There was no responding neigh. Thunder took off into a canter then slowed back to a trot. He was obviously getting tired from the journey. The helicopter casually pursued the horse.

"Gold leader," Jackie announced into her headset. "Jackrabbit is on the move."

There was no response.

Monroe glanced at her. "They must be away from the jeep," he remarked.

"Keep trying him," Jackie informed her friend and concentrated on flying. Now that the horse was moving slower, she had to maintain a slower speed.

Monroe was finally able to contact Ross about the horse continuing onward. The second half of the horse's trek took almost an hour. The horse stopped on top of a ridge, stood straight and rigid, letting out a fierce neigh. There was a responding neigh. The helicopter hovered a moment. Thunder raced down the hillside for the abandoned amusement park below. The moment the amusement park came into view, Jackie lowered the helicopter, touching ground. Monroe and Bogart leaped from the helicopter with their assault rifles in hand before Jackie completely shut it down. Jackie finished her landing, tore off her headset, and ran after the men. All three approached the ridge near some rocks and looked to the abandoned amusement park below in the distance. Its very sight was almost chilling. Bogart watched through his binoculars as the black horse raced across the plains, entered through the opened main gates, and ran straight for the chain link fence surrounding the generator building. Storm Cloud squealed loudly and ran across the fenced area, greeting his friend.

Within their basement prison, Monique and Colleen had been dozing when Storm Cloud's loud, shrill neigh woke them. Both girls tore their mattresses from the bunks, piled them in front of the window, and jumped on top to look outside. Their eyes lit up to the sight of Colleen's black horse touching noses with Storm Cloud through the chain link fence.

"It's Thunder," Colleen cried out softly and turned to Monique. "We're saved!"

Both girls looked around outside but quickly became concerned.

"I don't see anyone," Monique remarked. "Where are they?"

"Maybe he got ahead of them."

Monique suddenly groaned and felt defeated. "Maybe he broke through the fence and took off."

"No," Colleen protested. "They're coming! They're out there. They're just--waiting."

"Waiting for what?" Monique demanded then groaned.

She removed the hoof pick from her boot and started scraping vigorously at the concrete surrounding the bars.

†

*J*ackie stood by the helicopter attempting to reach anyone on the radio while Monroe and Bogart hid behind a large rock and kept watch on the old amusement park below. Jackie became disgusted and approached the guys, lowering herself near them behind the rocks.

"I can't reach anyone on the radio," she remarked with annoyance.

"Beck has the tracking device on the horse," Monroe reminded. "They'll find us."

"It's not just that," Jackie remarked and sank into her own concerns.

Monroe looked back at her and appeared curious. "What then?"

"I can't reach anyone at the Cooper farm," Jackie informed him, again feeling that pang in the pit of her stomach. "They were adamant we contact them the moment we found anything. They said they'd be waiting by the radio. Three people and no one can answer the call they were anxiously awaiting?"

Monroe sank into thought then looked into her eyes. "Go, Jackie," he announced. "I'm making the call. You can be there and back in less than an hour. We'll be casing the place a little while anyway."

Jackie nodded and hurried for the helicopter. The helicopter no sooner lifted off and headed back toward the farm when the jeep pulled up. All four men piled out with their assault rifles slung over their shoulders and hurried to where Monroe and Bogart lie in wait. They crouched alongside the men, keeping their heads down.

"What do we have?" Ross asked.

"The horse found his friend," Monroe informed him. "The pinto is still under saddle, but he appears to be locked inside that fence beyond the building and truck."

"No sign of life," Bogart informed him then returned to his stakeout.

"Okay," Ross announced. "We're going to flank the area, but we're not moving in until we know what we're up against."

All six switched on their hand radios and placed their small transmitters into their ears.

"Watch for lifeforms," Ross announced. "I want to know how many men are down there, if any, and how heavily armed before we go in." He then looked at Zack. "If nothing moves in the next hour, Zack, you're on point."

Zack nodded.

"Two-by-two formation," Ross announced and gave the signal.

Kirk and Zack went south while Ross and Beck went north. It would take them several minutes to make their way around the park while keeping out of sight. There was too much open terrain to make the move any faster. Monroe now watched the park while Bogart watched the men depart. He glanced at Monroe.

"Guess it's just you and me this time," Bogart remarked.

"Yeah," Monroe scoffed without looking at him. "Don't accidentally shoot me."

Bogart sneered at him even though he couldn't see it. "Very funny."

Chapter Ten

*T*he helicopter lowered in the yard not far from the barn, since the horse was no longer around to be spooked by it. Jackie cut the engine and jumped out of the pilot's seat. She tossed her headset aside and stared at the quiet farmhouse. No one came out to greet her. Uncle Dave's pickup truck was still parked before the garage and possibly hadn't moved since they'd left. She assessed the farmhouse and outer buildings a moment then reached back inside the helicopter. She removed a double nylon gun holster containing two semiautomatics. She connected the belt around her waist and attached the straps around each of her thighs. Attached to the back of the holster were two eight-inch tactical batons. Jackie approached the house while removing both tactical batons from their rightful spot on the holster. As she flicked her wrists, the batons extended to two feet each.

Rather than walk onto the porch, she rounded the house and peered into several windows. The house was eerily silent, which made no sense. Both women and Colleen's uncle were anxiously awaiting news of their findings. It seemed odd they would leave. Since the guys had Donna's jeep and Uncle Dave's truck was still parked by the garage, either the women walked to Donna's house or someone had picked them up. Neither story sounded plausible to Jackie. She finally reached the back of the house, still with no sign of life inside. Jackie approached the back, kitchen door, stood to the side, and tried the knob. It wasn't locked. She took a deep breath then pushed the door inward and slipped into the kitchen. She assessed both entrances to the kitchen. When no one came at her from either doorway, she proceeded in the least logical direction, in case someone was waiting to jump her.

She crossed the empty dining room and approached the living room archway. Her boots made little to no noise as she crossed the hardwood floor. She entered the living room and saw Uncle Dave reclined in his easy chair in the corner. His head rested back and his mouth hung open as he snored softly. Jackie stared at the sleeping man with disbelief. He hadn't heard the helicopter?

"Dave," she announced firmly. He still didn't wake. "Dave!"

Uncle Dave flew up in the chair, the footrest crashing to the floor with a thump. He looked around with surprise.

"What? What?" He looked at Jackie then groaned softly. "Oh, it's you."

"You didn't hear me arrive?" Jackie demanded.

He gently rubbed his eyes. "No, I must've dosed off," Uncle Dave replied. "I haven't slept much the last few days." He looked at her and quickly sprang to his feet. "Did you find them?"

"We found the second girl's horse," Jackie replied while eyeing him with distrust then looked around. "Where are Donna and Marie?"

"Donna's husband received a ransom demand," Uncle Dave reported. "He thought it best to take the women someplace safe."

"Why didn't you go?"

"I thought someone should stay here and see what you guys found," he replied.

"What did the ransom note say?"

"I don't know," Uncle Dave replied. "He didn't offer that information. Although, it looks as if the girls were abducted because of him."

Jackie eyed him suspiciously. "What does Donna's husband do for a living?" she asked while tilting her head. It seemed odd that no one mentioned his profession until now.

"Well, he's, uh, you know," Uncle Dave fumbled. "He works for the government."

"Care to narrow that down?" Jackie demanded.

"It's, well, classified," he replied almost timidly.

Jackie glared at him, growing impatient. She intended to tell Ross about her suspicions involving Uncle Dave. He certainly wasn't acting normal. Before she could press him further for a decent response, they heard a plane in the near distance. Jackie became alert. Just by the sound, she knew it was a private plane, but certainly larger than a two-seater style plane most private citizens would own. She hurried from the house onto the front porch with her batons firmly in hand. Uncle Dave was only two steps behind her. Both looked to the sky. What was easily a ten-passenger plane flew overhead. Jackie and Uncle Dave ran into the yard and looked past the house to watch the plane. On cue, it circled and came back.

"Inside!" Jackie ordered and forced Uncle Dave back onto the porch.

Jackie replaced the retracted batons to her holster and ran for the helicopter. She jumped into the back, grabbed an assault rifle, and leaped out the opposite side. She ran for the barn and hid just inside the open doorway. As she peered out, the plane was already touching down on the long, dirt driveway. The Grand Caravan EX was a 10-passener single-engine prop plane with non-retractable wheels, wings attached on the top, and doors in the front and back. The body length was 41' with a wingspan of 52'. It was an impressive plane. Jackie clutched her assault rifle and watched as the plane turned and taxied toward the helicopter. Something wasn't right. She waited a moment for the plane to stop and shut down. As the plane door opened lowering into steps, she positioned herself just outside the barn door and aimed the assault rifle.

A silver sable German shepherd dog, sporting the latest in K-9 bulletproof vest wear, leaped down the steps and sniffed around the area. Jackie groaned and lowered the rifle while allowing a soft laugh to escape. She slung the rifle over her shoulder and left the barn. The dog saw her, became excited, and ran for her. He barely stopped before jumping on her. She affectionately scratched the dog's scruff.

"Hey, Darth," she announced while laughing. "When did you learn to fly? That landing needs some work."

"Bullshit," came a gruff male voice.

Jackie looked toward the plane as Gil approached her. Being one of the stylish ones, he too wore tan cargo pants and a button shirt. Jackie grinned, met him halfway, and hugged him. He returned the embrace.

"Happy birthday, Jackie."

"Thanks, Gil."

Jackie pulled away and took in a sweeping glance of the newly bronzed man. She had to admit, he looked good with a tan. She was certain a week of sex with the ex did wonders for his personality as well.

"What are you doing here?" she finally asked with a curious look. "I thought you were indulging in a couple's vacation full of sun, surf, and sex."

"I was," he replied, "but then I heard the assignment involved kids." Gil frowned. "The thought of any of those guys interacting with children prevented me from sleeping." He folded his arms across his chest and stared at her with disbelief. "How the hell did the old man get you to ride along? Didn't Holden put you on house arrest?"

"You mean, will he kill me if he finds out I'm running amuck with you guys?" she suddenly asked while raising a clever brow. "Oh, definitely, but as you said, how could I refuse helping find two girls."

"Want to bring me up to speed?"

†

*B*ogart sat casually spread out with his back to the rock while Monroe kept watch over the abandoned amusement park through the binoculars.

"Anything yet?" Bogart muttered.

"No," Monroe snapped with annoyance. "Stop asking. You're worse than a two-year-old."

Bogart sighed deeply. "Shouldn't we be storming the place searching for those kids?" he asked, appearing mildly frustrated. "It seems to me that every minute we waste sitting here, they could be suffering."

"Yeah, let's do it your way," Monroe scoffed lowly. "Guns blazing."

"Hell yeah," Bogart launched and looked at Monroe's profile. "We've been sitting here nearly an hour. There's no telling what those bastards are doing to those girls." He angrily tossed a rock. "Pisses me off just thinking about it."

"So stop thinking about it," Monroe remarked sternly. "We don't even know that they have those girls. We don't even know if there's a 'they' down there. You don't rush in shooting off your guns." Monroe glared at Bogart then drove the point home. "That's how people *accidentally* get shot."

Bogart sneered at Monroe then groaned and rested his head against the rock behind him. Monroe suddenly became interested in something he saw.

"Who has eyes on the truck?" Monroe asked into his transmitter. "I thought I saw something."

"We have activity," Ross was heard responding through their ear transmitters. "Zack, where are you?"

"Hiding high," came Zack's calm voice.

Monroe searched the park with use of the binoculars. One of the Ferris wheel carts rocked slightly. Monroe lowered the binoculars.

"How the hell did he get up there?" Monroe demanded more to himself, causing Bogart to turn and look as well.

Within the highest cart on the Ferris wheel, Zack remained curled up on the seat of the round, covered cart while watching the park from his elevated view. As the cart rocked, the faint squeaking sound indicated a heavy buildup of rust on the bolts and chains. He should have been concerned for safety reasons, but Zack rarely was.

"I see two men coming out of that large building," Zack announced. "They're smoking by the truck."

Once the cart stopped rocking and squeaking, Zack purposely rotated his body, allowing the cart to continue to rock and squeak. He was much like a child on a swing set.

"Zack," Kirk announced over his ear transmitter. "Can you see the alleyway between the first building and the kiddy rides?"

Zack shifted slightly, allowing the cart to rock a little harder. He looked through his small binoculars. A camouflaged tarp covered something within the alley.

"Looks like we're hiding something," Zack replied. "Want me to investigate?"

"Negative," Ross replied over his ear transmitter.

Toward the rear of the park, Ross stood in the tall grass near the last curve of the wooden roller coaster. He watched the rest of the park from afar.

"Monroe," Ross announced while watching the park through binoculars. "See if you can reach Jackie in the helo. I'd like her to do a flyby. Might draw some people out. Give us a better idea of what we're dealing with."

"Roger that," Monroe chirped through Ross's transmitter.

Back on the ridge, Monroe handed Bogart the binoculars and hurried for the jeep parked several yards away. He removed the radio and attempted to hail Jackie.

"Eagle eye one, this is Prince Charming," Monroe announced. "Do you copy?"

"Prince Charming?" came Jackie's response over the radio. "What are you smoking?"

Monroe grinned at the comment. "Gold leader wants to give this place a buzz cut. What's your ten-twenty?"

"I'm about two minutes off your ass," she replied. "I'll give you that buzz cut and raise you an enema."

Monroe appeared bewildered. "A what?" He shook his head and grinned while speaking into the handheld radio. "Seriously, Jackie, you need to learn actual military terms."

She was heard laughing over the radio. "Heads up," she announced.

The faint sound of a plane was heard in the near distance. Monroe and Bogart both looked to the sky. The ten-passenger plane came into view, surprising both men.

"Uh, where'd you get the new wings?" Monroe asked into the radio.

"A special guest appearance," Jackie teased back. "Special airborne coming to an amusement park near you."

The plane's engine suddenly cut out, leaving the plane gliding quietly through the air. Something dropped out the back. A parachute opened almost immediately.

"What the--?" Monroe gasped.

From his perch on top of the Ferris wheel, Zack immediately straightened and watched the man parachute into the back of the park with the silver sable German shepherd harnessed to his chest. Zack suddenly frowned.

"Why does the dog get all the fun?" Zack pouted.

The dog was released just before Gil hit the ground. Darth took off across the clearing and ran behind the bumper cars. Gil skillfully collected his parachute into a messy bundle and slipped out of sight, joining the dog. The plane's engine started up, sputtered, and again went in and out. The plane teetered and eventually glided to a landing in the large open space that was once the parking lot outside the amusement park.

"Ah, Christ!" Ross's voice cursed over everyone's ear transmitters.

Back on the ridge, Bogart signaled to Monroe, who still held the radio. "Four men on ATVs are mounting up to greet her," Bogart called to him.

"You have company, Jackie," Monroe announced into the radio.

"How many weapons?" Jackie asked.

"Gun count," Monroe announced through his ear transmitter.

"Possibly handguns," Beck responded to the question from his vantage point. "No heavy firepower on them."

"Handguns, Jackie," Monroe informed her through the radio. "I think Triple A is coming out to assist the damsel in distress."

"Just applying my lipstick now," she teased.

Within the abandoned park, Darth trotted along the backs of old rides while sniffing the ground. Gil slipped along the sides of buildings and remained out of sight while keeping his eyes on the tablet in his hand. A camera affixed to the dog's vest allowed him to see everything Darth was seeing. Gil flattened himself against a concession stand and watched the monitor.

"New toy?" Zack asked from over Gil's shoulder.

Gil jumped with surprise and looked at Zack, who now peered over his shoulder. "Damn it, Zack," he grumbled. "I wish you'd stop playing ninja around me. You're gonna get shot one of these days."

"What's he tracking?" Zack asked without regard to the comment.

"We let him sniff some of the girls' dirty clothes back at the house," Gil replied.

"Uh, huh," Zack remarked showing little interest. "Unfortunately, everything they own smells like their horses."

They watched as Darth approached the generator fence. He excitedly watched the horses. Gil groaned softly. There was a soft whistle. Darth suddenly turned and ran for the large building. As he closed in on the building, Monique and Colleen were seen through the small, barred window level with the ground.

Within the cell, Monique and Colleen excitedly pet the dog through the bars.

"He's wearing a vest," Monique cried out softly. "That means he's a police dog."

Colleen then pointed to the camera. "It's a camera!"

Both girls became excited and waved at the camera. "Help us," both girls cried softly. "We're down here!"

Chapter Eleven

*J*ackie stood on a small step stool just outside the plane's engine compartment. She tinkered around within the engine as the four men on ATVs approached. She had discarded her leather jacket on the pull-down steps near the flight deck, allowing the men to get a full look at her in her white tank top. Her top hung down to her hips, just far enough to cover the gun holster in the back of her pants. Her white tank top was nearly see through and easily revealed her lacy, white bra beneath. Her formfitting black pants were tucked inside her knee-high black boots. She certainly gave the illusion of being unarmed and non-threatening. The men, all dressed in store-bought Army fatigues, stopped their four wheelers and took in an eyeful of Jackie as she casually turned on the step stool. One man remained serious, although the other three couldn't hide their grins at the attractive woman with her awe-inspiring cleavage staring them in the face. Jackie appeared relieved and smiled sweetly at the men, who dismounted their ATVs.

"Aren't you boys a sight for sore eyes," she announced and carefully walked down the three steps from the stool, taking extra care to give them maximum view of her cleavage.

"You're lucky you didn't crash," the first man announced, easily falling for her damsel in distress charm.

Jackie grinned and raised her brows seductively. "Technically, I did." She approached her jacket on the steps, picking it up while being careful to keep the semiautomatic beneath it concealed. She turned toward the men while maintaining her smile. "I busted a waterline," she informed them. "I have duct tape, which should temporarily fix it long enough to reach the nearest airport, but I'm a little low on water." She grimaced slightly. "You boys wouldn't happen to have a gallon of water I could borrow, would you?"

"You're in luck," the first man replied cheerfully. "We have plenty of water."

"Toby will get that for you," the serious man informed her. He obviously wasn't as trusting or nearly as taken by her seduction act.

The first man, who was obviously Toby, appeared disappointed and reluctantly drove back to the abandoned amusement park.

The serious looking man indicated her plane. "Mind if I check her out?"

His *request* wasn't as much curiosity as distrust. Jackie shrugged and gestured toward the entrance near the flight deck.

"Be my guest," she announced simply.

The serious man wasted little time climbing the few steps into the plane. The remaining two men took advantage of the other man's departure to put the moves on the attractive, female pilot. Jackie couldn't help but wonder if her boys were so easily distracted by strategically placed cleavage. She assumed if they were that they probably wouldn't have lived as long as they had.

†

*Z*ack and Gil joined Darth outside the small barred window where Monique and Colleen eagerly awaited their rescue. Both girls were relieved to see the two, heavily armed men approaching. The men crouched low to the ground on either side of the window. Zack kept his back to the wall and surveyed the area while clutching his semiautomatic. His assault rifle remained casually slung over his shoulder while not in use. Gil glanced through the window at the two girls below.

"Thank God," Colleen gasped.

"You girls okay?" Gil asked gently.

Both nodded.

"I'm Gil and that's Zack," he informed them. "We're going to get you out of there, but we need you to remain calm and stay quiet. Okay?"

"Just get us out of here," Monique whispered with a sense of urgency.

"We will," Gil announced in a calm, reassuring tone, "just as soon as the rest of our team arrives. We don't know how many men are inside the building."

"There were at least eight men here the day they captured us," Monique informed him.

Colleen was suddenly staring off. "What's he doing?" she asked, catching Gil's attention.

Gil and Monique looked across the small courtyard to the tractor-trailer. Zack opened the back door and peered inside. Gil groaned softly.

"Just being nosy," Gil informed Colleen.

Zack hurried to join them as Ross, Kirk, and Beck approached, keeping low to the ground. Zack appeared excited for the first time and grinned at what he'd discovered.

"That truck is filled with weapons," Zack announced gleefully. Most things that went boom were enough to make Zack giddy with delight.

"Well, at least we know what's so damned important here," Ross muttered.

Monroe and Bogart soon joined them. It was difficult to tell if the teenage girls were impressed or frightened by the sheer number of weapons their rescuers carried.

"Jackie's entertaining three of the guys," Monroe announced. "The fourth one came back to the park."

"There are at least four more men," Gil informed Ross.

"Okay," Ross announced then indicated the door. "That's our exit point."

"What about the guns?" Zack eagerly asked.

"We're not worrying about the guns," Ross informed him in a stern tone.

"Stealing the truck would be a great diversion," Beck announced casually.

"You're right," Ross replied while glancing at Beck. "Good idea."

Zack appeared offended. "Why wasn't it a good idea when I suggested it?"

Beck glanced at Zack and offered a sly grin. "Because you're, well, you," he replied then looked back at Ross. "Give me five minutes to hot-wire it."

"Keys are in the ignition," Zack muttered, clearly annoyed.

Beck gave Zack a look then hurried for the semi-truck.

"Watch for company once that truck starts," Ross informed the guys.

†

$\mathcal{J}$ackie casually leaned against the plane while the two men were eager to make small talk in a clumsy attempt to cozy up to the attractive pilot.

"What brings you out here?" the first man eagerly asked.

"Are you from around here?" the second man chimed in while giving her a quick once over.

Jackie heard the man within the plane thump around, but she didn't let the sound distract her. The sound of the tractor-trailer caught their attention. Unbeknownst to them, she had the semiautomatic beneath her jacket aimed at them. She smiled sweetly at both men.

"Actually, I volunteered for a search and rescue mission," she announced boldly. "Perhaps you'd heard about the two missing girls?"

Both men tensed but immediately covered with innocent looks with timid smiles.

"No, we hadn't heard about any missing girls," the second man responded.

"Oh," Jackie commented while raising her brows then smirked. "So how do you explain their horses over there by the chain link fence?"

Her words were enough to alarm them. Both men reached for the guns hidden down the back of their pants. Jackie had her gun aimed at the first man before he could even draw his weapon. She shot him in the chest then immediately turned toward the second man, who now had his gun drawn. Jackie squeezed the trigger and shot him in the forehead, exploding blood and brain matter out the back of his head. The man from the plane leaped down the steps with his weapon in hand, having heard the gunshots. Jackie spun into a roundhouse kick without barely looking at him, and kicked him in the chest, sending him to the plane steps. Despite the hard hit, he aimed his gun at her. Jackie fired first, shooting the man in the chest. He died almost instantly. Jackie hated the killing aspect, but she knew it was them or her, especially when there wasn't an opportunity to take prisoners. The last thing she wanted or needed was a man she thought was down coming back and killing one of her guys. She frowned and shook her head.

"You couldn't just stay down, could you?" she muttered with disgust.

Jackie casually collected weapons from the three dead men then watched as the tractor-trailer sped past her, its air horn blowing.

Beck grinned sweetly and waved to her. A jeep with two men and two four wheelers were soon following after the truck. Jackie remained just out of sight by the steps, but the men in the vehicles didn't give her or their men a second glance. They undoubtedly assumed the men had the situation under control, perhaps because they knew she was a woman. Bad assumption.

Chapter Twelve

*T*he six men and Darth entered the building with their assault rifles leading the way. The building was quiet and empty, providing no resistance as they approached the basement door marked 'employees only'. Once they passed through the door, Ross signaled for Kirk to remain just inside the basement door. He remained hidden behind the door and kept watch on the room beyond it, allowing him to see the main entrance as well as the back corridor to the rear exit. The other five continued down the stairs to the basement with Darth leading the way. He was stealth and took his job seriously. They reached the security office, discovering it too was empty. One door led to the accounting office, which contained the park safe and the area used to count revenue. The second door led to the holding cells containing the two girls. Gil and Darth stood guard in the security office doorway, with clear view of Kirk at the top of the stairs.

The four men swept the security office for keys to the holding cell door and the cells themselves, but they came up empty. Zack already had his lock pick device out and worked on the outer cell door. It didn't take long for him to manipulate the lock. He opened the door, grinned, and extended his hand for Monroe to enter. Monroe hurried into the holding cell area and approached the girls, who now collected by the cell door.

"Oh, thank God," Colleen gasped.

"Hurry," Monique whispered with mounting concern.

Zack worked on the lock to the cell door while Monroe questioned the girls to their condition.

"Are you both okay?" Monroe asked while glancing over them for any visible signs of abuse. "Any injuries?"

"We're fine," Monique replied.

Zack opened the cell door. Both girls ran out of the cell while securing their cowboy hats firmly on their heads.

"If you can just get us to our horses--" Monique began but was interrupted.

"The only place you're heading is to our getaway plane," Ross informed them firmly.

Both girls appeared alarmed. "We can't leave our horses," Colleen proclaimed louder than intended.

"We don't have to take them with us," Monique announced. "We just need to set my horse free. They'll go back home on their own."

Bogart gave Ross a stern look. "We can certainly open the gate for the other horse," Bogart announced to his boss.

Ross glared disapprovingly at Bogart then shook his head. "Only if it doesn't put any lives in danger," he replied.

He herded the girls into the security office where Gil waited by the door with Darth. Colleen saw her bullwhip lying on top of the nearby desk. She grabbed her whip and clung to it. Ross nodded to Monroe. He headed for the door and slipped out, checking with Kirk to see if the coast was clear. Ross appeared stern while looking at both girls.

"We're going to move out in pairs," he informed them. "There are only two ways out of this fun park. The downed gate in the rear beyond the roller coaster and the main entrance. We're heading for the main entrance and an awaiting plane. You're going to keep down and stay quiet." Ross indicated Monique. "You're with Zack. No matter what happens, you remained glued to him." He then looked at Colleen. "I want you to stick with--" Ross looked at Bogart then pointed across the room to Gil. "You're with Gil."

Bogart appeared offended, his mouth hanging open in protest. "Hey," he immediately proclaimed. "I can do this. Let me protect the squirt."

"Squirt?" Colleen demanded while gripping her bullwhip.

Bogart's eyes pleaded with Ross. "Come on, Ross," he announced with conviction. "I've proven myself dozens of times. I can do this."

Ross groaned softly, although he didn't appear convinced. "Fine," he scoffed then looked at Colleen. "You're with Bogart."

"Clear," Monroe announced from the hallway just past Gil.

"Okay, men," Ross announced then hesitated, "and ladies. Move it out."

Ross led them from the room and headed up the stairs to join Kirk. Zack and Monique followed, with Colleen and Bogart behind

them. Gil and Monroe brought up the rear. They reached the top
of the stairs and headed for the back hallway. Men could be heard
approaching from the back of the building. Ross signaled to his team.
They headed for the front while keeping quiet. Gil and Monroe kept
watch on their rear flank in anticipation of the approaching men.
Ross checked to see if the front was clear. Zack removed an Uzi
from a hidden holster on his back, cocked it, and handed it to
Monique. She uncertainly accepted the weapon. He then approached
the door. Monique stared at the massive weapon in her hand and
exchanged looks with her friend. Kirk glanced at the Uzi in
Monique's hand, rolled his eyes, and took the gun from her while
shaking his head. He handed her a semiautomatic instead. Monique
again eyed Colleen. Colleen shrugged.

Monique hurried to keep up with Zack. The main street
beyond the building entrance was clear, allowing them to filter into
the main thoroughfare while keeping close to the building. Monique
kept close to Zack. As Colleen followed Bogart from the building,
two men appeared from the back hallway. Gil and Monroe fired
upon the men, taking the first armed man down. The second
returned to the safety of the connecting hallway and fired at them.
Now that gunshots were fired, others would be alerted to trespassers.
Monroe and Gil fired back while making their way to the front door
with the others.

Once outside, more men on four wheelers came at them from
the front of the park. There were six on ATVs and more than ten
on foot. Ross signaled to his men. They split up and ran into the
park, taking opposite sides. Zack hurried Monique inside one of the
concession stands where they hid. Both flattened against the stand
and watched several men run past on the main thoroughfare. They
heard a four wheeler approaching. Zack looked at Monique.

"I'm going to commandeer a vehicle," he informed her.
"Can you drive a four wheeler?"

Monique nodded.

"Straight back to the roller coaster and out the back
opening," he informed her. "No matter what happens, don't stop
and don't look back. We're heading up the hill to the jeep on the
ridge. Got it?"

Monique again nodded and clutched her gun. He glared at
the gun. She nodded and stuck it down the back of her jeans.
Monique remained behind Zack and waited for him to put his plan in
action. The four wheeler zipped past the concession stand. Zack
leaped over the counter, kicking the man from the ATV. As the four
wheeler rolled to a stop, Monique leaped out from behind the

concession stand and jumped on the vehicle. Before she could even question his next move, Zack leaped onto the back behind her, facing backwards.

"Go, go!"

Monique sent the four wheeler flying along the main thoroughfare toward the distant roller coaster while Zack sprayed the approaching men with assault rifle fire. Most of the men leaped to safety and were unable to fire back. A man appeared on the street in front of them and aimed his gun at them.

Monique screamed, "Zack!"

Zack turned on the seat behind her, now riding on his hip and aimed his semiautomatic just past her face. She cried out and shut her eyes as his gun fired. When she opened her eyes, the man was on the ground, and their ATV was running over his fallen body. Both clung to the vehicle to keep from being bucked off. There was a round of gunfire from somewhere beyond the tilt-a-whirl. They heard a loud popping sound. Monique attempted to keep the vehicle going straight, but the four wheeler veered sharply to the right from the blown front tire. As the vehicle flipped, Zack tackled Monique to the ground and shielded her from the rolling ATV. Monique looked up and watched the ATV roll several times before striking a rotting, wooden bench, exploding the wood. Zack rolled off Monique, reclaimed his discarded assault rifle, and fired at the men by the tilt-a-whirl.

"Go! Run!" Zack cried out.

Monique scrambled to her feet without hesitation and instinctively did as she was ordered. Zack ran behind her for the nearby roller coaster. More men fired from nearby. Zack grabbed Monique's arm and tossed her with him into the brush beneath the massive roller coaster overgrown with vegetation. Zack pointed to the area beneath the roller coaster with the most supports intersecting, offering the most cover. Both crawled on their bellies through the tall grass to remain hidden.

"Where are we going?" Monique gasped softly, now fearful since they were heading away from the opening in the fence.

"I need to get higher, so I can pick them off," Zack informed her. "You just stay in the brush."

They reached one of the support beams for the roller coaster. There were cross supports in every direction towering up the massive coaster. Both paused in the grass on their bellies and looked at the support. Zack glanced back at Monique, studied her a moment, and appeared curious.

"Can I ask you a personal question?" Zack asked while tilting his head.

"I guess so," Monique replied with uncertainty as she stared at the odd man.

"Are you afraid of snakes?"

"Snakes?" She appeared bewildered then shook her head. "Only the poisonous ones."

"Oh, good," Zack replied then casually indicated her back. "There's one slithering on your back."

Monique looked back and saw the snake slithering across her. She let out a tiny, shrill scream and cast it from her body. Zack stared at her with a look of disappointment.

"I thought you said you weren't afraid of snakes?" he almost demanded.

"Maybe next time you should lead with, 'hey, there's a snake slithering across you'," Monique snarled.

Zack studied her a moment, considered, and then nodded. "Okay, fair enough," he replied then pointed. "There's a snake on your leg."

Monique again jumped and kicked the snake off her leg. She glared at Zack.

He grinned, pleased with himself. "You're welcome."

Chapter Thirteen

Bogart and Colleen hurried alongside the large, mansion-like house halfway down the main thoroughfare. Both flattened themselves against the building and watched the armed men running through the street past them. Bogart paused and touched his ear transmitter in response to Ross's enquiry.

"Yeah, Ross," Bogart announced. "I have the squirt. We're by some big house on the right side of the park." He listened to his boss a moment then nodded. "Copy that. We'll meet you there." Bogart looked at the nervous girl alongside him. "It's too dangerous to go for the plane," he informed Colleen. "Ross already instructed Jackie to take off the moment she sees them coming. We'll have to make it to the ridge and try to reach the jeep. Zack and your friend are heading there now."

Colleen nodded while clutching her bullwhip like a security blanket. Bogart turned toward the building and tried the side door near him. It wasn't locked. He hurried her inside and shut the door behind them. Bogart and Colleen headed along an oddly narrow, windowless hallway before reaching another door. Bogart stopped and looked at the nervous girl. He attempted to sound confident for her sake.

"We'll slip out the back of this building," he informed Colleen. "The others will keep the guys busy on the main thoroughfare while we move along the back fence toward the roller coaster." Bogart opened the door, peered into the next room, and stared a moment with some surprise. He snorted a soft laugh. "Oh, this day just keeps getting weirder by the minute," he remarked.

As he passed through the doorway, Colleen appeared curious and followed him. Colleen stared at the haunted house exhibit they now stood within. The creepy dining room was filled with cobweb infested, animatronic mannequins seated at the table. Another mannequin was bound and tied on the table, apparently the main course.   Chariot style carts meant to deliver guests through the haunted house were spaced every ten feet on a track.   The door shut behind Colleen, causing her to jump with surprise.   Bogart hurried past one of the carts on the track.   Colleen eyed the macabre scene then hurried after Bogart.

"Monique would love this place," Colleen remarked, although not sharing the sentiment.   "She's into wild and creepy."

"Huh," Bogart remarked from in front and grinned.   "She'll get along great with Zack then.   He both wild *and* creepy."

They heard someone storm in through the front door.   Bogart hurried Colleen up the stairs alongside the ride track.   They entered the hallway, now out of sight of anyone entering the house.   Bogart peered down to the first floor below.   Two men with assault rifles walked along the hallway, obviously looking for them.   He hurried Colleen along the upstairs hallway and past several bloody displays.   They darted into one of the gruesome bedroom displays.   A blood-covered corpse lie beneath the sheets, undoubtedly fixed with hydraulics to rise when the carts rolled past.

"What did you do to piss these yahoos off?" Bogart muttered softly while keeping watch along the upper hallway.   He glanced back at Colleen.   "Why do they want you so badly?"

"We saw them kill a man in the building near the generator," Colleen informed him.

"Still," Bogart muttered with limited understanding, "to these guys, that's nothing.   They probably kill people every day.   They're risking an awful lot, considering they could've just taken their guns and ran.   Why worry about your butts?"

Colleen slowly shook her head, obviously at a loss for answers to his questions.   "Beats me.   All I know is two guys in suits killed two other guys in suits."

"Guys in suites?" Bogart asked and eyed her suspiciously. "Expensive suits?"

"No," Colleen replied mechanically.   "Off-the-rack, department store suites.   You know, the kind Monique's father wears."

"Whoa, wait," Bogart stopped her and appeared concerned. "The sort of suits Monique's father wears?   Monique's father the federal agent?"

"Yeah, why?" Colleen asked not understanding his logic.   "Is it important what sort of suits they were wearing?"

"If they were federal agents being executed, yeah, it's kind of important," Bogart remarked then snorted a laugh.   "It'd certainly explain why they're hell-bent on keeping you from leaving."

They heard movement on the stairs. Bogart suddenly became alert, flattened himself against the inside wall, and returned his gun to his holster.

"Why don't you just shoot them?" Colleen asked softly as she flattened herself alongside him.

"If the others hear gunshots coming from this direction, we'll have more company on our ass," Bogart whispered then glared at her with disappointment. "You need to watch more zombie movies, Squirt. They'll teach you everything you need to know about survival."

Colleen groaned softly. "God, you sound like my Uncle Dave."

Bogart motioned her back into the corner. Colleen backed up several steps and crouched on the floor within the corner, keeping her eyes glued on Bogart, her only chance for survival. The nervous look on her face was easily explained. As the first man approached the open bedroom exhibit, Bogart grabbed his arm, keeping the gun away from him, and kneed him in the thigh, narrowly missing the man's groin, his intended target. The man responded to the pain but recovered far too quickly and punched Bogart in the face. Bogart easily took the hit and returned with his own flying fist. The second armed man appeared in the display opening with his gun aimed at the fighting men. Bogart punched the first man several times, driving him onto the floor. He straightened while grinning then saw the second man with the gun aimed at his face. His expression suddenly dropped. A loud cracking sound startled both men. The bullwhip latched onto the man's wrist, knocking the gun from his hand and pulling him off his feet. Bogart looked back at Colleen as she skillfully flicked her wrist, releasing the bullwhip from the man's arm.

"Christ," Bogart gasped with surprise.

The man scrambled to his knees and went for the discarded gun, alerting the girl. Colleen coiled back with the whip, and with a mighty crack, the whip caught the man around the neck. She pulled vigorously, and rolled him off his knees. Bogart grabbed the discarded gun and hit the man on the back of the head with it. He collapsed to the floor out cold. Bogart straightened and again stared at Colleen.

"Where'd you learn to do that?" he asked with surprise while breathing heavily and flexing his fist.

Colleen released the whip from around the unconscious man's neck and coiled it in her hands. She shrugged and showed little emotion.

"My father was a huge Zorro fan," she replied gently. "He showed me all sorts of tricks. I practiced every night for years while waiting for him to come home."

"He must be proud," Bogart announced with his best country boy grin.

Colleen attempted a smile, but it came off insincere. "Yeah. Can we go now?"

"Uh, yeah," Bogart replied and indicated the opposite direction. "The tracks go that way, so there must be back stairs." He peered into the hallway then hurried her further into the haunted house. "Do me a favor, will ya?"

"Yeah, sure."

"Don't tell Ross *you* saved *me*, okay?" Bogart remarked looking tense. "He's very difficult to please, and I already have a few strikes against me."

Colleen snorted a soft laugh. "I doubt I exactly saved you," she gently replied. "I was just helping you take them down with little noise."

Bogart suddenly grinned in response. "Hey, I like that."

✝

*G*il and Monroe ran after Darth through the tall grass just beyond the massive Ferris wheel. All that was seen of Darth was the tops of his ears as he left a trail through the tall grass. The base of the Ferris wheel left enough cover from the four men following them to avoid the shots being fired. As they came out of the tall grass, both men suddenly stopped at the two-foot drop leading into the murky green water below. Darth stood on the other side of the three-foot channel, waiting for them on the ledge of the flume canal. Monroe looked into the murky water below.

"What a lovely shade of toxic green," Monroe muttered then eyed Gil, who studied the jump across the channel where Darth waited. "That's the last time we follow the dog."

"I trust his instincts over yours," Gil remarked without looking back at him.

Monroe stared at Gil's profile with a look of disbelief. "That dog isn't nearly as smart as you give him credit," Monroe bluntly informed him then looked back at the area before them. "What now?"

Gil glanced back at the men closing in then looked at Monroe and shrugged. "We jump."

"Terrific," Monroe muttered.

Both men slung their rifles over their shoulders, took a running start, and jumped the channel. They landed on the other side with Darth and immediately rolled into the dry canal filled with years of dried leaves. From the safety of the log flume canal, they removed their rifles and fired at the approaching men. The men darted back into the wooded, grassy area, retreating to the safety of the Ferris wheel structure. Monroe and Gil jumped to their feet and ran through the leaf coated, log flume canal. The canal took them across the murky pond to the other side of the ride. Partially sunken paddle boats with duck heads and duck bodies rose up from the green ooze, indicating the pond was possibly only a few feet deep. What lie beneath the murky surface was possibly more frightening than the men with the guns. As the men followed Darth around the curve in the log flume canal, they stopped at what lay before them. Darth scaled the conveyer belt up the slope.

"No, no, no," Monroe suddenly announced and vigorously shook his head. "Bad idea."

"We can't stay here and we can't go back," Gil insisted with a wild look in his usually calm eyes. "If those guys suddenly get creative, they'll climb the Ferris wheel and shoot at us. We'll be sitting ducks."

Both men glanced at the partially submerged duck boat staring back at them. Monroe sharply eyed Gil.

"Have you ever been on a log flume ride before?" Monroe demanded.

"Maybe as a kid," Gil replied. "Big deal."

"Yeah, it is," Monroe informed him. "Because at the top of that hill is the drop off, which typically falls into the water below." Monroe indicated the lime green water alongside them. "Into *that* water."

"This isn't Florida, Monroe," Gil calmly informed him. "There aren't any alligators or sharks in this pond."

"No, but there are probably snakes and God knows what else."

The men started shooting at them. Gil and Monroe instinctively ducked and looked back at the men now firing at them from near the Ferris wheel. One man was climbing up the wooden brace. Gil glared at Monroe.

"No time to debate this," Gil announced and charged up the slope after Darth.

Monroe groaned and ran after him. They reached the top and stood alongside one of the empty log boats. The steep drop led to a pool of murky water below. On the other side of nearly fifty feet of green water was the remaining log flume canal.

"That's pretty gross," Gil muttered.

"I tried to tell you," Monroe launched back.

Gil indicated the boat near them. "We'll use the boat."

"It may not float," Monroe warned him with concern.

"We don't have a choice," Gil reminded firmly.

As the men climbed into the intact log boat, Darth jumped into the boat in front of them, placing his front paws on top. He panted and wagged his tail with excitement. Monroe and Gil rocked the log boat until it toppled forward, falling down the metal canal at frightening speed toward the murky water below. Gil pulled Darth into the boat and shielded him. Monroe screamed the entire way down. The plastic log boat struck the green water, parting it in a wave of murk nearly six feet high. The boat safely sailed across the green water until it hit the dry canal on the opposite side. Darth jumped out of the log boat into the safety of the dry canal. Gil followed the dog while wiping some water from his hands onto his pants. Apart from that, he was almost completely dry. Monroe stepped out of the boat and flicked water from his drenched body. Gil eyed Monroe and made a face.

"Oh, man, you stink," Gil boldly announced then hurried after the dog.

"Next time," Monroe announced as he followed Gil and Darth, "I'm partnering up with someone else."

Chapter Fourteen

Random gunfire was heard throughout the park, lending an eerie backdrop to the already creepy area, but none of the sounds indicated a strong firefight. Four armed men hurried across the main thoroughfare. Two headed for the tilt-a-whirl, while the other two headed for the nearby pirate ship. As the two men approached the pirate ship, Kirk suddenly poked his head up from behind one of the partitions and fired at them. The first man went down from a head shot, nearly exploding his skull, allowing the second man time to run for cover. The two men by the tilt-a-whirl turned when they heard the gunfire. The first man ran toward the pirate ship. Ross leaped out of one of the tilt-a-whirl carts, grabbed the second man around the neck, and pulled him into the cart with him. The cart rocked violently, creaking on rusty fixtures, as several grunts and groans were heard. The first man turned back toward the tilt-a-whirl with his gun aimed.

The gunfire from an assault rifle echoed in the sky. The first man took a shot directly through his heart, exploding out his back, and dropped to the ground. Ross poked his head out of the tilt-a-whirl cart and looked toward the roller coaster in the near distance. Zack was perched halfway up the structure with his assault rifle at the ready. Ross grinned at his counterpart and shook his head. Four men on ATVs raced toward the roller coaster to join the other men, who were already closing in. Ross frowned and touched his ear transmitter.

"Zack, you have company rolling in," Ross announced. "Where's the girl?"

"Waiting for her ride," Zack casually replied over Ross's transmitter.

Ross looked around for signs of Monique. From his position on the roller coaster frame, Zack aimed his rifle at an approaching ATV. He shot the man in the chest, which knocked him from the vehicle, allowing the ATV to slow. Monique sprang up from the tall grass and jumped onto the four wheeler. She rode away through the grass beneath the roller coaster while heading for the opening in the back fence. Zack rapidly fired at any man attempting to approach the girl on the four wheeler. Two men on four wheelers seemed to appear out of nowhere and blocked Monique's path to the opening. She screamed but didn't slow as Zack's shots struck the men's ATVs. One man was hit and fell from his ATV but Monique was in Zack's line of fire for the second man. Another shooter fired at Zack where he was carefully perched. He took shelter and was unable to fire at the man blocking Monique's path.

Monique screamed at the sight of the man's gun aimed at her and made the bold decision to dive off the four wheeler. The vehicle crashed into the two ATVs blocking the exit. The man dived to the ground to avoid the crash then fired at Monique. She panicked and ran for the roller coaster steps. She swiftly scaled up them while holding back her frightened screams. Zack got one shot off before taking more fire. That one shot was enough to slow the man down, allowing Monique added seconds to scale the rickety, old steps of the roller coaster.

"Son-of-a-bitch!" Zack cursed and began climbing higher up the roller coaster frame.

Back at the tilt-a-whirl, Ross watched helplessly at the situation unfolding at the roller coaster, shook his head, and touched his ear transmitter.

"Where is everyone?" Ross demanded. "We have a situation at the roller coaster."

Just a little distance from the tilt-a-whirl, the remaining armed man kept low and crept up to the pirate ship for a surprise attack on Kirk. The man leaped up, aiming his rifle at the empty seat. Kirk was gone! The man looked around with surprise. Kirk was standing behind him. Kirk hit him in the face with the butt of the assault rifle, knocking him back several steps. He then kicked the man in the abdomen. As he doubled over, Kirk struck him on the back of the head with his weapon, driving him to the ground. Kirk hurried to join Ross just a few yards away.

"What's the situation?" Kirk asked.

Ross frowned and pointed up the roller coaster. Monique ran up the three flights of steps to the loading platform with two men chasing after her. Thankfully, she was faster than they were.

"I'm on it," Kirk announced and ran in the direction of the roller coaster.

Several shots were fired at Kirk. He threw himself to the ground near the tilt-a-whirl, sought cover, and fired back. Ross joined him and leaned against the rusted cart.

"Two shooters," Ross announced.

"I can count," Kirk muttered.

More shots were heard in the distance from the flume ride. Ross touched his ear transmitter while looking across the area to the men pinning them down.

"Monroe, Gil," he announced with urgency in his tone. "What's your twenty?"

Across the park at the flume ride, Monroe and Gil scurried along the flume canal while firing at the men who were behind them now on top of the ride's peak. The men fired at them while they took cover.

"Hey, Ross," Monroe announced while Gil fired back at the men. "We're just over here at the flume ride taking in the sights. What's the situation at the roller coaster?"

"Two non-friendlies chasing our blond teen up to the loading platform," Ross announced over Monroe's transmitter. "Kirk and I are pinned down. Zack's on his way, but he's not going to make it before they intercede."

"Yeah, we're definitely too far from the party," Monroe informed him and joined Gil in firing back at the men. "We'll send in the second string. Give your best whistle."

From across the park, Ross was heard whistling. Darth's ears perked up.

"Go get him!" Gil announced to the dog.

Darth took off through the leaf-coated canal. Once he rounded the curve, all they saw were leaves being kicked up in the air.

†

𝓜onique reached the top of the loading platform and ran past a parked string of roller coaster cars. She headed to the end of the platform and suddenly stopped. All that remained before her was the old wooden tracks on a sharp downward descend. The sounds of thundering feet were heard behind her on the platform. Monique spun around while removing the gun from the back of her pants. She aimed it at the two men running for her. They weren't deterred by her holding the semiautomatic, although they did slow their approach, and kept their own weapons on her.

"Drop the gun, kid," the first man announced. "You aren't going to--"

Monique squeezed the trigger before the man could finish his assessment of her young mind. The bullet ripped through the man's knee, dropping him to the platform in agony as he clutched his bleeding leg. The second man prepared to fire at her. Zack leaped over the railing and struck the man in the chest with both feet, hurling him into the string of cars on the platform. The cars creaked and rolled several feet along the rusty track. Zack rolled with the kick and sprang to his feet as the man recovered from his position against the cars. Zack aimed his assault rifle at the man and pulled the trigger. It clicked empty. The man realized Zack was empty, pulled a knife from his boot, and lunged for him. At the same time, another man appeared on the loading platform with an assault rifle. Zack whipped his empty assault rifle at the approaching man. The rifle pin wheeled through the air and struck the man in the legs, taking him down. Zack faced the man with the knife, spun into a roundhouse kick, and struck the man's arm, knocking the knife from his hand. He went for the return kick and again threw the man into the cars.

The cars groaned from the force and again moved along the track, getting closer to the edge. Another man appeared on the platform and aimed his assault rifle at Zack. Monique screamed, dove into the first car, and fired back at the man, surprising him. He aimed the assault rifle at her, but she was already lining up her next shot. The gun fired and the shot struck the man in the hand, knocking the rifle from his bloodied grip. Zack looked behind him with surprise on his face and saw the man clutching his bleeding hand. He looked back at Monique and grinned his approval.

"Nice shooting!"

"Behind you!" Monique screamed.

Zack spun into a roundhouse kick and knocked the man backward. The first man returned to his feet and lunged for Zack. He fought both men with amazing karate skills, his fists flying and his feet kicking. Monique kneeled on the seat of the car and watched Zack handle both men with ease. She marveled at his fighting abilities and quick reflexes. The second man tackled Zack into the cars. The cars again groaned and moved. Monique looked around then to the front of the car at the steep drop before her.

"Time to vacate," Monique muttered.

Before she could jump out of the car, two more men appeared on the platform and fired at Monique and Zack. Zack punched the man on top of him in the throat then leaped into the car four rows behind Monique.

"Down!" Zack screamed at her.

Monique dived to the floor of the car. Both men jumped into the car to tackle Zack. The cars groaned and lurched forward on the track. Monique poked her head up and saw the car pointing down the steep incline. She screamed. Zack looked up. As the cars lurched down the hill, he dove into the seat and clung to the lap bar. The cars rocketed down the hill with Monique screaming hysterically. The first man was thrown from the car on the steep drop, screaming the entire way before his sudden impact with the ground. The second man clung to the lap bar and aimed his gun at Zack alongside him. Zack released the lap bar as they reached the bottom and kicked the man in the chest just as the cars barreled around a sharp curve. The man flew from the car and onto the track below them, lying limp and broken across the track. Once the cars rounded the curve, Zack scaled the individual cars despite the speed and joined Monique in the front. She continued to scream while clinging to the lap bar. Zack pulled the bar down over their laps as they raced along the track, gravity barreling them through another curve.

"We're going to be okay," Zack cried out above the sound of the roller coaster cars vibrating on the rusted track. "The track is holding!"

Monique suddenly screamed and pointed ahead of them. The track was missing. Zack clutched the bar in front of him and screamed in unison with Monique. The cars jettisoned through the air with its screaming passengers. As the string of cars hit the ground ten feet below, the last half of the cars broke free and crashed into one of the support beams. There was a loud crack and a deafening groan. All eyes within the park were suddenly on the rollercoaster as it toppled to the ground in a massive pile of wood, dirt, and debris. A cloud of dirt exploded into the air high above. The cars containing Zack and Monique jetted from the cloud of dirt and rocketed safely away from the disaster.

As they hurtled along the overgrown concrete, Zack and Monique looked from the crumbling roller coaster behind them and exchanged horrified looks. Their car continued to race through the main thoroughfare at high speeds. Several men on four wheelers stopped to aim their guns. Zack grabbed Monique's gun and fired at them, skillfully hitting each one like some sick shooting gallery. As the car finally slowed, they jumped out. Monique was moderately rattled but remained composed. Zack hurried her for the first abandoned ATV while tapping his ear transmitter.

"We're clear," Zack announced. "Heading for the original extraction point."

They jumped on the ATV with Monique driving and Zack riding shotgun with his semiautomatic. As they drove across the overgrown parking lot, they could see the plane ahead. Several men on ATVs surrounded the park side of the plane.

"Zack, look!" Monique screamed almost hysterically.

Zack turned to see the trouble ahead. Monique slowed the ATV, looked back, and saw Zack's grin. The men sitting on the four wheelers were slumped over and positioned to look as if they had the plane on lockdown when, in fact, the men were all dead. Jackie walked down the plane steps with an assault rifle slung over her shoulder.

"Where are the others?" she asked.

Zack hurried Monique to the plane. "Getting out of a tense situation," he replied. "Bogart said he's on his way, but no one's heard from him since."

"Colleen," Monique suddenly gasped.

Zack caught her by the shoulders, spun her toward the plane, and herded her up the steps, not giving her a chance to protest her missing friend.

†

*T*he men continued to fire upon Ross and Kirk by the tilt-a-whirl. Ross held his assault rifle in the air to surrender. The gunfire stopped. Ross straightened, allowing the men firing at them to straighten as well.

"Smart move," the man called to him while keeping his weapon aimed at Ross.

Ross smirked and nodded. "Angriff," he remarked loudly.

The man appeared baffled. Darth suddenly leaped on top of the man from behind, riding him to the pavement while sinking his teeth into the screaming man's arm. Once he had him on the ground, Darth viciously slung the man by the arm while tearing into his flesh. The second man aimed his gun at the dog. Kirk sprang up from his position behind the ride and fired multiple shots into the man. His body jerked and jolted from several shots before hitting the ground in a moderately bloody heap.

"Darth, freilassen!" Ross called out.

Darth released the man's arm and ran to Ross. Monroe and Gil pulled up to them on borrowed four wheelers.

"Did someone call a cab?" Monroe asked while grinning.

Kirk jumped onto the ATV behind Monroe.

"Zack got his girl to the plane," Ross informed them. "Any word from Bogart?"

"No, none," Gil responded.

Ross cursed under his breath and eyed his men. "You three head to the plane and get that kid out of here. I'll stay behind and locate Bogart and the other girl. When I find them, we'll take the jeep on the ridge."

"Darth and I--" Gil began but was interrupted.

"Don't argue with me," Ross snorted then snapped his fingers at the four wheeler. Darth jumped onto the ATV in front of Gil, who partially clung to the excited dog. "Just go. If Bogart is alive, I'll deal with him."

Chapter Fifteen

*B*ogart and Colleen remained flattened against the corner of the larger building near the generator fence not far from the main entrance. Bogart glanced around the corner toward the generator several yards away. The black horse stood outside the fence separating him from the saddled horse. Both horses had their heads up high and their ears perked while listening for further gunfire, but everything was now quiet. Bogart looked back at Colleen and grimaced.

"If Ross finds out about this, he's going to kill me," Bogart muttered to Colleen.

"Hey, this is all me," Colleen whispered back. "I took off, and you had no choice but chase after me."

Bogart stared at her with some surprise. "And I thought I was a good conman."

"We can compare offenses later," Colleen replied. "All we need to do is open the gate and set Storm Cloud free. The horses will go back home. I'm not leaving without my horse."

"You've got a stubborn streak, Squirt."

"Stop calling me that," she growled softly.

Bogart took a deep breath and clutched his semiautomatic close to his chest. "Okay, once I open the fence, you do your whip thing to make them run."

Colleen nodded and flexed her hand on her bullwhip. Bogart and Colleen kept low and ran for the generator fence. Thunder saw Colleen and neighed a loud greeting. The large, black horse galloped for her, skidded to a stop, and head butted her chest. Colleen clung the horse's halter and held back her tears.

"I missed you too, buddy," she announced softly. "It's time to go home."

An armed man suddenly appeared out the back door from the nearby building and grabbed Colleen around the waist. He placed a gun to her head. She let out a startled scream, surprising Bogart, who had just opened the gate to the generator fence.

"Toss the gun down!" he shouted to Bogart.

Bogart sneered with disgust and tossed the gun to the ground. The black horse squealed as his ears flattened back against his head. Thunder reared high into the air with his hooves thrashing at the man holding his friend. The man panicked to the sight of the thrashing hooves and the horse's underbelly in front of his face. He cried out and aimed the gun at the horse. Colleen screamed and rammed her elbow into the man's ribs. She hit him hard enough to free herself and interfere with his aim. The gun fired near the horse, spooking him enough to halt his rearing. Colleen dove to the ground. The large black horse again reared, his thrashing hooves crashing down on the armed man. Bogart stared in disbelief as the horse repeatedly struck the fallen man, crushing him with powerful blows. Four wheelers were then heard approaching.

"Son-of-a-bitch," Bogart cursed, tearing his eyes away from the bloodied man on the ground and looked at Colleen. "They know where we are! We have to go! Now!" The sound of the plane's engine was heard across the parking lot. Bogart threw his arms in the air. "And there goes our ride."

Colleen ran to Bogart and indicated the saddled horse as she grabbed the reins. "Get on!"

Bogart swung onto the saddled paint horse without use of the stirrups, momentarily impressing the teen. Colleen grabbed his hand and swung onto the horse's back behind him. She was barely seated when she cracked her whip. Storm Cloud took off into a gallop from a dead standstill. Thunder stomped on the man lying on the ground once more for good measure then whirled around and chased after the paint horse.

In the parking lot just outside the main entrance, the plane began its taxi away from the amusement park. Ross sat on his four wheeler and watched the plane preparing to depart. Out of the main entrance appeared the paint horse and its two riders with the black horse galloping after them. Ross straightened on his four wheeler and stared.

"I'll be damned--"

Four men on ATVs filed in after the black horse by fifty yards and gaining.

Ross cursed softly and touched his ear transmitter. "Guys, Bogart and the girl are riding up on your left flank. They've got company. I'm going to divert."

The plane continued to taxi but didn't gain speed. The rear left door opened partway to reveal Zack and Kirk. Bogart and Colleen galloped after the plane, attempting to catch them as they slowed. The men in pursuit fired at them from behind. Ross fired at the men with his assault rifle in one hand while steering the ATV with the other as he chased after them.

Within the plane from her pilot's seat, Jackie looked back into the fuselage at the guys hanging out the back door. Panic was starting to set in as they rapidly approached boulders that would destroy the plane.

"We have to do this fast," she cried out. "I'm running out of runway!"

Lagging behind the plane, Storm Cloud raced up to the back door with the two men half hanging out the doorway. Despite having two riders, the horse still remained ahead of the black horse without any rider. The horse was part thoroughbred, and that made him fast. Catching the plane was a challenge Storm Cloud readily accepted. They gained on the plane with Zack hanging half off the partially lowered steps. He had his hand extended while Kirk braced himself against the doorway, holding onto Zack. Although keeping pace, the horse still wasn't getting close enough.

"Jump!" Zack called out while reaching for Colleen's extended hand.

Colleen pulled her arm back with frustration, clutched her bullwhip, and cracked it for the wing's vertical support. The bullwhip snagged the support. Colleen dove off the back of the horse and swung for the opening and the men. Zack caught her. She released the whip from the support and disappeared into the plane. As the steps pulled up and sealed the door, Bogart veered the horse to the left and away from the plane. The plane picked up speed and began to lift off. Bogart raced the horse toward the ridge with the black horse on his heels. Ross shot the last pursuing ATV, blowing a tire, and causing the vehicle to flip with its rider. Both the man and the ATV rolled together for several yards, crushing the rider. Ross veered to the left and followed Bogart and the black horse. The plane pulled up and narrowly avoided the massive boulders, signifying the end of the makeshift runway.

Within the plane, Monique and Colleen jumped into seats on the left side and watched through the side windows as their beloved horses raced up the ridge. From their rapidly elevating view, both girls witnessed Bogart riding Storm Cloud to the top of the ridge. He stopped the horse at the top and gave his best cowboy wave while making the horse rear up. Monique and Colleen gasped simultaneously at the impressive cowboy move.

"I think I'm in love," Monique gasped softly, capturing Colleen's sediments.

Zack sat half turned in his seat and stared at the girls with a dumbfounded expression. It was difficult to tell whether he was shocked or appalled by the comment. While the girls looked on, taking in an eyeful of their hero cowboy, Bogart tumbled off the back of the horse, striking the ground and landing on his ass. Storm Cloud took off, leaving Bogart lying on the ground. Both girls frowned and turned forward in their seats.

"Another fantasy dead and buried," Colleen muttered.

Zack grinned and held back his chuckle.

†

*W*hat would have been a two-hour drive back to the Cooper farm took about thirty minutes by plane. Ross and Bogart would be nearly two hours behind them, making a conscious effort to herd the two horses back to the farm. There had been an odd silence among the others regarding the decision, and it was abundantly clear that Bogart was getting the reaming of a lifetime whether he blamed Colleen for their foolhardy actions or not. The plane touched down and came to a stop within yards of where Gil had originally landed not far from the helicopter. By the way Jackie and Gil smirked at each other, they'd obviously made it into a competition. Beck had radioed ahead from the tractor-trailer once he'd lost his following and confirmed his position at a roadside rest. He'd await further instructions from Ross about what to do with the semi-truck filled with weapons.

Monique and Colleen were excited to be home and practically ran off the plane with Darth in tow. Zack and Kirk kept time with the girls while heading for the house. It was with great certainty that the two men would be raiding the family frig. The girls were eager to shower and change after spending three days in the same clothes. Jackie and Gil brought up the rear, not nearly in as much of a hurry as those in need of a shower or food. Monroe, who had been trailing behind, eyed the garage suspiciously and made a side trip to investigate.

"So this Uncle Dave will be able to contact the parents?" Gil asked as they approached the porch.

"I certainly hope so," Jackie replied with a deep sigh. "He's not the most sound minded fellow." She then glanced around the farm. "His truck is gone. He might be at Donna's farm next door." Jackie shook her head while rubbing her arms as she looked around the farm. "Something about this place just give me the creeps."

Gil snorted a soft laugh. "It's called peace and quiet," he informed her. "You and Holden need to spend some time at the lodge. You'll learn to appreciate peace and quiet."

"Yeah, well, peace and quiet gives me the willies," she remarked.

"God, you've been hanging around Zack too long," Gil muttered. "As long as Zack can eat, there's nothing to worry about. I trust his gut over your instincts any day."

Jackie glared at Gil and frowned. "The longer I'm around you; the more I like the dog."

He glanced at her with a sly look. "Do I still rank above Bogart?"

She groaned softly and reluctantly replied, "Yeah."

He snorted a soft laugh and grinned. "Then I'm good with that."

Jackie smacked his arm then affectionately clung to it as they headed to the house. Gil pulled his arm free, caught her around the neck as they walked, and rubbed his knuckles over her head while she screamed. She laughed while pulling away as they entered the house. Jackie and Gil walked down the hallway toward the kitchen in the back of the house. Both stopped when they saw Kirk alone in the kitchen fixing himself a sandwich. Darth sat by his feet watching him stack lunchmeat on bread. The dog licked his muzzle in response, keeping his eyes glued on the sandwich.

"Go away," Kirk snarled at the dog.

"Where's Zack?" Gil asked and looked around, suddenly appearing tense.

"Taking a piss," Kirk muttered without concern. "Damned if I know. Keeping tabs on him would be a full-time job."

Gil and Jackie exchanged looks. Jackie didn't hide her uneasiness for the situation.

"I'll be upstairs keeping an eye on the girls," she announced and hurried out of the kitchen and for the stairs.

†

$\mathcal{M}$onroe walked across the moderately cluttered, detached two-car garage. There were two 1967 Pontiac GTOs parked side-by-side. One was clearly stripped for parts, while the other was being restored. Apparently, Uncle Dave was into classic muscle cars. Monroe looked at the concrete floor containing several fresh oil stains. Among the stains and random car parts, he noticed several red spots. He crouched down and touched one of the spots. He studied the fresh blood between his fingertips. Monroe straightened, removed his gun, and aimed it deeper into the garage. He looked around while remaining silent then followed the fresh blood trail toward the back of the car. Monroe reached the back of the car and spun to his left with his gun aimed.

Uncle Dave was propped against the left wall not far behind the car. His eyes were closed, but he held a crowbar in his relaxed, bloodied hand. Uncle Dave was bleeding from his temple and had several lacerations on his arms and scrapes on his face. He opened his eyes and looked at Monroe.

He groaned softly. "Oh, I'm glad it's you," Uncle Dave announced and slowly attempted to straighten.

Monroe lowered his gun and approached the fallen man. "What happened?"

"I saw someone lurking around at the Harris farm next door while on my way out," he announced and managed to sit forward, although it caused him some pain. "At first I thought it was Blake. It looked like his black SUV in the driveway. I went to check it out, and the next thing I know, I'm being chased in my truck by the SUV. I gave them a good run, but they drove me off the road and into a ravine nearly a mile from here." He groaned softly while holding his head. "I don't know if they thought I was dead or just didn't care. They took off. I dragged myself back here, but I couldn't make it any further." He hesitated and indicated the nearby wall. "There's a first aid kit on the wall."

Monroe hurried to the kit he indicated and returned with it. "I'll get you patched up," he announced and routed through the kit. "Did you get a good look at any of them?"

He slowly shook his head and instantly regretted it. "Looked like they were wearing suits though. Seemed odd."

"We'll get you to the nearest hospital," Monroe informed him.

"No, I'm fine," Uncle Dave reported. "You need to find my niece and her friend."

"We found them," Monroe informed him. "They're here. They're both fine."

Uncle Dave sighed with relief and allowed his head to fall back against the wall. "Thank God."

"Tell me more about these guys who were chasing you," Monroe remarked.

Chapter Sixteen

Once at the top of the stairs, Jackie found Monique within one of the upstairs bedrooms routing through Colleen's dresser drawer for a change of clothes. Although both were 'the only child' in their houses, the girls were almost like sisters. Jackie was envious of their relationship. Moving from one army base to the next, Jackie didn't make many friends and almost never any female friends. Her closest friends were the men raiding the Cooper's refrigerator. Friends her own age came and went, but her father's team always came back to her.

"Hey," Jackie announced gently while pausing in the bedroom doorway, catching Monique's attention. "I guess we haven't been properly introduced."

Monique appeared slightly startled, not expecting to find someone standing in the bedroom doorway. The girl smiled at Jackie with a strange admiration in her eyes.

"Yeah, you were busy, you know, flying the plane and all. That's pretty cool," Monique announced cheerfully. "So you're like one of those guys?"

"I suppose I am," Jackie replied while leaning against the doorframe and folded her arms across her chest. She then considered the comment and chuckled softly. "You know, when they need a favor." She then offered a pleasant smile. "I'm Jackie."

"I'm Monique, but I guess you already knew that," she announced, laughing at herself, and then appeared curious. "So where are our parents? I thought they'd be here to greet us."

"There were some complications," Jackie informed her. "The men holding you and your friend sent a ransom note, and your father thought it best to get both your mothers away from here until he was sure it was safe."

Monique managed a smile and laughed softly while casting a clean pair of jeans onto the bed. "Yeah, that's my dad. He's always one step ahead of the game." She collapsed onto the bed and studied Jackie. "Sometimes I wish he wasn't so good at his job."

"Being a father?"

"No, being a fed," Monique replied.

Jackie slowly straightened in the doorway and allowed her arms to fall to her sides while studying the teenage girl. She tilted her head in curious response.

"Your father works for the FBI?" Jackie nearly gasped but attempted to appear calm.

Monique mechanically nodded.

Jackie's mind was now reeling with the new information. She could feel her irritation rising. "Here in the Colorado Springs branch?" she attempted to confirm what she already suspected.

The young girl again nodded then stared at Jackie with apparent humor at the expression on her face. "Don't they tell you anything?"

Jackie frowned and kept from sneering. "I'm on a need to know basis. When they need something, they don't want my husband to know."

"How's that?" Monique suddenly asked a little bewildered by the comment.

"I heard the name Harris mentioned earlier." Jackie's look turned serious. "Is your father Blake Harris, head of the Colorado Springs Bureau?"

"Yeah, do you know him?"

"We've never officially met. He's my husband's boss," Jackie remarked while gritting her teeth. "A little fact the guys didn't want me to know."

"Why?"

"Good question," Jackie grumbled while sinking into thought. Her fingers tightened into a fist. "You can bet Ross won't be too happy when or *how* I ask either."

Both heard a vehicle approaching in the distance. It definitely wasn't Ross and Bogart. They wouldn't be along for almost two hours. Monique became enthusiastic and hurried to the window.

"Must be Uncle Dave," she announced and looked out the open window.

Jackie approached the window and looked out as well. A black SUV drove the long driveway toward the house. Jackie recognized it as an official federal vehicle.

"Is it your father?" Jackie asked.

"Looks like his SUV," Monique replied excitedly and ran for the door.

Jackie stared out the window then saw movement in the tree near the porch roof. She didn't have to see him to know it was Zack. That he was playing sniper in the tree didn't put her mind at ease any. Zack was known to be paranoid, but was it really paranoia if he was always right? Jackie turned and hurried out the bedroom door as well. She stopped by the bathroom door in the hallway and knocked loudly.

"Colleen," Jackie announced through the door. "Get dressed and wait at the top of the stairs until I call you."

"What? Why?" came Colleen's voice through the door. "Is something wrong?"

"Probably not," Jackie called back. "Just being cautious." She then hurried down the stairs.

Jackie reached the front door and was immediately greeted by Kirk and Gil. Monique stood impatiently by the door with her hand on the knob while casting hostile looks at the guys.

"I don't understand," Monique almost demanded. "It's my father. Why can't I go see him?"

"Once we establish it's your father," Gil calmly informed her, "then you can go out and see him."

"I'll greet him," Jackie announced.

She removed the Glock semiautomatic from the back of her pants, checked the clip, and then returned it to the concealed holster. Jackie then turned her attention to Monique.

"You wait at the top of the stairs with Colleen until we say it's all clear," she announced to the girl.

"Wow," Monique remarked while shaking her head. "You guys are paranoid." She grumbled the entire way up the stairs.

Jackie opened the door and walked onto the porch, remaining in line with the doorway for a hasty retreat, if necessary. She casually leaned against the support beam near the steps and watched the SUV pass the barn then the garage. It eventually pulled up to the house. From Jackie's position, she could see two men in the front of the vehicle. She'd never met Blake Harris, so she wouldn't know him if she tripped over him. Agents Dodson and Metzger got out of the SUV and approached the porch. Jackie didn't know the men, but she easily pegged them for federal agents. Bogart had been right with his assessment; eventually all feds looked alike. Being married to one made them that much easier to detect in a crowd. Jackie had never met any of Holden's co-workers at his new job, so she couldn't attest to their identities.

Both men wore pleasant smiles as they approached her on the porch. She didn't straighten, allowing her right arm to remain at her side, hidden behind the post and her fingers delicately touching the grip of her firearm. She returned the pleasant smile despite catching a glimpse of someone just within the garage beyond the moderately dirty window. She was counting on that someone being Monroe, as he had entered the garage rather than the house when they arrived. If she were wrong, Zack probably already had that someone in his sights. Dodson and Metzger flashed their badges, allowing Jackie to relax her fingers on the grip of her gun.

"Good afternoon," the first agent announced. "I'm Agent Dodson and this is my partner, Agent Metzger. Forgive me, but you're *not* Mrs. Cooper," he informed her while attempting to feel her out.

"No, I'm Jackie," she casually replied. "A family friend. How may I help you gentlemen?"

Agent Metzger cast a glance to his right, causing Jackie's eyes to stray briefly. Darth sat on the ground a few feet away from the men and watched them, seemingly innocent, but she was certain he was standing guard, figuratively, of course.

"Agent Harris sent us to collect his daughter and her friend," Agent Dodson replied. "He wanted us to take them someplace secure until he could make other arrangements for their safety."

Jackie eyed the men with bewilderment. Had Ross gotten a hold of Monique's father already? She hated that she was generally suspicious of everyone. Undoubtedly, these men were Holden's new co-workers, and it would be in her best interest to make a good first impression. She shamed herself for her untrusting nature and vowed to work on that...eventually.

"They're showering," Jackie easily lied. "But, of course, you're more than welcome to wait inside."

She stepped aside and extended her hand toward the front door. Both men walked up the porch steps, passed Jackie, and entered the house. Darth trotted onto the porch and followed them with Jackie bringing up the rear. Once inside the house, both agents looked around. The downstairs appeared void of life, but Jackie knew it only seemed that way. As much as she hated to admit it, she'd grown so used to the guys and their tricks; she could almost guess where they were lurking. After a morning like theirs, as gross as it was, she could actually smell their location. Jackie escorted the two agents into the kitchen just down the hall and offered them seats at the table. They reluctantly pulled out chairs and sat down. Darth sat not far from both men and stared at them, causing them to eye the dog and his untrusting nature. It was almost as if he'd been sizing them up for his next meal.

"Could I make you some coffee while you wait?" Jackie asked while smiling sweetly.

"No need to trouble yourself," Agent Dodson replied while remaining pleasant.

Jackie considered the comment and nodded. "Yeah, you're right," she replied.

Agent Metzger seemed more interested in assessing the layout of the house from where he sat. Jackie casually leaned against the kitchen counter and studied both men. Their suspicious nature only increased her suspicious nature.

"Is it just you here with the girls?" Agent Metzger finally asked and looked back at her.

"Of course," she replied casually. "Who else would be here?"

"The girls' mothers," Metzger remarked, allowing his gaze to fall upon her. "Aren't they here?"

Jackie felt her body tense at the question. Wouldn't Harris have mentioned whisking the women away to a secure location to his trusted men? Then again, shouldn't Ross have mentioned she was working for Holden's boss? Maybe she was judging them too harshly. She smiled sweetly all the same.

"They're on their way from the Harris house," Jackie easily lied. "There was some miscommunication regarding our rendezvous." She cocked her head slightly and sized them up. "Surely Harris told you to wait for their mothers."

"Yes, of course he did," Dodson announced without hesitation. "That's why we were sort of surprised that they weren't here."

Jackie smiled knowingly and nodded. Obviously, they weren't at the house on Blake Harris' orders or they'd know they weren't meant to pick up the women. It was all Jackie needed to hear to put her concerns to rest.

Agent Metzger then stood, appearing slightly tense. "I should probably wait outside for the women and keep an eye out for trouble."

Jackie's cell phone vibrated in her pocket. She knew who was calling, but she certainly couldn't answer her phone at such an inopportune moment. There were more urgent matters.

"Darth," Jackie casually announced.

Darth stood rigid and snarled at Metzger, startling him. Dodson sprang to his feet and reached for his gun. Jackie kicked the gun from his hand, sending it flying across the kitchen, nearly striking the dog. Darth yelped and dodged the flying gun, allowing Metzger the opportunity to reach for his gun. Darth snarled viciously and attacked the man, savagely tearing into his arm to keep him from reaching his holstered weapon. Kirk stepped around the corner with his assault rifle casually resting in his arms and watched the ensuing fight. As Jackie went for a return kick, her cell phone flew from her pocket and struck the floor as her foot struck the man in the chest. Dodson hit the floor with a groan near her phone.

"Jackie?" came Holden's voice from the phone on the floor near the fallen man.

Jackie stared at the phone with horror and leaped for it. She snatched the phone while placing her knee into Dodson's throat, keeping him silent. Kirk slung his assault rifle over his shoulder before punching Metzger in the face, stopping Darth's attack. He then leaped to the floor, placing Metzger in a chokehold to keep him quiet.

"Shh," Kirk whispered pleasantly in Metzger's ear, "the lady's on the phone."

"Holden, hey," Jackie announced in a cheerful tone despite the man gasping beneath her knee.

"What's going on there?" Holden asked through the cell phone. "I thought I heard groaning."

"Oh, that's just the guys," Jackie replied in as natural a tone as she could manage. "They stopped by to spend a couple of days. You know, for my birthday."

"Hey, Holden," Kirk called out in a cheerful tone. "Monroe would say hi, but he's in a chokehold right now." Kirk loosened his chokehold just enough that the man would groan.

"Great," Holden muttered through the phone. "Keep Bogart out of my things and don't let Zack play with my guns."

"Way ahead of you," Jackie replied as Dodson attempted to punch her thigh to move her knee from his throat. With her free hand, she grabbed the man's crotch and gave a firm twist. He suddenly gasped and stopped fighting her. Jackie removed her knee from his throat, since he was now disabled. "Uh, Bogart found your good scotch," she quickly announced. "I should probably go. I'll call you later, okay?"

"Yeah, sure," Holden replied from the other end. "I love you."

"I love you too."

Metzger attempted to shout something. Kirk released him from the chokehold and punched him in the face, once again silencing him. Jackie disconnected the call and groaned softly while glaring at Kirk.

"I hate lying to him," Jackie muttered to her teammate.

"You weren't lying," Kirk replied while giving her an innocent look. "All those things will eventually happen. You were just foreshadowing."

She glared at his twisted smile and shook her head. "And you wonder why you're not married."

Jackie collected Dodson's gun and straightened. Both men slowly sat up, neither feeling too good. One clutched his bleeding arm, while the other clutched his crushed testicles. Darth kept close watch over the men and snarled his disapproval. They didn't move far.

"I don't suppose you boys are going to willingly spill your guts," Jackie announced while sighing.

Neither man spoke. That they didn't look the least bit concerned was troubling to Jackie. Kirk eyed both men with a steely gaze and cracked his knuckles.

"Of course not," Kirk announced casually to Jackie. "That's why you keep me around." He gave her a serious look. "I'm going to need a corkscrew, some duct tape, and table salt."

She nodded without hesitation. Dodson and Metzger exchanged looks. They appeared slightly tense now, but neither man was nearly as alarmed as they should have been. Kirk immediately noticed their moods and touched his ear transmitter.

"Who has eyes outside?" Kirk suddenly demanded. "Do we have company?"

"I have two men in my crosshairs just south of the farm," Zack announced over Kirk's transmitter. "Should I engage?"

"On my command," Kirk replied.

"I have another three north of the farm beyond the barn," Monroe responded.

"Four to our rear," came Gil's response.

"Hold your position," Kirk informed them then looked at Jackie across the kitchen. "We're about to have a gunfight on our hands. We don't know how many others are out there."

"We need to evacuate the girls," Jackie replied with concern.

Kirk touched his ear transmitter while removing zip ties from his side leg pocket. "How's our path to the plane?"

"Clear for the moment," Zack replied.

Kirk looked at Jackie as he tied the first man's wrists behind his back and nodded to her. She ran from the kitchen and hurried down the hall for the stairs. She looked up the stairs to the second floor.

"Monique, Colleen!"

Both girls appeared at the top of the stairs, alarm clearly on their faces.

"Who were those guys?" Monique asked. "We saw them from the upstairs window. I didn't recognize them."

"It's not important," Jackie replied, feeling pressed for time. "We're bugging out--now."

They thundered down the stairs to join her. Colleen had changed into clean clothes after her shower, but Monique still wore the same clothes from three days ago. Colleen carried her bullwhip while Monique held Uncle Dave's rifle cradled in her arms. Jackie opened the front door and slipped outside with the girls directly behind her.

"Darth!"

Darth joined them on the porch. Jackie hurried the girls toward the plane just beyond the barn. Monroe and Uncle Dave filed in behind them as they passed the garage. Uncle Dave needed some assistance despite Monroe's first aid. As if on cue, the men from both edges of the property started driving toward them. Uncle Dave secured his rifle from Monique and joined Monroe as he fired at the men with his assault rifle. Zack joined in the gunfight from his position on top of the porch roof. Jackie ushered the girls and Darth onboard the plane and started the engine. Monroe and Uncle Dave remained near the helicopter and fired at the approaching men. Gil and Kirk soon joined them, firing at the other men approaching from the rear. Gil and Kirk ran for the helicopter, jumping inside. Uncle Dave joined them. Monroe ran for the plane and remained within the open doorway until they were able to taxi. Gil gave Jackie a twirling finger, indicating for her to take off.

Gil jumped into the helicopter and started her up while Kirk, within the helicopter, and Monroe, from the plane doorway, continued to fire upon the approaching vehicles and men. The helicopter lifted ahead of the plane with Kirk sitting in the open rear doorway. The helicopter hovered over the plane while Kirk fired at the men from above, allowing Jackie time to prep the plane. Monique and Colleen jumped into their seats and tightened their seatbelts. Monroe climbed the few steps and looked around.

"Where's Zack?" he suddenly demanded.

"He'll have to catch the helo," Jackie called back while flipping switches. "Secure the door. We have to go--now!"

Monroe reached to close the door when he saw a jeep with men rapidly approaching. He aimed his assault rifle to stop their approach when Zack appeared in the jeep behind the driver. Without even exerting himself, Zack easily snapped the man's neck. The jeep veered and flipped as Zack dove out the side. He rolled across the ground and ran for the moving plane. Zack jumped inside the plane as it started to taxi. Monroe groaned and closed the door behind him.

"Cutting it a little close?" Monroe remarked.

Zack casually flopped into one of the seats and cast his legs over the seat arm. "Someone has to bring up the rear, Monroe," he announced simply. "You should try it every now and then."

Just above the farm, Kirk remained hanging outside the open door of the hovering helicopter and fired a barrage of bullets at the men in jeeps, covering the plane as it taxied along the dirt driveway. A jeep stopped in the plane's path. Kirk stepped into a harness, attached it to the bracket on the helicopter floor, and grimaced his annoyance.

"You don't *need* a rocket launcher, Kirk," Kirk snarled, mimicking Ross. "It's just a search and rescue, Kirk." He slapped the magazine into the assault rifle with added vigor then cocked it. "I want my fucking rocket launcher!"

Kirk leaned out the helicopter door on a nearly vertical angle and fired at the jeep with a round of precision shots. The jeep suddenly exploded and propelled the men through the air. Hunks of debris were scattered across the dirt driveway. The plane taxied through the debris and lifted off. As Kirk pulled himself back inside, the helicopter flew after the plane.

Chapter Seventeen

$\mathcal{W}$ithin the plane, Monroe joined Jackie on the flight deck. He collapsed into the co-pilot's seat, belted himself in, and put on the extra headset. He flipped a few switches and attempted to radio Ross, who would still be in the jeep. Jackie sniffed the air, became concerned, then leaned closer to Monroe, and smelled him. She wrinkled her nose and made a face.

"What's that god awful stench?" she gasped.

Monroe glared at her then continued to fiddle with the radio. "It's called *Eau de never listen to Gil*," he muttered then tried the radio. "Ross, do you copy?" There was a static-filled response. Monroe shook his head and groaned. "I'll try him again in a few minutes. Maybe Gil's having more luck with his radio."

"What now?" Jackie asked while glancing at Monroe in the seat next to hers. "It's obvious the Bureau has been compromised. I don't think those guys were just posing as agents. I think they were the real deal." Her heart sank at the thought. "Someone in the agency wants those girls."

"Head for the lodge," Monroe instructed while leaning back in his seat. He groaned softly and stared at the buttons and switches above him. "It's the only place that's safe."

Jackie flipped several switches, glanced at him, and then shook her head with annoyance. "I can't believe you lied to me," she muttered.

Monroe looked at her and appeared surprised. "What do you mean?"

"Don't play stupid," she huffed. "You knew Monique's father was Holden's boss. You, all of you, purposely kept that information from me. Why?"

"Because you would have felt obligated to tell Holden," Monroe remarked. "Then Holden would have kept you from helping us. I think the term is 'plausible deniability'. The less you knew; the less you'd be lying to Holden. It was for your own good."

"Yeah, I'm sure you see it that way," she scoffed. "Remind me to punch you when we land."

"It was Ross's idea," Monroe remarked. "Hit him."

"Don't worry, I intend to," she grumbled and turned her head to glare at Monroe. Zack's face was inches from hers. Jackie cried out with surprise. "Damn it, Zack!"

His look was stern and more serious than usual. "You'd better do something about those two rug rats before I toss them out the hatch."

"They're kids, Zack," she snapped hotly. "They're practically your peers. Can't you get along with a couple of kids?"

"They're not kids," Zack announced boldly. "They're Tasmanian devils in very horsy smelling jeans. You have two minutes. The blond one goes out the door first."

Zack disappeared before Jackie could respond. She groaned softly, removed her headset, and glared at Monroe.

"You've got the bridge," she muttered.

Monroe appeared horrified and stared at the controls. He placed his hands on the wheel and looked back at her. "Jackie, I don't know how to fly!"

"It's on autopilot, Monroe," she snarled back as she headed into the fuselage.

Monique and Colleen stood in the aisle arguing with Zack, who did his best to ignore them, but they were extremely confrontational. Jackie would have found the sight comical if she knew it'd only amount to an hour-long round of 'I know you are, but what am I'. That probably wouldn't be the case. It wasn't as if Zack had *never* thrown someone out of a moving plane before, so there was cause for alarm.

"I mean it, kid," Zack growled at Monique while pointing a warning finger at her. "You're about to join the 54th airborne."

Jackie tapped Zack on the shoulder, essentially tapping him out of the argument. He cast himself into the nearby seat. Monique and Colleen immediately ambushed Jackie, bombarding her with questions.

"What about our horses?" Monique asked, showing a mixture of fear and hostility with her tone. "If they go back to the farm, those men could kill them."

"They're not going to kill your horses," Jackie bluntly informed them. "Those men are probably already gone. Why would they harm your horses?"

"Haven't you seen "The Godfather"?" Colleen interjected with alarm.

"You must have more compassion than *that* one," Monique snapped while gesturing at Zack. "He said they'll probably eat the horses."

Jackie looked at Zack with her mouth hanging open. "Did you say that to them?"

Zack immediately turned defensive and shifted in his seat, casting his leg over the arm. "No, I didn't say that--" he boldly announced then muttered, "--exactly."

"No," Monique launched back while folding her arms across her chest and glared at him. "You just said it'd be a shame to waste perfectly good meat."

"Taken completely out of context," Zack casually remarked and placed his hands comfortably behind his neck.

Jackie shook her head with disgust while glaring at Zack. "You're like that nasty older brother no girl ever wanted." Zack was about to open his mouth when Jackie pointed a warning finger at him. "Zip it, Zack," she snarled. "I don't want to hear another word out of you on the subject."

Zack growled softly at her then repositioned himself more comfortably and closed his eyes. Monique glared at him and sneered. Jackie drew a deep breath and studied the two girls.

"Our options are limited," Jackie informed them. "We have no choice but to take you to a secluded safe house several hours north of Denver. Even if Ross agreed to trailer your horses, it's a long trip to the safe house."

"My cousin lives only an hour from my place in a town called Stony Ridge," Monique informed Jackie. "They could take the horses there. She'd look after them. They'd be safe with her."

Jackie stared at the girls then groaned softly. "I'll talk to Ross once he makes radio contact. I can't promise anything. I'm guessing he's not going to be in a very good mood about our situation as it is."

"He'll listen to you," Monique announced.

Jackie eyed Monique with a curious look. "What makes you so sure?"

"Because he needs you," Monique quickly replied. "Isn't that why he lied to you about my father being a fed? Because he needs you?"

Jackie groaned while running her fingers through her hair. "Yeah, and then I'll have to give up my right to ream him out in order to pull that one off."

"We'll make it up to you," Colleen offered without hesitation.

"Just name it," Monique added.

"For now, you can start by staying away from Zack," Jackie informed them. "He's not real good with kids." She hesitated then considered. "Or people in general."

Despite giving the appearance of sleeping, Zack's lips curved into a grin.

$$\dagger$$

The tractor-trailer was parked at a secluded rest stop attached to a small diner. Only one other tractor-trailer had been parked at the stop before Beck had arrived with his tractor load of coveted, illegal assault weapons. Beck sat on the semi's step, casually reclined, and ate a hamburger that he'd gotten to-go from the diner. Endless sitting around and awaiting orders seemed to be pretty much the norm in Beck's world. At least at their fixer-upper lodge, he'd have never-ending projects to keep his mind and body entertained. His cell phone rang, almost startling him. Ross wouldn't be in range that soon. He removed his cell phone and looked at the caller ID. A boyish grin crossed his face at the name 'Pinto'. He eagerly answered the phone.

"Hiya, babe," he announced cheerfully and with an added tone of affection. The name on the caller ID was enough to bring color to his cheeks.

"I wish this were a social call," Pinto announced with an odd urgency in her tone.

Beck dropped his hamburger into the bag and quickly sat forward on the step of the truck cab. Her tone immediately concerned him.

"What's wrong?" he suddenly asked and looked around as if half expecting to find a way to reach her at a moment's notice. "Did something happen? Are you okay?"

"I'm fine," she announced gently. "It's just--" She hesitated, and he heard her take a deep breath. "Some men showed up at the lodge in a helicopter a few minutes ago."

"Some men? Who were they?" he demanded. "Did they hurt you?"

"No, nothing like that," she replied. "They said they were with the FBI. They had badges and everything. They were looking for you and the guys, although they didn't ask for any of you by name. I told them you weren't here. I thought they left, but they landed in a secluded spot at the end of the driveway. I can see their helicopter through your telescope."

"Okay," Beck announced in rushed speech as he sprang to his feet and ran his fingers through his hair. "I'm, uh, I'm coming to get you. I want you to keep the doors locked. Go to the banister and push that hidden red button."

"There's no need to push the panic button," she informed him. I'm fine, really." Pinto hesitated and drew a deep breath. "I don't think you should come back, at least not for a while."

"I'm not leaving you there unprotected," he announced firmly, nearly choking on his emotions into the phone while starting to pace the length of the truck.

"I'm hardly unprotected," she announced with a slight laugh in her voice. "I have enough weapons and ammo here to start a war. If they come around again, I'll go into the bomb shelter like you taught me." She hesitated. "Please. Don't come back here. Since they didn't know any of your names, I'm guessing they're just fishing. You'll be safe if you just stay away. Just stay away until this is cleared up. I'm begging you."

Beck again ran his fingers through his hair, looked to the sky, and fought his emotions. He nearly choked on his words. "Okay, babe. I'll stay away. We'll straighten this out. Just--don't go outside. Stay away from those men."

"Way ahead of you." There was a moment's pause. "If you run into trouble," she announced gently, "you know who to call. Someone who has a long reach and plenty of space for you to crash for a while."

It had obviously dawned on his girlfriend that the men waiting at the bottom of the driveway, if official, could have her phone tapped. Her words appeared to resonate with him. He knew just who she meant.

"That's a very good idea." Beck took a deep breath and fidgeted. "I love you."

"I love you too," she replied. "Stay safe."

He managed a soft laugh even though his emotions were getting to him. "That's supposed to be my line."

"I'll see you soon," she replied.

"I promise you will," he said softly. "Bye."

Beck disconnected the call then clenched his jaw in anger. He wasted no time climbing into the cab and snatching the radio from its holder.

"Ross, you copy?"

There was a moment of silence.

Ross finally responded. "Yeah, ridge runner, I copy. We have a slight situation, so I'm going to need you to sit tight a while longer."

"Yeah, well, your situation just got worse," Beck announced into the radio. "Lola just informed me that Rico arrived at the Copacabana."

There was a long silence.

"Well, fuck me," Ross finally exploded through the radio. "What's Lola's situation? Does she need extraction?"

"No, Lola has a level head and knows the drill," he replied while fidgeting. "Although I'm unhappy about it, she insists we stay away."

"Okay," Ross announced then sighed deeply. "I'm going to need about thirty minutes to come up with plan 'B'. I'll need to stop eagle one from her current flight pattern."

"Lola did make a suggestion," Beck announced gently. "You may not like it, but it's not without merit."

"Oh, God," Ross muttered then groaned with defeat. "I'm listening."

"She suggested you call her father for a favor," Beck replied and immediately grimaced to hear the response that was sure to come.

There was a long silence.

"Hmm," Ross muttered. "Asking her father 'the Godfather' for a favor. This day just keeps getting better." He sighed deeply. "I suppose if you want to cheat the grim reaper, it's lucrative to make a deal with the devil."

"Our options are limited," Beck reminded him.

"Yes, I agree," Ross replied and fell silent a moment. "Considering you're the one sleeping with his daughter, I'll leave the honor of calling him up to you."

"Thanks, Ross," Beck muttered with defeat and disconnected the call.

He sat in the driver's seat a long moment while staring out the windshield then finally pressed a single button. The phone rang only once before being answered.

"Hello, honey?" came the enthusiastic male voice.

Beck forced a smile and gently cleared his throat. "Hello, darling."

There was an awkward pause.

"Beck--?" came the cheerful male voice of Sal Romano, although there was skepticism in his tone. "Sorry, I thought you were my daughter. How's she doing?"

"Oh, uh, Pinto's doing very well, Sal," Beck replied. "She's been spending a lot of time at the lodge decorating. I think she found a new calling."

"Splendid! I'd love to get her out of that club," Sal replied then suddenly fell silent. "Something's wrong, isn't it? Did something happen to my daughter?"

"No, absolutely not," Beck quickly replied. "She's fine and in good spirits. You can call her after I hang up. She'd love to hear from you, although--" Beck drew a deep breath. "Her phone might be tapped, so you should probably watch what you say."

"I always do," Sal responded, although his tone sounded stern. "You're sure she's okay?"

"Yes, absolutely," Beck again confirmed. "It's the rest of us that are in a bit of a bind." He fidgeted and looked out every window in the cab. "We have two kids in protective custody, but they're being hunted by a mole in the Bureau. We can't go back to the lodge or any of our other safe houses. Although they haven't made us yet, there's always the chance they're watching the rest of our sanctuaries."

"I see," Sal replied with little hesitation. "And you need a favor from your girlfriend's old man."

"I hate to even ask--"

"Why?" he suddenly demanded. "We're practically family. At least, I hope we're *practically* family." His tone was curt and insinuating.

"Yes, we're practically family," Beck confirmed with confidence.

"Then consider it done," Sal replied in a jovial tone. "What major city are you near? I'll see what I have available to you that's reasonably close."

Beck sighed with relief. "Thanks, Sal."

"No need to thank me--" Sal announced a little too cheerfully, "--son."

Beck shut his eyes and held back his groan.

"You can owe me one," Sal chirped with enthusiasm.

Beck placed his hands over his eyes and allowed his head to fall back against the seat. He mouthed a curse then straightened, forcing a smile, although his caller couldn't see it.

"Of course, Sal."

Chapter Eighteen

$\mathcal{A}$s their temporary safe house came into view, Jackie stared out the windshield with amazement. Monroe remained in the co-pilot's seat and shared the same expression. The abandoned casino was situated in the middle of nowhere, which was just north of Cripple Creek, Colorado. They had flown over a small town before arriving at the large casino owned by Salvatore Romano. Although the casino and hotel were completely finished, the parking lot hadn't even been started and there wasn't any landscaping surrounding the property. It looked as if Sal had built the place and then walked away. Essentially, he had walked away. When plans for a factory were scraped, the highway was diverted away from the small town, and Sal's plans for the casino fell apart as well.

As Jackie circled the massive property, she noted the odd placement of a small farm. Had the casino been finished, the farm would have been sitting on the edge of the parking lot. Jackie took the plane in for a landing on the stretch of dirt road leading to the casino. Gil and Kirk would join them in a couple of hours. The men in the helicopter intended to meet Ross and Bogart at the cousin's farm in Stony Ridge, where they planned to drop off the girls' horses. They would then fly back to join the others at the remote casino. No sooner had the plane come to a stop when Zack appeared on the flight deck.

"Looks like the neighbors are dropping by to say hello," Zack casually informed them.

"Are you serious?" Monroe suddenly asked while staring at his odd friend.

"A couple of women in a jeep," Zack announced then grinned in a mocking manner. "I'm guessing they baked a pie to welcome us to the neighborhood."

"Now you're just screwing with me," Monroe muttered with annoyance.

They left the flight deck and headed for the main door. Monroe opened the door and paused on the first step. The jeep containing three women had already stopped and the two female passengers, one in the front passenger seat and one in the back, stood while aiming shotguns at them. Monroe tensed with surprise and held his hands up to appear less threatening. Zack stood just beyond the entrance with his assault rifle ready for a gunfight. Jackie glared at Zack and shook her head. There was no end to his paranoia. Jackie stepped into the doorway and observed the three women.

The driver of the jeep was a simple looking woman in her early fifties. Betty had long black and gray hair worn in a granny bun on top of her head. Although she wasn't much older than Zack, the years had clearly taken their toll on her. Her skin was leathery in texture, ashen in color, and further aged with wrinkles along her mouth and in the corners of her eyes. She wore an old, classic granny shirt with worn, faded flowers. The two young women holding shotguns aimed at Monroe looked to be in their late teens to early twenties, undoubtedly the woman's daughters.

Lexie looked to be about twenty years old. She had dirty blond hair or perhaps blond hair that was excessively dirty. Her long hair was slightly unkempt, giving her a jungle woman appeal. Not necessarily unattractive, she kept her farm girl look simple and moderately masculine. If not for her long hair and ample breasts, she might be mistaken for a man. Build sturdy from a lifetime of farm work, there was nothing feminine about the girl from her stubby fingernails containing dirt beneath them to her bold eyebrows begging to be sculpted. Her wardrobe appeared to be from the men's department back in the 1970's. Kathy, on the other hand, was slightly dainty. She was built smaller, being less robust than her older sister was, and more feminine with naturally softer facial features. Her light brown hair was worn in a messy ponytail, much like Jackie's, indicating the girl had been working hard prior to their arrival. She wore crudely cut jean shorts that were perhaps shorter than they should have been. The sleeves on her tattered flannel shirt had been cut off and the bottom was tied in a knot at her abdomen, showing off her bellybutton.

"This is private property," Betty boldly announced in a gravelly voice and indicated a sign on a stick fifty yards away. "This is not the casino's property, so you'd better move that contraption off my land."

"We didn't mean any disrespect," Jackie informed the woman while studying her.

"Yeah, sure you didn't," Betty snarled with limited patience. "None of you ever do."

"Can we assume you aren't the caretakers Romano mentioned?" Monroe remarked while keeping his hands open and raised in front of his chest to remain non-threatening to the armed women.

"Those heathens?" Betty suddenly demanded. "Certainly not!"

"Okay then--" Monroe muttered.

"We'll move the plane," Jackie informed the woman while remaining polite despite their obvious irritation.

Monique and Colleen stuck their heads out the open doorway of the plane and gazed at the nearby farm, studying the grazing horses in particular.

"You have beautiful horses," Colleen announced.

Jackie unsuccessfully attempted to push the girls back inside the plane. The older woman saw the teenage girls and motioned to her daughters with the shotguns. Both lowered their weapons, allowing Monroe to lower his hands as well. Betty glanced at the two girls.

"They belong to my youngest daughter," Betty replied. "Got them from an auction when they were just colts. Like big dogs, really. My husband died before he had a chance to break them to ride."

"The term 'breaking' is outdated," Monique boldly informed the woman. "If they have good ground manners and a solid relationship with your daughter, there's nothing to putting them under saddle."

Betty stared at Monique and appeared slightly surprised by the comment. Jackie again attempted to push the girls back into the plane.

"I don't think they want your advice, Monique," Jackie muttered to the girl.

"I honestly figured it'd be too dangerous to let her get on top of the horses," Betty informed Monique. "You know a lot about horses?"

"We were riding before we could walk," Colleen informed the older woman. "We raised our horses from colts when we were pretty young."

"I'm sure my daughter would welcome a few pointers," the woman replied as her mood softened. She actually smiled. "It's okay if you want to leave your plane there. It's not really hurting anything."

"We'd love to help your daughter with the horses," Monique quickly chirped.

"Monique--" Jackie softly scolded.

"Can we come over later this evening?" Colleen asked with enthusiasm.

"Colleen," Monroe grumbled while eying the girl, who easily ignored him.

"That'd be wonderful," the woman replied cheerfully. "I'm Betty and these are my daughters, Lexie and Kathy."

"You have three daughters?" Jackie couldn't help but ask the older woman.

"Yes, my youngest, Lilly, is back at the house. She's fourteen." Betty appeared slightly ashamed while indicating the shotgun relaxed in Lexie's arms. "I'm sorry about the rude greeting. We don't get a lot of visitors out this way, and we can't be too careful, but seeing you have your own kids with you--"

Jackie was slightly surprised. Did Betty actually think she was old enough to have two fifteen-year-old daughters? She was only twenty-four herself. She caught Monroe's sly grin and wished she could wipe it off his face.

"Well, we'll let you to your business," Betty announced then smiled at the girls. "After you've finished your dinner, you're welcome to come over anytime this evening."

"Thanks," both girls announced in unison.

Jackie had to refrain from rolling her eyes. Honestly, the girls were acting as if they were on vacation. Socializing while men were hunting them was not a good idea, and Ross wouldn't allow it. Betty turned the jeep around and drove back to her farmhouse. Jackie and Monroe exchanged looks.

"That was interesting," Monroe remarked.

Zack leaned just within the plane doorway with his arms folded across his chest, clinging to his assault rifle like his cherished baby.

"A woman and her three daughters," Zack announced then shook his head while frowning. "That's nothing but trouble, I guarantee it."

t

$\mathcal{T}$he casino hotel lobby was massive by any standards and despite being nearly two years old, it remained in brand new condition. It contained mostly marble floors and walls. Several large chandeliers lined the ceiling, although none were lit. The furniture, which was scattered throughout the lobby, gave the impression of smaller gathering areas. The sofas and oversized chairs were of the highest quality and consisted of a durable leather-like material. Jackie and company were greeted by a ravenous beauty in her early thirties. Katrina's outfit could only be described as business sexy. She wore a simple, black dress that hugged her curves, but the healthy slits on both sides up to her thighs allowed for maximum movement. The V-neck dipped low enough to reveal plenty of cleavage possibly further elevated with the help of a push-up bra. She wore high heels that had to be uncomfortable. Jackie stared at the picture perfect woman with carefully styled reddish blond hair and flawless make-up. It was one of those few times Jackie felt completely inadequate but at the same time, she couldn't help but wonder who the woman was trying to impress.

Monroe made every effort not to stare at the gorgeous woman, but the sweat on his upper lip indicated he was already entertaining some seriously inappropriate fantasies. Monroe was a stylish man who appreciated expensive taste in clothing. A well-dressed woman always made an impression on him, and when they looked as good as Katrina did, he was reduced to a helpless little boy. Zack was a different breed of man altogether. By the way he scanned the lobby it was possible he hadn't even noticed Katrina was a woman. Zack was notorious for only being attracted to women who could kick his ass. Once he shifted out of warrior mode, he'd almost certainly start pushing Jackie's buttons. Provoking her into a fight ranked high on his list of favorite pastimes. She didn't doubt he could easily defeat her, but that wasn't his endgame. To him, it was almost a twisted form of foreplay. Just another one of Zack's 'Jekyll and Hyde' personas.

"I'm Katrina," the attractive woman announced and seductively extended her hand to Monroe.

He looked as if he'd melt just by touching her. Monroe managed his best charming smile and shook her hand.

"I'm Monroe," he announced then introduced the others to the attractive woman.

Katrina must have noticed the odd stench from Monroe's clothes. She made a slight face but seemed to brush it aside. The woman then gave Jackie a sweeping look, which was quickly followed by what could only be described as pity. Jackie was dressed in her finest workout pants, scuffed boots, and her worn, leather bomber jacket over a dirty, white tank top. Her dark hair was pulled back into a ponytail that had been put through hell the last few hours. Her ensemble was completed with her father's old Navy SEAL dog tags. The attractive woman glanced at Zack, who didn't bother acknowledging her existence. He was too busy studying a naked Roman male statue standing boldly in a small, marble fountain. The fountain was dry and had probably never contained water. Zack's hand was to his chin as he stared at the statue's painfully small genitals. He shook his head.

"That's just sad," he muttered while walking away, catching the woman's attention.

Jackie could only imagine what the fashionable woman was thinking about Zack. He currently looked like the poster child for guerilla warfare in his favorite, excessively worn and undoubtedly bloodstained military jacket. If a forensic swab were ever done on the treads of his comfortably worn-out combat boots, the results would be frightening.

"Sal mentioned more than just five of you," Katrina informed Monroe.

Monroe was so smitten with the woman; he probably didn't hear a word she said. "Oh, well, uh, the others--"

Zack finally looked at Katrina, possibly curious by Monroe's sudden inability to complete a sentence. He gave the woman a quick, sweeping once over and immediately raised his brow in question by her attire.

"You didn't have to dress up on our account," Zack announced. "Sal's not with us."

Katrina eyed Zack and appeared uncertain what to make of him. "I didn't dress up on your account."

Zack appeared surprised and raised a challenging brow. "You seriously stuffed your feet into those uncomfortable shoes for the sheer joy of it?"

She stared at him a moment with her mouth hanging open then looked in silent question at Monroe, who was close to blushing with embarrassment.

"He's, uh, seen a lot of combat," Monroe gently informed her while fidgeting.

She managed a smile and nodded. Zack didn't seem offended by the comment and brushed it off with ease. The statement was, after all, true.

"The rest of the team will be along in a couple of hours," Monroe replied.

Katrina then smiled pleasantly and approached the massive check-in desk, which took up nearly half the back wall. The check-in desk also consisted of white marble and gold accents to create a feel of wealth.

"Why don't I get you some rooms, so you can clean up and get settled before your friends arrive? Once you're settled, I'll introduce you to the other caretakers." She gave Jackie a strange look that again conveyed pity. "Did you bring any bags? A change of clothing, perhaps?"

"In the other transport," Jackie casually informed her.

She hated to admit that her change of clothes was pretty much similar to what she was already wearing, just without the dirt and bloodstains. Then again, she didn't need to impress this woman, and it didn't matter what she thought. She also didn't need validation from men drooling over her. She just needed them to respect her, which sometimes involved kicking their asses.

"Colleen and I don't have any clothes," Monique reminded Jackie. "I'm still stuck in the same clothes I was wearing three days ago."

"We'll find something for you to wear," Jackie gently informed Monique.

"I'm sure I have something you can wear," Katrina informed the teenager while smiling pleasantly.

Monique stared at the attractive woman. It was obvious the young girl's mind was reeling. "No offense, but I don't wear dresses."

Katrina laughed softly. "I think I can find something less dressy."

"I'm glad," Monique announced with a soft gasp. "I wouldn't be caught dead in a dress."

Zack placed his arm around Jackie's shoulder and playfully pulled her to his side while grinning. "Awe, the sassy blond one takes after you. That's so sweet."

Jackie glared at him, their eyes locking from only inches away. He chuckled at the look she gave him then kissed the top of the head. Zack suddenly gave her an odd look, pulled back, and removed something from between his lips. He stared at the pinkish object between his fingers then showed it to Jackie.

"Is that a fingernail?" he asked.

Jackie looked at the torn fingernail with some flesh still attached on the back as he held it. He casually glanced over the top of her head then poked around in her hair, looking for more gross treasures.

"What else you got hiding in there?"

Katrina suddenly looked at them and stared at the fleshy fingernail Zack held. She gave Jackie a look of distaste. Jackie turned and walked away with annoyance. Once she was away from the others, she subconsciously ran her fingers through her hair, checking for more foreign bodily objects.

Chapter Nineteen

$\mathcal{W}$ithin the hour, the tractor-trailer rolled down the long, dirt road to the casino. Beck pulled the semi-truck around back near the loading dock, parked it, and climbed out of the cab. He was greeted at the loading dock by Jackie and Monroe. Beck looked around as he approached them by the open, large bay door. The loading dock contained several crates that had possibly been there since the place was first built. Undoubtedly, they contained personal touches for the hotel or supplies for the casino.

Beck smiled and nodded his approval. "This is some little hideaway Sal's loaning us," he remarked.

"Does Ross know you were bringing that truck here?" Monroe asked in a somewhat demanding tone as he folded his arms across his chest.

Beck glared at Monroe with a look of annoyance and possible impatience. "Yes, Monroe," he scoffed with noted irritation. "Ross is aware. We'll turn the truck over to Blake when we return the kids."

Jackie eyed both men suspiciously. She didn't know why they seemed to be in a pissing match lately, but it didn't pay to ask with the guys. They'd kill and die for one another, but there was always one pissed at another for some reason. It usually turned out to be something trivial involving a poker game or someone flushing a toilet while the other was in the shower.

"What's the safe house situation?" Beck asked, giving Jackie his full attention, intentionally excluding Monroe.

"Three caretakers," she informed him. "Two men one woman. Each one as questionable as their 'goodfella' boss. I'm sure Zack's poking around as we speak. The only neighbors are a woman and her three daughters, who promptly greeted us with shotguns, but the situation was defused by our horse loving witnesses. Keeping those two away from the neighbor girls and their horses is going to be a bit of a challenge."

Beck nodded in agreement then considered his next question as he studied Jackie. "Did Ross notify Blake of the situation at the Bureau yet?"

"We're not sure. We haven't heard from Ross since you spoke to him last," Jackie replied with some reluctance. "Supposedly, Stony Ridge is a bit of a cell phone dead spot, and he wouldn't trust using any landlines."

"Without my things from the helo, I don't have access to my laptop," Beck announced then looked around. "I'll scout the area, maybe see what Zack located. Where are the girls?"

"With Katrina attempting to find some suitable clothes," Jackie replied. "I don't think either are going to be happy with anything they find in Katrina's closet."

"Oh?"

Jackie shook her head while making a face. "The woman dresses awfully nice for someone who doesn't have contact with the outside world. Seems strange."

"Don't start that again," Monroe muttered under his breath while rolling his eyes.

Beck cast a glance at Monroe then looked back at Jackie and grinned. "Oh, so she's hot," he announced simply then added a throaty chuckle.

"She's attractive, yes," Monroe replied then glared at Jackie. "So, naturally, Jackie's suspicious of her."

Jackie turned to face Monroe with a slight fire in her eyes. "I have good instincts," she snapped hotly. "Whether or not she's attractive has nothing to do with my suspicions."

"No, but her being hot has everything to do with Monroe's judgement," Beck remarked with a hint of a grin.

Monroe's expression suddenly dropped as he glared at Beck. "What's that supposed to mean?"

Beck casually shrugged with little emotion. "I thought it was self-explanatory."

"When have I ever allowed an attractive woman affect my judgment?" Monroe demanded.

"We could start alphabetically with Afghanistan," Beck remarked while placing his hands casually on his gun holster securely around his hips. "Or we could go chronological and start with Jackie."

Jackie was nearly as stunned as Monroe was. Both stared at Beck.

"What?" Jackie suddenly lashed out, feeling her cheeks redden at Beck's insinuation.

"It's not like it was a secret about you two a few years back," Beck replied simply then suddenly silenced and shot a glare at Monroe. His look was stunned yet almost mocking. "Wait? She doesn't know that we all knew?"

Monroe's anger showed as he glared at Beck and his jaw clenched. Jackie stared at both men as her mind reeled with the new information. She wanted to hit Monroe, having felt betrayed that he had bragged to the guys about their one night together before she went off to college. Maybe she shouldn't have expected any less. After her father had died a few years ago, Monroe undoubtedly saw little reason to withhold their activities. It wasn't as if her father would come back from the grave and kick his ass--again. Jackie knew she needed to let it go. She shouldn't have expected Monroe to keep his mouth shut out of respect for her, especially since he was the one who wanted a relationship and she didn't. She knew the guys talked about their sexual conquests and sometimes bragged. She just needed to let it go and walk away. Monroe stared at her while fumbling for something to say as he subconsciously ran his fingers through his hair. Jackie turned to leave.

"Jackie, let me--"

Jackie spun into a kick, striking Monroe in the abdomen. He clutched his stomach and doubled over in pain. Jackie held her head high and walked away. Monroe slowly straightened while rubbing his sore abdomen. It could have been a lot worse, as Jackie obviously held back with the fierceness of her kick. Monroe turned toward Beck and glared at him. Beck folded his arms across his chest and smirked.

"Now we're even," Beck cheerfully replied.

✝

*J*ackie walked along the broad first floor corridor lined with a wall of windows. The view was of mostly nothing with distant mountains as a backdrop. She already felt guilty about striking Monroe. When her father found out Monroe had slept with his daughter, he was obligated to give Monroe a substantial beating. You didn't sleep with your commander's daughter. It was just wrong. Jackie had attempted to deny what happened with Monroe to her father, but she could never successfully lie to the commander.

Monroe received the beating partly of his own doing. Jackie didn't want to go off to college without experiencing certain things. It was important to her to lose her virginity to someone she genuinely cared about, and Monroe had been attentive. He seemed the logical choice. She had no idea he'd mistook what happened as the prelude to a relationship. He made her father genuinely suspicious, which is what started the entire downward spiral. She never regretted sleeping with Monroe, and after he got used to the idea that they weren't going to live happily ever after, they shared a special friendship. The more she thought about it, the angrier she became that Monroe bragged to the others about their special moment. She now wished she'd kicked Monroe in his lady parts. Jackie approached the first guestroom on the right and knocked on the door.

"Monique? Colleen?"

There was no response. Jackie knocked a little louder then considered checking to see if the door was locked from the inside. Katrina entered the hallway from the nearby linen closet, saw Jackie at the girls' guestroom door, and approached while carrying a set of sheets.

"If you're looking for the girls," Katrina announced, "they went outside for a while."

Jackie felt her heart pound with concern as she stared at the woman. "Outside?"

"They said they were going outside to play with the dog," she replied then indicated the sheets. "I brought sheets for their beds. I'll just leave them inside the room for them."

Katrina opened the guestroom door without use of an electronic key. The hotel ran on a generator, which only powered up the necessities. The electronic door locks were not among those necessities, considering the hotel was abandoned before it was even open. Jackie was annoyed with the girls for leaving the hotel without checking with one of them first. Katrina hardly counted, since she didn't know their reason for hiding out in the first place.

"Oh," Katrina then announced and paused in the doorway. "Tell the girls to stay away from the neighbors. Terrible people. Always causing trouble for us here." She shook her head and made a face. "That woman is just plain rude and nasty. I wouldn't hold out much hope for her daughters either."

A horrible thought then swept over Jackie. What if the girls had gone next door to visit the neighbor girls? What were the chances they were drawn to the horses? They knew they weren't supposed to leave without permission and someone to keep an eye on them. Jackie only had to consider it a moment. Of course, they went to the neighbors! She cursed under her breath and hurried along the corridor for the lobby entrance. If Ross discovered she'd allowed them out of the building, he'd be furious. She needed to find and return them before Ross arrived.

Chapter Twenty

$\mathcal{J}$ackie approached the plane and paused alongside it, covering her real reason for being there. She casually scanned the nearby farm for signs of the girls. She didn't want to cause problems with the odd family if the girls hadn't actually gone to their farm. She saw the horses in the fence grazing. It was little surprise to Jackie when she saw Monique and Colleen standing outside the fence with Darth and a young teenage girl. Jackie shook her head with annoyance. They knew better! She heard a faint thumping sound and immediately recognized it as an approaching helicopter. Jackie looked to the sky and shielded her eyes from the sun. Within a moment or two, the helicopter came into view. Jackie easily recognized it as hers, which meant Gil was arriving with the rest of the team. It was too late for Jackie to make it to the farm and retrieve the girls before the helicopter landed. Ross wouldn't be happy.

The helicopter approached and landed not far from the plane. Ross, Bogart, and Kirk got out of the helicopter as Gil shut it down. Ross approached Jackie as the others began unloading their gear. He gave Jackie a warm hug, being happy she was okay after the tense rescue. He then pulled away and attempted to remain pleasant, although something was obviously bothering him.

"What's the safe house situation?" he asked.

"Comfortable," Jackie replied. "Plenty of room to spread out, that's for sure."

"Good, I'm glad to hear," Ross responded. "We may need to make ourselves comfortable for a while."

Jackie was surprised and stared at him. Not just for personal reasons, she was concerned about the possibility of being stranded for days or even weeks. It meant there was more bad news coming.

"That doesn't sound good," she remarked and shifted uncomfortably. "Is something wrong?"

"I honestly wish I knew," he replied with a deep sigh as the guys approached from the helicopter each carrying several duffel bags. "I've been unsuccessful reaching Blake. I tried his radio frequency, his cell phone, and his office number. My calls keep going to voicemail."

"He could be with the women at their safe house," Jackie suggested, although she knew that was a pipe dream.

Ross nodded but didn't appear convinced either. "I'll keep trying to contact him throughout the evening. I hope I'm just being paranoid," he announced.

"You and me both," Jackie informed him while insecurely folding her arms across her chest. "This place is unsettling."

"Oh?" Ross enquired.

"I haven't met the two male caretakers yet," she announced while glancing back at the massive hotel and casino, "but the woman gives me a bad vibe."

"In what way?"

"She's dressed to the nines in a place where there's no one to impress."

"So she's attractive," Gil casually remarked.

Jackie glared at him. By his expression, he was only making an observation and not attempting to ruffle her. She felt a little guilty about giving him a dirty look.

"How attractive?" Bogart suddenly asked, barely able to control his lustful grin.

"Not important," Ross muttered, his words wiping the smile from Bogart's face.

"Was Monroe tripping over his tongue?" Kirk teased, enjoying his comment.

"Can we stay on subject?" Jackie demanded.

Ross disapprovingly glared at the three men alongside him. "You heard the lady. Stay on subject." He looked back at Jackie while maintaining his commanding attitude. "Anything else?"

Jackie groaned softly then gave a slight nod to the farm nearby. "Then there's the neighbors."

All four men cast casual glances toward the farm, but easily conveyed that they weren't looking. It only took a sweeping glance for Ross, Kirk, and Gil to notice what most wouldn't. Bogart remained clueless.

"Why is Darth at that farm?" Gil almost demanded then whistled.

"More importantly," Ross almost snarled while glaring at Jackie, "why are Monique and Colleen over there?"

"I was just on my way to retrieve them," Jackie replied. "A woman and her three daughters live on that farm. They have it out for Sal, the casino, and the caretakers. Somehow, the girls weaseled their way into the woman's heart. It's going to be tough keeping them away from those horses."

Ross rolled his eyes and shook his head. "So the natives aren't friendly, huh?"

"They are for the moment," Jackie replied gently, "but they're going to be offended when they discover the girls aren't allowed over there."

"We'll deal with that later," Ross announced.

Darth ran to Gil and greeted him with enthusiasm. Gil happily scratched the dog and lightly wrestled with him. Monique and Colleen jogged toward the plane. Both girls were enthusiastic about their visit.

"Betty's younger daughter is really nice," Colleen announced cheerfully.

"She wants us to help train her horses," Monique informed them. "Isn't that great?"

Ross glared at both girls. His stare was enough to wipe the smiles from their faces.

"What?" Monique suddenly asked. "Did we do something wrong?"

"The list is growing," Ross remarked curtly then indicated the hotel. "I want the two of you in that hotel yesterday. We're going to discuss the dangers of talking to strangers and making new friends while trained killers are hunting your asses."

The girls exchanged looks and appeared to debate a response. Neither seemed brave enough and headed toward the hotel. Ross nodded to Bogart and Kirk. Both men gathered their bags and followed the girls in their trek to the hotel entrance over one hundred yards away. When Jackie looked back at Ross, Zack was standing alongside her puffing on his cigar.

"Kids suck," Zack muttered.

Jackie looked around with surprise. "Did you go to the farm with them?"

"Did I *follow* the brats to the farm?" he reconfirmed. "Yes, I followed them. With Monroe following his divining rod and you being so trusting of the tom girls, I took it upon myself to keep an eye on the future criminal minds."

Jackie felt the color rushing to her cheeks from Zack's assessment. Maybe she had given the girls too much credit for maturity. They obviously felt safe in their new environment, which was a distinct possibility, but it was a bad idea to put their guard down even for a moment. Jackie knew that all too well from her own encounter while in witness protection.

"Did you happen to learn anything about the neighbors during your stakeout of the girls?" Ross asked and appeared curious.

"The apple pie smelled delicious," Zack replied simply. "They keep a clean farm, and one of the daughters takes a liking to thong panties."

Ross and Gil eyed Zack in silent question. Jackie had to look away, wanting no part of Zack's intimate observation. Zack noted the looks he received.

"I wasn't rummaging through their panty drawer," he scoffed. "Get your minds from the gutters. They had wash hanging on the line," Zack announced firmly in his defense. "Just seemed kind of odd."

"Hanging wash on the line?" Gil suddenly asked.

Zack stared at him in disbelief. "No, the thong panties," he snapped then shook his head with irritation. "Haven't you been paying attention?"

"The nearest town is almost an hour's drive from here," Jackie informed them. "There aren't any men within miles."

Ross and Gil stared at her with less of a clue than before. Jackie groaned softly wanting to give up her explanation. The conversation was embarrassing enough as it was.

"Imagine Jackie wearing thong panties," Zack attempted to explain.

Jackie glared at Zack. Why did the point he was attempting to make have to involve her and such a visual image? Ross and Gil both came to the same conclusion and nodded.

"Why would a young woman need sexy undergarments when she spends most of her days on a farm so far from male company?" Ross questioned.

"Exactly," Zack replied firmly. "Sort of like the princess at the hotel. If there isn't anyone around to impress, why be uncomfortable when you don't have to be."

Jackie was happy that *someone* finally got it. She didn't know why they automatically had to assume she was jealous of the woman. She was very disappointed in her father's team. She always thought they were above petty lust. Jackie then thought about her own insecure thoughts and felt a crushing blow. Was it true? Was she jealous?

"So it's possible we could have company during our stay," Ross muttered then shook his head. "Additional visitors are something Sal should have mentioned. The more people who are aware of our presence; the greater chance of our location getting out." He glanced at Zack. "I want you, Kirk, and Bogart to take turns keeping watch for visitors. I'll see what our caretakers are willing to offer about other people coming and going."

As the guys approached the helicopter to remove more bags containing personal items and possible weapons, Jackie tugged on Zack's jacket and gave a nod toward the plane. She walked toward the plane with Zack following her. His look was curious yet playful. Jackie hurried up the plane steps with Zack on her heels. She turned just inside the fuselage and nearly collided with him. He wore a devious smile on his face.

"Hmm, secret meetings," he teased while placing his hand against the wall near her head as he leaned closer to her. "What will Holden think?"

Jackie ignored the comment, brushed his hand away from the wall, and removed the photo of Bogart's mother from her pocket. She showed it to Zack.

"Do you know this woman?" she asked.

He glanced at the photo then looked back at Jackie and snorted a soft laugh. "Oh, yeah," Zack announced with a soft groan. "A real Southern bell. Every Navy man's fantasy."

Jackie shifted slightly. "I hate to ask, but was she popular with anyone we know?"

Zack stared at Jackie a moment and seemed to consider his answer carefully, which wasn't like him. When it came to the topic of sex, he was usually rather blunt and uninhibited.

"Where did you find this picture?" he asked rather than answering her question.

Jackie stared at him with surprise. Why was he avoiding the question? "Does it matter?" she asked.

Zack leaned against the doorway while studying her. "It was long before your mother," he bluntly replied. "Your father never cheated on your mother."

Her mouth suddenly fell open as she stared at him. "What? Wait," she nearly stammered. "Are you telling me *my* father slept with this woman?"

He groaned softly and ran his fingers through his hair. "Oh, Jackie," Zack muttered softly. "We were all young horny Marines back then. Your father, Ross, and myself." He casually shrugged. "During that week on shore leave, it was one big party. She offered and none of us refused." He straightened and studied the shocked look on her face. "Are you upset about it?"

She stared back at him, uncertain what to think. The possibilities were frightening. Could one of them be Bogart's father? Could Bogart be her brother? Jackie attempted to cover, although she'd already piqued Zack's curiosity.

"It wasn't as if it was an orgy," he quickly announced in an attempt to curb her concerns. "Just some lonely guys seeking the company of an attractive woman."

"I'd feel better if you stopped trying to explain," Jackie remarked. "I'd rather not think about my father that way."

Zack placed his hands on her shoulders and smiled reassuringly. "I promise, your father never cheated on your mother," he announced then grinned deviously. "Too many of us would have lined up at her door to steal her away. The commander loved your mother very much."

His assurances didn't comfort her, since he didn't know the real reason for her concern. She put on a false smile and made a hasty attempt to end the conversation. The possibility of Bogart being her brother was too much information for her to process.

"I appreciate that," she replied gently then kissed him quickly on the cheek.

Zack attempted to hide his pleased grin, possibly forgetting the entire conversation the moment she kissed him. He was easily distracted by the slightest display of affection from her, almost like a dog with his favorite squeaky toy.

Chapter Twenty-one

Monique and Colleen kneeled on one of the lobby sofas and peered out the large wall of windows. Both leaped off the sofa in unison as the front door opened and awaited the men's arrival. Kirk and Bogart entered carrying several duffel bags each. They dropped the bags on the floor near the fountain and looked around the massive, elegant lobby.

"Not half bad," Bogart announced.

Kirk wasn't nearly as interested in the comfortable lobby. "Where are the caretakers?" he muttered with irritation.

Monique and Colleen started their approach to question the men on what happened with their beloved horses.

"If I don't get a shower and something to eat soon," Kirk growled, "I'll have to hurt someone."

Both girls stopped in their tracks and quietly slipped off to the side to avoid the large, hostile man. The elevator dinged. As the door opened, Katrina stepped out as if on cue. She smiled sweetly at both men, giving them more than a quick once over. Kirk had the body of a Greek God, and Bogart had the looks of a male model. Her sweeping gaze over the men was her silent approval.

"Oh, you must be the rest of the team," Katrina announced in a sexy, sultry voice she hadn't used earlier and paused before them.

Kirk swept a look over the woman in the sexy outfit and stiletto heels, showing little interest in the attractive woman. "And you *must* be Katrina," he remarked.

"Yes, I'm Katrina, one of the caretakers here. You must be exhausted. The electronic door locks on the rooms aren't on the generator, so you won't need keys." She gave them each another sweeping glance and smiled lustfully. "I'll put you in rooms 110 and 112. I'll show you to the rooms. This way."

She turned and headed down the connecting hallway to the first floor rooms where Jackie and the girls were staying as well. Katrina walked in such a manner that it was difficult not to admire her backside in the tight dress. Bogart grinned his approval, but Kirk's reaction was oddly indifferent. Kirk collected his share of the bags and followed Katrina. Bogart attempted to grab his bags as quickly as possible, so not to miss a moment of the woman's captivating booty, but fumbled with the heavy duffel bags and their twisted straps.

"Bogart," Colleen called softly to him.

He picked up the last of the bags and looked across the lobby where the girls partially hid and vigorously motioned him over. Bogart looked back down the hall at the disappearing woman, whimpered softly, and then groaned with defeat. He dropped the bags and approached the girls.

"Yeah, Squirt? What do you want?" he muttered with noted irritation in his tone.

"I wish you wouldn't call me that," Colleen remarked under her breath.

"And I wish Ross hadn't chewed my ass off," Bogart snapped hotly, losing patience, "but I guess we all have our little problems. What do you want?"

"Did you get the horses safely to my cousin's house?" Monique asked in a more delicate tone, attempting to appease the irritable man.

"Yeah," he groaned softly. "The horses are fine." He then considered and grinned. "Your cousin's pretty fine too. We left your Uncle Dave at the farm with her. She said she would care for his injuries."

"What injuries?" Colleen asked with surprise. "What happened to my uncle?"

Bogart fumbled with a response. "His truck went into a ditch. He's fine." He didn't want them to know that their abductors had gone after Colleen's uncle or they might start worrying about their mothers.

"Oh, that's a relief. He's a terrible driver," Colleen replied. Her look then turned sorrowful. "We're sorry you got into trouble with your boss."

"Uh, huh," Bogart remarked and raised his brows. "You should probably be worrying more about yourself."

"What do you mean?" Colleen asked.

"Ross is pissed at you," Bogart informed her. "That little stunt with the horses--" He shook his head. "The man is not happy."

"Let him yell," Colleen replied and folded her arms across her chest. "I wasn't leaving our horses behind. Besides, what's he really going to do to me?"

"I don't know," Bogart announced while shaking his head, "but he made me jog five miles alongside the jeep before finally letting me get inside."

Both girls stared at the handsome country boy with equally concerned looks. They obviously weren't expecting to hear that. Monique gently nudged Colleen.

"I think we should let Bogart get showered and settle in," she gently informed her friend. "He's had a rough day."

"No kidding, Twinkie," he grumbled to Monique. "Just do me a favor and stay far away from me for a while. I don't need your help getting into trouble with the boss."

Bogart returned to the discarded duffel bags, collected them with some effort, and hurried down the connecting hallway to catch up with Kirk and Katrina. The girls sighed simultaneously while watching Bogart disappear.

"There's no way he was going to help us sneak over to the neighbor's farm," Monique informed Colleen. She shook her head with annoyance. "I can't believe he called me Twinkie."

"I'd rather be Twinkie than Squirt," Colleen remarked. She then hesitated and sank into thought. "Do you think Ross is pissed enough to do something irrational?"

"I don't know," Monique replied gently. "Maybe we should hide behind Katrina for a few hours until he cools off. I don't think he'll turn all Dirty Harry in front of the caretakers. Especially a woman."

They were about to head down the connecting hall when the door opened. Ross, Gil, and Jackie entered with Darth on their heels. Jackie gave the girls a timid, sad look then hurried down the hall with Gil and Darth in tow. Ross stopped before the girls with a broad stance, folded his arms across his chest, and gave Colleen a cold glare. Both girls tensed at the harshness of his stare.

"I get that you love your horses," Ross remarked sternly, "but you risked the lives of my team with that stunt you pulled. We've survived every third world shithole out there, because we don't run fool's errands."

Monique opened her mouth to speak. Ross pointed a warning finger without even looking at her.

"Think twice before you say something stupid," Ross warned Monique but kept his eyes locked on Colleen. "Until I can safely turn you over to your parents or the authorities, you two are my responsibility. My men are also my responsibility. Don't ever again do anything so stupid that puts my men at risk. This isn't a game. All of our lives are officially on the line, and you will *not* make a move that I don't know about." He inhaled deeply and straightened, looking even more intimidating. "I'm not your father, and I'm not your friend. I am your commanding officer until this mission is complete. You step out of line, and I'll knock you back in it. I'll have you scrubbing the commode with your toothbrushes if you piss me off. Are we clear?"

Colleen stared at him and held her breath. She slowly nodded. He then looked at Monique.

"Are *we* clear?"

Monique nodded as well. Ross nodded then turned and walked away. Both girls exhaled simultaneously then looked at each other with wide, horror-filled eyes.

"Let's try not to piss him off," Monique muttered softly.

Colleen nodded, still unable to speak. Ross walked down the main corridor and nearly collided with Jackie as she filed into the hallway from the nearby lounge, joining him on his walk.

"Don't you think you were a little tough on them?" Jackie remarked while casting a quick glance at him.

Ross casually shrugged. "Possibly," he replied without looking at her, "but if I didn't put a little fear into them, they'd undoubtedly con Bogart into doing something stupid again. Honestly, Jackie, I have no doubt Bogart will eventually get himself killed, but I really don't want it to be me who kills him. I have a better chance of getting through to those girls than I do Bogart."

"You need to stop being so hard on Bogart," Jackie remarked then felt a chill running down her spine at the things she'd recently discovered. "He tries so hard to please you."

"He tries so hard to annoy me," Ross easily corrected then glared at her. "How can you defend him after everything that's happened?"

Jackie shrugged and considered the possibility that he could be her only living relative or even Ross's only son. "He grows on you after a while," she replied almost defensively. "He did get Colleen out of that battlefield." She raised a brow and grinned. "And you have to admit, that was one hell of a rescue with the horse and the plane."

Ross considered the comment and hid his smile. "Yeah, it was pretty impressive," he remarked. "I'm guessing he missed his calling as a rodeo clown." There was a moment of silence. Ross finally looked at her. "Am I getting any closer to the kitchen?"

Jackie smiled and pointed down the hall.

Chapter Twenty-two

$\mathcal{I}$t was later that evening. The team and the girls had a chance to shower, change into clean clothes, and have something to eat. The kitchen was well stocked despite only accommodating the three caretakers. Around dinnertime was the first any of them had met the two remaining caretakers. It seemed odd that the team had been around several hours and hadn't run into either man. It was no surprise that both men were Italian descent. Their boss, Salvatore Romano, was as Italian as a 'goodfella' could be. The team knew of Sal's rumored mob ties, but he was the only one they could count on in their current situation. With Beck dating his daughter, they felt relatively confident they weren't in any danger from Sal or his employees.

Alfonzo, or Fonzi as he preferred to be called, was attractive from a distance, but he lost his appeal close up. He had dark, slicked back hair and seemed in excellent physical shape. His age was difficult to tell by the wear and tear on his face. He'd suffered terrible acne in his youth, leaving pocks covering most of his face. He was almost certainly in his thirties if not older. He tried a little too hard to live up to his 'Fonzi' nickname, keeping tradition with the standard, black leather jacket, white tee shirt, and blue jeans. His black cowboy boots were excessively shinny and killed the entire ensemble. Clarke, which could have been his first or last name, was built muscular, although not nearly as tall and buff as Kirk. He kept his head clean-shaven for an intimidating look and sported a dirty blond goatee. He was possibly in his late thirties or early forties. He had a gruff, gravelly voice to match his tough appearance. He too preferred jeans but chose black work boots. He wore a button shirt untucked with the sleeves rolled up to his elbows.

With the casual dress of the two men, Jackie was still left bewildered about Katrina's wardrobe choice. It was possible she just enjoyed dressing feminine. Jackie always felt she had limited knowledge of women, since she didn't spend much time in the company of women and she was raised by men, but something about Katrina's appearance nagged at her. She was almost positive it didn't have anything to do with being jealous of the woman.

After dinner, Monique and Colleen were introduced to a wide assortment of DVDs the caretakers had collected during their two year tour of keeping the casino and hotel from falling apart. It was possibly Sal's hope that a highway would eventually be built close enough to give his casino relevance. The girls took a few movies and Darth with them to their room and retired for the evening. Beck had the connecting room to theirs and happily retired with his laptop. Someone had to remain close to the girls, and Beck had plenty of work to do on his computer that he didn't mind leaving the gathering early. He also assumed responsibility for attempting to reach Blake Harris, which all attempts had still remained unsuccessful.

Jackie joined the others in one of the elegant lounges. Although there were several lounges, only one was stocked. There were pub tables along the edges, a few small tables toward the center of the room, and sporadic sections of sofas and chairs surrounding coffee tables throughout. The entire back wall was encased in glass with double doors leading out to what should have been a patio, but the patio had never been completed. Ross, Kirk, and Gil sat at the old-fashioned, detailed wooden bar, had a few drinks, and smoked cigars with Fonzi and Clarke. As social as the gathering appeared, Jackie was almost certain the guys were probing for information.

Not far from the bar, Monroe and Bogart sat on the comfortable sofas while making spectacles of themselves fawning over Katrina. Jackie sat on a sofa across the room and watched the pitiful display. It wasn't as if Katrina didn't show an interest in either man, on the contrary, she was extremely flirtatious. Judging by the glances Ross, Kirk, and Gil gave their teammates flirting with the attractive woman, Jackie didn't doubt they were taking bets on which of the two would secure the woman's overnight company. Zack was conveniently absent, which was normal for the abnormal man. He didn't function well in social situations, particularly with strangers. It was unclear if he was uncomfortable or just disinterested.

A serving tray containing a china teapot and teacups on saucers was placed on the coffee table before Jackie. She looked up and met Zack's moderately playful grin. He sat on the sofa alongside her and poured each of them a cup of tea. Without a word, she watched him add a lump of sugar to each and creamer to hers. He handed her the delicate teacup on the saucer. Jackie held back her laugh and accepted it. He picked up his teacup, sipped his tea in a refined manner, and casually glanced around the room. She was convinced Zack could play any role required of him, even that requiring sophistication, when called upon.

"Doesn't look as if I've missed much," Zack muttered then indicated his team with the male caretakers. "A battle of testosterone at the bar." He then indicated Monroe and Bogart with Katrina. "And a game of 'who can sink the submarine' being played over there."

Jackie sipped her tea and showed little reaction to the sexual innuendo. "Thanks for that descriptive assessment," she casually remarked.

"Anytime," Zack replied, possibly unaware of his distasteful remark.

They sat several minutes in silence while sipping their tea and observing the others. For a moment, Zack almost passed for a refined gentleman.

"Are you jealous?" Zack casually asked without bothering to look at her.

Jackie eyed him with some surprise then demanded, "Why would I be jealous?"

"I'll take that as 'yes'," Zack replied and still didn't look at her. He preferred to keep an eye on the room.

Jackie set her teacup down and turned on the sofa to face him, finally catching his attention. "If this is about what happened between me and Monroe--?"

Zack's expression suddenly dropped as he stared at her. "You and Monroe?" he nearly gasped then cast his teacup down on the coffee table with some vigor. They received several looks from the others, but none were interested in their conversation. "What happened between you and Monroe?"

Jackie stared at him with her mouth hanging open. Her mind raced to process the question. Beck said the guys knew, so why was Zack acting as if he didn't?

"I thought Monroe bragged about what happened before I went to college," Jackie remarked with surprise while staring at him. "Beck said--"

"Beck and Monroe have been in a pissing match ever since Monroe walked in on Beck's girlfriend in the shower last week," Zack informed her. "If there had been something between you and

Monroe way back when, Beck didn't know anything about it. He was just grasping for anything to get even with Monroe."

Jackie stared at Zack with disbelief and then shook her head. She wasn't sure which man she wanted to hit.

"You and Monroe," Zack suddenly scoffed while making a face. He then considered his comment and had a slight revelation. "That *would* explain why the commander beat the crap out of Monroe when we arrived in port a few years back." His expression once more turned irritable and he again glared at her. "You and Monroe?" he announced with a little more vigor. "What the hell were you thinking?"

Jackie shrugged and attempted to compose herself. "I didn't want to go off to college a virgin," she gently replied. "Monroe seemed like the logical choice."

She was about to reach for her teacup when she noticed the hostility on Zack's face.

"Monroe was the logical choice?" Zack suddenly demanded. "Monroe?"

Jackie tensed slightly as she stared at his expression. He was undoubtedly pissed at her. Zack had never shown hostile feelings toward her before, and it was a little frightening.

"How can you even say that while keeping a straight face?" Zack scoffed, clearly offended. "You don't send a boy to do a man's job."

Jackie immediately felt uncomfortable and shifted on the sofa. "All things considered," she firmly announced, "I think my father wouldn't have been nearly as forgiving with the other, more mature men in his team."

Zack studied her in silence, but he was clearly considering the comment. He then relaxed. "You may have a point."

She held back her smile and refrained from laughing. She was grateful he was willing to let it go. "Are we good?"

He considered the question only a moment before shaking his head then responding. "No, I've been offended," Zack announced firmly. "I demand retribution."

"Retribution?"

He stared into her eyes with a serious look. "This hotel has a fancy gym downstairs with mats--"

She should have seen that one coming. Her eyes narrowed. "No, Zack," she firmly replied.

His expression hardened. "You don't even know what I was going to say."

"I'm pretty sure I do," she replied, "and the answer's no. I'm not going to spar with you."

"Why not?" he asked clearly disappointed.

"Because I don't feel like having my neck broken."

"I wouldn't break your neck," he scoffed then grinned. "I'd be willing to take it easy on you." His look turned playful. "Please, Jackie. It'll be so much fun."

"No, I'm not sparing with you," she remarked firmly.

"Just a little workout."

"The answer is still no."

Zack flopped back on the sofa and folded his arms across his chest. "You're no fun," he pouted.

Jackie couldn't help but smile at his boyish tantrum. She placed her arm around his neck and gently pulled his head to her shoulder. He showed no resistance as he placed his head on her chest, allowing her to hold him.

"I'm still mad at you," he muttered softly as he wrapped his arms around her and made himself comfortable.

She gently patted his head and smiled only because he couldn't see it. "I'm good with that."

Chapter Twenty-three

$\mathcal{R}$oss, Kirk, and Gil remained at the lounge bar with Fonzi and Clarke over the next hour. Despite being friendly, the caretakers seemed to be oddly quiet at times and took great care with what they said to the men. Kirk and Gil sipped their whiskey and puffed on the expensive cigars, compliments of the casino, while Ross did most of the talking with the two caretakers.

"It must be pretty dull living here in the middle of nowhere," Ross remarked to both men.

The irony of the statement was the team's own living arrangements were fairly similar in that they too lived in the middle of nowhere, and they preferred it that way. Ross owned a gentleman's farm where he lived with his girlfriend and his brother-in-law, and the others spent most of their time at the old lodge far from civilization. Monroe divided his time between the Colorado lodge and his beach house on a remote island off the coast of Florida.

"What do you do for fun?" Ross enquired.

Both men laughed and raised their glasses and cigars. "You're looking at it," Fonzi replied.

"There's more to do here than you think," Clarke offered. "We have a section of video poker machines connected into the generator; the indoor pool is filtered and cleaned, although it's not heated, fitness center, and game room. The countryside is great for hiking."

"If you had a lake nearby, I could live here," Kirk remarked, being the first comment he'd offered all evening. Perhaps it was the whiskey fueling his sudden urge to talk.

"There's a lake, although it's a twenty minute ride by dirt bike or quad," Clarke informed him.

"Dirt biking," Kirk remarked and nodded his approval. "I could get into that."

"We'll take you out if you're here more than a few days," Clarke replied.

"Sal was vague on how long you'd be with us," Fonzi remarked while glancing at Ross. "If it's longer than a week or two, we'll need to adjust our grocery list."

Ross was aware that the man was attempting to find out how long they intended to stay, which wasn't an unreasonable question. Why he didn't just come out and ask was uncertain.

"Well, we're hoping to only be here a few days," Ross replied, "but we're having some trouble contacting the man who hired us."

"What's the situation?" Fonzi asked then immediately held his hands up in the air. "If you're allowed to discuss it. I don't mean to pry. I know the drill working for Sal."

"No, that's okay," Ross announced while grinning. "We're all on the same team, right?"

Fonzi smiled his response, although he didn't agree nor disagree with the statement.

"There's a feud brewing among the families," Ross easily lied, "and, naturally, our boss wanted his daughters removed from the situation. Once things blow over, we can return them to their parents. We've been experiencing radio silence since yesterday afternoon and the feds have been crawling all over our safe houses. Sal was nice enough to give us a place to keep the girls out of harm's way."

Gil smirked into his glass, apparently amused by the story that was at least partially true but mostly bullshit.

"So you guys work for one of the families?" Clarke asked with a curious look.

Ross smiled and nodded. Clarke and Fonzi appeared relieved by the response.

"That does make things a bit easier on us," Fonzi remarked while studying Ross. "The casino sees a bit of action on Friday and Saturday nights. Nothing wild; just some gambling with a known crowd of regulars. We didn't know what we were going to do about this Friday, if you were still here."

"Oh, I see," Ross announced and grinned. "Is that why your neighbors were upset by our presence?"

"The neighbors," Fonzi groaned softly and shook his head. "It'd be in all our best interests if you avoided that nutcase and her daughters."

"Nothing rowdy or out of hand," Clarke interjected while eyeing the men at the bar. "Those girls and the young lady are perfectly safe in their company."

"Though I suggest keeping the girls away from the casino," Fonzi informed Ross with sincerity. "It's just not the proper environment for kids, and I wouldn't want to upset their father by exposing them to something he wouldn't approve."

"I understand," Ross replied. "And I agree 100%. Thanks for being upfront about the situation. We'll see that the girls confine themselves to the hotel portion of the property while you're entertaining."

"Mind if we join in?" Kirk asked with interest. "We enjoy taking other people's money."

"You're more than welcome to join us," Fonzi cheerfully informed them. "The more the merrier."

"Just, uh, don't tell anyone about our situation," Ross gently informed them, his concerned look remained genuine. "Protecting those girls is our number one priority. It's a matter of life or death. We keep them alive or it's our death."

Gil snorted a soft laugh and finished his drink. He stood and slapped Ross on the back. "I'm going to see how Beck's doing with the kids and then turn in."

"You're on the morning shift," Kirk remarked while glaring at him. "Make sure there's coffee."

Gil nodded and crossed the room, pausing before Monroe and Bogart, who were still competing for Katrina's attention. Neither man looked prepared to back down without a fight. Gil placed his hand on Monroe's shoulder and gave it a firm squeeze.

"I'm checking on the girls then heading to bed," Gil announced with little emotion then locked eyes with Monroe. "We may be in for a storm."

Monroe was suddenly interested in what Gil had to say while Bogart remained happily clueless.

"Did he need me to check that the plane and helicopter are secure?" Monroe quickly asked.

"Nah," Gil casually replied and straightened. "Just a heads up. You know how those kids can be during storms."

"Got it," Monroe replied with a reassuring nod.

"I don't think we're getting any storms tonight," Katrina informed Gil.

Gil looked at her and offered a tiny, charming smile. "Ross thinks he can tell the weather by the arthritis in his shoulder. We like to humor him. Good night, Katrina."

Bogart didn't even give Gil's comment a second thought and returned to flirting with the attractive woman. Monroe watched Gil approach Jackie and Zack on the sofa across the room. Jackie was comfortably reclined in the corner of the sofa with her feet propped on the coffee table while Zack slept with his head nuzzling her chest and his arms securely around her waist. He was locked onto her like a python.

Gil leaned down and whispered into Jackie's ear. "Looks like our caretakers are on Sal's dirty payroll," he gently informed her. "Probably nothing to worry about but keep alert."

He kissed her warmly on the cheek. She met his gaze and patted his hand on her shoulder then watched him leave the lounge. Jackie glanced across the lounge to Monroe, who now stared back. He raised his brow in silent question. Jackie nodded. She knew Monroe was subtly asking if she was armed, and she responded she was. Both knew Gil was on his way to alert Beck of the situation, if it even was a situation. Jackie drew a deep breath and looked at Zack clinging to her while he slept. He looked like an innocent little boy. She also knew she was never going to get him to let go of her either. Jackie attempted to make herself comfortable while lazily playing with Zack's slightly spikey hair. He nuzzled her chest in response. It took a lot to relax Zack. She just wondered why all his relaxation techniques somehow involved her.

From across the room at the bar, Ross and Kirk watched Zack sleeping while entwined around Jackie on the sofa. Ross snorted a soft, humored laugh then glanced at Kirk while indicating the odd couple.

"Think we should rescue her?" Ross asked teasingly as he sipped his drink.

"Fuck that," Kirk muttered and refilled his glass, no longer paying attention to the couple on the sofa. "Jackie knows to keep arms distance from Zack. If she gets too close, she's on her own." He took a swallow of whiskey. "I'm not pissing that boy off when he's sleeping. Jackie can fend for herself."

"You're the last of the true gentlemen, Kirk," Ross remarked with a sigh.

"Hey, she's perfectly safe," Kirk informed him in a defensive tone. "I don't want my hand bitten off. Never come between a dog and his favorite toy. If you're feeling all chivalrous and shit, be my guest."

Ross again glanced back at the couple on the sofa. He casually shrugged. "She seems fine."

Bogart approached them at the bar with a frown etched on his face. He wore a defeated look. Kirk and Ross eyed him then chuckled softly.

"I'd know that look anywhere," Ross remarked while studying Bogart. "Get shot down?" He seemed to take a little too much pride in the question.

"I don't want to talk about it," Bogart muttered then looked across the lounge.

Kirk and Ross followed his gaze across the room. Monroe and Katrina left the lounge together. Kirk suddenly groaned and rolled his eyes.

"Ah, hell, no," Kirk muttered.

Ross chuckled softly and extended his hand. Kirk slapped a twenty-dollar bill into his palm then glared at Bogart and pointed a warning finger at him.

"You," Kirk snarled. "You disappoint me."

Bogart eyed both men with surprise and possible annoyance. "Did you two take bets on which of us would bag the babe?" he suddenly demanded.

Both shrugged. Bogart considered the comment then smiled at Kirk.

"Thanks for the vote of confidence, man," Bogart cheerfully chirped.

"That reminds me," Ross announced to Kirk. "Tell Gil he owes me twenty bucks."

Bogart shook his head with disbelief and seemingly pouted. "I don't get it," he remarked. "If I had two thirds your votes of confidence, how did Monroe end up with the girl?"

"I was counting on guys in boots and jeans being a dime a dozen around here," Ross announced. "That gave 'flash in the pan' the advantage." Ross casually stood and stretched his sore back. "Well, I'm beat." He then looked at Bogart. "Since you're not busy tonight, you can tell Zack he's on second watch."

Bogart stared at Ross with surprise as his mouth hung open. "You want me to wake Zack?" he suddenly demanded then pointed to the sofa. "If I try to pry him off Jackie, he'll turn my body into a jigsaw puzzle."

"I give you one simple task--" Ross muttered then walked away while shaking his head.

Bogart gave a dumbfounded look at Kirk, who also stood while finishing his drink. He pointed after Ross and appeared defensive.

"I'm not crazy, right?" Bogart suddenly asked Kirk. "He's trying to get me killed, isn't he?"

Kirk playfully slapped him on the back and grinned in response. "Yep."

Chapter Twenty-four

Ross, Kirk, and Bogart walked along the first floor corridor toward the front guestrooms that they were assigned. Jackie and Zack were conveniently missing. Before the guys even reached their guestroom doors, Beck and Gil entered the corridor from Beck's room. Both men appeared moderately tense, which was odd for either man.

"We have a problem, Ross," Beck announced gently while attempting to keep his voice down.

Ross held up his finger and silenced them. "Where are Monroe and Katrina?"

Beck waved him off. "They're at the other end of the hall," he announced softly. "I saw them head into her room ten minutes ago."

Ross motioned them into Beck's room. All five entered, allowing the door to close behind them. Ross made a motion to the connecting door to the girls' bedroom.

"What's the problem?" Ross asked in a soft tone, so as not to alert the girls to their conversation. "Is it Blake?"

"That's only part of it," Beck announced gently. "I can't reach Blake on the radio or his cell phone, and their Uncle Dave has been calling the Bureau all day with no success. The last time anyone saw Blake Harris was when he showed up at the Cooper farm to pick up the girls' mothers. Their Uncle Dave hasn't heard from his sister, Donna, or Blake since they left."

Ross groaned softly and placed his hand over his eyes. He lowered his hand, drew a deep breath, and looked at his men.

"I don't want anyone telling those girls about this," Ross remarked softly. "We don't know what's happened. There's no point alarming them just yet."

"Well, we may know something that's happened," Gil informed them, "but it's not good."

"What's that supposed to mean?" Kirk demanded.

Beck hurried to his laptop setting on the small table. He clicked on several files.

"I was talking to Pinto a little while ago, and she showed me this," Beck informed them then stood aside.

Ross, Bogart, and Kirk stared at the computer screen, which showed grainy footage of Bogart and Monroe from the building where the girls were being held. They were clearly holding guns in their hands, which was probably taken during the first shootout.

Bogart suddenly groaned while throwing his arms in the air. "Why is it always me?"

Beck clicked on another file. "And this was from the nightly news." He played the video file of the news report.

"Six or more men are wanted tonight in connection with a shooting that has left two federal agents dead along a back road," the female newscaster announced in the video. The grainy images of Bogart and Monroe were again flashed. "If anyone knows the identity or whereabouts of these two men, please call local authorities. They're armed and extremely dangerous."

Beck stopped the video and looked at Ross. "I don't think it's a coincidence that we can't locate Blake Harris," he announced gently. "I think this goes deeper into the Bureau than we had imagined."

Ross gently scratched his graying hair and remained deep in thought. "This is not good," he muttered.

"At least the pictures are lousy," Gil announced with a sigh. "I don't think anyone will be able to recognize either as Bogart and Monroe."

"It's interesting that they didn't mention the girls or give the plane information," Ross remarked and sank into thought.

"The rental information on the plane must be how they located the lodge," Gil informed them, "but because of the corporate information we use, they weren't able to identify us or get our names."

"It's almost as if they wanted to put us into hiding but not enough to have us found," Beck remarked while folding his arms across his broad chest.

Bogart sank into thought a moment then glanced at the others. "Squirt said she thought the men who captured them reeked of fed," he informed them. "Witnessing two feds killing two other feds would certainly garner all the attention our girls are getting from these guys."

All eyes were suddenly on Bogart. "Are you telling me those girls witnessed a fed on fed assassination?"

"Yeah, Squirt told me at the amusement park," Bogart replied then hesitated, giving him an odd look. "She didn't tell you? I thought she would."

Ross folded his arms across his chest while glaring at Bogart. "I would think you'd tell me an important detail like that," Ross snarled.

"Yeah, and I probably would have, if I wasn't busy running behind you in the jeep," Bogart snapped back. "Squirt probably didn't tell you herself, because you chewed her out for the whole horse thing."

There was an odd silence as Beck, Gil, and Kirk stared at Ross waiting for the explosion. Ross locked eyes with Bogart. The explosion never came.

"What's done is done," Ross muttered and allowed his hands to fall to his hips. "We need to find Blake Harris. We don't know who we can trust with what the girls witnessed. Anyone at the Bureau could be involved in the murders and gun trafficking."

"There is one person at the Bureau you can trust," Gil remarked gently.

They all exchanged looks. Ross inhaled deeply and shut his eyes almost as if in pain at the thought.

Gil's look was serious. "Ross, we need to involve Holden."

✝

*I*t was a little after three in the morning. Jackie remained sleeping peacefully on the lounge sofa with Zack still nuzzled against her. Even she hadn't been brave enough to attempt to wake him. Zack suddenly woke and looked around the partially lit but empty lounge. He reluctantly pulled away from Jackie and approached the large wall of windows. Jackie felt unusually cold and slowly woke. She looked around the room with some disorientation then saw Zack staring out the window. She straightened on the sofa and ran her fingers through her slightly mussed hair.

"Something wrong?" she asked with concern.

"I'm not sure," he replied.

Jackie sprang to her feet and hurried toward the window to join him. She looked outside into the darkness in the direction he stared. Beyond the woods, she saw a faint glow. The glow of the moon provided just enough light to see smoke billowing above the tree line. Wherever the fire was coming from, it was beyond the casino property and almost certainly not on Betty's land either.

"What do you make of it?" Jackie asked. "Brushfire?"

"No, it's too small," Zack muttered while staring out the window. "Can you smell it?"

Jackie sniffed the air, but with the windows closed and sealed, she couldn't really smell anything. It was obvious Zack smelled something.

"I should check it out," he informed her.

"I'm coming with you," she quickly announced.

Zack eyed her as if taking her comment as a request. "Are you armed?"

"You were fondling my Glock the last few hours," she remarked. "I'd think you'd know."

"It's probably nothing," he informed her, "so I'll let you tag along."

"You act like you could actually stop me."

Zack grinned and cleverly raised his brows. "That challenge will have to wait for another time."

He motioned for her to follow him. Jackie followed him to the side door and slipped out behind him. Once they stepped onto the unfinished patio, the smell was a little stronger.

"That's a strange smell," Jackie remarked.

Judging by the look on Zack's face, he was familiar with the smell, but seemed unwilling to share its origin.

"Yes, it is," he replied with little emotion and walked across the property.

Jackie had to hurry to keep up with his fast gait. He wasn't a tall man, so his strides weren't long, but he moved in stealth mode. Quick and silent. As they neared the woods, he took her hand, surprising her.

"What you smell," he announced softly, "is burning flesh and hair or fur."

Jackie held back her startled gasp and squeezed his hand in response. It was almost as if he predicted she'd need a little comforting at that moment.

"What do you think is burning?" she gasped softly, not sure she really wanted to know.

"I'm not sure, but we're about to find out," he muttered.

It took them several minutes at a brisk walk to reach the clearing mostly filled with smoke. Whatever flames they had seen had already diminished. Zack stopped her before the clearing, forced her to crouch alongside him, and took a moment to survey the area. She clung to his hand and attempted to see what was burning, but the smoke appeared to be coming from nowhere. She wanted to ask him if he saw anything, but she didn't want to speak. The woods were quiet and sound would travel. She didn't know how long they remained crouched alongside a large tree, but Zack wasn't in any hurry to rush into a situation.

"We're alone," he finally informed her and straightened, releasing her hand.

Jackie straightened as well and looked around. "What's burning? I don't see anything."

"There's a pit up ahead," he replied and entered the clearing.

She slowly followed him while removing her gun from her concealed pants holster. Zack didn't bother removing his gun. They approached the smoky pit, stood on the edge, and looked at the smoldering remains. The smell was worse than horrendous. It was something Jackie had never smelled before. Zack walked along the edge of the pit for a better look beyond the billowing smoke. Jackie hurried after him. They found a less smoky spot and looked into the pit at the charbroiled remains of a man. Jackie gasped softly and stifled her emotions with her hand to her mouth. As they scanned the pit, they saw nearly a dozen burned remains.

"Oh, my God," Jackie gasped softly. "What the hell?"

"Yes," Zack replied lowly. "What the hell indeed?" He inhaled deeply despite the awful stench and looked around. Zack nodded into the woods. "The neighbor's property is about half a mile that way." He then looked back the way they came. "The hotel is about half a mile that way."

"So you think it could be the Hatfield's or the McCoy's?" she questioned.

"My money is on the psycho women from hell," Zack remarked simply, "but I can't imagine either the farm girls or the caretakers having motive for mass murder."

"It would make sense if they're mob hits," Jackie remarked. "If Sal really is a kingpin, this could be his body dump."

"And we came along, so they decided to burn the evidence in the middle of the night," Zack added then looked around while processing the information.

"It could also explain why we didn't see the two guys all day," she remarked.

"That would be a neat and tidy explanation," Zack replied while deep in thought, "but that still doesn't explain the thong panties on the wash line."

"Zack," Jackie snapped hotly. "This has nothing to do with a country girl wearing thong underwear."

He turned and glared at her. "Give me one good reason why any of those girls would wear thong panties."

Jackie stared at him and struggled for an answer. He was right, and he had excellent instincts. A young woman spending all her days tending to crops and farm animals without male companionship would have no reason for sexy undergarments.

"Okay, I can't explain it," Jackie caved. "But I also can't imagine those women being serial killers either."

"Well, there could be a very good reason there aren't any men around," Zack informed her. "Betty could be the world's biggest man-hater and does everything in her power to keep men away from her daughters." He was silent a moment. "So if we find Bogart in that pit, we'll know."

Zack turned and headed back toward the woods, surprising Jackie. She didn't understand how he could show so little reaction to what they'd just discovered. Jackie looked back at the pit, grimaced, and then hurried after Zack before he disappeared forever.

Chapter Twenty-five

Early the following morning, Jackie sat on the unfinished back patio overlooking the small grassy patch of land and watched Darth trotting around from weed to weed, marking his territory. Beyond the small grassy patch was a large field. The area was supposed to be the garden and pool, neither of which were started. Jackie hadn't slept after her grisly discovery with Zack. It was unclear if Zack had woken Ross to inform him of what they had found. What it meant regarding their current situation was frightening. They couldn't exactly leave, since they had no place to go, and remaining came with a new set of challenges. Ross walked onto the patio, placed a cup of tea on the table before her, and sat in the vacant chair alongside her with his own mug of coffee. She eyed the cup of tea then cast a look at Ross.

"Is this bribery or an apology?" she asked while cleverly raising her brow.

"Both," he replied while managing a smile.

She sipped the tea, hesitated, and again eyed Ross. "Zack made this," she announced and set the cup back down. "It must be one hell of a favor."

"It feels like the situation is falling apart," Ross informed her. "I need to man up to my mistakes and take responsibilities for the lies I've told."

"Which lies?" she asked with a slight bite to her words. "The one where you forgot to mention that Monique's father is Holden's boss?"

"That would be a start," he calmly replied while avoiding looking at her. He blankly stared at the field beyond the hotel and drew a deep breath. "I've done a bad thing, Jackie." Ross finally looked at her.

She could see the guilt in his eyes and immediately felt an ache in the pit of her stomach. Jackie wasn't sure how things could get much worse, but she was almost certain he was about to find a way to do just that.

"What did you do?" she gasped slightly as she felt her anxiety increasing.

"You're an important part of our team," he began and immediately hesitated.

Jackie stared at him and felt her heart pounding heavily in her chest. Several scenarios raced through her mind. None of them were good.

"Ross," she growled softly. "What did you do?"

"When Blake Harris came to us about his missing daughter, he asked if there was anything we needed from him," Ross blurted out the words.

Jackie's eyes widened but she held back her gasp. "You didn't!"

Ross looked away and ran his fingers through his graying hair. "I asked him to send Holden on a two-week tour of duty, so we could sneak you on the mission."

"Oh, Ross!"

His words nearly crushed her. He purposely had her husband sent away, so he wouldn't be around to protest their little 'flight issue'. Then it suddenly hit her. She turned sideways in her chair and stared at him.

"Did Blake Harris send him on a fake assignment?" she suddenly demanded.

Ross smiled weakly. "I certainly couldn't ask to send him someplace dangerous," he remarked. "I'd feel terrible if something bad happened to him."

Jackie shook her head with disbelief. "You're unbelievable," she scoffed then turned facing forward in her seat and refused to look at him.

Ross squirmed in his chair. "Well, as long as I'm confessing and you're going to be mad anyway, I may as well get it all off my chest."

She glared at him with alarm. "All of what? How can there possibly be more?"

"I don't know," he groaned softly. "Somehow, with me, there always is." He tensed and stared at her. "I sort of pulled some strings to get Holden the job here in Colorado," he gently informed her then straightened proudly. "You were too far away living in Chicago."

Jackie groaned and sank in her seat. She cast a glare at him. "And you thought a cup of tea would soften the blow?"

"No, the tea was Zack's idea," Ross replied gently. "Look, I'm sorry I deceived you with everything I did. When Holden freaked out about you being shot on our last mission, I didn't know how to fix things. I gave him a few weeks, but that didn't seem to be working, so I took drastic steps to bring you into our backyard." He sighed softly. "I know it was wrong, but sadly, I'd do it all over again if I had to."

"You're not winning any points, Ross," she muttered and finally straightened in her chair. "Why are you confessing this to me now?" Her eyes narrowed. "What is it you want?"

Ross gently placed the satellite phone on the table before her. "I need you to involve Holden."

She stared at him with surprise. "What?"

"I need you to call Holden where he's working undercover at that mansion, confess everything, and convince him to help us," Ross gently replied.

"And why would he want to help you?" she suddenly demanded. "What makes you think he's not going to go ballistic and kick both of us to the curb."

"The most important reason being he's madly in love with you," Ross announced and again shifted in his seat as he stared into her eyes. "Jackie, we can't locate Blake Harris. Holden's boss is MIA. The girls' mothers are MIA. The FBI has wanted posters for Monroe and Bogart implicating them in the murders of two federal agents."

She could barely comprehend what she was hearing as she stared at him with horror. "Are you serious?"

"Yes, Jackie," he replied gently. "Although I haven't spoken to either of the girls yet this morning, Bogart told me that they witnessed two men murdering two other men. We're certain all four were feds, just like the guys at the Cooper farm. We don't know who at the Bureau is involved, but those girls aren't safe. Holden needs to find out what happened to his boss and find out who those men were that the girls had seen."

Jackie picked up the phone and frowned. "Is this thing untraceable?"

"Absolutely," Ross replied.

"You know he's never going to trust you again," she announced.

Ross nodded and slid a piece of paper on the table in front of her. "I know," he replied softly. "I'm prepared to accept the consequences of my actions. Holden is the only person in the FBI we can trust right now. I have no other choice."

Jackie picked up the paper containing the phone number and groaned softly. "This is going to suck," she muttered.

Ross stood and offered a sympathetic smile. "I'll give you some privacy." He turned and headed back inside.

She turned on the phone and punched in the numbers, feeling an ache in her stomach with each button she pressed. She placed the phone to her ear as she stood and started to pace as it rang.

†

*H*olden crossed the mansion's large kitchen and approached the phone on the wall near the island counter. Holden was dressed in an expensive butler's uniform that almost certainly cost more than his entire wardrobe.

"Marble Crest Manor," Holden announced into the phone.

"Hi, Holden," came Jackie's voice.

Holden's entire body sprang to attention as well as the enthusiasm showing in his eyes. "Jackie," he gasped softly and smiled with relief. "I've been trying to reach you, but your phone's been disconnected."

"Yeah, it's a long story," she remarked timidly.

Holden's eyes suddenly narrowed. "I saw Monroe and Bogart on the news," he growled into the phone. "Please tell me you're not with them."

She inhaled deeply from the other end. "I wish I could," Jackie replied softly.

"Damn it, Jackie--"

"We're in trouble, Holden," she announced softly, the fear in her tone.

Holden's mood immediately changed. "Okay, tell me where you are, and I'll come and get you with as much backup as you need."

"It's not that simple," she informed him. "The guys are working for your boss."

"Blake Harris?"

"His daughter and her friend disappeared a few days ago," Jackie announced. "We rescued them from some pretty seedy characters." There was a long silence. "They witnessed two feds killing the dead agents that were found. Now your boss is missing. The guys can't get a hold of him or the girls' mothers."

"What?"

"The last time anyone heard from your boss was when he went to the farmhouse to pick up the girls' mothers and take them someplace safe," Jackie replied. "No one's heard from him since, and we don't know who to trust at the Bureau."

"You suspect something happened to Blake?" Holden asked with concern. "I need to find a way to get out--" He suddenly hesitated and looked around. "Wait a minute. Blake hired the guys to find his missing daughter and it just happened to coincide with my undercover assignment?"

"There is no assignment, Holden," she informed him gently. "I just found out from Ross. Blake sent you away at Ross's request, so they could get me to fly them on what was supposed to be a search and rescue mission."

Holden's jaw tensed and his eyes narrowed. "Your devious, conniving friends and I are going to have a talk when this is all over," he growled softly. "If they're lucky, I won't arrest them."

"I'm sorry, Holden," Jackie announced gently from the other end. "I thought I was just doing them a favor. Once I heard there were kids involved--"

"I understand, Jackie," he grumbled then ran his fingers through his dark hair. "I'm not mad at you. You just don't know how to tell them no."

"I tried," she announced, "but they bribed me by cleaning and unpacking the house."

"Okay, you just watch your ass," Holden informed her. "I have the satellite phone number. Is that how I reach you?"

"Yes, but use the special cell phone the guys gave you," Jackie replied. "The untraceable one."

"I'll get it on my way to the Bureau," he replied and fidgeted within the kitchen. "Anything else I need to know."

"Once you get the special cell phone, Beck is going to send you a picture Kirk took of the two guys who jumped us at the farmhouse," Jackie informed him. "I'm pretty sure they were feds. Whoever they are, they're in on it, but they're not the ones who whacked the other feds. The girls didn't recognize either. If you could get Beck access to the Bureau's agent database, the girls could look at some pictures and maybe identify the agents they saw."

"That's going to be tough," he replied with a groan. "Those computers are monitored. They may be able to locate your safe house."

"If there's a way, Beck will find a way around it," she replied. "I'm really sorry, Holden."

"Don't worry about that now," he announced gently. "I just want to get you out of there in one piece." He hesitated and stared blankly at the floor. "I love you, Jackie."

"I love you too."

Holden hung up the phone, sank against the wall, and groaned softly. "I'm going to kill Ross."

Chapter Twenty-six

$\mathcal{J}$ackie brutally assaulted the punching bag within the expensive fitness room. She was already moderately sweated in her shorts and tank top, and her ponytail was determined to slip out of its scrunchie. She stood in bare feet on the mats, as it was more natural while working out, and wore her fingerless, leather gloves to protect her knuckles. Most of the fitness room equipment was brand new, although, judging by their moderately used condition, it was evident the caretakers had been using some of the machines as a form of entertainment. The punching bag had been manhandled, but it was obvious the caretakers weren't nearly as aggressive with the punching bag as Jackie was. She continued her assault on the bag with a vengeance. She was no longer mad at Ross, but she did feel as if she had betrayed her husband. Despite his supportive words, she'd lied about the company she'd been keeping. She was starting to wonder if it was in her best interest to sever ties with her father's former SEAL team.

She loved spending time with them, even the dangerous ventures, but that really wasn't being fair to Holden. He came first, and it was becoming obvious she'd need to make the ultimate sacrifice if she wanted to keep him. She'd need to apply for a job with the FBI! Somehow, the thought turned her stomach. She punched the bag then immediately spun into a roundhouse kick, striking it hard. She sneered at the bag, drew an 'x' on the bag's perceived groin area, then stepped back, and rammed her knee into the 'x'.

"Oh, that's gotta hurt," Monroe announced from across the fitness room.

Jackie looked behind her to where Monroe leaned against one of the treadmills. She wasn't sure how long he'd been standing there, but it couldn't have been more than a few seconds. Zack was the only one who could sneak up on her. She turned back to the bag and punched it a few more times as Monroe approached.

"I hope you weren't thinking about me at that moment," he announced.

"Sorry to disappoint you, Monroe," she remarked and punched the bag with vigor. "Not everything that pisses me off involves you."

"Actually, I'm glad to hear that," he replied and hid his smile.

"I'm surprised you're up so early," Jackie announced while concentrating on assaulting the bag. "Katrina shoot down the early bird special?"

Monroe stepped behind the punching bag and held it in place for her. "Can I talk to you about that?"

Jackie suddenly straightened and glared at Monroe behind the bag. "Uh, no," she snapped with distaste. "I don't want to hear details about your X-rated adventures. Try Kirk."

"There aren't any details," Monroe announced firmly then hesitated a moment while appearing slightly guilt-ridden. "I know you're mad, but you have to know I didn't tell the guys about us. I'd never do that. Not to you."

"Yeah, I know," she muttered, again feeling bad about kicking him. "I heard about your little tiff with Beck."

"Not my fault," he protested. "Please, Jackie," Monroe practically begged. "I really need to talk to someone, and I'd rather discuss something like this with you than the guys."

She stared at him as her mind reeled from the comment. She blurted out the first thing that came to her mind, although it shocked even her.

"*You* had performance jitters?" she gasped then hide her mocking smile, because it wasn't funny.

Monroe groaned and allowed his forehead to hit the bag. "No," he moaned softly then lifted his head and met her gaze. "It never got that far."

Jackie studied him and became increasingly curious. Now he had her attention. "What *did* happen?"

"We went back to her room," he announced then drew a deep breath. "Things were progressing nicely, and then she stops me and said she needed three hundred dollars to *complete* the transaction."

Jackie's mouth fell open as she stared at him with surprise. She wanted to laugh, but it was just one more troubling piece to the puzzle.

"She wanted you to pay her?" Jackie gasped. "Seriously? How much of a market is there out here for that sort of thing? There are only two men for fifty miles, and she lives in the same hotel with them."

"I know," Monroe remarked. "It's strange."

"Very strange," Jackie muttered and leaned on the punching bag. "Although it does explain the way she dresses, but to impress who? You're sure you heard her right?"

Monroe tilted his head and glared at her with annoyance. "Yeah, I heard her right."

"You need to tell Ross."

"Are you kidding?" Monroe suddenly cried out. "Do you have any idea how embarrassing that's going to be?"

"It's Ross," Jackie scoffed while giving Monroe a look. "He's not going to gloat."

"Yeah, the Ross you know won't gloat," Monroe scoffed. "You've never met the Ross I know."

She had to admit, he could be right. She was sure they practiced better behavior while she was around. Well, excluding Zack and Kirk. Those two didn't have any qualms being themselves around her.

"Still," she announced, "he needs to know."

Monroe frowned. "Yeah, you're right," he muttered and moved out from behind the bag. "I'll tell him then."

Once Monroe left, Jackie returned to her all-out assault on the punching bag. She kicked the bag several times then went for a punch. Her arm was suddenly grabbed from behind, startling her. Before Jackie could even react, she was thrown to the mat by her arm. Jackie rolled across the mat and into a crouching position. Zack stood over her and grinned.

"Morning, dear," he announced cheerfully.

She glared at him while straightening. Zack wore his black combat pants and his black tee shirt, but was missing his shoes and socks. Jackie felt a slight pang in her stomach. He wasn't without his socks and shoes for no reason. He was almost certainly stalking his prey; and she was his prey.

"I'm not in the mood, Zack," she remarked firmly, attempting to squash his little fantasy involving her and the mats. "Don't do anything stupid--"

Before she could even finish her sentence, Zack swept her legs out from beneath her. Jackie landed on her backside on the mat. She looked up at Zack and sneered at him, irritated by his devious grin.

"Not funny, Zack," she snarled and slowly pulled herself to her feet.

Before she even straightened, Zack grabbed her by the arm and slammed her back onto the mat. Jackie rolled across the mat and sprang up into a crouching position while glaring at him.

"Now you're just pissing me off!"

Zack grinned and took a defensive stance. Obviously, pissing her off was part of his plan. Jackie wasn't in the mood to play his game. He was baiting her, and she knew it. She couldn't let him sucker her into a sparring match. As she straightened, Zack attempted to again kick her legs out from under her. Jackie blocked his kick with her leg and instinctively kicked him in the side with a warning jab. Before she could even plant her foot back on the mat, Zack kicked her in the shoulder and sent her back several feet. He'd successfully baited her into a fight! Jackie spun into a roundhouse kick, which Zack successfully blocked. She spun back for the return kick and nearly clipped him in the face. Zack grinned with enthusiasm and attempted to kick her in the abdomen.

Jackie blocked his foot and the second kick that immediately followed. She then attempted to sweep his legs out from under him. He jumped her foot and kicked her in the shoulder, sending her backwards. Jackie attempted to kick him in the chest. Zack caught her ankle and tried to throw her off balance. Jackie kicked out with the leg she stood on, struck Zack in the shoulder, and then rolled across the mat. Zack hit the floor. She'd successfully taken Zack down! As she sprang to her feet, Zack was already up and throwing a karate punch. Jackie blocked several punches and kicks as he drove her backward several feet from the fast, hard shots. When she'd reached the tipping point, she came back at him, returning the same fast kicks and punches, putting him on the defensive. With her final kick, he grabbed her leg and knocked her down to the mat. With little hesitation, she swept his legs out from beneath him from where she lie, taking him down to the mat just a few feet away.

They both sprang to their feet at the same time and went after each other with a series of hard kicks and punches, successfully blocking each blow. She had to wonder if he was holding back, or was she actually matching Zack blow for blow? The punches, kicks, and defensive blocks happened faster and faster. Both were completely focused on their kicks and punches that they didn't see the guys filtering into the fitness center. They leaned against the back wall near the door and watched the match in progress. By their reactions and grins, they were obviously placing bets on who would end up victorious. Jackie attempted to kick Zack in the face with a little more vigor and irritation than before. Zack caught her ankle and smiled mockingly just to irritate her further. Jackie suddenly threw herself into a backward flip, kicking Zack in the face with her free leg, and breaking free her captured ankle. It was a stunning backward flip which, despite the kick, she nailed the landing.

The guys applauded and whistled at the impressive move. Zack was momentarily stunned by the kick and the maneuver. Jackie barely straightened, catching her balance, when Zack flipped through the air, flung himself around her body, wrapping around her like a python, and took her to the mat with him. Jackie remained entangled in Zack's legs and arms, uncertain how to free herself from the human pretzel into which she'd been twisted. With the position of his leg around her neck, she was certain he could easily break her neck. She was almost positive he'd done it before to some poor fool who attempted to fight him. She could feel the tightness of his leg against her throat, and it frightened her. She feared he'd accidentally kill her while playing his little game. A survival instinct within her suddenly kicked in, and she was no longer playing.

Unable to get in a good hit or kick with the way he had her twisted, Jackie saw only one move she could play. Jackie grabbed Zack's crotch with her hand in a wide, claw-like grip, clamping down. Surprisingly, he endured the pain a good thirty seconds before crying out and releasing her. Jackie released his crotch and rolled into a crouched position, prepared to defend herself. Zack writhed around the mat while clutching to himself in agony.

"Son-of-a-bitch!"

He panted a moment and slowly moved to his knees without releasing himself. Zack met her gaze, and for a moment, she felt bad for hurting him. She didn't know how she could do something so horrible to someone she'd always looked up to.

"Cut those fucking claws!"

Five of the guys appeared irritated and slapped money into Gil's outstretched hand. Gil grinned and awaited his payment, being the only one having bet on Jackie. Jackie eyed the guys and shook her head with annoyance. Gil grinned at her and waved his fist full of money. Jackie caught her breath and again looked back at Zack, who continued to clutch himself, but seemed to be enduring the pain better.

"What's wrong with you?" she demanded and slid across the mat, moving alongside him.

He shrugged finally releasing his crotch and glanced at her, a strange grin on his face. "I can't resist an aggressive woman," he replied teasingly. "It's my weakness."

"No, your balls are your weakness," she remarked.

Zack laughed softly, although he was obviously in some discomfort. "Now don't start with the dirty talk," he teased. "You know it turns me on."

"I somehow doubt you'd be in any condition to do anything about it," she remarked while playfully patting his face.

Jackie leaned heavily on his shoulder, using him as support while pulling herself to her feet. She grabbed a towel from the nearby rack and tossed it to Zack, who easily caught it. She snatched her own towel, wiped her sweated face, and then glared at the guys as they watched while grinning. Jackie tossed the towel aside and straightened proudly.

"Who's next?" she snarled.

All six men placed their hands over their crotches and darted from the fitness center to avoid Jackie's wrath.

✝

*T*he black sports car pulled off to the side of the road on the busy street in Colorado Springs and parked. Holden sat behind the wheel of Jackie's car as he watched Dodson and Metzger get out of their government issued, black SUV and approach an outdoor food stand. He groaned softly, picked up his travel mug, and took a sip of his lukewarm coffee as he watched the two men order their breakfast. Stakeouts were never fun. Holden removed his cell phone and pressed a number. The call was quickly answered.

"Uh, yeah, this is Agent Holden Falcone," he announced. "I'm calling for Blake Harris. He hasn't returned my calls." Holden was silent and listened to the response. "He's going to be out for a few days on personal business?" he repeated the response then frowned. "It's important I talk to him. Is there an alternate number?" He listened to the response again. "No, that's okay. I've already left a number of messages. Just let his next in command know that I'm still on assignment, and I'll be available by voicemail only."

Holden disconnected the call and frowned. He watched Dodson and Metzger take their food to an outdoor table and sit to eat. Holden made himself comfortable in the seat then eyed the interior of the car.

"Gone a few days, and she already bought a sports car without telling me," he muttered then hesitated and eyed the car suspiciously. "This car looks familiar."

Holden looked back across the street and saw two men in suits and sunglasses, definitely agents, approach Metzger and Dodson. Holden took pictures of the four men with his cell phone. As they removed their sunglasses, he immediately recognized Agents Tremaine and Hoffman. Holden found their meeting curious, took a few more pictures, and then sent the pictures to Beck's secured email. He knew it could be an hour or longer before Beck even checked the secured server for new messages. So now he just needed to sit back, enjoy his coffee, and wait.

The four federal agents in their standard, off-the-rack suits sat at the outdoor table together and ate their food in a casual manner. It seemed almost natural, although the conversation was far from usual. Dodson and Metzger were battered and bruised from their encounter with Jackie, Kirk, and Darth. Both men were obviously subconscious about how they would explain their injuries, especially the dog bite.

"We have to find those girls," Agent Hoffman informed the other agents in a firm but soft tone. "Once we have them, everything else will fall into place."

"We've been looking," Dodson grumbled while picking at his food. "No one told us we'd have our asses handed to us by a woman and her dog."

"Who the hell are these people that have those kids?" Metzger demanded with annoyance. "Do you know something you're not telling us?"

"The lodge in the mountains is owned by a corporation," Agent Hoffman informed them. "There's little information on that corporation. Either these guys enjoy their privacy or they're just a bunch of nobodies."

"Well, they don't fight like a bunch of nobodies," Dodson snapped hotly. "They have a plane, helicopter, and automatic weapons. Do you know how many men they took out at that farm? Our friends are demanding answers."

"It's our asses I'm worried about," Tremaine boldly announced. "To hell with the cartel and his scummy lot. Those girls *saw* us."

"And now they've seen you too," Hoffman remarked to Dodson and Metzger. "You're in this as deep as we are. We have to shut this down and fast."

"They couldn't have disappeared off the face of the earth," Tremaine remarked. "Not without help. Find them. Someone is helping them."

"We'll solicit a few more sources," Dodson replied. "Maybe call in a few favors."

"Yeah, whatever it takes," Hoffman remarked. "Just find them."

Chapter Twenty-seven

Beck jumped up from the laptop in his guestroom and hurried to the connecting door to the girls' room. He urgently knocked on the door. It opened only a moment later to reveal the weary teenage girls.

"What time is it?" Monique muttered.

"Almost nine in the morning," Beck informed them. "You should have been up hours ago. You're burning daylight."

"Big deal," Colleen groaned. "We can't do anything anyway."

"Well, you can look at some pictures I just received from one of our sources," Beck informed them then motioned for them to follow him.

They entered Beck's guestroom and approached the laptop on the small table. Both girls stared at the picture of Tremaine and Hoffman, appeared alarmed, and immediately started pointing.

"That's them!"

Beck studied both girls and their expressions as they stared at the men on the screen. Their emotions were mixed between fear and rage.

"That's a big help," Beck gently informed them. "Why don't the two of you get yourselves together, and I'll share this information with our guy in the field."

"He's going to arrest them, right?" Monique suddenly asked. "Then we can go home."

"Well, let's not jump the gun," Beck announced, withholding information they wouldn't be able to handle. "You can't just accuse feds of murder and kidnapping. Our man will need to gather some evidence first. You're safe here. This is the best place for you right now."

"Can't we call our moms?" Colleen asked.

"I wish you could, but Monique's father has them stashed someplace safe," Beck announced in a calm and soothing tone. "They need to remain hidden as well. We need to be very careful about who we talk with. You never know who's listening on the other end."

Colleen nodded. Monique just stared at Beck. "Are our mothers okay?"

"I have to assume they are," Beck replied without hesitation. "We weren't given their location as a safety measure. We couldn't contact them even if we wanted to, but it's for the best."

Monique didn't appear satisfied with his answer, but she didn't press the issue. Both girls headed back for their room through the connecting door. Beck shut his laptop and removed the satellite phone. He pressed a button and waited for an answer.

"Holden," Beck announced eagerly. "We have confirmation on the subjects. Proceed with extreme caution." He paused and listened to the response. "If you need backup, Gil can be there in thirty minutes by helicopter. Keep us informed."

✝

*L*ater that same morning. Within the empty casino floor, Gil stood behind one of the blackjack tables that, despite being brand new, had incurred much wear and tear. He dealt blackjack to Jackie and the rest of the team, who sat around the front of the table. Beck was the only one missing. The casino floor consisted of over thirty table games in an oval directly in the center of the room. The interior 'pit' was a large area in the center of the oval where the 'pit boss' could keep an eye on the games during play from behind the dealers. Above the large area of table games was a cathedral ceiling consisting of a large glass skylight, allowing sunlight in during the day. There were rows and rows of slot machines on both sides of the casino floor. Certain banks of machines appeared to have power to them while others were void of life. The guys played blackjack while sipping coffee and smoking cigars. Jackie smoked a cigar along with them. Holden didn't approve, but she always felt included when she smoked a cigar with the guys. Zack, who sat alongside her, watched her puff on the cigar and grinned almost lustfully. She cast a look at him then straightened and glanced around the table.

"Will someone switch seats with me?" she grumbled while avoiding looking at Zack.

"It's your own fault," Monroe announced and tapped the table indicating for Gil to hit his two cards totaling twelve. Gil dealt him a king, busting his hand. Monroe groaned with disgust.

"How is it my fault?" she demanded.

"You grabbed the man's crotch," Kirk blurted out without care.

"I nearly ripped off his testicles," Jackie launched back. "I wasn't initiating foreplay."

"Same thing is Zack's warped mind," Gil finally added and dealt Kirk a queen, busting his hand as well.

Jackie glared at Zack. He stared at her and maintained his grin. She'd created a monster. Gil glared at Zack and cleared his throat. He continued to stare dreamily at Jackie with his chin resting in his hand as he leaned on the table.

"Zack," Gil snarled with impatience. "Hit or stay."

Zack snapped out of his puppy love induced trance and looked at the table before him. He had a pair of sixes and Gil had a king showing.

"Split," Zack replied and placed another chip alongside his original bet.

Gil rolled his eyes and shook his head. "You really don't get the concept of this game, do you?"

Gil split the sixes and placed a card on each. Both cards were jacks, giving Zack sixteen in each hand. Zack tapped his finger to the first hand. Gil dealt him a two, giving him eighteen. He tapped the table again. Gil glared at him.

"Idiot," Kirk launched. "You have eighteen."

"Yes," Zack replied casually, "but the dealer could have twenty. Eighteen doesn't beat twenty." Zack again tapped the table with added conviction.

Gil groaned and dealt another card, revealing a three card. Zack motioned to stay then tapped the table by the second hand. Gil dealt a four card. Zack indicated to stay and leaned back in his chair while puffing on his cigar. Gil flipped over his bottom card to reveal a ten card. Ross snorted a laugh while rolling his cigar within his mouth. Gil shook his head and paid Zack his winnings.

"You do realize he was counting cards," Ross informed Gil and Kirk.

Gil collected the cards. "I knew there was a reason why we never played cards with Zack."

Zack grinned through the cigar pinched in his teeth and collected his winnings. Beck entered the casino and approached them at the table. He took the vacant chair on the opposite end of Jackie and Zack.

"The girls are watching a movie in their room," Beck informed them.

"And the cameras?" Ross asked while pointing to the ceiling with his cigar.

"None of the cameras are operational," Beck informed him. "They were never connected. We're free to talk."

"We need to make sure last night's bonfire isn't going to come back around and bite us in the ass," Ross informed them. "We're going to do a little recon just to be safe."

"Recon," Bogart announced excitedly. "I'm all for some recon."

"Don't be," Kirk muttered. "Low ranking man gets the shit detail." He cast a look at Bogart and grinned. "You're the low ranking man."

Bogart frowned.

"Bogart, you're going to spend the afternoon with Katrina. I want you to find out what she's willing to tell you about the neighbors," Ross informed him. "She seems to despise them, so I'm sure she'll be more than willing to spread some gossip."

Bogart leaned back in his chair and lacked enthusiasm. "Gossip detail? Won't that make her suspicious? Me wanting to gossip with her? How do you get women to gossip?"

Ross placed three hundred dollars on the table before Bogart and grinned. "I'm sure you'll think of something."

Monroe placed his hand over his eyes and groaned softly at Ross's mocking smile. Bogart picked up the money and chuckled. Apparently, Ross had told everyone about Katrina's profession, officially signifying that they all knew Monroe hadn't scored with the attractive woman last night. Jackie fidgeted slightly in her chair at Ross's casual suggestion. She disliked knowing certain details about the guy's intel gathering methods.

"That sort of gossip, I can handle," Bogart teased then cast a look at Monroe and mocked him with his grin.

Kirk removed something from his pocket. He tossed a condom onto the table before Bogart. Bogart picked up the condom and chuckled.

"Good idea," Bogart remarked cheerfully. "Can't be too careful with ladies of the night."

"I was actually thinking of her protection," Kirk announced casually.

"I'm getting images burned into my head," Jackie informed them while tensing. "Please make it stop."

"Okay, everyone behave," Ross gruffly bellowed. "Who wants the girls from "Deliverance" next door, and who wants the bowery boys?"

"Clarke offered to take me out dirt biking," Kirk replied. "We can ride out to the lake. I can gauge his reaction by veering off in the direction of the fire pit."

"Not alone," Ross announced then glanced at the guys. "Who's good on a dirt bike?"

"I'll go with Kirk," Beck offered. "It's been a while, but I'm sure I can keep up." He glanced at Kirk. "Think we can get Fonzi to go along?"

"Yeah, I think so," Kirk replied.

Ross glanced at the remaining four. "Two of us should stay here to watch over the girls. The other three will go to the farm and get to know the neighbors."

"I'm with Jackie," Zack casually announced and placed his arm over the back of her chair.

Jackie shifted in her chair but refrained from commenting. Ross eyed Jackie and then looked back at Zack.

"Zack and Monroe will stay with the girls," Ross announced, causing both men to groan with displeasure. "Monroe should remain under the radar, in case the neighbors have a television."

"Why me?" Zack suddenly asked, almost pouting.

"Because, Jackie needs a break from you," Ross replied simply.

"I hate kids," Zack muttered.

Ross slammed his palms on the table and stood. "Okay, we have our assignments. Let's get nosy."

As the others left, Jackie caught Bogart's arm and held him back. He didn't make a big deal about it or even comment until the others were out of earshot. He glanced at her and tilted his head.

"Something up?" he asked.

Jackie smiled gently and handed him the photo of his mother. "You dropped this at my house in the hallway," she replied. "I just wanted to return it."

He groaned softly and accepted the photo. This time he placed it in his sock just inside his boot. "I'm always losing things," he replied. "Thanks for not returning it in front of the guys."

"Trust me," she announced with a soft groan. "It never crossed my mind." Jackie held her breath a moment then forced a smile. "You never mention your father."

Bogart shrugged. "I never knew my real father," he replied casually. "My mother never talked about him much, and as I said, she died when I was little. I was raised by my stepfather. He married my mother when I was just a baby."

Jackie fidgeted slightly. "So you don't know anything about your birth father?"

He shook his head then appeared curious. "Why do you ask?"

Jackie forced a smile and shook her head. "I guess I know how you feel, in a way. I never really knew my mother," she replied. "She died when I was little, so I suppose I can relate to what it was like for you not knowing your father or your mother, for that matter."

Bogart grinned. "Yeah, we're a lot alike you and I."

Jackie felt a knot in the pit of her stomach. What if they actually were? She wasn't sure how she felt about having Bogart for a brother.

Chapter Twenty-eight

Bogart entered the kitchen and paused near the door. The kitchen was massive, although the caretakers only used a small portion of it. Across the room, he could see Katrina sitting at the broad island counter with her late morning tea and a magazine before her. She wore yet another sexy, form fitting dress with a plunging neckline and her insanely high heels. Bogart assessed the situation a moment before putting on his best country boy grin and crossed the kitchen to where Katrina flipped through her magazine. He gave her a polite smile and nod as he helped himself to some leftover coffee warming in the pot from that morning. He cast a glance at her over his shoulder and then joined her at the island counter.

"Is this seat taken?" he teased as he sat down.

She smiled in response.

"I heard what happened with Monroe last night," Bogart announced.

Katrina stared at him, undoubtedly surprised by his forwardness, and fumbled for a response.

Bogart maintained his grin and shook his head. "Turned him down flat, huh?" he suddenly announced with a pleased look. "I know it's wrong, but Monroe needs his ego deflated once in a while."

Katrina was baffled by the response, but she managed a smile and played along with the story. "He seemed too needy," she easily replied. "A woman doesn't want that in a man."

"Understood," Bogart replied and sipped his coffee.

Katrina set her magazine aside and seemed to take a renewed interest in Bogart. Perhaps she saw her chance to recoup some of last night's losses.

"Not that there's anything wrong with a man wanting an aggressive woman," Katrina informed him while smiling lustfully. "I know I enjoy an aggressive man now and again."

"You do?" he asked while grinning slyly. "Nice to know. I know I enjoy an aggressive woman myself, but I have to ask, honestly, what's up with your neighbors?"

She was taken by surprise by the question. "They're sociopaths," Katrina informed him. "Not much else to tell." She then appeared curious. "Why do you ask?"

He waved her off and took another sip of coffee, almost as if he was finished with the topic. Bogart then glanced at her, shifted in his chair, and sat forward.

"I went out for a walk early this morning," he informed her, "and one of them approached me. I mean, this girl was all over me. I thought those girls were, you know, reserved."

"Oh, you must mean Lexie," Katrina announced while rolling her eyes. "That girl has a serious sex addiction."

Bogart was genuinely surprised by the remark but quickly covered with a look of disinterest. "As I said, I like aggressive women, but that girl put me on edge. What are those spiders that kill their mates?"

"The black widow," Katrina replied.

Bogart snapped his fingers and pointed at her. "Yeah, that's it. I felt like she was a black widow spider luring me back to her web." He shook his head and sipped his coffee. "Gave me a serious case of the creeps."

"You should probably avoid Betty and her daughters," Katrina informed him. "There's something strange going on over at their farm. I think they practice witchcraft or something."

"Really?"

"Oh, yeah," Katrina chirped with a serious look on her face. "They have midnight bonfires, and I often hear gunshots in the middle of the night. Even Clarke isn't bold enough to go over there by himself. Some nights, I swear I see men at the farm, but they're never there in the morning."

"I should probably warn the guys," Bogart announced. "Some of them ain't so bright. They might fall for their little seduction act and end up roasting on a spit." He sipped his coffee and appeared to sink into thought. A tiny grin crossed his face. "Although, it sort of sounds adventurous." He glanced at Katrina and chuckled softly. "The girl ain't much to look at, but sometimes a guy could use a little walk on the wild side. Might be an exciting experiment. Psycho women can be fun, if you know how to avoid being killed."

Katrina tensed and didn't seem to appreciate his renewed interest in venturing next door to visit the neighbor women. A strange smile crossed her face. She reached across the counter and placed her hand on his.

"You don't need to go over there for a wild time," she announced in a seductive tone. "All this talk about aggressive sex is turning me on." She affectionately caressed his hand and lower arm. "I saw the guys leaving on the dirt bikes, and your friends headed out to the plane. Why don't you and I take advantage of the empty hotel and have a wild afternoon?"

Bogart stared at her a moment then grinned. "Now you're speaking a language I understand." He was quick to spring to his feet and join her on the opposite side of the counter.

Katrina stood and immediately jumped into his arms, nearly knocking him backward onto the island counter as she tore at his clothes. Bogart kissed her aggressively while taking a fistful of her hair, which seemed to turn her on more. She eagerly pulled his belt open, unzipped his pants, and nearly tore them off.

†

$\mathcal{R}$oss and Gil stood outside the plane while Jackie remained just inside the entranceway at the top of the steps. Gil played with Darth at the bottom of the steps while casting glances toward the nearby farm. It was a gorgeous morning, so their presence outside by the plane didn't seem suspicious. Darth was enjoying his playtime with his best friend, Gil.

"I thought you said those reclusive women would come to us," Gil remarked softly while attempting to give the impression of disinterest in the farm.

"Have a little faith," Jackie announced while leaning against the nearby seat just inside the plane and kept watch over the farm as well. She could see two of Betty's daughters roaming around the farm. "Betty's daughters are suffocating for attention. I'm sure the younger one is wondering why Monique and Colleen haven't been over yet today." She then eyed both men. "Why don't the two of you act less intimidating?"

Ross and Gil exchanged looks then eyed Jackie.

"I'm playing with a dog," Gil protested softly. "Women love that crap." He then indicated Ross with a nod. "Ross looks like he's itching to kill something though."

Ross eyed his folded arms across his chest then groaned softly and allowed his arms to fall to his sides. "I'm sorry if a pit full of burning bodies puts me on edge."

"We'd get a lot closer to them a lot faster if we just brought the girls out here," Jackie informed Ross.

"No," Ross announced firmly. "I don't want those girls exposed to whatever could be going on over there."

"You don't know that what's going on isn't coming from Sal's goodfellas at the hotel," Jackie reminded. "They could be sitting in a powder keg for all we know." Jackie suddenly perked up and gave a general nod. "They're getting in their jeep." She hesitated. "And they're coming this way."

Jackie disappeared inside the plane as the jeep approached with Betty's three daughters. They stopped the jeep before the men by the plane's entryway. Betty's daughters got out of the jeep and approached while carrying two pies. Lexie seemed to be the most outgoing of the three.

"Our mother said we should bring you some pie," Lexie announced with a slightly embarrassed smile. "To make up for how badly we treated you yesterday."

Gil was quick to offer a smile and accept one of the pies. "It's still warm."

"Our mother does most of her baking in the morning," Kathy replied.

"Are Monique and Colleen up yet?" Lilly, the fourteen-year-old, eagerly asked.

"I'm sure they are," Ross replied while offering a tiny smile, "but they're grounded at the moment."

"Oh," Lilly replied with a defeated sigh.

Lilly was the only daughter they hadn't met upon arrival. She was a moderately cute, young teenage girl. Although tomboyish in many ways, she had softer, feminine features like her sister, Kathy. She had slightly darker hair then the other two, which she wore in a neatly brushed ponytail. She dressed almost similar to Monique and Colleen. It didn't appear as if the harsh farm life had caught up with her yet. Jackie appeared in the plane doorway and gave Ross a disappointed look along with a disapproving frown. He caught her look but didn't let it bother him.

"We don't get many people my age around here," Lilly informed them almost sadly.

Jackie walked down the plane steps and accepted the second pie. "I'll make sure they get some pie," she announced. "And I'll tell them you said hello."

"I hope they're not in trouble for offering to help me with the horses," Lilly then remarked, turning concerned. "I didn't mean to get them into trouble."

"No, it didn't have anything to do with offering to help with your horses," Ross replied. "They were caught misbehaving at the amusement park."

"Do you have a smokehouse?" Gil then asked and appeared curious. "I thought I smelled something burning in the middle of the night."

"We had a bonfire early in the evening," Kathy informed them then continued with her explanation. "We burn most of our garbage; what we can't recycle."

"Though I can't imagine that would smell like a smokehouse," Lexie replied.

"You know, I smelled something weird last night too," Kathy informed them. "I looked outside around one o'clock, but I didn't see anything on fire, so I went back to bed."

"Mother asked us to invite you and your friends over for dinner tonight," Lexie informed them cheerfully. "We're having a BBQ. Your friends look like meat eaters."

Darth licked his muzzle, almost as if understanding. Gil looked at Ross, almost begging with his eyes.

"We could get to know the neighbors," Gil gently remarked, although he was obviously more interested in grilled meat.

"Surely you can let the girls off probation for one evening," Jackie chimed in.

It was really the only way to explore the farm without sending Zack on another covert mission. Ross glared at both then looked at Darth, who again licked his muzzle. Ross groaned softly then looked at the girls and smiled politely.

"That's very generous of you," Ross replied. "I think I can allow the girls out briefly tonight."

Lilly became excited.

"How many of you will there be?" Kathy asked.

"Did you want us to ask the caretakers?" Jackie enquired, almost certain of the response.

"We'd rather you didn't," Kathy replied while offering a timid smile. "Mother wouldn't be very happy about that. She really doesn't like Katrina."

"Eight to ten," Ross replied.

Obviously, Ross was still debating whether or not to allow Bogart and Monroe out in public, even though the neighbors probably never saw the broadcast showing them wanted for murder.

"Great," Lexie chirped cheerfully. "We'll let mother know."

All three waved then returned to the jeep. Ross, Gil, and Jackie watched them drive back to the farm. Gil sniffed the pie and grinned.

"God, that smells good," Gil remarked with enthusiasm.

"I'm glad," Ross announced while smirking. "You can have the first piece. If you're not sick in an hour, the rest of us can enjoy it."

Chapter Twenty-nine

Monroe hurried from the kitchen and nearly collided with the girls, who were on their way to join him. The expression on his face was hard to read although he appeared slightly shocked. He took each girl by the arm and turned them in the opposite direction and away from the kitchen.

"I thought we were having brunch? You said you'd make chocolate chip pancakes," Monique remarked with surprise, his firm hand guiding her further away from the kitchen.

"We'll have to wait on that," Monroe informed them while appearing tense.

"But we're starving," Colleen remarked. "Why can't we get something to eat?"

Monroe fumbled for an answer while hiding his disgusted frown. "Because Bogart's giving Katrina a hard time, and there's a lot of cursing going on."

Monique and Colleen exchanged bewildered looks. Zack approached from the opposite end of the corridor and gave them strange looks.

"I thought we were having chocolate chip pancakes," Zack remarked with the same look of disappointment as the girls had.

"Bogart and Katrina are doing the nasty in the kitchen," Monique casually informed Zack.

Zack stared at her a moment with little reaction then looked back at Monroe. Monroe's mouth hung open with surprise as he stared at Monique.

"And they say I'm bad with kids," Zack scoffed. "Nice way to corrupt a minor, Monroe." Zack shook his head with disgust then turned and walked away.

Monroe ran his fingers through his hair, fidgeted slightly, but readily left Monique's observation slide.

"Why don't we watch a movie," Monroe suggested. "We can have lunch after the movie."

Both girls reluctantly agreed, but it was obvious they were already bored with movie marathons. The girls exchanged looks, as if reading each other's minds. They looked back at Monroe.

"We want to watch "Gone with the Wind"," Colleen boldly announced.

Monroe appeared surprised. "We just watched that this morning," he remarked. "I could barely keep my eyes open the first time through."

"No one says you have to watch it with us," Monique reported. "You can hang out in Beck's room."

"Then I'll fall asleep for sure," Monroe muttered.

†

*A*s the movie played, Monique and Colleen cast looks at the second bed. Monroe was stretched out while sleeping on the next bed over, as promised. The girls exchanged grins then silently moved off the bed and hurried into the connecting room. They crossed Beck's room and approached his bedroom door, which would make less noise when the outer door was opened. They quietly opened the door and slipped into the empty, first floor corridor. Both girls giggled and hurried down the hall.

"We're going to get into trouble with Ross again," Colleen informed her friend.

"I don't care," Monique announced firmly. "I'm bored to death. Besides, Jackie won't let him punish us. We're safe." They approached the connecting corridor. "We'll slip over to the neighbors and be back before anyone knows we're gone."

They rounded the corner to the connecting corridor and nearly collided with Zack, who casually leaned against the wall with his arms folded across his chest. Both girls screamed, jumping backwards and away from him.

"Going somewhere?"

As Zack straightened, both girls screamed and ran away from him.

†

$\mathcal{T}$he four men rode their dirt bikes away from the casino and toward a worn path in the woods. Once in the woods, Beck steered his bike in the direction of the kill pit. As Fonzi and Clarke followed him, Kirk hung back and brought up the rear, keeping an eye on both men. The men didn't attempt to stop Beck, only keep up with him. Beck rode the dirt bike through a large clearing of fresh dirt with unusual tire marks along the entire area. He stopped his dirt bike, tearing up dirt as he spun the back end around. Beck removed his helmet and looked around with surprise as the others approached. He hid his surprise with a more natural, curious look. All three stopped as well and removed their helmets.

"What's wrong?" Clarke asked while looking around.

"These tire marks," Beck informed them and glanced around the entire area. "Looks like someone was back here recently." He then looked at Clarke. "I thought you said there was no one around." He then looked around as if paranoid. "Are we safe staying at Sal's place?"

Fonzi waved him off and offered a sly grin. "Just those crazy women next door," he announced simply. "Don't be surprised when you find the remains of some steer they butchered. They dump animal carcasses in the woods off their property all the time. We can't really complain, because it's not on Sal's property either. It's state land out here."

"Are you sure it's them?" Beck asked and continued to observe the area. "Those don't look like jeep tire tracks. They look more like a tractor or skid steer."

Clarke indicated the tire marks. "Those tire tracks came from their tractor, I'm almost positive," he replied. "They're always running around on the state game land doing God knows what. I wouldn't worry about them. They're just nutcases. Nothing for you to worry about."

Fonzi and Clarke put their helmets back on and drove away. Beck and Kirk exchanged looks while eyeing the area.

"This is the place," Beck informed Kirk. "Someone covered the pit, burying the burned bodies."

"Sounds like it's the crazy neighbors," Kirk remarked. "Should I go back and tell Ross?"

"No, we'll tell him this afternoon after our ride," Beck announced. "No need to make the caretakers suspicious."

They replaced their helmets and raced after the two men, who now had a healthy head start.

†

$\mathcal{R}$oss, Gil, Jackie, and Darth entered the lobby to see Zack with Monique in a headlock from where he stood behind her. She thrashed around wildly, attempting to get out of her predicament. Colleen was nowhere to be found. Darth ran up to Zack and barked at him as he held the girl immobile.

"Zack!" Ross cried out with alarm.

Zack didn't release Monique, although he did casually look up. Keeping the girl contained required little exertion on his behalf. "Oh, hey," he chirped. "Did you learn anything?"

"Would you mind releasing the kid?" Ross demanded in an angry tone.

"No, I got this," Monique gasped from beneath Zack's hold around her.

She thrust her elbow backward and completely missed Zack. He tightened his grip around her neck and rubbed the top of her head with his knuckles, severely messing her hair.

"Sorry, kid," Zack announced then released her. "I just broke your neck. Better luck in the next life."

Monique caught her balance, straightened, and rubbed her neck while frowning. "What did I do wrong?"

"You took too long to react," Jackie informed her. "He anticipated your move and took a step back. Next time, try stomping on his foot before going for the backward elbow thrust. With those old-fashioned, wooden heels on your cowboy boots, you could probably inflict a lot of pain."

"Where's Colleen?" Ross demanded.

Before Zack could even respond, they heard the bullwhip crack from one of the nearby areas. Gil, Ross, and Jackie ran for the corridor with Darth leading the way. Monique and Zack didn't even react to the sound; instead, Zack grabbed her arm and twisted it behind her back. She again thrashed around while attempting to get out of his tight hold. The others ran along the corridor and into the nearby lounge. Bogart leaned against the bar while holding a cloth to his bleeding cheek. Colleen placed ice inside another hand towel from where she stood behind the bar. Monroe sat on one of the bar stools and showed little reaction to what was going on.

"What happened?" Ross suddenly asked and looked at his injured man.

"Just a little accident," Bogart muttered with defeat.

182

"He wanted to learn the bullwhip," Colleen announced then frowned. "He needs to practice wrist control."

"You did this to yourself?" Gil suddenly asked then hid his smirk.

"It's not as easy as it looks," Monroe reported and indicated the tear on his pants leg.

Ross groaned and shook his head. "Okay, everyone just take a break from combat training." He then turned and left the lounge without another word.

Bogart returned Colleen's bullwhip to her and grinned slyly. "We'll practice later when El Comandante isn't around."

Colleen returned the smile then left the lounge as well. Bogart sat at the bar and dabbed the cut on his cheek while Monroe poured drinks for them. Gil and Jackie joined them at the bar.

"Ross is awfully sour today," Bogart announced and sipped his whiskey.

"Not everyone had the opportunity to get laid today, Bogart," Monroe scoffed lowly. "Maybe we should discuss boundaries. Primarily those that forbid sexual acts on the kitchen counter."

"Oh, like you wouldn't have done Katrina right then and there if she'd come on to you," Bogart snorted.

"What the hell did I miss?" Gil suddenly asked while eyeing each man.

Neither seemed willing to elaborate. Bogart sipped his drink and shook his head.

"I feel sorry for Squirt," Bogart announced while eyeing the guys. "From what I've gathered, her father died when she was young. In a lot of ways, she's like me."

"God, let's hope not," Gil muttered into his glass of whiskey.

Bogart sneered at Gil.

"Her father didn't die," Monroe reported while leaning on the bar. "He was an Army deserter."

Bogart and Gil appeared surprised and stared at Monroe.

"How do you know that?" Gil suddenly asked.

"I read it in Monique's journal," Monroe replied. "Colleen's mother bought her that horse to soften the blow of her father abandoning them. I guess he's still wanted by the Army."

"Poor Squirt!"

"Some guys just snap," Gil replied while shaking his head. "PTS affects everyone differently."

"It wasn't PTS," Monroe announced and offered an annoyed look. "Sounds as if he was selling weapons they'd confiscated, and he was about to be arrested, so he took off."

Bogart lowered his head and sighed softly. "I know how the kid must feel," he announced gently. "My father abandoned me too. By the time I was her age, I'd already been in a ton of trouble. My father was a real bastard too."

Jackie cast a look at Bogart. "You said you didn't know your father."

"I didn't," Bogart replied in a harsh tone while glaring at her, "but he abandoned me and my mother, so that makes him a bastard in my book."

She considered pulling him aside and having a talk with him, questioning him about certain details, but she didn't feel that would be fair to Ross. If Ross had been involved with Bogart's mother, he should hear her suspicions first. The only thing stopping her from having that talk with Ross was her own concerns to what she'd possibly learn about her father.

"I think she has her head on straight," Monroe replied. "He may not be the sharpest tool, but her uncle's been doing a decent job standing in for her father."

"Having Twinkie and her family around probably helps," Bogart announced then drifted into his own world. His look conveyed years of childhood trauma and sympathy for what the girl must have gone through at a young age.

Jackie suddenly felt bad for the secret she may have been holding. She wasn't sure about any of her suspicions. Maybe none of them were Bogart's father. It was best just to keep it to herself for now. There wasn't any logical reason to upset anyone at the moment.

Chapter Thirty

*D*espite the neighbors having limited contact with the real world, Ross felt it was best if Bogart and Monroe remained back at the hotel. His decision was met with protest on both men's behalf. Monroe prided himself on being a 'grill master' and was upset that he wouldn't be able to share his expertise with the neighbors. Bogart was once again feeling excluded from bonding with the team in a social setting. Compared with their initial meeting, Betty and her daughters were pleasant and hospitable toward their guests. Monique and Colleen hung out in the paddock with Lilly and her two horses. They were showing her training techniques, which she was excited to learn.

Their outdoor picnic style dinner consisted of a variety of fresh grilled meats, homegrown vegetables, and homemade alcohol that was almost certainly moonshine. Betty and her two older daughters, Kathy and Lexie, were gracious hostesses and almost too friendly, in Jackie's opinion. As she picked at her slice of homemade apple pie, Jackie started observing the woman and her daughters more closely. As far-fetched as it seemed, she'd have sworn the older woman was flirting with Ross and Zack. Although polite, Ross wasn't the flirtatious type. He also had a hot girlfriend almost half his age waiting for him back home. Zack, known for his animalistic sexual desires, was only interested in women who could kick his ass. If it hadn't been for the bountiful buffet of meats and desserts, he would almost certainly have found some perch to observe the festivities from a safe distance.

Kathy and Lexie were enjoying fawning over Gil, Beck, and Kirk. It was like watching a train wreck. Gil and Beck each had women they loved back home, so neither were showing the sort of interest the women had anticipated from mature, healthy men. Kirk, although happily single, was mostly indifferent as a general rule. Jackie knew of Kirk's reputation with women. Although he was not nearly as loose and free as Bogart, Jackie had never actually seen him cozy up to a woman. It started her wondering how he ever got from 'hello' to 'good morning'. Beck abandoned Gil and Kirk, leaving them to fend for themselves with the two young women and joined Jackie at the picnic table. He leaned in close to her, touched her arm, and offered a soulful look.

"Hide me," he whispered softly. "Those girls are sex-starved."

"I can imagine," Jackie replied and glanced at the girls with Gil and Kirk.

Kathy and Lexie were turning up the charm to maximum. Their eyelashes were batting and their hands were traveling. It was difficult to tell if Kirk was uncomfortable or not, but Gil was starting to fidget.

Beck rested his head on Jackie's shoulder. "They won't take 'I have a girlfriend' for an answer."

Jackie eyed his head on her shoulder, smiled sweetly, and patted his face. "You poor thing." Before Jackie could comment further, Gil slid onto the bench alongside her, sitting as close as he could without sitting on her lap.

"What are those girls on?" Gil muttered to Jackie. "Homegrown hormones?"

"Ross picked one hell of a time to exclude Monroe and Bogart," Beck announced while lifting his head. "They'd be perfect picnic companions for those girls."

"So is this what we're going to do all evening?" Jackie asked while eyeing the men on either side of her. "You two seeking me to shelter you from the love-starved girls?"

Beck and Gil exchanged glances over Jackie then looked back at her and nodded.

"Uh, huh," Gil announced.

"Yep," Beck replied. "Pretty much."

Kathy approached their table, startling them. She sat alongside Beck, smiled sweetly, and cozied up to him while clinging to his arm.

"So how about that walk?" Kathy asked while grinning lustfully.

Beck managed a tiny smile. "I don't think my girlfriend would approve," he announced. "She's the jealous type."

"What she don't know won't hurt her," Kathy teased and placed her hand on his thigh.

Beck jumped up from the bench and quickly excused himself. "I, uh, think Ross called me."

Jackie and Kathy watched him hurry away. Kathy appeared slightly disappointed then glanced past Jackie to Gil. To both their surprise, he was gone.

"Your friends come and go like the wind," Kathy remarked to Jackie.

"Yeah, they're pretty quick on their feet," Jackie replied then glanced at the other table. Kirk and Lexie were gone. She looked back at Kathy with some surprise. "Where did Kirk and your sister go?"

Kathy grinned and shrugged. "I'm guessing the barn loft," she announced while raising her brows suggestively.

Jackie found that surprising yet not so surprising. Kirk was difficult to read, and once again, she missed what happened between 'hello' and 'good morning'.

"I didn't realize they were hitting it off so well," Jackie announced, feeling curious enough to seek answers.

"Honestly, I thought he was taking an interest in me," Kathy informed her, "but Lexie said something to him and he got up and left with her." She cocked her head, giving a look of surprise. "He's tough to read, huh?"

"Yeah, a little."

"You know," Kathy boldly announced, "you can tell your friends I'm eighteen. By the way they're acting, they must think I'm not legal or something."

"Oh," Jackie remarked, taken slightly off guard by the comment. "Well, they're all in committed relationships. I think they're just trying to do the honorable thing."

"Really?" Kathy questioned with surprise. "I didn't think guys cared about doing what was right. Mother says men only care about whoring around."

"Oh?"

"Yeah, our father left when we were young," Kathy replied. "He wanted to be where the action was. Our place was too remote for his womanizing."

Jackie was slightly surprised to hear Kathy candidly talk about her father's adulterous behavior. She shifted slightly on the bench and pushed her empty plate away.

"Some men might be that way," Jackie informed her. "Some women too, but it's my experience that most are committed in their relationships. I know my guys are."

"Your guys?" Kathy asked, her eyes lighting up. "You have several boyfriends?" She then giggled. "Of course you do! You're so pretty."

Jackie blushed slightly. "That's kind of you to say," she replied. "No, I don't have multiple boyfriends. I'm happily married to a wonderful man who worships me. I'm very fortunate. I meant 'my guys' as in those guys." Jackie gave a general nod to the guys within the yard. "I've known that bunch most of my life. Some like uncles; others like annoying big brothers."

Kathy rested her chin on her fist while leaning on the table studying Jackie. "Do you believe in true love?"

"Definitely," Jackie replied without hesitation.

"You mean there is such a thing?"

Jackie stared at the girl a long moment then realized that she was serious. The girl never really had the chance to experience anything that didn't involve her sisters and solitude. Her mother resented their father, so she poisoned them with everything bad about men, leaving them to think there were no good points. The poor girls would probably never have a successful relationship.

"Yes, there's such a thing," Jackie gently informed her. "I know it's difficult for you to see living so far from town."

"I sometimes wish I lived where there were more men," Kathy announced. "I like men. They're a lot of fun, but there's never really any around." She suddenly straightened and looked uncomfortable. "I mean, there's those who show up on weekends at the casino, but they're awful."

"I suppose I'll find out tomorrow night," Jackie announced with a heavy sigh.

"We have to stay inside when they show up," Kathy informed her. "Mother doesn't like us even going out to the barn after they arrive. She says they're bad men."

Jackie studied Kathy while sinking into her own thoughts. She felt some concern for the safety of Monique and Colleen. She didn't know if they were actually bad men or just Betty's version of bad men. Betty joined them at the table, sitting across from them, and looked around with a puzzled expression on her face.

"What happened to that short cute guy?" Betty asked. "Zack?"

Jackie laughed softly. "We've given up keeping tabs on him," she informed her. "Too much effort."

"Ah," Betty announced with a frown. "I was hoping I'd get to know him better." She grinned. "I like the quiet ones, especially ones with healthy appetites. That boy can eat."

"A man burns a lot of calories flying in stealth mode," Jackie announced while softly chuckling.

✝

*K*irk and Lexie rolled around in the loose hay within the barn's second floor hayloft. They kissed passionately while groping each other. Lexie wasted little time pulling Kirk's shirt off. She was eager to throw herself at him, possibly afraid he'd change his mind, leaving her alone once again. Kirk slipped her out of her shirt, revealing her lacy, black bra. He once again sought her lips and kissed her passionately as she kneeled on the hay. As she attempted to open his pants, he wasted little time slipping her out of hers, revealing the matching lacy thong panties. Kirk ran his hands along her buttocks, pulled her legs up to his hips, and lowered her to the loose hay on the loft floor.

Chapter Thirty-one

$\mathcal{T}$he following evening, the black sports car pulled up to the curb not far from an old warehouse, which was located on the outskirts of town in a remote area. Holden sat behind the wheel and watched Agents Dodson and Metzger leave their SUV and enter the building through a side door. Once they were inside, Holden got out of the car and approached the SUV. He looked into the vehicle through the rear window. A black, tactical duffel bag lie on the floor between the first and second row of seats. Holden removed his cell phone and pressed a button. He held the phone to his ear while keeping close watch on the building.

"Yeah, this is Agent Falcone," he announced. "I need assistance with door locks on vehicle number twenty-two. Authorization HF4489." There was a pause. The vehicle doors electronically unlocked. "Thanks."

Holden disconnected his call and opened the rear door on the driver's side. He pulled the duffel bag across the floor and unzipped it. The bag contained several illegal handguns, two cell phones, black hooded masks, a large bundle of cash, a smoke bomb, and some plastic explosives. Holden stared at the bag's contents then looked at the building with concern.

"Ah, hell," he muttered softly.

He slung the bag over his shoulder and closed the vehicle door. Holden removed his gun and hurried for the side entrance. He entered the warehouse and immediately darted behind some crates to keep out of sight. Voices were heard across the large interior. Holden stashed the duffel bag then followed the voices while remaining hidden behind the crates. There were only two distinctive voices, indicating Holden wouldn't have much company. He paused behind one of the crates and looked toward a small clearing in the center of the warehouse. Blake Harris was tied to an old metal folding chair. He appeared conscious but slightly battered. Agents Dodson and Metzger stood over him, each taking turns asking Blake questions. A third man stood by, keeping watch of the area with his gun accessible. Blake refused to answer any of their questions. After a quick visual sweep of the area, Holden was confident Blake was the only hostage, indicating he'd gotten the girls' mothers to the safe house before being captured by his own men. Unaware of traitors in his ranks, Blake hadn't stood a chance against them.

There was no time to solicit help from Whiskey Tango Foxtrot. Holden was almost certain Blake didn't have half an hour before they intended to terminate his life. His men intended to set up his death, possibly making it look like he'd stumbled upon a drug deal gone bad. They'd shoot Blake with an untraceable gun, leave unidentified cell phones scattered about along with a wade of cash, and blow up the building to make sure the evidence required weeks to sift through. Holden didn't have any trustworthy backup, and even if he did know who he could trust, it was unclear if he had time to spare waiting for them. He could take out one man, but either of the other two could easily kill Blake before he took them out. They were federal agents with the same training as Holden had. An equal playing field wasn't what Holden needed right now. Holden needed a loose cannon. What he needed was Zack. Something suddenly occurred to Holden. He didn't need Zack; he just needed a Zack-like diversion.

Blake stared at his men as they stood over him. Despite being battered, he remained strong.

"You're out of you mind if you think I'd ever give up my daughter's location," Blake informed them. He then grinned in a devious manner, blood staining his teeth. "And the men who have her won't give her up without a fight." Blake chuckled softly. "You couldn't hope to beat them; not on your best day."

"Who are the men that have your daughter and her friend?" Dodson demanded. "We'll eventually figure it out. We know what they look like, and we know the location of their home base in the Colorado Mountains. It's only a matter of time before they screw up."

"Good luck with that," Blake muttered and refused to look at them. He was obviously finished talking.

Something metallic rolled along the crates alongside them. Blake and his three captures followed the sound and saw the rolling object as it fell from the crates and rolled across the floor toward them. All four appeared terrified when they saw the round metal disk roll to a stop. The three men cried out and leaped away from the device. Blake cried out and threw his weight against the chair, toppling it away from the black disk. A large volcano of smoke poured from the fallen object, quickly filling the area. Two shots were fired from the right. All three men took cover and fired in the direction of the gunshots despite being unable to see anything. Holden slipped out from between two crates near Blake and cut the zip ties binding him to the chair. The three men continued to blindly fire across the warehouse as Holden hurried Blake back to the safety of the nearby crates in the opposite direction.

The smoke began to clear, and the men would soon realize no more shots were coming from across the warehouse where a semiautomatic was taped to a crate. Holden had rigged some string to the trigger that, on a moment's notice, created the illusion of a shooter off to the right. Divert and distract. Holden gave Blake one of the illegal guns from the fed's duffel bag. Blake cocked the gun and grinned at Holden.

"I owe you, Holden," he announced.

"More than you think," Holden remarked while glaring at him, "but we'll discuss your deal with those devils after we take down these bastards."

Blake nodded in agreement. Holden motioned for Blake to follow him. They slipped along the back of the crates toward the area of the gunfire. The sound of gunfire filled the old warehouse. They were nearly upon Dodson and Metzger when they were spotted. Holden and Blake opened fire on the men. Dodson and Metzger returned fire, but they had seen them too late. Blake shot Metzger in the chest, sending him to the floor. In the split second that Dodson took to look at his fallen partner, Holden fired and shot Dodson in the forehead. His head snapped back as blood spurted out his forehead. The third man fired at them from a more secured location, making it difficult to get a clean shot. Holden removed his cell phone and pressed a button. He looked at Blake.

"Get ready."

"Ready for what?" Blake asked.

Holden listened to the phone on the other end as it began to ring and waited. Across the warehouse, a lone cell phone duct taped to a support beam just behind the shooter emitted the sound of loud, rapid gunfire as its ring tone. The shooter turned and fired behind him. Blake suddenly straightened and took his only clean shot, striking the man in the temple. The man's eyes rolled back before he sank to the floor. Holden cast the stolen cell phone aside and patted Blake on the back.

"Nice shot," Holden announced as he straightened.

They kept their guns aimed as they hurried toward the fallen men. All three were dead or mostly dead, their blood rapidly spilling out onto the concrete floor. Holden scanned the area while Blake lowered his gun and sighed softly. He then looked at Holden and appeared concerned.

"They wanted to know where my daughter and her friend were. I was hoping that meant they got away," Blake informed Holden but remained tense. "I could only assume the team found the girls. Are they safe?"

"Yeah, they're safe," Holden informed him.

Blake appeared relieved and sighed, his entire body sagging with relief. He then looked at the dead men and shook his head.

"My own men," Blake scoffed then eyed Holden. "All of this because of some loser scumbag I arrested last week?"

"This had nothing to do with you, Blake," Holden informed him. "The girls witnessed two feds executing two other feds at an abandoned amusement park an hour or so from your house. You were just a liability they couldn't afford, because you'd never let them get away with killing your daughter. They needed you out of the way. With you dead, they could make it look like the girls died because of something you'd gotten into and not the other way around."

"But they're safe now?" Blake reconfirmed. "Metzger said they knew where the safe house was."

"The guys knew the safe house had been compromised and found an alternate place to stay. The girls are safe with the men you hired," Holden announced then sneered his disapproval as he glared at his boss. "Along with my wife."

Blake fidgeted and appeared embarrassed that he'd been caught in his lie. "I'm sorry about that, Holden," he replied gently. "I had to find my daughter, and they were my best option. Lying to you was an easy call in the grand scheme of things."

"I know why you did it," Holden replied. "You're not the one I'm mad at."

"I knew you'd understand. Let's get my daughter back," Blake announced while appearing relieved.

"It's not that easy," Holden informed him. "Metzger and Dodson weren't the agents they witnessed killing the others. The two men responsible are still out there. We need to contain them and find out who else at the Bureau is on their payroll. The girls are safe where they are. They need to stay there until we get this wrapped up."

"Who are the agents involved?"

"Tremaine and Hoffman."

"I can't believe it," Blake gasped and shook his head. "This whole time? They've been out there helping the search party. Those bastards."

"The sooner we clean house at the Bureau, the sooner we can get your daughter out of hiding," Holden informed him. "You and I have our work cut out for us."

Chapter Thirty-two

*L*ater that evening, the guys and Jackie hung out in the lobby while the caretakers prepared the casino for their visitors. Since they didn't know what to expect, they wanted to be prepared for just about anything. Although, by the way Zack was positioned at the window, it looked more like a briefing before battle. Bogart stared at Ross and appeared offended by the current assignment he'd been given.

"How do I always get stuck babysitting?" Bogart demanded and folded his arms across his chest.

Ross turned to Bogart and glared at him. "Because you and Monroe are the only ones the authorities are searching for," he announced boldly.

"Idiot," Kirk snapped, clearly irritated at Bogart. "We can't risk having any of the casino guests recognizing either of you. Think, Bogart!"

Bogart frowned while seemingly pouting. "I sometimes think you purposely exclude me."

"You're right," Gil announced while grinning slyly.

Ross ignored Bogart's comment and looked at the others. "We're going to split up and keep an eye on the place," Ross informed them. "Bogart will remain in the hotel with the girls. Monroe will maintain a presence here in the lobby keeping an eye on any casino activity spilling into the hotel. The rest of us will act naturally, join in the festivities, and keep an eye on the guests in the casino."

They inserted their ear transmitters.

"What about our weapons?" Beck asked and appeared curious. "Clarke indicated they didn't allow weapons. They saw our weapons when we arrived. They know we're armed. They might do a 'stop and frisk' at the door."

"Taken care of," Zack remarked and handed Beck a crude drawing of the casino floor. "I've taken the liberty of stashing a few weapons earlier in case of emergency."

Beck glanced at the paper then handed it to Jackie. She studied the locations of more than a dozen weapons then rolled her eyes at the crudely drawn dead body on the floor. She handed the paper to Kirk.

"Planning a third world takeover, Zack?" she muttered.

He casually shrugged and grinned at her. "Eventually, but tonight I'm just looking to make a few bucks."

Ross eyed the map of the weapons stash, familiarized himself with their location, and then glared disapprovingly at Zack.

"No cheating at cards," Ross scolded with a stern look on his face. "Don't do anything to unnecessarily piss off our hosts. We don't know what sort of crowd we're dealing with."

"Yeah, you might end up in a pit with a hole in your head," Monroe muttered.

"And I'm telling you it's those crazy neighbor women," Kirk announced firmly while glancing around the lobby. "Everything they do sets my short hairs on end."

"You didn't seem all that worried last night when you were violating the eldest fruitcake daughter," Beck remarked casually as he folded his arms across his chest.

"That's different," Kirk announced boldly. "I was just being polite."

There was a round of moans throughout the room, including from Jackie as well. In his defense, Jackie thought it was possible Kirk honestly believed it.

"These are Sal's people," Jackie informed the guys. "I'd say that's more than enough reason to suspect them of burning those bodies in that kill pit."

"They may be Sal's people, but I don't think Sal would approve," Beck informed her firmly.

"Standing up for your girlfriend's mob boss father?" Monroe muttered under his breath.

Beck turned toward Monroe with hostility and pointed a warning finger at him. "Hey, anytime you want to take a swing, take it."

"That's enough from you two," Ross growled softly. "I swear *I'm* the one babysitting."

Zack stepped away from the lobby windows and eyed the group. "There's a conga line of vehicles coming this way," he announced. "I think the party's about to start."

"All right then," Ross announced and straightened his dressier casual jacket. "Let's mingle, boys."

Bogart and Monroe watched the team head through the corridor to the connecting casino. Bogart frowned and sulked, once again feeling excluded. Monroe snatched a magazine and tossed himself onto a comfortable sofa.

"Aren't you the least bit bothered that we're left behind all the time?" Bogart demanded.

"Nope," Monroe casually replied and flipped through the magazine.

"Why not?"

Monroe glared at Bogart and raised his brows. "Because this isn't a social gathering. Our assignment is to protect those girls," he announced. "I'm sorry if this job isn't exciting enough for you, but exciting puts our clients' lives at risk. Enjoy the boredom."

"Fine," Bogart scoffed. "But if those girls want to watch "Gone with the Wind" again, I'm throwing the television out the window."

Bogart left the lobby and headed for the connecting wing toward the guestrooms. Bogart paused before the girls' guestroom door, tapped twice, and then entered. Colleen read a book while sitting on the bed alongside her friend, who was tucked beneath the covers on the opposite side of the bed closest to the wall. The covers were up over her head, indicating she didn't want to be bothered.

"Is Twinkie asleep?" Bogart asked with surprise.

"Cramps," Colleen casually replied then grimaced. "I suggest you don't bother her. She gets mean."

Bogart rolled his eyes and collapsed onto the second bed. "What are we watching tonight?"

"Whatever you want," Colleen replied without care. "I'm just going to read before going to sleep."

"Oh," Bogart announced and then grinned with enthusiasm. "I can live with that."

He jumped up from the bed, approached the dresser, and sorted through several DVDs lying scattered on top. He inserted one into the machine and returned to the bed. Colleen cast a glance at the lump as it moved under the covers in the bed alongside her. She gently tugged on the sheet to hide Darth's head, so Bogart wouldn't realize Monique was missing. Darth looked at her from beneath the covers and panted happily.

✝

Monique hurried down the back set of stairs on the first floor of the hotel. She paused before the exit door and pushed it open to reveal Lilly, dressed casually in jean shorts and a tank top, as she stood in the doorway just outside.

"What took you so long?" Lilly asked and entered the hallway with Monique.

"Colleen and I couldn't agree on which one of us had to stay behind and entertain Bogart," Monique replied then reached for the exit door. "Are you ready?"

"Oh, no, we can't work with the horses tonight," Lilly informed her.

Monique appeared surprised at the announcement and studied the girl. "I thought you said you needed my help tonight," she remarked.

"I do need your help," Lilly informed her. "My mother would kill me if she ever found out, but I help Katrina on the weekends when they have people over. The pay is good and the work is super easy."

"I thought you didn't get along with the caretakers?" Monique remarked.

"My mother and my sisters don't," Lilly replied casually. "But we really need the money. That's why I don't tell my mother that I help out over here. I know she would be upset if she found out."

"Well, I suppose I could help out," Monique replied with a soft sigh, although she seemed disappointed that they weren't working with the horses tonight.

"Don't worry," Lilly announced cheerfully, noting Monique's disappointment. "We can sneak out to the horses later. We'll only work here a couple of hours at most."

Lilly grabbed Monique's hand and pulled her along the hallway. Monique reluctantly followed the girl. They headed up the stairs to the second floor and approached one of the guest suites near the back of the hall. Lilly knocked on the door. The door opened without hesitation to reveal Katrina dressed stunningly in a formfitting dress with plenty of cleavage and leg revealed.

"You're late," Katrina huffed then eyed Monique. She looked back at Lilly with surprise. "What's going on?"

"You said you needed more help," Lilly announced cheerfully and indicated Monique. "Monique said she'd help out."

"Really?" Katrina remarked skeptically then eyed Monique with concern. "Do the others know you're here?"

"Don't be silly," Lilly answered for her and entered the room with Monique following. "They're almost as controlling as my mother."

Monique glanced around the elegant room and appeared curious. Katrina tossed a uniform at Lilly.

"Hurry up and get ready," Katrina announced in a gruff tone. "We're already running late."

Lilly took the uniform and hurried into the first bedroom. Katrina glanced at Monique, sized her up, and then removed another uniform.

"This will suit you," Katrina announced. "You can use the second bedroom. Go on. Hurry up and change."

Monique uncertainly accepted the clothing she was given then entered the second bedroom. Monique shut the bedroom door and studied the uniform presented to her. She appeared mostly puzzled as she stared at what was clearly a prep school uniform with a short plaid skirt and white blouse.

"Like I'm wearing a dress," Monique muttered. She tossed the outfit onto the bed without care then hesitated and again stared at it with a puzzled look. "Why that outfit?" she asked softly aloud to herself. "I don't get it."

Chapter Thirty-three

7he casino floor had only eleven tables open for the decent-sized crowd that had arrived. There were four poker tables, four blackjack tables, two Pai Gow poker tables, and one craps table open for play. Several scantily dressed cocktail waitresses served drinks. The hired dealers dressed professionally and took their jobs seriously. The caretakers had quite the operation going, undoubtedly on Sal's behalf. Clarke and Fonzi patrolled the pit located between the tables, keeping an eye on the gathering to ensure everything was kept honest. Gil and Beck sat at a poker table playing draw poker with a group of seedy looking men. An overwhelming majority of the crowd, however, looked to be just average guys. Most of the predominantly male crowd were bored locals seeking a little excitement on a Friday night.

Ross remained at the blackjack table and joked around with the other players. Kirk played craps and was either winning or losing with vigor. His shouts matched those of the other players, and it was hard to tell whether the game was going in his favor or not. Jackie attempted to play Pai Gow poker, but Zack felt the need to hover over her shoulder and tell her how to play each hand. She was certain if she saw his finger point at one more card while he whispered instructions in her ear, she was going to bite his finger. Zack wasn't like the other guys. He didn't feel it necessary to protect innocent women, which left Jackie wondering why he was always hanging over her shoulder. Maybe he figured she was the only one left who could stand him, so she won him by default. Jackie watched the dealer take her money. She groaned with disgust and leaned back in the chair. Zack massaged her shoulders and leaned closer to her ear.

"Should have listened to me," he said in a soft, mocking tone.

"If you value your life--" she began but refrained from finishing the threat. He might take it as a challenge and attempt to sucker her into another sparring match.

Jackie saw a small, black disk light up and vibrate on the table before one of the men. He was a large, husky man with curly, stringy hair. The other players were alerted to the sound, but none seemed to comment on it. The object she originally mistook for a drink coaster reminded Jackie of the pagers used at some restaurants indicting when a patron's table became available. The large, husky man looked like a cross between a biker and a deranged hillbilly. He didn't seem the type to be a high roller, if that's what the pager system indicated. She hadn't noticed any special room for high rollers either. Jackie caught Zack's hand on her shoulder and gave it a firm squeeze. He didn't mistake her actions as playful and followed her attention to the large man with the lit pager. Both watched as the man collected his chips and nearly sprang up from the table. Zack again leaned close to her ear.

"I'm going for a walk, darling," Zack announced and kissed her quickly on the cheek.

He was gone before she could protest his actions. Jackie received several looks from the other men at the table. She fidgeted slightly. Why did Zack insist on turning them into a couple while undercover? Jackie collected her cards for the next hand. Once she arranged her cards and laid them out, she noticed another similar coaster, although unlit, setting on the table alongside one of the other players. When the grungy looking man caught her look, she initiated with a tiny smile and indicated the device.

"What's with the pagers?" she asked. "Some sort of high stakes poker game with limited seating?"

The man stared at her a moment, grinned, and chuckled softly. "Nothing that would interest you, sweetheart," the man remarked, gaining snickers from another man at the table.

Jackie was feeling particularly confrontational at the moment, but she knew she had to behave. What the burly creep didn't realize was that she could beat him at any card game *and* kick his ass without breaking a sweat. Ross would be very disappointed in her if she did the latter. She smirked at the man, although it came across as more of a sneer, and minded her cards.

†

$\mathcal{M}$onique held the skirt and blouse up to her body while looking at herself in the full-length mirror. She remained puzzled by the situation and the bizarre outfit; although it was obvious she was attempting to figure it out. There was a soft tap on the bedroom door, causing her to jump and spin to the sound.

"Have you changed yet?" Katrina announced through the door.

Monique eyed the skirt and blouse then looked back at the door. "Uh, one more minute."

As soon as she heard Katrina's high heels clopping away from the bedroom, she tossed the clothing onto the bed and hurried to the door. She quietly opened the door a crack and peered into the living room. Monique stared in horror at the sight of Lilly, who was dressed in a similar schoolgirl outfit, sitting on the lap of a man almost as old as her father was. They kissed passionately as his hand caressed her bare leg just beneath the skirt. Katrina allowed another man into the room and flirted with him. The man kissing Lilly picked her up and carried her into the first bedroom. Katrina guided the newly arrived man toward the third bedroom. Monique shut the bedroom door, leaned against it, and held her chest.

"Shit," she gasped softly, finally putting it together. "What the hell--?"

Monique hurried across the room toward the window. To her surprise, it didn't open. Most hotel windows didn't open, but Monique didn't travel much. The bedroom door opened, startling her. She whirled around and saw the husky, hillbilly biker standing in the doorway. He was younger than the man she'd seen with Lilly, but he still had to be in his thirties. The man was grotesque, particularly to a young, teenage girl. He grinned when he saw her.

"She wasn't kidding," the man announced while studying her, "you are young."

"Yeah," Monique announced boldly. "And there's been a big misunderstanding."

The man shut the door behind him and maintained his grin, revealing heavily stained teeth. "It's okay," he replied. "I don't mind that you're underage. I'm paying extra for it."

"Yeah, and I was just leaving," Monique bluntly informed him as she headed past him for the door.

The man suddenly grabbed her by the arm and stopped her. She stared at him with surprise. He laughed in his throat. He smelled badly of body odor, cigar smoke, and alcohol.

"You aren't going anywhere until I've gotten my money's worth out of you," he announced almost playfully.

Monique tensed with fear as she stared at the large man. She suddenly stomped on his foot, turned her back to him, and rammed her elbow into his abdomen. She grabbed his arm and, with all her strength, flipped him over her hip. Once he was on the ground, she stomped on his crotch. The man howled while clutching himself. Monique straightened proudly and stared at the writhing man with some surprise.

"What do you know--?" she gasped then snorted a soft laugh as she ran from the room.

Monique entered the living room, which was now quiet and empty. Both bedroom doors remained closed. She ran for the main door, threw it open, and hurried into the hallway. Monique ran along the corridor as fast as she could and only slowed when she reached the corner. She spun the corner and collided with another man. Monique screamed hysterically as the man grabbed her arms, keeping them both from falling.

"Hey, hey!" Zack cried out.

Monique stopped struggling and stared at Zack standing before her. She was breathing heavily and appeared uncertain what to say. Zack touched his ear transmitter.

"Damn it, Bogart," Zack snarled. "Why do I have one of your rug rats on the second floor?"

Monique pointed back the way she had come and appeared overly animated. "Katrina tried to sell me to a man for sex! Lilly's in trouble!"

Zack stared at Monique a brief moment in silence. Although his expression never changed, his mind could almost be seen racing with the information.

✝

*W*ithin the casino, Jackie placed her hand to her ear transmitter as her expression dropped, having heard Monique's plea through Zack's transmitter. There was a crash across the room. Jackie whipped her head in the direction of the crash. Ross was hurrying through the casino. It appeared as if he were muttering to himself, but each member of the team had heard Monique's comment to Zack. From her vantage point, Jackie could see the other guys sitting tense while watching Ross leave and awaiting further orders that never came.

"Zack," came Ross's harsh but soft voice over Jackie's ear transmitter, "stand down!" There was no response from Zack. "Monroe, intercept!"

Jackie attempted to act casual and stood from the table. As she walked away, the others at her table called to her reminding her that she'd forgotten her chips.

"I'll be right back," she barely gasped and attempted to keep a calm appearance.

Jackie could see the others had remained seated, although watching intensely. Jackie caught up to Ross near the casino door.

"Will Monroe make it in time?" Jackie gasped softly.

Ross gritted his teeth and shook his head.

†

Zack stormed into the suite with the appearance of a raging bull while Monique hurried after him. She pointed to the first bedroom door. Zack approached the door, barely stopped, and kicked it open with one foot. The door nearly broke off its hinges. Lilly screamed from within the room. Zack entered the bedroom. Monique ran after him and stopped at the busted door. She was nearly struck by the still fully dressed man as he flew backwards from the room. Monique screamed and jumped against the nearby wall. Zack emerged from the room as the man attempted to scramble to his feet. The man was nearly on his feet when Zack kicked him in the leg. The crunching of breaking bones caused Monique to scream. Lilly ran from the room, saw Monique, and joined her alongside the wall. The man clutched his leg and collapsed to the floor while begging for his life. Zack grabbed the man by the shirt, pulled him to his feet, and punched him twice in the face. The third bedroom door opened.

Katrina and her 'date' entered the suite from their bedroom. The man with Katrina attempted to stop Zack's assault on the injured man. Zack released the first man and spun into a roundhouse kick, striking the second man in the chest. He sent the man flying across the room. The second man struck the wall with enough force to crack the drywall. Katrina removed a gun and aimed it at Zack. Zack snap kicked the gun from her hand. The return kick sent her onto the nearby sofa with enough force to move the sofa an inch or two. Zack lunged for Katrina where she'd fallen, grabbed her by the throat, and pinned her down. She gasped and fought his grip on her throat. The look in his eyes was wild and unpredictable.

"Is this what you do?" he demanded in an evil, harsh tone. "Sell little girls? You and your kind are despicable human beings and should be eradicated from the face of the earth," Zack lashed out like some deranged lunatic. "There's a special place in hell for people who target children. Would you like to see it?"

Katrina gasped and thrashed, fighting the hand tight on her throat. Her eyes were wide as she stared at the frightening man hovering over her.

"Zack, stop!" Monique cried out in horror. "You'll kill her!"

†

*J*ackie and Ross ran into Monroe, Bogart, and Colleen in the hotel's second floor hallway. Darth ran along the hallway ahead of them while barking, possibly hearing the commotion coming from the other end of the second floor.

"They have to be down this hall," Monroe called out. "Darth thinks there's something this way."

They hurried through the hallway while following the dog on his search and rescue. They rounded the corner and suddenly stopped. Monique stood in the hallway outside the suite while holding the sobbing fourteen-year-old girl. Darth was already inside the room. Colleen ran to her friend and hugged her. Monroe and Ross approached the open suite door. Monroe was the only one with a gun, so he led the way. As they entered the suite, they saw Zack casually reclined in a plush chair facing them. He cleaned dirt out from under his fingernails with his Bowie knife and barely acknowledged them as they entered. Monroe and Ross looked around the room as Jackie stood in the doorway behind them. The three men were bound with their own shoelaces and sat on the floor against the wall on the opposite side of the room. Monroe appeared alarmed while looking around then looked back at Zack.

"What did you do, Zack?" Monroe gasped with horror, unable to take his eyes off his friend. "Where's Katrina?"

Katrina's faint muffled screams were heard. Jackie then saw Darth run to the broken window. He stood on his hind legs and peered at something below. The internet cable was tied to the corner of the bar leading out the window. Jackie and Ross hurried to the window and looked out. Katrina dangled alongside the window from the cable tied around her ankles. She attempted to scream through the knee-high sock stuffed in her mouth. Monroe continued to stare at Zack, who remained calmly seated.

"I'm sorry," Zack informed Ross while frowning and pointed with his knife, indicating the first tied man. "I think I broke his leg. I fucked up the mission."

Zack replaced his knife to his boot and appeared disgusted with himself. Ross looked back at Zack, exhaled softly, and scratched his gray hair. He managed a tiny smile and shook his head.

"I'm just grateful cleanup didn't require a mop," Ross replied.

Zack rolled his eyes and shook his head. "It was just one time," he scoffed. "Are you ever going to let it go?"

Ross nodded for Monroe to help him pull Katrina back inside. Jackie glanced at the tied men while Bogart remained in the corridor with the girls.

"What do we do now?" Jackie asked gently while glancing at Ross. "With that pager system, someone's going to eventually complain. Clarke and Fonzi will come to check on Katrina to see what happened."

"I know," Ross muttered as they pulled Katrina back into the room. He then looked around. "I'm guessing we have an hour or so before the situation implodes on us. We'll prep the transports and leave before that happens."

"And go where?" Monroe asked.

"I don't know, but we can't stay here," Ross replied. "We can't afford anyone asking questions."

"Taking off in the dark is a bit risky, Ross," Jackie announced. "Neither Gil nor I are familiar with the terrain."

"Well, we can buy a few more hours if we clean up the room and move these four someplace else," Ross announced with a defeated sigh. "Clarke and Fonzi may be too busy to search for them right away."

"Someone needs to drill Sal a new asshole too," Zack muttered as he sprang up from the chair. His look was demanding and hostile. "What the hell was he thinking?" He looked away and waved off Ross. "Don't get me started again. I was just calming down."

"Yes, you work on keeping calm," Ross informed Zack while maintaining a stern expression. He then looked behind him. "Jackie, take the kids back to their room. We'll escort the young lady back to her mother once we've cleaned up this mess."

Jackie nodded and hurried into the hallway with Darth on her heels to collect the three girls. As she entered the hallway, Bogart pulled her aside and away from the three girls, who now appeared calm.

"Did Zack flip out?" Bogart nearly whispered to Jackie with a stunned look on his country boy face.

"Yeah, just a little," Jackie replied softly so the girls wouldn't hear. "He has a few buttons you never want to push." She hesitated and drew a deep breath. "Those guys in there were very lucky. Ross wasn't kidding about the mop."

As Jackie approached the girls and guided them down the hall, Bogart stared after her with his mouth hanging open.

"Jesus," Bogart muttered softly then shook his head. "Zack the Ripper."

Chapter Thirty-four

$\mathcal{I}$t was possibly the most awkward moment of Jackie's life, and there had been many awkward moments being raised by her father and his SEAL team. Jackie stood on the dark farmhouse porch alongside Lilly awaiting someone to answer the door. It was a little after midnight by the time they finished cleaning up Zack's mess and hid all evidence of what had happened. Ross leaned against the corner of the barn in the near distance with his arms folded across his chest while keeping an eye on Jackie and the young girl. The porch light came on, sending a nervous pang through Jackie's stomach. The door was finally opened to reveal Betty in her tattered housecoat. She stared at her daughter still wearing the schoolgirl uniform, knee-high socks, and high heels. The amount of make-up on the young girl's face was staggering to her mother. She looked from her fourteen-year-old daughter to Jackie standing on the porch alongside her.

"What's going on?" Betty suddenly demanded and again looked at her daughter. "Why are you dressed that way?"

"This is so hard to say," Jackie announced gently then drew a deep breath. "Katrina tricked your daughter into entertaining men for profit."

The look in Betty's eyes showed her horror. She looked from Jackie to her youngest daughter. The shattered look in her eyes was heartbreaking.

"I didn't know it was wrong, momma," Lilly blurted out, nearly down to tears. "Monique and Colleen explained it to me. I know it was wrong now. She just offered me so much money. I didn't know it was wrong."

It was obvious Betty wanted to be mad. Her expression indicated she was wrestling with whether she wanted to scream or cry. She wiped a tear from her eye and nodded, all emotion seeming to disappear.

"It's not your fault, Lilly," Betty finally responded, her voice cracking. "I'll deal with Katrina."

"He nearly killed her," Lilly again blurted out as the tears now flowed. "The man from Jackie's group did horrible things to the man I was with, and then he almost killed Katrina."

Betty glanced at Jackie. She offered a slight nod, although the words coming from the girl's mouth caused her to squirm slightly. She couldn't even imagine what Zack had done before they'd arrived at the suite. Betty looked back at her daughter, placed a reassuring hand on her shoulder, and managed a smile despite what was going through her mind.

"Then I'm grateful to Jackie's friends," Betty announced almost gently. "Get out of those clothes and get into a bath. Once you've washed the filth from yourself, we'll have a nice long talk over hot chocolate."

Lilly smiled gently and nodded. She skulked into the house and disappeared from Jackie's sight. Betty's expression turned cold and vengeful.

"Did your friend punish Katrina and the man who'd touch my daughter?" she demanded.

"I can assure you, Betty," Jackie announced and immediately rubbed her chilled arms. "Whatever my friend did to Katrina and that man tonight will emotionally scar them for life."

"You know I want them dead," Betty remarked firmly.

Jackie nodded with understanding. "Yes, I'm sure you do," she replied then hesitated and drew a deep breath. "To avoid a riot with the caretakers' unsavory guests, we thought it best not to involve the authorities until morning. My friends have the situation under control until an arrest can be made. I promise you, they're not getting away with any of this."

Betty stared at Jackie with an unpredictable look on her tired face. "You're barely old enough to have children of your own," Betty announced gently. "I'm not sure you can understand what I'm going through right now." She cast a look past Jackie to Ross leaning against the barn. "You can!"

Ross straightened and approached the lit porch, joining Jackie where she stood before the woman in the worn housecoat.

"Everything okay?" Ross asked gently.

"I don't have much, but you're welcome to anything I have," Betty informed Ross. "Is there any way I can appeal to your sense of decency to deal with this situation?"

"I'm not sure I understand," Ross informed her while glancing at Jackie, although he'd undoubtedly been listening to the entire conversation via Jackie's ear transmitter.

"You know what I'm asking," Betty sharply informed him while folding her arms across her chest. "I want Katrina to pay for what she did to my daughter. Dispense a little justice. If you're not man enough to do it then stand aside and let me have her."

Jackie and Ross were stunned by the comment coming from the older woman. The burned dead people within the pit immediately came to mind. Blaming the seedy caretakers for those deaths may have been a hasty conclusion.

"I'm afraid I can't do that," Ross gently informed her. "Trust me when I say she's paid a steep price for her crimes tonight. In the morning, the legal system will take it from here."

"The legal system," Betty scoffed hotly. "What's the punishment for pimping out underage girls? A hefty fine and a year of probation? The legal system is a joke!" Betty attempted to contain her anger and drew a deep breath while staring into Ross's eyes. "If you don't have the stomach to do what needs to be done, maybe your two friends do."

There was an awkward silence from Jackie and Ross as they attempted to understand the woman's remark.

Betty raised her brows in a cocky manner. "I get the newspaper from a woman a few miles down the road," she informed him. "I saw your two friends on the front page. Bad picture, but I know it was them. The good-looking one and the snappy dresser. Wanted by the FBI." She casually placed her hands in her housecoat pockets. "I'm not asking much. I've sat on this information, so you know I really don't want to turn them in. You need to do this favor for me."

Ross stared at Betty with a look Jackie couldn't read. The look almost frightened her. It was uncanny how much he resembled her father at times. Jackie looked back at the woman in the doorway and spoke without hesitation.

"She'll be in your barn first thing tomorrow morning," Jackie announced firmly.

Betty looked at Jackie with some surprise.

"Alive," Jackie remarked boldly. "You can do with her what you please, but I'll have no part of what happens to her."

The relief showed on the older woman's face. It was as if a heavy burden was suddenly lifted from her shoulders.

"And I have just the thing to make that job easier for you, dear," Betty announced then hurried inside.

Jackie and Ross waited on the porch. Ross glared at Jackie with disapproval on his tough face, causing her to tense.

"How could you?" he demanded.

"You know she has a pistol in her housecoat pocket," Jackie remarked.

He nodded in response. "I was confident she had a gun aimed at my crotch," Ross confirmed.

"I can have us out of here just before sunup," Jackie informed him while smirking slightly. "It'll work out. Trust me."

Ross inhaled a deep breath and shook his head. "You're too much like your father," he muttered. "It's frightening."

Betty returned to the doorway with a small kit. She opened the kit to reveal a large bottle and several syringes.

"This is horse sedative," Betty informed them. "There's a chart with dosage according to weight. You just inject the proper dose into the muscle, and it's nighty night time. Should last for a few hours." She closed the kit and handed it to Jackie.

Jackie accepted the kit and offered an approving grin. "You know, this *will* come in handy. Thank you."

Betty offered a pleased smile and shut the door behind them. Jackie and Ross walked off the porch. As they passed the barn, the porch light went out. Ross eyed Jackie and the twisted smile on her face. He hid his grin.

"I know that look," he announced. "What's going through that evil head of yours?"

"Betty just solved our problem with Katrina's call for sex system," Jackie announced cheerfully.

✝

Monroe stood before Ross with a demanding look on his face. His hands were firmly on his hips. He wore the schoolgirl skirt and low-cut blouse with extra padding stuffed to give the illusion of cleavage. His moderately hairy legs stuck out above the knee-high socks, although he was unable to fit into any of the shoes.

"This is crossing the line, Ross," Monroe launched with hostility.

Jackie attempted to attach hair extensions in the form of ponytails to the sides of his head. Ross kept his hand near his mouth to cover his grin.

"You know," Jackie announced as she applied the ponytail extensions, "with a little bit of make-up, you'll make a nice looking woman."

"This is ridiculous," Monroe bellowed. "I'll deal with the one hundred gamblers downstairs. Just let me get out of this ridiculous getup."

"Oh, stop your fucking whining," Beck cried out from across the room.

Jackie and Ross glanced at Beck near the first bedroom. Beck stood with his hands firmly on his hips in his own schoolgirl outfit complete with ponytails and a layer of make-up, including bright red lipstick. There was a tap on the suite door, which was immediately opened to reveal Gil.

"How's it--?" Gil stared at Beck with surprise. A broad grin crossed his face. He burst out laughing and immediately reached for his cell phone.

"Don't you dare!" Beck cried out.

Gil snapped a picture then ran from the room as Beck charged after him. Ross stepped into his path and stopped his pursuit.

"Don't get your panties in a bunch," Ross remarked firmly. "I'll get Gil to delete that picture." He then looked at Jackie. "How long for the make-up on our little princess there?"

Monroe sneered at Ross. Jackie eyed Monroe, grinned slyly, and then looked back at Ross.

"Ten more minutes," she replied.

"Perfect," Ross announced then touched his ear transmitter. "We'll start resuming the beeper system in thirty minutes."

Jackie eyed Ross with some surprise. "I only need ten for Monroe-Ann's make-up."

"I know," Ross replied while grinning. "But you're going to need a few minutes to slip into something a little less comfortable yourself."

Jackie stared at him with horror on her face. "Excuse me?" she suddenly demanded.

"We have a lot of guys waiting," he informed her. "They're a bit backlogged. We need to move this along before Fonzi and Clarke become suspicious. We need a third hooker, and I'm not brave enough to go near Zack with a dress, so that leaves you." His teasing smile mocked her. "Our only *real* woman."

Monroe and Beck were momentarily dumbfounded. Both gave Jackie a quick once over then burst out laughing.

"Totally worth it," Beck announced, barely able to control his humor.

"Yeah, come on, Jackie," Monroe teased while grinning. "Fair is fair."

Jackie felt the heat rise to her cheeks. She glared at Ross. "I'm afraid there aren't any more outfits."

"That's okay," Ross casually replied. "I'm sure Katrina has something slutty in her closet for you to wear."

Beck jumped around excited while raising his hand in the air. "Oh, I'll find something! Let me pick out something for her!"

Ross grinned and nodded. Beck ran into the first bedroom. Jackie folded her arms across her chest and glared at Ross.

"You're going to pay for this," Jackie snarled.

Ross laughed softly. "To quote Beck, 'totally worth it'," he announced.

†

*R*oss stood inside the suite by the doorway and studied the clipboard. He crossed off another name then picked up the phone on the table near the door. He pressed in a number, which would trigger the pager of another man. There was a knock on the main suite door. Ross touched his ear transmitter.

"Okay, Jackie," he announced softly. "I'm sending another one your way."

"Yippy," came her response.

Ross chuckled softly and opened the suite door to reveal a large, eager looking man. Ross maintained a stern look and indicated the third bedroom with a firm nod.

"Knock once then enter," he informed the man.

The man approached the third bedroom door and did as he was told. He entered the dimly lit bedroom with only a few lit candles to brighten it. Jackie lie on the bed in a seductive position. She wore nothing but a black, lacy bra and a matching micro miniskirt, which revealed a garter belt attached to black fishnet stockings. Her black calf-high boots added a certain toughness to her sexy appeal. The man grinned his approval while shutting the door behind him. Jackie smiled lustfully and pawed at the bed as the man approached. Zack stepped out of the darkness behind the man and jabbed a syringe into his buttocks. He barely flinched before collapsing to the floor. Jackie frowned and sat up on the bed.

"Whose idea was this anyway?" she muttered.

Zack eyed Jackie and seductively raised his brows. "Do that 'crawly' thing on the bed again."

She glared at Zack, but he wasn't the least bit intimidated by the killer look he received. Jackie touched her ear transmitter.

"Ross, I want to trade-in Zack," she muttered.

"No can do, my dear," Ross replied over her ear transmitter. "Kirk and Gil are having too much fun with their assignments. I could send Bogart--"

"We're good here," Jackie snapped.

Chapter Thirty-five

 $\mathcal{I}$ t was a little after four o'clock in the morning as Jackie sat up in bed trying to convince herself to get up. Ross wanted to leave in an hour, just prior to sunrise, even though most of the team had only gotten two hours sleep. Leaving half an hour before sunrise would enable Jackie just enough light to see for takeoff, and it would give them a healthy head start on the remaining caretakers. A large group of guests had left around two in the morning, although some did pay extra for overnight accommodations. Whether they intended to or not, those seeking Katrina's services had spent the night in bedrooms on the second floor, which remained mostly unused. A dozen or more men would be waking up with nasty sedative hangovers by late morning, that went without say. There was a soft tap on Jackie's door. Jackie climbed out of bed wearing only a tank top and sleep shorts. She removed the dead bolt and opened the door to reveal Ross, who looked a little too cheerful for a man with only two hours of sleep.

"One hour," he announced softly.

Jackie nodded and leaned against the doorframe, barely awake. "Are the others up?"

"Yeah, they're up," he replied. "Zack's already collecting his hidden arsenal from the casino floor. The place is a ghost town. No one else is up." He took a deep breath and straightened proudly. "I intend to make one phone call right before we leave."

"Cutting it a bit close," Jackie remarked, wishing she could fall asleep against the doorframe, "calling the authorities on Katrina while we're on our way out the door."

"No, that call will wait until we're half an hour in the air, just to be safe," Ross replied. His look then turned hateful. "This call is to Sal, and I intend to let loose with both barrels over Katrina's underage prostitution ring."

"I doubt he knows she solicited a fourteen-year-old girl," Jackie informed him.

"Well, I'm going to make sure he knows," Ross replied hotly. "Zack has his methods, I have mine."

Judging by his tone, Jackie had to wonder if Ross was secretly disappointed Zack hadn't killed the woman. Although he kept his cool last night, it was possible his rage had a chance to fester. Ross typically had a short fuse, blew up fast, and cooled off quick.

"Meet us in the kitchen at o-five hundred hours. We'll regroup there before heading for the lobby," he informed her. "Fonzi and Clarke shouldn't be up before noon, but we don't want to take any chances."

Jackie nodded then watched Ross walk away. She shut the door, leaned against it from the inside, and groaned softly. Thankfully, she was tired and unable to think straight; otherwise, she may have reconsidered and delivered Katrina to Betty as she had promised.

†

$\mathcal{I}$t was ten minutes before five when Jackie entered the kitchen with Bogart, the girls, and Darth, who was sporting his fashionable, K-9 bulletproof vest. Jackie wore her bomber jacket with her leather shoulder holster hidden beneath, her Glock in the hidden holster down the back of her pants, and the double hip holster with leg tie-down attached to each of her thighs. Her dual tactical batons were in the back of her holster, and her assault rifle was slung over her shoulder. Her backpack contained extra rounds and clips for each gun, just so she was prepared. None were expecting trouble, but they were all prepared for it. Jackie was surprised that Gil and Monroe weren't among those present within the kitchen. Zack was missing as usual, but he was probably outside the lobby scoping out the area for their departure. Ross held the satellite phone to his ear while leaning against the counter in his best intimidating pose, even if the caller couldn't see it.

"Yes, I know what time it is, Sal," Ross muttered into the phone, lacking patience.

It was almost six in the morning Chicago time for Sal. Still an ungodly hour to call a person, but at least Ross didn't call him in the middle of the night. Jackie paused alongside Kirk by the large island counter while looking around the kitchen.

"Where are Gil and Monroe?" she asked.

"They're loading some gear into the plane," Kirk replied while sipping his coffee. "Gil wanted to give the plane and helicopter a quick visual inspection before departure."

Ross straightened with the phone still to his ear. "You knew what we were up against when you offered to put us up, Sal," he announced firmly into the phone. "I could care less about the illegal gambling you have going on over the weekend, but I'm more than pissed about your girl Katrina involving minors in her little prostitution ring. I certainly hope you weren't aware of what she was doing--and with a fourteen-year-old girl no less."

"What?" Sal could be heard exploding from the other end. There was an odd silence. "Ross, I would never condone something like that--ever. You should know that." He could almost be heard breathing through the phone. It was the heavy breathing of a man whose heart was pounding. "And what's this about illegal gambling? At my abandoned casino? Are you telling me the caretakers are involved in illegal operations behind my back?"

Ross was silent a moment and glanced at the others around the kitchen, who now watched him. "You didn't know about the gambling either?"

"Absolutely not," Sal exploded. There was another pause. "I'm shocked. Absolutely appalled to hear something like this. Who would expect a nice old couple like that be capable of such devious behavior--and with their mentally disabled son, no less. I can't believe they'd expose him to something like that. They've sheltered him from just about everything bad in this world. That's why they wanted a job with so much solitude. It's absolutely shocking that they'd do something like that."

Ross collapsed against the main counter while staring blankly as he held the phone to his ear. "Old couple? Mentally disabled son?" he gasped, his mind searching for answers. "Sal, the people here are in their thirties at most. There isn't any old couple with a disabled son here."

There was a strange silence. "Ross," Sal lectured, "Katrina and Clarke have to be almost seventy years old by now, and their son is in his late forties."

Ross stared at the others, catching their curious looks. He then returned to his caller. "Then I don't know who these people are, but I think I have a pretty good idea what happened to your elderly caretakers."

The others were now staring at Ross and the strange look on his face. His words were concerning.

"Listen, Sal," Ross announced quickly. "We need to get out of here. Do me a favor and call the police in an hour. We'll be long gone by then."

"Yeah, Ross, sure," Sal replied, although he sounded tense. "Give me a call once you're in the air. I'll see if there's someplace else I can redirect you that's safe."

"Thanks, Sal." Ross disconnected the satellite phone and looked at the others who now stared at him with concern. "I guess you heard the important part. The caretakers aren't who they say they are, but it's no longer our problem. It's time to bug out."

"What's the plan?" Beck asked.

Ross removed his assault rifle from over his shoulder and looked from Beck to Kirk. "You two will take the tractor-trailer. Wait for Gil and Jackie to fire up the plane and helo before starting the truck. The truck is closer to the building and it might wake the others. We'll ditch the truck somewhere secure about an hour from here. It can wait there until Holden finds someone trustworthy to impound it."

Beck and Kirk nodded, grabbed their rifles, and hurried out the back kitchen door, which was the quicker route to the tractor-trailer parked alongside the building near the loading dock.

"I'm on point," Ross announced firmly. "Jackie is fifty feet behind me with the girls. Bogart will bring up the rear." He glared at Bogart and pointed a warning finger at him. "Keep alert. Got it?"

Bogart nodded and removed his semiautomatic from his hidden shoulder holster, keeping his assault rifle slung. "Yeah, I got it."

Colleen clung to her bullwhip while Monique clung to her friend's arm. Jackie touched their shoulders and offered a reassuring smile to relax them.

"It's going to be fine," Jackie announced gently. "Ross is just being cautious, that's all. We don't expect any trouble."

Both girls breathed a sigh of relief. Ross headed through the main kitchen door. Jackie waited ten seconds then guided the girls behind him. Darth trotted alongside them from the kitchen. Bogart then followed while keeping close watch behind them.

Chapter Thirty-six

Moonlight shined upon the large open area surrounding the plane and helicopter. There was a hint of sunrise approaching. Monroe stood outside the plane and kept guard while Gil puttered around inside. Monroe glanced at his watch then looked around the desolate area. The morning was quiet, as were all mornings in the middle of nowhere. A few animals from the nearby farm were rustling around, but even most of them were still asleep. The farmhouse remained dark, although Betty and her daughters would undoubtedly be up within the hour to start their chores. Gil walked down the plane steps and glanced at Monroe.

"She's prepped and ready to go," Gil announced to his friend then looked at his watch. "They should be gathering in the lobby about now."

Both men looked toward the distant hotel entrance. There was only one light on, which was left on intentionally, leaving the lobby only dimly lit. The sound of vehicles were heard in the distance, surprising both men. Gil and Monroe eyed each other and hurried to the front of the plane. They looked down the long roadway and saw several vehicles approaching just fast enough to keep the noise to a minimum.

"Ah, hell no," Monroe muttered then touched his ear transmitter. "Ross, we have company. A lot of company. Could be hostiles."

Gil tossed Monroe an assault rifle. Both men hid alongside the plane and awaited the approaching vehicles. One of the trucks headed for the plane and stopped directly before its nose. They weren't even aware of Gil and Monroe's presence. The visitors seemed interested in blocking the plane so it couldn't take off. A second truck parked behind the tail, successfully blocking the plane.

The remaining trucks headed for the hotel. The guys lost count after the first dozen.

"Definitely hostiles," Gil reported softly into his ear transmitter.

Men from the first truck, parked in front of the plane's nose, hurried for the helicopter, not even bothering to look for anyone up at the early hour. The trespassers must have assumed they had the element of surprise on their side. Gil and Monroe secretly watched the men, who were dressed similar to those back at the amusement park. As the trespassers hurried for the helicopter, Gil and Monroe exchanged looks and nodded. Both moved away from the side of the plane and fired at the men. They took down both men before those within the second truck jumped out and fired back at them. Gil crawled under the plane and returned fire while Monroe ran up the steps inside the plane and fired at them as well. The remaining men went down relatively fast, minimizing damage to the plane. Fortunately, the sounds of the trucks racing for the hotel prevented the others from hearing the gunfire and backtracking to assist them. Gil and Monroe checked on the dead men lying on the ground. Gil saw something in one of the man's hands, kicked the object, and then groaned with disgust as he stared at the explosives. He touched his ear transmitter as he looked around.

"Ross, they intended to blow up the helicopter," Gil announced. "One of the dead guys had C4 in his hand."

Monroe routed through an old backpack worn by the second man then whistled to Gil, indicating the bag. "There are more here and some detonators."

"I'll send the girls someplace safe," came Ross's response through their transmitters. "Get that helicopter airborne. We can't risk something happening to it. We're going to need it for our escape," Ross informed them. "Fly it someplace safe, wait twenty minutes, and then meet us on the hotel roof for extraction."

"Roger," Gil responded and nodded Monroe to the helicopter.

Both men ran for the helicopter and climbed inside. Gil started the engine and prepared for takeoff while Monroe prepared his assault rifle in the event of another firefight. Neither seemed to notice that the farmhouse lights were now on. It was possible that the sounds of gunfire traveled as far as the farmhouse and awoke those inside.

†

$\mathcal{B}$eck and Kirk stood on the loading platform by the tractor-trailer and listened to the reports through their ear transmitters. They exchanged concerned looks.

"We have a dozen or more trucks approaching the front of the hotel," Kirk informed Beck.

Both men eyed the parked tractor-trailer. Beck touched his ear transmitter while anxiously pacing.

"Ross, can you make it to the truck at the loading platform behind the hotel?" Beck asked.

"Negative," Ross replied. "We could make it to you, but there are too many trucks approaching. We'll never outrun them in that rig. I can't risk the girls' lives."

"Want us to run interference?" Beck asked while looking around and listening to the distant sound of trucks near the front of the hotel.

"If you could lead a few of them away, I'd be grateful," Ross replied.

Kirk and Beck eyed each other and nodded. Both men climbed into the truck cab with Beck in the driver's seat. He started the truck and pulled away from the hotel. Kirk lowered his window and aimed his assault rifle out the opening, prepared for a firefight. Beck drove the tractor-trailer slowly around the side of the hotel then stepped on the gas as they neared the front, wanting the element of surprise. The tractor-trailer drove straight toward the oncoming trucks, plowing through several of them and left them in a mess of twisted metal. A few trucks turned and chased after the tractor-trailer. A dozen or more remaining trucks continued toward the hotel. As the tractor-trailer flew past the trapped plane surrounded by four dead men, the helicopter lifted off. The tractor-trailer raced along the roadway toward the woods, which would make it difficult for any of the enemy pickup trucks to pull alongside the rig.

An enemy helicopter suddenly dropped down in front of the entrance to the woods and a man fired out the side. Within the tractor-trailer, Kirk fired back at the helicopter while Beck stepped on the gas, aiming to ram it if it didn't move. Several bullets struck the windshield, causing Beck to shirk in his seat, but not deterring his current path. The helicopter was suddenly under fire from above. Gil zipped overhead while Monroe fired out the side at the helicopter blocking the tractor-trailer's path. The helicopter lifted and chased after Gil and Monroe. The men in the trucks continued shooting at the tractor-trailer. What sounded like an explosion rocked the truck.

The wheel attempted to turn in Beck's hand. He fought to control the tractor-trailer, but the blown front tire was too much for him to handle. The tractor-trailer swerved just enough, forcing it to hit a tree near the roadway in the woods. Beck and Kirk were tossed around the cab despite their seatbelts.

$$\dagger$$

*J*ackie and Ross stood before the window not far from the main lobby door. They had bolted the door, but the windows would eventually shatter with enough gunfire. Bogart kept the girls away from the windows while Jackie and Ross watched the approaching trucks. Ross turned to Jackie.

"I want you and Bogart to take the girls up to the penthouse and make your way to the roof," Ross informed her.

Jackie stared at Ross with concern. "Gil has a helo on his tail," she practically gasped. "Is the roof extraction still a viable option?"

"We have to hope Gil's the better pilot and wins that race," Ross replied and again glanced out the window. "You have to be ready to get those girls out in that helicopter. Once he reaches the roof, he may not have much time."

Jackie reluctantly nodded. It was Ross's call. Bogart appeared anxious and stared at Ross.

"Shouldn't I stay here with you?" Bogart asked while clutching his assault rifle. "You need backup."

"I have backup," Ross replied. "Zack is out there somewhere just itching to play sniper."

"Are you sure?" Bogart questioned.

A shot rang out from the second floor. They looked out the window and saw a truck with a blown tire suddenly flip over and roll several feet. Ross looked back at Bogart and grinned.

"I'm relatively confident," he replied then turned serious. "Protect those girls. Go, now. I've got this."

Jackie and Bogart hurried the girls to the elevator. Just as the elevator doors open, more gunfire was heard from outside. Jackie and Bogart forced the girls into the elevator and looked back just in time to see Ross leap away from the window. A truck plowed through the large windows and came to a grinding halt inside the lobby, striking the fountain and the naked Roman statue. Jackie tossed Bogart into the elevator and dove in behind him. The door immediately shut. Bogart stared at Jackie with surprise as the elevator headed upward.

"You left him!" Bogart suddenly proclaimed. "How could you just leave him there?"

Jackie refused to look at Bogart. "Ross can take care of himself." It wasn't a decision she made lightly. "Getting the girls killed isn't going to help anyone."

"I could have stayed!"

She suddenly glared at Bogart. "And do what? Get yourself killed?" Jackie demanded. "You're not equipped to handle a gunfight, Bogart. You're not a soldier; you're a conman. When you learn to handle yourself, you'll have your chance."

Bogart frowned and looked away, because he knew it was true. Monique and Colleen looked from Bogart to Jackie with surprise by the comment.

"I know I screwed up," Bogart announced gently without looking at Jackie. "I'm trying to right my wrongs."

Jackie glanced at the sulking man. She groaned softly while fidgeting. "I'm not mad at you, Bogart," she informed him in as calm a voice as she could manage. "You've been put into situations you're not trained for. Everyone makes mistakes. You just have to learn from them; not attempt to right them."

He stared into her eyes with a look of defeat. Jackie inhaled deeply and felt her entire body twitch. She was suddenly looking at the conman in a different light. She didn't want things between them to end with hateful words. Even if it turned out that he wasn't her brother, he was still one of her boys.

"Whatever happens," she informed him gently and with a serious look, "you and I are good, okay?"

Bogart forced a smile and nodded. "Yeah, okay," he replied softly.

It was in that moment as she stared into his eyes, she realized she saw her father's eyes staring back at her. Somewhere, deep inside, she knew the truth. Bogart was her brother. The moment was short lived as the elevator suddenly stopped on the second floor. All four looked at the doors with alarm. Jackie and Bogart raised their weapons as the doors opened. The corridor was empty. Bogart relaxed his weapon and was about to speak. Jackie silenced him with her hand while keeping her eyes and weapon locked on the open doors. As the doors were about to close, Fonzi leaped in front of them with a gun in his hand. Monique and Colleen screamed. Jackie fired at Fonzi, winging him in the arm and sending him flying backwards. Colleen rapidly pounded the 'close' button. Fonzi came back at them, but the door was already closing. Jackie and Bogart fired several shots, keeping him from attempting to stop the doors from closing. The girls huddled in the corner by the control panel and attempted to contain their fear.

"They'll know by the floor we stop on that we're heading for the roof and ambush us," Jackie informed them. She pressed the button for the eighth floor and looked at Bogart. "I'll get off on eight and draw their fire. You take the girls to the penthouse on ten and get to the roof. Barricade the door with anything you can."

"Then you won't be able to get through," Bogart announced with concern.

"The mission is to get the girls out of here," Jackie informed him firmly. "I have four semiautomatics, an assault rifle, and a bag of ammo. I'm good for the entire afternoon. Just get the girls on that helicopter."

Once the elevator reached eight, Jackie stepped out with her semiautomatic aimed. The corridor was empty.

"Jackie," Monique gasped with fear and pleaded with her eyes, "please don't do this."

Jackie looked from Monique's pleading eyes to Bogart and gave a firm nod. He frowned and hit the 'close' button. Monique attempted to bolt out of the elevator, but Bogart caught her by the shoulders and held her back. As the doors closed, Jackie darted into a nearby guestroom, propping the door open just a crack with the dead bolt. She kept her handgun aimed out the opening, directly at the elevator, prepared to pick off whoever stepped out first.

Chapter Thirty-seven

Kirk and Beck took cover in front of the heavily damaged tractor-trailer grill smashed against the large tree and returned gunfire. The men in the truck, who'd been chasing them, were now parked and stood behind their pickup truck, shooting at the guys with their own assault rifles. It was difficult for Kirk and Beck to get a decent shot at the men behind the truck, although the bad guys weren't fairing much better with their shots either, despite being heavily armed.

"It'd be nice if we were at the back of the truck," Kirk announced to Beck as he aggressively reloaded. "You know, where all the guns and ammo are."

"It's not in the cards, man," Beck replied and reloaded as Kirk took his turn shooting at the men. "Only one thing could make this day any worse."

They heard an approaching truck from the opposite side of the crashed tractor-trailer, indicating they were about to be pinned down with gunfire from both sides. Kirk plastered himself against the damaged grill and glared at Beck.

"Another truck of heavily armed men coming up our right flank?" Kirk casually asked.

Beck groaned softly and listened to the approaching truck. "Yeah, that'd do it."

"We need to take out these bastards before their friends arrive on our ass," Kirk informed Beck. "Ready?"

Both men inhaled deeply and stared at each other. They nodded their intent then moved into position to fire at the men with everything they had. Beck crouched low, resting on one knee, and Kirk prepared to fire from overtop of him. They heard the sound of rifle fire but not the automatic weapon fire they'd been hearing for the last ten minutes. It was actual rifle fire with the sound of cocking between each shot. One of the men behind the parked pickup truck suddenly went down. The other three men turned to face their surprise attack. Betty and her three daughters walked together while simultaneously firing their rifles at the men behind the truck, keeping a steady pace and steady gunfire. The remaining three men didn't get a shot off before going down. The older woman and her daughters stopped just short of the fallen men and looked at Kirk and Beck behind the severely damaged truck.

"What the hell is all the noise about out here?" Betty suddenly demanded. "Can't an old woman get a decent nights' sleep?"

The second truck approached from Beck and Kirk's right flank. Beck offered a pleasant smile.

"Can you wait ten minutes for an explanation?" Beck asked then turned and joined Kirk in firing at the truck attempting to slip around them.

Betty grabbed one of the dead man's assault rifles and looked at her three daughters.

"Lock and load girls," Betty announced while grinning. "We have some foxes in the henhouse."

The girls grabbed the remaining discarded assault rifles and ran to the front of the truck to join Kirk and Beck. As their assailants jumped out and fired at them from the opposite side of their pickup truck, Betty leaped into the clearing and fired a rapid spray of bullets at them. She gleefully hollered as the rounds rapidly flew from the barrel. Kirk and Beck flattened themselves against the front of the truck and watched the woman and her daughters firing the assault rifles with sheer joy.

"Where were these women when we were in Afghanistan?" Kirk remarked.

"I don't know," Beck gasped softly while watching the women pulverize the pickup truck. He slowly shook his head. "I'm a little frightened right now."

"We'll just keep this between us," Kirk replied and watched fourteen-year-old Lilly fire the assault rifle with a sparkle in her eyes and a twisted grin on her face.

"We're going to need a truck," Beck informed his partner. "It's going to be a warzone at the hotel. They're going to need us."

Kirk indicated the truck behind them by the dead men. "One truck coming up," he announced cheerfully.

t

*R*oss crouched behind the front desk and fired at the men on the opposite end of the smashed pickup truck in the middle of the lobby floor. Darth remained by his side, patiently waiting for some secret signal that didn't seem to come. Four men returned fire with automatic weapons, leaving Ross spending most of his time ducking behind the solid check-in counter. Ross touched his ear transmitter while the four men fired at him.

"How are we doing?" he casually asked. "I'd like to move someplace a little less noisy."

"By all means," Jackie announced over his ear transmitter, "move. I'm on the eighth floor. Bogart is taking the girls to the rendezvous."

Ross hesitated and appeared annoyed. "What they hell are you doing on eight?"

"We had company," Jackie replied over his transmitter. "I'm running interference. Will you just worry about your own ass for ten minutes?"

Ross groaned and looked at the dog crouched alongside him. "I have the commander to thank for her lovely disposition," he informed the dog then touched his ear transmitter. "Zack," he boldly announced. "Will you smoke these fuckers?"

"I thought you'd never ask," came Zack's response through his ear transmitter.

A metal object whizzed down the broad staircase and struck the smashed truck. Ross covered his ears. There was a loud bang as the truck blew up. Ross slowly straightened and looked across the lobby at the exploded truck. There were truck and body parts covered in blood scattered along most of the lobby reaching as far as the elevator and the front desk. Darth placed his front paws on the desk and peered across the lobby alongside his commanding officer. Ross touched his ear transmitter.

"You took me too literally," Ross muttered. "Where the hell did you get grenades?"

Zack appeared at the top of the stairs, looked down to the lobby below, and grinned while clinging to his newly found assault rifle with grenade launcher. Darth barked softly at Zack, alerting Ross to his presence.

"I took the liberty of removing a few toys from the truck," Zack announced from where he stood by the railing.

Ross and Darth hurried across the lobby and paused by the bottom of the stairs. Both looked up at Zack.

"Get your ass upstairs and assist with the welcome wagon," Ross announced. "I'll backup Jackie."

"Backup Jackie," Zack replied firmly and cradled his large weapon of mass destruction. "Got it."

Before Ross could protest, Zack disappeared into the nearby corridor. Ross shook his head while muttering under his breath. He motioned to the dog then ran for the elevator. More men began filtering into the lobby from the large opening left by the truck. Ross saw them and groaned.

"It's going to be one of those days," Ross muttered then ran down the hall with Darth on his heels.

Taking the elevator would only giveaway the girls' position to the newly arriving men. At least ten heavily armed men entered the lobby with their assault rifles aimed and ready to fire. They scattered throughout the tattered lobby, looking for the team and the girls. Tremaine and Hoffman entered behind them and looked around as well. Hoffman noticed the elevator doors were open.

"Four of you take the stairs; two on each end of the building," Hoffman announced then indicated the elevator. "Two take the elevator." He then looked at the other four as the first six took off. "You four are with us. We'll search the first floor. Keep alert. These guys are highly trained and heavily armed."

The four men nodded and followed Tremaine and Hoffman down the corridor. More trucks were heard outside.

†

*J*ackie remained hidden behind the partially open guestroom door just across the hall from the bank of elevators. She watched both elevators while frowning.

"Typical men," Jackie scoffed softly. "Leave a lady waiting-- and with an itchy trigger finger no less."

The light above the elevator finally lit and the familiar ding sounded just before the doors to the second elevator opened. Jackie kept her gun trained on the elevator and watched the first man cautiously step out. To her surprise, it wasn't Fonzi. Somehow, the intruders looking for the girls had made it past Ross and into the hotel. She hadn't heard from Ross. She hadn't heard from anyone since she heard the explosion within the hotel. She refused to believe the others were dead. It was possible her transmitter wasn't working properly. She waited for the second man to step out of the elevator. Both were heavily armed with assault rifles. Jackie couldn't use her assault rifle in the confined space by the door, so she was outgunned, but she had the element of surprise on her side.

Once the first man took two steps in her direction, the second man was just far enough from the open elevator to be a prime target. Jackie chose her target and shot the man closest to the elevator first, so he wouldn't have a chance to flee back into the safety of the elevator. That would give her enough time to pick off the second man before he could retreat. The bullet tore through his chest, although off center. The first man fired blindly while backing toward the elevator, uncertain where the shot came from and not wanting to give her a chance to get off a second round. Jackie crouched down to avoid the random gunfire and squeezed off a second round, taking the first man down with a chest shot as well. Jackie slowly straightened, waited a moment, and then slipped out of the guestroom. She approached the two dead men outside the open elevator.

A third man suddenly appeared from the elevator with his assault rifle aimed and ready to fire. Jackie didn't like surprises. She instinctively struck the rifle with her left arm, causing it to fire haphazard across the hallway, startling the man. She caught his wrist, spun her backside into him, and flipped him over her shoulder. The assault rifle fell from his hands and struck the floor. Jackie's own assault rifle clattered to the carpeted floor from the force of the flip. As she reached for her rifle, the first elevator arrow lit up along with the familiar ding. At the same time, she heard the stairwell door opening.

"You've got to be kidding," Jackie muttered.

She left her assault rifle where it fell and darted into the open elevator without a second to spare. She hid around the corner opposite the control panel with her semiautomatic close to her chest. Either the doors would close, or she'd need to get some clean shots. She heard someone from the first elevator bolting into the hallway. The doors closed before she even saw him. Jackie leaped to the opposite side to the control panel. The elevator was already indicating it was going up, so she needed to maintain that direction or risk the doors again opening on the eighth floor to some bad company. She pressed the button for the ninth floor, uncertain that she wanted to lead the men to the penthouse in case Bogart and the girls hadn't been rescued on the rooftop. She tapped her ear transmitter several times.

"Anyone out there?" she announced.

There was no response. She realized she was officially cut off now. As the doors opened on the ninth floor, Jackie stepped into the corridor with her gun aimed and looked both directions, prepared to fire. Normally, she'd be a little more cautious, but the guys on the eighth floor would easily make it up one flight and be on her tail in a minute or two. She didn't have time for cautious. As she ran down the corridor, the first elevator dinged. Jackie briefly glanced back and groaned.

"Are we going to play this game all morning?" she muttered then darted into a nearby suite.

Bolting the door behind her would only buy a few seconds against their assault rifles, and a locked door would certainly give her location away. She'd have to play a little game of cat-and-mouse with them. To her surprise, and with a little amount of luck, she discovered she had entered a high roller suite. It was larger than her new house with multiple floors and rooms. She had wandered into the second floor bedroom area. There were bedrooms along the upper floor and an open balcony before her with a staircase leading down to the living room below. She ran down the stairs but had little cover. The upstairs door was heard opening.

Jackie scanned the living room then bolted for the main entrance. She took only a moment to position herself alongside the door and cautiously open it. As she peered into the hallway, a gun was aimed in her face. Jackie grabbed the man's wrist and twisted, forcing the gun away from her, and also making him drop the gun. Although only a handgun, the soft thump was enough to alert the man on the second floor above them. Without releasing the man's wrist, Jackie rammed her knee into his ribs and then flipped him by his already bent arm. He crashed to the floor. Jackie leaped over the man and ran into the hallway. She heard the fire door to the right open followed by the one to the left. The sound of thundering feet on the stairs within the suite was almost deafening to Jackie, considering her current situation. The first elevator dinged, alarming her. Jackie's expression shattered.

"You've got to be fucking kidding!"

Jackie ran down the main corridor and darted into the first room she reached. She shut the door as quickly and quietly as possible and applied the bolt. She had no choice this time. She looked around the suite then to the balcony. Jackie groaned softly at her only option.

"This just doesn't get any better, does it?" she muttered then ran for the balcony doors.

Jackie unlocked the glass doors, exited through them, and silently closed them behind her. She approached the end of the balcony and considered her next move. There were other balconies attached to other suites. If she were lucky, one would be unlocked. Jackie took a deep breath, climbed over the metal balcony railing, and stood on the edge. She looked across the gap to the next balcony over. It was only a four-foot jump, which she was confident she could make. She then looked down. It was the nine-story drop that frightened the hell out of her! She took a deep breath and leaped to the next balcony over, easily catching the rail. Her backpack slipped from her shoulder and fell to the ground below. Jackie groaned softly with defeat. Her luck just wasn't getting any better.

She held her breath a moment before climbing over the rail onto the adjoining balcony. Jackie peeked into the suite through the glass doors. The suite looked empty. She tried the door. Naturally, it was locked. Breaking the glass would be easy enough with her firearm or her tactical batons, but the shattering glass would alert every goon on the floor to her whereabouts, and she was currently lite on ammo. Her semiautomatic in the shoulder holster was empty, leaving her with her two side arms, and the Glock in her pants holster. Jackie crossed the balcony and looked at the line of balconies before her. There were four more balconies before the end. At the end was salvation. From her position, she could see an access ladder leading to the casino roof just a few stories below. Jackie again looked down to the ground below, groaned, and climbed over the railing.

Chapter Thirty-eight

Bogart cautiously opened the rooftop door and looked around while holding his handgun close to his chest. When nothing moved, he motioned for the girls to join him. Monique and Colleen stepped onto the roof. He indicated for them to wait by the door then approached the corner and peeked around the side. Two men quietly patrolled the roof with their assault rifles. Bogart grimaced and returned to the girls by the door. Monique stared at something attached to the wall near the door hinge. She appeared slightly pale as she pointed.

"Bogart, what's that?" Monique asked softly with concern in her tone.

Bogart glanced at the object attached to the wall. His expression immediately dropped as he stared at the C4 explosive planted on the wall.

"That's our cue to leave, Twinkie," he softly replied and ushered them through the door.

They quickly and quietly hurried down the steps to the tenth floor. Bogart checked the corridor before ushering the girls into the safety of the tenth floor hallway. He opened the linen closet door and pushed both girls inside. Once the door was securely closed, Bogart touched his ear transmitter.

"Ross, we have a situation with the rooftop evac," Bogart announced softly and awaited a response. Once Ross acknowledged his transmission, Bogart continued. "They're planting explosives along the rooftop. I don't know whether they're waiting for the welcome party of if they just intend to set it off for shits and giggles." Bogart listened a moment then nodded. "My thoughts exactly. We're on our way."

Bogart turned to the girls and forced them to look into his eyes. Both remained terrified.

"We're heading for the loading dock for extraction," Bogart informed them gently. "We need to take the corridor beyond the kitchen. You know which one?"

Both girls mechanically nodded.

"Ross is going to meet us there," Bogart continued while attempting to remain calm for the girls' sake. "Beck and Kirk are on their way there now. If anything happens, no matter what, I want you two to get to that loading dock."

"You mean leave you?" Colleen suddenly gasped with horror in her eyes.

"You do what you have to do to make it out of here, Squirt," he firmly informed her.

"We can't leave you," Monique whispered, sharing the same expression as her friend.

"If this goes sideways, you just keep going," Bogart lectured firmly. "You don't stop, and you don't look back. If there's trouble, I'll find my way out, I promise." He straightened while clutching his gun. "Now, I'm going to check the hallway. We're going to turn left and head for the fire stairs on the far end of the hall. The kitchen is only a short distance from where the stairs end. Once we pass the kitchen, the loading dock is down the left corridor." Bogart drew a deep breath and clutched his handgun. "Are you ready?"

Both girls shook their heads, indicating they weren't ready. Bogart offered a sympathetic smile then slowly opened the door. When he saw the corridor was clear, he ushered them into the hallway. They quietly hurried along the empty corridor for the opposite end of the tenth floor. Bogart stopped by the intersection in the hallway and glanced around the corner. Two men with automatic rifles saw him, pointed, and ran for him.

"Ah, hell," Bogart muttered.

He shoved Monique and Colleen into a nearby bedroom, gave them a quiet sign, and then ran down the hallway while exchanging his pistol for the assault rifle slung over his shoulder. Monique and Colleen ducked into the nearby bathroom and listened to the sound of gunfire from several automatic weapons. They clung to each other and listened to the haunting sounds. There was no telling who was winning. The gunfire suddenly stopped, which was almost more chilling. Someone was victorious. Monique and Colleen exchanged frightened looks.

"They got him," Monique gasped softly.

"We don't know that," Colleen whispered back.

Monique glared at her friend and raised her brows. Colleen frowned, having been unwilling to accept Bogart's lack of skills, and looked down when she accepted defeat. After a brief moment, both girls slipped out of the bathroom and took turns looking through the peek hole in the door. They saw two men punching Bogart into submission. The first man removed Bogart's ear transmitter and spoke into it.

"I know you can hear me," the man announced. "We have one of your men. If you want to see him alive, you'd better bring me those girls."

The man dropped the transmitter to the floor and stomped on it, crushing it. Monique now watched through the peek hole and her obstructed view. The first man nodded to someone else in the hallway with him.

"You two check the rooms on this floor," the man announced. "If he was up here for a rooftop extraction, he may have hid the girls."

Monique turned away from the peek hole while appearing deep in thought.

"They're going to kill him," Colleen whispered.

"I know," she whispered back while continuing to consider their options.

Monique looked back through the peek hole and saw the man, possibly by himself, holding a gun on Bogart, who was now forced onto his knees. Monique quickly looked back at her friend.

"If we're going to do this, we only have one shot," Monique informed Colleen.

Colleen nervously nodded and coiled her bullwhip. "What's the plan?"

"He sent the other men to the end of the hall to search the rooms," Monique announced softly. "Bogart is with one man outside the door."

Colleen looked through the peek hole then backed away and nodded. "I can do it."

"One shot, Colleen," Monique sternly informed her. "You need to make it count."

Colleen took several deep breaths and focused on the door. Monique returned to the peek hole while gripping the doorknob. She watched the man with the gun standing over Bogart. When he turned his back to them, Monique threw open the door. Colleen leaped into the doorway and cracked her bullwhip at the man, who was turning to the sound of the door opening with his gun aimed.

She caught him around the ankle with the whip and pulled his legs out from under him. As he crashed to the floor, Bogart leaped for his gun. Bogart and the man rolled around the floor attempting to punch each other while wrestling for control of the gun. Colleen frantically attempted to untangle her bullwhip for a second crack. One of the doors just down the hall opened. Colleen pulled her whip free and ran down the hall to greet the man before he could aide his partner. As the large, muscular man stepped into the hallway with his automatic weapon raised, Colleen cracked her whip, slashing him across the face. It was enough to throw the man to the floor, allowing his weapon to fall from his hand.

Monique saw the discarded gun just beyond the wrestling men. She leaped for the gun, but the third man from the opposite end of the hall grabbed her around the waist from behind and pulled her off her feet. The man wrestling with Bogart was able to grab the gun on the floor. Monique thrashed wildly against her attacker. She coiled back with her right foot and thrust it behind her with all her strength, connecting with the man's knee. He dropped her to her feet but refused to release her. Monique rammed her elbow into his ribs, clutched his arm while casting herself forward onto her knee, and tossed the man over her shoulder. He roughly struck the floor and writhed with agony. Monique saw the discarded assault rifle. She leaped on top of the rifle and attempted to pick it up, although the weight stunned her.

Still on the floor, Bogart slammed the man's hand with the gun against the hall wall, forcing him to drop the gun as they continued to roll around the floor. Just down the hall, Colleen kicked the assault rifle from the reach of the burly man with the bleeding face. He gave up his quest for the assault rifle and set his sights on Colleen instead. The massive man charged for Colleen, grabbing her shoulders, and slammed her into the wall with tremendous force. Colleen was dazed by the hard hit. Bogart punched the man he wrestled with on the floor and turned in time to see Colleen slowly sinking down the wall.

"Squirt!" he cried out with horror.

Bogart became enraged and punched the man beneath him with fury until he stopped moving then scrambled to his feet. The large man at the other end of the hall released Colleen's shoulders, saw Bogart, and charged for him. As Colleen sank down the wall, she tossed the bullwhip across the floor, allowing it to slide past the charging man and for Bogart. Bogart saw the bullwhip, threw himself to the floor, and grabbed it. As he stood, the man plowed into him, throwing him into the wall not far from the man Monique had knocked to the floor. Monique attempted to hold the assault rifle, but it was bulky and awkward for the young girl. The first man was now returning to life and scrambled for his discarded semiautomatic on the floor.

As the muscular second man threw a punch for Bogart's face, Bogart ducked, allowing the man's fist to strike and crack the wall behind him. It was enough to cause him severe pain but not enough to stop him. Bogart leaped away from the wall and the big man. He coiled back with the bullwhip and cracked it. The whip tangled around the man's neck, startling him. As he struggled to loosen the whip around his neck, Bogart, who was a little more than surprised that it had worked, suddenly grinned and pulled back with all his might. The large man was thrown off his feet and struck a wall table with his head. The man with the semiautomatic aimed it at Bogart and was about to pull the trigger.

Monique cried out and squeezed the trigger on the assault rifle. She was thrown back against the opposing wall as a barrage of bullets shot from the weapon, seemingly all at once, first up the wall and then down the wall. The first man looked at the girl with the large weapon and aimed the gun at her instead. Bogart looked at Monique, who was clearly not in control of the firing weapon, and threw himself to the floor. The bullets rapidly struck the wall horizontally and tore into the man with the gun. His body jerked and jolted from the gunfire as blood sprayed across the wall behind him. Monique slid down the wall as the bullets continued to shoot up and into the ceiling. Her finger finally released the trigger and the deafening sound ceased.

From where he lie, Bogart stared with surprise at the fallen girl with the large weapon. He scrambled to his feet and hurried for Monique. He removed the assault rifle from her arms and pulled her to her feet.

"Are you okay?"

She nodded while trembling. A strange smile suddenly crossed her face. "That was oddly invigorating."

"I'm glad you're feeling empowered, but we have to go," Bogart announced. "Everyone knows where we are now."

Monique collected both discarded semiautomatics then hurried down the hall with Bogart to collect Colleen, who was slowly pulling herself to her feet. She was slightly dazed but far from incapacitated. Bogart took a quick second to assess her injuries before returning her bullwhip to her. He turned her in the right direction and motioned for the girls to hurry.

"That way! Go!"

✝

*R*oss paced the open door to the loading dock and alternated glancing at his watch, the sky, and the hotel entrance. Darth sniffed around the loading dock, looking for some predator that didn't exist, at least not yet. Darth suddenly stood rigid and stared at the main entrance. He snarled softly. Ross aimed his assault rifle at the door and took two steps behind a supply crate. The door opened to reveal Bogart with his assault rifle aimed. He looked around, saw there was no one in the loading dock, and then motioned the girls inside when the area was secured. Ross shook his head and stepped out from behind the crate.

"Your skills need refining," Ross announced, obviously disappointed that Bogart hadn't realized he was there.

Bogart cried out and aimed the assault rifle at Ross. Ross raised his hands in the air and immediately became annoyed.

"You idiot," Ross snarled, momentarily concerned he'd be shot by accident. "It's just me."

Bogart attempted to relax and lowered his weapon. "I'm sorry," he scoffed with annoyance while cocking his head to the side. "It's been a rough morning."

Darth ran across the loading dock and greeted the girls. They happily patted the dog, almost as a gesture to calm their own rattled nerves.

"Are you scared, boy," Colleen announced to the dog. "We won't let those bad men hurt you."

"Where's the helicopter?" Bogart asked while looking out the open door.

"Gil's trying to lose some airborne hostiles," Ross informed him. "We just need to keep quiet and wait it out. Beck and Kirk will be here soon."

"What about Jackie and Zack?" Bogart asked with concern. "Have you heard from either?"

"Zack knows the plan," Ross replied.

Both girls straightened from petting Darth and shared the same look as Bogart.

"What about Jackie?" Bogart again asked in an almost demanding tone.

"I'm sure she's fine," Ross muttered.

"We need to find her," Bogart blurted out with concern.

"We will."

"We're not leaving without her," Bogart announced more firmly with conviction.

Ross glared at Bogart and turned hostile. "When that helicopter arrives, your job is to get those girls out of here, do you understand?"

"But Jackie--"

"Zack and I will make sure Jackie isn't left behind," Ross informed him. "You're not ready to take on that many armed men. I don't need to worry about you going off half-cocked. I've got Zack for that."

Bogart frowned and paced the loading dock while running his fingers through his hair. He was clearly upset by Ross's orders.

Chapter Thirty-nine

*J*ackie swiftly climbed down the ladder to the casino roof below and jumped the last few feet. She remained close to the wall while scanning the flat roof for any visible way into the casino apart from the skylight. She spotted a small hatch, which was probably intended for maintenance to gain access to one of the many industrial sized air-conditioners. Jackie ran for the hatch, easily opened it, and climbed down another ladder. She continued down the narrow passageway and finally understood what it must have been like for the guys when they were stationed on ships. There was little light at the bottom, but it was enough for her to see the rungs as she climbed down. Jackie reached the bottom and looked around the maintenance closet. Its sole purpose was to house the ladder to the roof. She removed one of her semiautomatics from her side holster and cautiously opened the door. When nothing moved in the corridor, Jackie hurried along the hallway, keeping close to the wall. If her transmitter had worked, she'd know where to find the others, apart from Bogart and the girls on the roof. Unfortunately, she was flying blind without any contact to her team.

None of the guys knew where she was, and with lack of communication, they might just assume she was dead. She wandered onto the casino floor and looked around the large, empty area. She didn't see or hear anyone. She heard faint gunfire from outside, but it seemed further away than she thought it should have been. If she were lucky, the guys had the deadly intruders on the run, but she knew she wasn't that lucky. She took note to the room's many exits in the event of a hasty departure. Her best bet was to stay put until she heard gunfire close by, and in true military fashion, run toward the sound rather than away from it. It would be her best chance of regrouping with the guys. She had no idea how many armed men were crawling around the hotel, but she knew the number was staggering. Wandering around blindly looking for the guys while low on firepower would be suicide. Jackie found a quiet spot near a bank of slot machines. She sat on the floor between the machine and the chair, which offered some camouflage. She could watch the main entrance from her position. It was a good place to wait for something, whether good or bad, to happen.

Jackie allowed her head to rest against the hard slot machine behind her. She shut her eyes while running her fingers through her rumpled ponytail. Sitting still was a bad idea, allowing her adrenaline rush to fade and exhaustion to take over. When she opened her eyes, Zack sat in the chair across the aisle from her. She gasped with surprise and attempted to leap up but struck the chair and the coin tray with her shoulders. Zack shook his head as he stared at her with disapproval.

"It's a fucking warzone out there, and you're in here taking a nap," he casually remarked then gently spun his chair in a childlike manner.

Jackie pulled herself out from under the chair and the slot machine. She stared at him with disbelief. Part of her wanted to throw her arms around him and hug him, but another part of her wanted to smack him silly. Since it was Zack she was dealing with, she chose hostility.

"How the hell did you find me?" she demanded.

Zack grinned and playfully waved her off. "I tagged you with a tracking device a few months back," he replied without care. "I do it with all my favorite pets."

"Funny," she scoffed, refusing to let him know she was still happy to see him.

"Were you just ignoring Ross?" he teased then grinned lustfully. "Or are you just playing hard to get?"

"My transmitter stopped working," she informed him, ignoring the sexual innuendo. "Where are the others? Did Gil extract the girls on the roof?"

"The roof's been wired to blow, so they're meeting with Ross in the loading dock instead," Zack announced and stood, slinging his fancy, new assault rifle into his hands from over his shoulder. "If we don't want to be left behind, we should probably join them."

"For once, we actually agree on something," she remarked and joined him.

They headed across the main casino floor past the open area containing the table games and approached the main doors. Both kept their weapons at the ready and watched all corners of the room, just in case. As they approached the door, Zack suddenly grabbed Jackie's arm, stopping her. She knew better than to speak, since he obviously heard something. Zack took her hand and pulled her across the room. They dove behind a blackjack table, which, being enclosed on the bottom, offered some cover. The main casino doors were thrown open. Katrina, Clarke, and Fonzi hurried onto the casino floor. As Jackie peered out from behind the enclosed blackjack table, she saw Katrina's high heels. No doubt, what Zack had heard clomping along the tiled outer corridor. Both men were armed and appeared moderately tense as they followed Katrina to the cashier's cage. Fonzi had patched the gunshot wound to his arm, which was easily seen beyond the bloodstained tear in his black, leather jacket. Katrina unlocked the cashier's cage door with vigor and disgust.

"I can't believe you turned them in," Katrina snarled at Fonzi with hostility.

"After what that psychopath did to you last night, I'd think you'd be onboard. We'd get the reward and get them out of our business at the same time," Fonzie lashed back. "How was I supposed to know the feds would send an entire army out to kill them?"

"It was a stupid call. You should have waited to talk to me. Now our entire operation is ruined," Katrina snapped back at him as she entered the cashier's cage.

Clarke stood guard outside the cage door while Katrina and Fonzi stuffed money from the safe into a black rolling suitcase.

"That's all we need is for Sal Romano to find out we've been hustling him for nearly a year," Clarke offered from outside the cage. "You don't mess with a guy like that. He wasn't supposed to find out we've been posing as his caretakers. His men will make these gun happy assholes look like Boy Scouts."

"We'll be long gone before Romano ever finds out," Katrina announced and finished loading all the money into the rolling suitcase. "We need to get out of here before those men decide to eliminate us along with the others."

Clarke glanced into the cashier's cage as they zipped the bag. "Almost finished?" he demanded.

"Yeah, just keep your pants on," Fonzi growled.

Clarke turned to keep watch on his post. A woman's black booted foot struck him in the face. He was thrown backwards against the cage doorframe. His large body hit the frame with more force than anticipated. Jackie grimaced at her own strength. Zack grabbed Jackie by the hand and pulled her around the corner where both ducked beneath the first teller window. Jackie watched Katrina and

Fonzi run from the cashier's cage and look at their fallen man. Clarke attempted to stand with some unsteadiness. The two aimed their weapons and looked around. Jackie looked behind her. Zack was gone! She looked up to the cage window and the small opening beneath the bars. He couldn't possibly have fit through there! Could he? When she looked back to the armed caretakers, she saw Fonzi by the casino cage door. He was suddenly thrown across the floor. Katrina turned back for the doorway while raising her weapon. Jackie leaped around the corner, flicked both her tactical batons, and struck her on the arm, knocking the weapon from her hand. Her gun flew across the floor. Katrina barely knew what hit her when Jackie punched her in the face then kicked her in the side, sending her flying to the floor near Fonzi. Clarke returned to his feet just in time to see what was happening. Zack appeared from inside the cashier's cage and kicked Clarke in the back of the leg, sending him to his knee. Zack then spun in a roundhouse kick and struck him in the head, knocking him to the floor. Zack looked at Jackie and grinned.

"Nice quiet takedown," Zack announced cheerfully. "Better than bringing the entire cartel down on us."

Two men with assault rifles appeared in the main doorway and aimed their weapons at Jackie and Zack. She darted a glare at him.

"You were saying?" Jackie muttered as the men approached from several yards away.

"Thank God you're here," Zack suddenly announced, sounding like a frightened little boy then frantically pointed at the two men on the floor. "We stopped them from escaping. I'm Fonzi. I called you. You're the feds, right?"

Jackie held back her surprise to Zack's transformation into something resembling a frightened child. Zack placed his arm around Jackie's waist from behind and pulled her to his side.

"Katrina and I were so worried when we found out who they were," Zack continued with his act.

Jackie tensed as she felt the Glock in her waistband being removed from its holster. She could now feel the barrel against her side. She trusted Zack, but she wasn't sure she wanted him doing a hip shot from *her* hip.

"Nice try," the first man remarked while grinning, "but we know who you are. Drop the weapons nice and easy."

Jackie frowned and tossed her tactical batons to the floor. Zack rotated his shoulder, allowing the assault rifle with grenade launcher to fall from his shoulder and into the crook of his arm. He gently tossed it to the floor just a few feet away. While both men kept their attention focused on the falling rifle, Zack fired several rounds from Jackie's semiautomatic from alongside her hip. Both men took shots to their upper bodies and fell to the floor. Jackie exhaled and felt her legs nearly give out.

"Damn it, Zack," she gasped.

"Time to move," he announced and tugged on her.

Before he could retrieve his assault rifle, the doors burst open to reveal three more men. Jackie and Zack ran across the casino floor and behind the safety of a long row of slot machines. Zack returned her gun to her and removed his own semiautomatic as the men fired at them. Zack fired back, forcing them to take cover behind more slot machines.

"We're seriously outgunned here," Zack informed her. "What do you have on you?"

"Just this," she announced and indicated the semiautomatic she held. "And a full clip in my left holster."

"You're kidding?" he suddenly demanded. "I thought women always over packed?"

"I'm sorry," she snapped. "I lost my 'morning after' bag when I was jumping across five balconies nine stories up." She gave him a firm once over. "Where's your arsenal? I thought you had a gun in every pocket and orifice."

Zack rolled his eyes while frowning. "Jesus, you're crabby this morning," he scoffed. "How does Holden put up with your mood swings?" He fired several shots at the men, who attempted to move closer, then looked back at her. "I used up my pocketful of tricks saving your ass."

"Saving my ass?" she suddenly demanded. Jackie poked her head around the corner and shot one of the men in the arm. She returned to the safety of the slot machine and glared at him. "My ass didn't need saving!"

"Okay, let's save foreplay for the dojo," he announced. "We need to get our hands on a few of those weapons."

"Brilliant observation," Jackie remarked with irritation. Why was he telling her what she already knew? "Do you have a plan?"

"Yeah, but you won't like it."

"Try me," she snarled.

"First, take all your clothes off--"

Jackie glared at him.

Zack grinned boyishly. "We'll just call that one plan 'B'," he announced then casually pointed with his gun toward the ceiling, indicating the skylight above the men by the table games. "How about some ventilation?"

Jackie looked up at the skylight above the men then smiled at Zack. "I could use some fresh air."

Both aimed their guns at the skylight and shot several rounds into it. The glass shattered, surprising the men below. As the men looked up, large chucks of heavy glass crashed down upon them, impaling them with larger sections of thick glass. Zack raised his hand to Jackie. She grinned and slapped it. He caught her hand, pulled her forward, and kissed her quickly on the lips. Jackie pulled back and glared her disapproval. Zack chuckled softly and headed onto the glass covered casino floor near the table games. Jackie followed him. Both stopped and stared at the two men writhing beneath the blood covered glass erupting from their arms, legs, and midsections. Zack shook his head with disgust.

"I'm going to hate myself in the morning," he announced then casually shot the man in the head. Zack took a deep breath and sighed. "Much better."

Jackie looked around with concern. "Wait a minute," she announced. "I thought there was a third gunman."

Shots from an assault weapon were suddenly fired, causing both to duck. A tactical baton struck Jackie on the head from behind, dropping her to the floor as the gun fell from her hand. Zack turned with surprise. Clarke suddenly tackled him to the floor near the blackjack table and punched him with fast hard hits. When Clarke took a second to catch his breath while straightening, Zack punched him in the face, instantly breaking his nose. Clarke clutched his bleeding nose and fell backward with surprise. The gunman, who had fired the shots, ran toward them while shooting at Zack. Zack rolled across the floor as the bullets tore into the colorful, tacky carpet. He sprang to his feet and into a roundhouse kick, striking Clarke in the chest and sending him flying backwards into the gunman. Both men caught their balance and charged Zack, knocking him into the blackjack table.

Despite her aching head, Jackie reached for her discarded semiautomatic not far from where she kneeled. She heard a gun cocking above her. Jackie slowly looked up and saw Fonzi standing over her with a semiautomatic pointed at her face. He tossed her tactical baton aside. Out of the corner of her eye, she saw Zack was busy fighting both man several feet behind her near the blackjack table. Jackie placed her hands in the air and slowly straightened. Fonzi grinned cheaply at the live capture of his female prisoner.

"I think our new friends will be pleased that I was able to take you alive," Fonzi informed her then gave her a quick once over along with a lustful smile. "You and your friends caused a lot of trouble for us, you know."

Clarke was kicked in the chest and thrown away from Zack, who now fought the last man. Clarke saw his assault rifle lying on the floor just a few feet from where he landed. He then looked up and saw Fonzi with the gun aimed at Jackie and the telltale grin on his face.

"Idiot," Clarke cried out in anger. "Just shoot her! She's a sneaky bitch!"

Fonzi maintained his cheap grin and chose to ignore Clarke, who now scrambled for his discarded assault rifle.

"I'm going to enjoy teaching you a lesson," Fonzi informed Jackie then grabbed her by her ponytail, pulling her head back sharply. "We'll see how rough you like it."

Jackie sneered at the man holding her hair in his fist as she was forced to meet his gaze. "I do like it rough," she hissed softly then grinned. "Just remember; ladies first."

She grabbed his wrist holding the gun and bent it back. The force and pain caused him to release the gun and her hair. Jackie elbowed him in the nose then punched him in the crotch. He attempted to clutch himself as he fell to the floor. Clarke grabbed the discarded assault rifle and aimed it at her as she threw herself to the floor and grabbed the semiautomatic. Jackie rolled into a crouched position and shot Clarke in the chest. He appeared momentarily stunned by the shot then collapsed to the floor. Jackie moved to one knee and hovered over Fonzi. She rammed the barrel of the gun into his groin causing him to gasp with pain and mild horror. She glared into his eyes.

"Lesson number one," Jackie snarled. "Don't ever point a gun in a woman's face." She rammed the barrel of the gun deeper into his crotch, causing him to twitch and cry out. "Lesson number two; don't *ever* piss off a woman." She cocked her head to the side and smirked. "She's liable to shoot off your dick."

Zack grabbed the last man around the neck and held onto him. He saw the situation with Jackie and Fonzi and watched with enthusiastic anticipation. Fonzi sobbed while pleading for mercy. Jackie sneered and straightened. She kicked him in the head with disgust, knocking him out cold. Zack frowned, effortlessly snapped the man's neck, and tossed him aside without care while glaring at Jackie.

"You're such a little tease," Zack scoffed and shook his head. "You should have ripped his nuts off."

Jackie glared at Zack then rolled her eyes. "There's an image I don't want in my head."

Katrina bolted for the door with her rolling suitcase behind her. Jackie saw her, aimed her gun, and pulled the trigger. Nothing happened.

"Son-of-a-bitch," Jackie cried out then ran after Katrina.

It was almost sad watching Katrina attempt to run in her high heels while pulling a rolling suitcase behind her. Jackie tackled her to the floor just short of the door. Katrina's rolling suitcase continued out the door. Jackie landed on top the woman and punched her twice in the face as the door started to close. Jackie pulled Katrina to her feet then saw the pickup truck approaching from outside. She released Katrina, screamed, and dove away from the windows as the men fired at her. The windows took several shots. Katrina crawled out the door, since they weren't interested in her. She watched the black suitcase roll across the crude pavement toward the stopped truck. The four men leaped out of the pickup with their weapons prepared to fire. The suitcase full of money wasn't worth trusting the men not to shoot her. Katrina sprang to her feet and ran away from the casino and toward the safety of the woods. As the four heavily armed men ran into the casino through the glass doors, they prepared to shoot the first thing that moved. Apart from a few dead men on the floor, the casino seemed abandoned.

"I saw the woman," the first man announced. "She's in here somewhere." He gave a general nod.

The first man went right while the second went left. The two remaining men broke off and headed in opposite directions toward the back walls on either side of the game floor. The first two men walked down the large, open casino floor past the table games on either side. A black, five-hundred dollar chip rolled across the carpet , causing the first man to aim his assault rifle at it. He then looked around to assess where it came from. The second man walked along the opposite side lagging behind by a few feet, glancing into each aisle of slot machines to his left and at the tables on his right. He was tapped on the shoulder from behind. The man spun with his assault rifle aimed, but there was no one there. He turned just in time to see Zack's boot striking him in the face. As the man stumbled backwards, Zack kicked the rifle from his arms, knocking it across the floor.

The first man heard the assault in progress and turned with his rifle aimed. Jackie leaped over the blackjack table and kicked the man in the chest with both feet, sending him flying backwards and into the bank of slot machines across the floor. The machine lit up, made noise, and flashed as coins dropped rapidly into the tray.

"Great," Jackie scoffed and ran for the fallen man before the others were alerted.

She threw herself to the floor, snatching the assault rifle, and aimed it across the casino. To her surprise, the third man didn't arrive. She scanned the area with the assault rifle, prepared to fire. The third man then poked his head out from behind a bank of slot machines and fired at her. Jackie gasped and pulled the unconscious man alongside her in front of her. He took several shots, shredding his body as blood seemingly exploded from his chest. Jackie aimed her own assault rifle from behind the now dead man, and fired several rounds at the man across the casino. She struck him twice in the chest, tossing him against the slot machine. His bullet riddled body slid down the machine to the floor. She looked across the casino to see how Zack was doing. He had the first man in a chokehold while firing at the fourth man hidden within the aisles of slot machines. Jackie ran across the casino floor to assist Zack when she saw the man he held remove a small caliber semiautomatic from a hidden boot holster. He attempted to turn it behind him at Zack, who was unaware that the man now had a gun. Jackie didn't have a clean shot with Zack holding the man, and he'd never hear her over his own assault rifle fire.

Jackie ran for Zack before the man could take his shot. She spun into a kick for the captive man's head. He aimed the small gun at her instead and pulled the trigger. The gun fired and the bullet tore into her leg. She cried out with pain and at the sight of her own blood exploding from her leg. Jackie clutched her bleeding thigh as she was thrown backward against the table. Zack saw Jackie go down. He appeared stunned initially then enraged. Without hesitation, Zack snapped the man's neck, released him, and fired wildly into the slot machines, taking down the last man with more bullets than necessary. Zack ran to where Jackie sat against the blackjack table, fell to his knees alongside her, and assessed her injury. He applied pressure to the bleeding wound and stared at her.

"What were you thinking?" he suddenly demanded while searching her eyes.

Jackie gasped in agony and glared back at him. "I was thinking about saving your ass, idiot."

Chapter Forty

Bogart continued to pace the loading dock before the open bay doors while Ross remained near some crates with the girls. Darth looked at the main entrance and snarled softly. Bogart and the girls instinctively looked at the doors. Ross motioned Bogart to take cover. Bogart barely made it behind the crate alongside them when the doors opened. Several men with automatic weapons entered with a mission to shoot anything that moved. Ross and Bogart waited until the men were unprotected in the center of the large bay before firing at them. The men attempted to dive for cover while firing back. Monique and Colleen crouched on the floor behind the crate and clung to the dog. Darth watched the action and seemed unaware of the girls clinging to him. More men filtered into the room and fired at them. Tremaine and Hoffman brought up the rear and immediately took cover, allowing the other men to do a majority of the dirty work.

Ross glanced behind him then looked at Bogart. "Out the bay door," he ordered softly. "Take the girls through the kitchen door and make your way to the casino. We can see them coming through the glass doors."

"What about you?" Bogart asked with surprise.

"I'll hold them off as long as I can," Ross replied.

Bogart wasn't pleased by his orders. He gathered the girls and positioned them by the bay doors.

"On Ross's signal," Bogart informed them. "We take this party to the kitchen just a few yards to the right."

Both girls uncertainly nodded.

"Darth too?" Monique asked in a timid voice.

Bogart glanced at Ross. He nodded.

"Darth too," Bogart replied while forcing a smile.

"On my signal," Ross announced then stood and rapidly fired at the men hiding behind crates.

Bogart hurried the girls from the loading bay doors down to the ground two feet below. Darth leaped the ledge and joined them. They ran around the side to the kitchen door. Ross took cover once they were clear. Tremaine nudged Hoffman and indicated the open bay door.

"I'm sure our kids went that way," Tremaine informed him.

Hoffman tapped the man next to him. "The rest of you finish off that one," he announced then touched his ear transmitter as he followed Tremaine to the main door. "I need every available man inside the hotel to meet me in the kitchen corridor."

Both men left the loading dock. Ross remained hidden behind his crate and frowned at the enormous amount of gunfire. A pickup truck approached the open bay door. Ross glanced behind him at the approaching truck and groaned softly.

"From bad to worse," he muttered.

Beck and Kirk dove out of the truck and fired rapidly into the loading dock, hitting several men as they joined Ross. Ross grinned at his men.

"Why must you cut it so close?"

"We like to make a dramatic entrance," Beck teased.

†

The helicopter zipped along the countryside with Gil at the stick. Monroe sat in the back within the open doorway, tethered to the floor with a cable attached to the harness he wore. He fired out the open side door at the enemy helicopter in hot pursuit. Two men fired back at them out the side of the pursuing helicopter. With Gil's maneuvering, they were avoiding most of the gunfire, but their assailants were closing the gap. Monroe looked back at Gil behind the controls.

"Those shots are starting to get close," Monroe announced to Gil through his affixed headset. "You'd better think of something amazing and do it fast."

"I'm working on it," Gil remarked with annoyance. "I'm better with a plane than I am with a helo. You want high-flying fun, fly Jackie's friendly skies!" Gil banked sharply, nearly toppling Monroe onto the seat. He hadn't been expecting the maneuver. "Why don't you help out a little by shooting those bastards?"

"You're not Jackie, and I'm not Zack," Monroe launched back. "I'm not real keen on heights or shooting from them."

"Yeah? Well, how do you feel about crashing from them?" Gil demanded.

Monroe sneered then leaned out the doorway and fired at the helicopter gaining on them. He shot one of the men leaning out the opening. The man tumbled from the open doorway and plummeted to the ground while screaming the entire way. Monroe grimaced, possibly envisioning his own fate.

"That's gotta hurt."

Gil banked to the left. Monroe lost his footing and fell from the opening. He cried out until the cable became taunt, stopping his fall. He was left dangling by the cable nearly twenty feet beneath the helicopter. Monroe screamed as he was towed through the air while frantically grasping for the cable. Gil looked out the window and groaned softly.

"Great, now I've got wind drag," he muttered.

Monroe spun around out of control on the cable attached to his harness. He attempted to keep a hold of his assault rifle while reaching for the cable as he twirled around in a circle. The entire time, the man in the second helicopter was shooting at him. Fortunately, being he was a spinning target, he was harder to hit. Monroe finally caught the cable and straightened himself. He raised his assault rifle, clenched his teeth, and fired back at the shooter while yelling like a madman. The remaining shooter took a bullet to the chest and fell back onto the seat. Monroe clung to the cable attached to his harness and wildly pointed with his assault rifle while screaming at the pursuing helicopter.

"There's more where that came from, you bastard!"

Monroe fired wildly at the helicopter that now attempted to get closer to him. It was possible the helicopter pilot wanted to get beneath him and slice him with the rotors. When he realized what the pilot was attempting, Monroe slung his assault rifle over his shoulder and cried out while frantically climbing the cable. The enemy helicopter flew beneath him and lifted upward. Monroe scrambled into the safety of his own helicopter and looked at the enemy helicopter several yards beneath them.

"Oh, you wanna play?" Monroe cried out. "I'll play!"

Monroe threw his assault rifle from the back and down upon the rotating blades beneath them. Gil cried out and veered sharply away from the enemy helicopter. The rotors caught the assault rifle. The horrific sound of metal chewing through metal could be heard even above the sounds of their own helicopter. Monroe stared out the side and watched as the rotors were torn from the craft, sending it spiraling downward. The enemy helicopter crashed into some rocks and exploded on impact. Monroe thrust his arms outward, revealing both middle fingers to the fiery inferno below. He caught his breath and collapsed against the seat.

"You know, I could be at my beach house soaking up some sun and getting plastered right about now," Monroe remarked with a groan.

"And yet you're always the first one to answer Ross's call to duty," Gil replied and cast a look back at Monroe with a mocking smile. His look then turned serious as he touched his headset. "I'm getting a transmission from Ross." He again looked back at Monroe, who now sat forward with a curious look on his face. "Loading dock evac has been scratched now as well. Too many hostiles hanging around. Do you have more weapons back there? We can offer some air support until they find a new evac site."

Monroe routed around within a duffel bag. "Yeah, I've got plenty of weapons and ammo." He cocked an assault rifle. "Let's circle the compound and see how many rats we can pick off."

†

*K*atrina ran through the woods, stumbling over tree roots and rocks in her less than desirable high heels. She finally stopped by a tree to catch her breath. The sounds of gunfire at the casino now almost a mile away had nearly silenced. She had covered a lot of ground in a short period of time considering her footwear. She shut her eyes and allowed her head to fall back against the tree while attempting to control her heavy breathing. The sound of a rifle cocking jolted her back into reality. Katrina stared at the barrel of an assault rifle directly in her face. She looked at Betty on the other end of the weapon, her finger tightly on the trigger. Betty grinned in a mildly psychotic manner.

"Now," Betty announced pleasantly to the once attractive, exhausted woman, "I think it's time you and I had a little talk."

Chapter Forty-one

$\mathcal{J}$ackie felt the sharp, hot pain shooting through her leg. The pain was so intense; she could almost feel herself about to black out. She sat rigid on the blackjack table alongside an industrial sized first aid kit kindly provided by Sal's casino. Zack, armed with a tweezers, dug inside the bullet wound on her outer thigh while catching as much blood as possible with a blood-soaked gauze pad. She pinched her eyes shut and held back her scream while gripping the foam edge of the table. Zack tried to convince her to lie down, but she admitted she was too stubborn to listen. Once he stopped digging with the blood-covered tweezers, she panted heavily. The agonizing pain was a welcomed relief to the excruciating pain Zack had been inflicting.

"Got it," he announced with a soft sigh.

Jackie opened her eyes and looked at the bloodied bullet between the equally bloodied tweezers. He tossed the tweezers aside and flushed the wound with a bottle of wound wash. She gasped softly, although the pain wasn't nearly as bad as it had been a minute ago. As he applied carefully cut strips of tape across her wound to hold it together, Zack cast several glances at her with a look she couldn't read. He wasn't mocking her pain. His look was almost sympathetic. Since he wasn't really the type to provide sympathy, his look was slightly troubling. He returned to patching her wound and avoided looking at her. Jackie felt a slight pang of concern sweep through her. She knew what happened when the guys became too attached. They started worrying about her, which allowed them opportunity to screw up. Maybe Holden had been right but not for the reason he'd given. Perhaps the team was better off without her. She didn't need the guys jeopardizing their lives because they were worried about her safety.

Zack placed a thick padding overtop the carefully patched wound, taped it securely to her thigh, and then straightened. He looked at her then frowned as he gently brushed the sweated hair from her forehead. His hand remained on her temple as his thumb touched her cheek. He again stared into her eyes with that hard to read expression. Jackie had never seen that look in his eyes before and felt compelled to stare back. It was possibly the longest she'd ever stared into Zack's eyes. For the first time in her life, she swore she saw into his soul. Although he never showed it, he cared. He cared too much. She somehow knew he'd be the first one to end up dead because of her, and the thought was frightening.

She looked away while tensing and subconsciously brushed his hand from her face. "I'm fine," she muttered softly. "We should get going."

"You're not fine," Zack informed her. "You can barely walk."

Jackie suddenly glared at him with unfounded hostility. "Don't think for one second about carrying me, Zachariah. I *will* hurt you."

"As much fun as that sounds, I'll have to pass," Zack replied, almost relieved to bury his emotions. "Ross just gave us our new orders. The extraction is happening just outside the game floor." He indicated the set of glass doors marked with bullet holes toward the back. "Gil's circling with the helicopter now. Once Bogart arrives with the girls, we'll only have a few minutes to make it to the extraction point before the guys in the trucks realize where the helicopter is landing."

Jackie glared at him with distrust. "Bogart is bringing the girls here?" she asked demandingly and raised her brow. "You're not just bullshitting me so I won't go after them."

Zack offered a humored smile and patted her good leg. "No bullshitting, darling," he informed her. "They're on their way, so let's get you positioned by that door. I'll cover your lovely little ass so no one shoots it."

She rolled her eyes at the comment and attempted to move off the table. It was harder than she anticipated, but she didn't want to admit she was in a lot of pain. Zack attempted to help her, but she resisted, causing her to lose her balance and fall to the floor. She cringed in agony. Zack stared at her a moment with a raised brow. *Now* he was mocking her. He extended his hand to her. She reluctantly accepted his hand. He easily pulled her to her feet. Jackie attempted to limp across the game room floor, but the pain was unbearable. It was almost worse than when Zack had been digging around for the bullet. Zack cut off her path and faced her. It wasn't as if she could do much to remove him either. His look was commanding.

"Look, I can either carry you military style or "An Officer and a Gentleman" style," he announced simply. "The choice is yours, but I *am* carrying you."

Jackie groaned softly and placed her arm around Zack's neck, submitting to his will. He easily scooped her up into his arms and carried her toward the glass doors. She didn't look at him, but she could feel his smirk burning into her skin.

He softly sang, "Where the eagles cry; on a mountain high."

She felt stupid, and there was no doubt she intended to hit him at some later date. They were halfway to the back glass doors when the main casino doors burst open. Zack spun while releasing Jackie's legs, although keeping his arm around her waist to balance her, and aimed his gun at the door. As Jackie's feet hit the floor, her gun was in her free hand aimed in the same direction. Bogart, the two girls, and Darth ran through the doors. Bogart stopped to bolt the doors with the floor and ceiling bolts then frantically motioned to the girls with his gun. Both girls ran across the casino and hid. Bogart saw Jackie and Zack halfway across the room. He motioned wildly with his gun.

"Take cover! Now!" he cried out. "They're right behind us!"

Bogart ran for cover. A split second later, there was a tremendous bang against the door. Zack whisked Jackie off her feet and carried her behind a bank of slot machines. He set her down, where she immediately allowed herself to drop to her knees while taking aim at the door. When she looked back, Zack was already gone. She looked up and saw his boots disappear over the bank of slot machines. That he managed to scale the wall of slot machines so stealth-like amazed her. If he ever officially retired from the team, he'd make a great cat burglar. Judging by the sounds coming from the right side of the room, Bogart had managed to lock the second set of doors as well. Men could be heard attempting to break through both sets of doors. The main doors cracked and flew open. Four men spilled into the room under a steady stream of bullets, allowing them to seek cover before Jackie or Bogart could even get off a shot. The glass doors to the back shattered under gunfire and more men spilled onto the casino floor from the rear.

As Jackie fired at random men barely poking out from behind slot machines, she was wishing she had her assault rifle now more than ever. Jackie heard a metallic clatter at the end of the aisle nearly fifty feet behind her. She looked down the aisle to see a man rounding the corner, his weapon hitting the edge of the slot machine. She spun around and aimed her semiautomatic at the man. A booted foot flew out from the end machine and struck the man in the chest. He was thrown across the aisle and into the opposing slot machine. Zack took one quick step across the aisle, spun into a roundhouse kick, and struck the man in the face. The man struck the machine hard. Zack grabbed the guy's head and, with one fluid motion, snapped his neck, allowing his lifeless body to drop. Zack casually snatched the discarded assault rifle, took a few steps closer, and tossed the weapon to Jackie. She caught the rifle and stared at Zack with surprise.

He grinned his pleasure. "Thought you might want one of those."

Before she could respond, he disappeared around the back of the aisle. That he had read her mind was scary enough. What really frightened her was that they apparently thought alike. The last thing she wanted was to be like Zack. The armed men from the glass doors started making their way closer, closing in on them. Jackie fired several shots at them, but she couldn't slow their approach even with the assault rifle.

On the other side of the casino floor, Bogart had his hands full shooting at the men making their way closer from the main entrance. The casino floor was now filled with the almost deafening sound of automatic weapon fire. Monique and Colleen clung to Darth while backing themselves into a corner, remaining close to the floor to avoid stray gunshots. Both watched Bogart fire at the men attempting to gain ground. The side door suddenly broke open and two more men filtered into the room with their weapons raised. Both girls screamed on cue. Darth pulled free from them and ran for the men with the guns while snarling viciously. As he leaped for the first man, the man fired at the dog, hitting him directly in the chest. Darth yelped while being thrown back to the floor where he lie motionless. Both girls again screamed while staring at the fallen war hero. As the men aimed their guns at the girls, Colleen suddenly cracked her bullwhip at the first man, catching him around the neck. She gave a firm yank using her entire body and pulled him off his feet. Bogart realized what was happening behind him and turned with his weapon raised.

The second man was about to shoot the girls despite his snagged partner. Darth suddenly leaped through the air and tackled him to the floor, viciously tearing into his shoulder. The man screamed as his blood was slung across the room by the viciousness of the attack. He hadn't considered that the dog was wearing a bulletproof vest, and he was only momentarily stunned by the chest shot. The man Colleen had snagged removed the bullwhip from around his neck where he remained kneeling on the floor and reached for his discarded assault rifle. Bogart shot the man multiple times, sending him the rest of the way to the floor in a bloody heap. Both girls screamed. Darth released the man on the floor, allowing Bogart to stand over him and shoot him between the eyes with his semiautomatic. When the blood sprayed across the floor, the girls were shockingly silent. A man appeared at the end of their aisle. The girls screamed and pointed. Bogart spun around and fired at the man, who now took cover.

Agents Tremaine and Hoffman entered through the broken side door with their semiautomatics in their hands. The girls saw the familiar men and gasped with horror. Monique fumbled with the semiautomatic she'd stuffed down the back of her pants. Zack suddenly appeared and kicked Tremaine in the face. He spun for the return kick and knocked the gun from Hoffman's hands. As Tremaine recovered, Zack punched him in the throat then kicked him in the chest. He pivoted on a hard angle and kicked the Hoffman in the head, dropping him to his knees.

At the other end of the aisle, Bogart finally got a lock on his target and fired several shots into the man seeking shelter behind the last slot machine. Bogart returned to the girls, shocked to see Zack had arrived on the scene. Darth watched Zack beating the two dirty agents and anxiously awaited to be tapped into the fight. While Hoffman was still on his knees, Zack grabbed him around the neck. Bogart gasped and covered both girls' eyes as Zack effortlessly broke Hoffman's neck. Despite the heavy gunfire within the casino, the sound of his neck snapping was almost deafening. Zack removed his knife from his boot and stabbed Tremaine through his eye. As he pulled the knife free, blood poured from Tremaine's eye socket and he collapsed to the floor.

Bogart removed his hands from the girls' eyes. Both girls saw the blood quickly pooling around Tremaine's head from his bleeding eye and cried out with horror. Zack wiped the remains of the man's eyeball onto the dead man's shirt before replacing his knife to his boot. Monique and Colleen gasped and nearly gagged. Bogart grabbed the girls and hurried them to the end of the aisle while Zack barricaded the door. Bogart looked past the slot machines to the main casino floor and fired at more men, who were attempting to move closer. From her position on the opposite side, Jackie had finally been successful at keeping the remaining men at bay.

Ross, Kirk, and Beck appeared in the back, entering through the broken glass doors, and took out the approaching men, who never saw them coming. Ross gave the signal, and even though Jackie didn't have a working transmitter, she knew he gave the order to evacuate the girls. The entire team concentrated a steady stream of fire on the men, keeping them behind shelter from the barrage of bullets while Monique and Colleen made their run for the broken glass doors. Bogart brought up the rear, firing wildly behind him. With the loud gunfire, the helicopter was barely heard approaching. Jackie attempted to straighten despite the pain then realized Zack was crouching alongside her.

"Time to go," Zack announced cheerfully.

Jackie eyed him then vigorously shook her head. "I can't make it that far," she informed him. "I'm a slow moving target. You certainly can't carry me and expect either of us to make it out in one piece."

"I had no intention on carrying you," he announced then grinned as he straightened to reveal the electric scooter sitting in the aisle just behind him. He seemed overly pleased with himself. "Do you want to drive or ride shotgun?"

Jackie suddenly grinned, feeling slightly giddy at the idea. "I'm riding shotgun."

Zack handed her the assault rifle containing the grenade launcher from over his shoulder. He'd managed to recover his new toy. "Then you're going to want this."

She eagerly accepted the grenade launcher and looked it over with a gleam in her eyes. And the transformation was complete. She'd officially become Zack.

"And, Jackie," he announced as he firmly placed his hand on her shoulders and looked deep into her eyes. A sly grin crossed his face. "Smoke those fuckers."

Jackie grinned in response. Zack jumped onto the scooter seat while Jackie placed her knee on the arm and, despite the pain, she put her other foot on the battery pack on the back. Zack kept his free arm around her waist to hold her steady then squeezed the power on the handle. The scooter launched from the aisle with more speed than Jackie would have thought possible. The team again fired vigorously at the guys across the casino floor to keep them from firing at the scooter with Jackie half propped and half clinging to the back. She fired a grenade across the casino floor and straight for a large cluster of men. They barely had time to leap from its path before it exploded on impact, tearing apart the casino floor and the men in its path. Jackie wasn't prepared for the body parts raining down upon the rest of the casino, but she couldn't let that interfere with their escape. She fired another across the room as Zack jetted the scooter for the broken glass doors. Ross, Kirk, and Beck fired randomly as they ran backwards for the opening after the scooter. The second grenade no sooner exploded, taking out an entire bank of slot machines, when Jackie fired a third grenade. With the third grenade, a majority of the men were blown up with it, taking out most of the table games. The casino floor was left in shambles with blood and body parts scattered everywhere.

Just outside, the helicopter lowered twenty yards from the shattered exit. Bogart tossed the girls into the helicopter as it hovered then helped Zack with Jackie into the co-pilot's seat. Trucks were heard approaching along with gunfire. Beck and Kirk jumped into the back of the helicopter and took positions at the open doors. They fired on the approaching trucks. Another helicopter was barely heard in the near distance. Ross and Zack stood just outside the helicopter and looked to the sky. The approaching helicopter soon came into view. Zack grabbed the discarded grenade launcher from the scooter seat and aimed it at the helicopter. He suddenly hesitated, surprising Ross. Zack quickly lowered his weapon.

"It says Romano Enterprises on the side," Zack announced with surprise.

Two men from the helicopter fired at the trucks with high-powered, military grade assault weapons. One of the trucks exploded on impact. The trucks made sharp turns and raced away from both helicopters. Several black federal SUVs and sedans containing Sal's men drove around the side of the building and chased after the trucks. As Romano's helicopter lowered, Jackie climbed out of the co-pilot's seat. She clung to the side of the helicopter and watched Romano's helicopter land. Holden and Blake jumped out of the helicopter. Jackie felt her entire body sag with relief. She had never been so happy to see Holden in her life! She attempted to run to him, although she mostly limped while clutching her leg. It felt as if her leg would snap in two, but she didn't care. Holden ran to her and gathered her in his arms. He held her against him, nearly smothering her. She felt compelled to sob on his shoulder but resisted. She groaned softly while clinging to him as if she'd never let go. Both girls saw Blake outside the second helicopter and became excited.

"Dad!" Monique cried out.

Monique leaped from the helicopter, ran for her father, and jumped into his arms. Blake held his daughter while nearly down to tears. Colleen joined them in the embrace. A slightly robust man in his mid-forties, Salvatore Romano, climbed out of the helicopter's co-pilot seat and approached the team. Sal had a baby face and moderately balding head, which gave him an innocent appeal. Although dressed casually neat, his clothes were expensive and in good taste. Beck smiled and extended his hand to Sal. Sal took his hand then immediately pulled him against him for a manly embrace. He pulled away while grinning then approached Ross while staring at his smoldering casino floor through the broken glass doors. His smile faded as he shook his head and sighed.

"You're the worst houseguest, Ross," Sal announced and patted him on the back as part of the ceiling caved in. Sal managed a tiny smile and eyed Ross. "The absolute worst."

Chapter Forty-two

$\mathcal{M}$onique and Colleen hugged Bogart, swarming the country boy with tearful goodbyes where they stood just outside the shattered casino doors not far from Jackie's helicopter. Bogart was a little misty-eyed himself, although he put on a tough act. The girls pulled away from him and wiped their eyes as they forced smiles.

"Will we ever see you again?" Colleen asked while fighting her tears.

"You never know, Squirt," he replied with only a hint of a smile, because he knew that day would probably never come.

"Promise you will," Monique insisted as she sniffed softly. She apparently knew it would be an empty promise.

"You've got it, Twinkie," he replied.

They hugged him again then reluctantly headed toward Blake and some of the guys by one of the many federal vehicles. Bogart secretly dabbed his eyes and looked away. Something then caught his attention. He cast a sideways glance at the oddly placed black rolling suitcase where it sat not far from the helicopter. The girls approached Blake and impatiently waited near the black SUV while he talked with Sal, Ross, and Beck.

"The girls are no longer in danger then?" Ross asked while folding his arms across his chest, again taking a broad stance.

"The traitors within the Bureau have been apprehended," Blake informed them. "The only ones who wanted them eliminated are in body bags thanks to you, so they're safe." He eyed Ross with humor and chuckled softly. "And your reputations have also been restored."

"Well," Beck teased while hiding his grin, "what was left of our reputations."

Beck's cell phone vibrated in his pocket. He removed the cell phone, pressed a button, and glanced at the picture of him dressed as a sexy schoolgirl. He casually replaced his phone, eyed the men, and offered a polite smile.

"You're going to need one more body bag," Beck announced with little emotion. "Excuse me."

Beck left the men and began his search for Gil. Blake inhaled deeply then smiled at Ross and extended his hand. Ross accepted his hand and shook it.

"Thanks again, Ross. For everything." He glanced at the girls leaning against the SUV with their arms folded across their chests. Both stared at him with the same impatient look. "I, uh, should get the girls back to their mothers," Blake informed him. "I'll have your money for you when I see you again."

Ross nodded and added a tiny smile. "Anytime you need anything, you know how to reach us."

"You can count on that," Blake replied then escorted the girls into the awaiting vehicle.

Alongside the helicopter, Bogart took a step closer to the suitcase, unzipped it, and peered inside. His eyes suddenly widened. He quickly zipped the bag and darted looks around the area to see if anyone was looking. He stepped in front of the suitcase and kept it hidden behind him while rolling it toward the awaiting helicopter. He paused near the bottom storage compartment, looked around, and then opened the compartment. As he reached for the suitcase, he saw Zack standing over him, glaring his disapproval. Bogart frowned and straightened. Zack turned his back to the compartment, slipped a duffel bag off his shoulder, and then turned and stuffed it into the compartment. Bogart stared with surprise then saw the muzzle of a grenade launcher sticking out of the overstuffed bag. Bogart grinned then stuffed the suitcase into the compartment along with Zack's newly found toys. It seemed Bogart and Zack each had their priorities. Bogart quietly closed the door while keeping his back to it and maintained an innocent appearance alongside Zack.

"You know," he announced to Zack. "The plane would have been closer to stash your coveted toys."

"Yeah," Zack replied with a sigh. "It's a little full already."

Bogart shook his head and chuckled softly.

Not far from the broken casino doors, Ross watched Sal assess the excessive damage to his casino floor.

"I don't suppose my hotel looks any better," Sal muttered while shaking his head.

"I sort of doubt it," Ross replied then inhaled a deep breath and straightened proudly. "So, about that favor--?"

Sal groaned, rubbed his weary eyes, and looked back at Ross. "Haven't you used up just about all your favors already?"

"Perhaps," Ross replied while grinning, "but it's just a small one. Besides, you have to admit, it could be fun."

Sal considered the comment then smirked and nodded. "All right, Ross," he announced in a jovial tone. "Count me in."

Ross chuckled, slapped Sal on the back, and walked him to his awaiting helicopter. Kirk, Monroe, and Bogart joined Ross and Sal. Gil argued with Beck over his broken cell phone as they joined the others. They saw the guys looking across the back property and felt compelled to look as well. The tension was thick as an odd silence fell over the men. Nearly twenty yards away, they watched Jackie where she sat on the ambulance tailgate while a paramedic checked her injured leg. Holden leaned against the side of the ambulance with his arms across his chest and a scowl on his face while watching the paramedic unwrap her wound.

"We really screwed the pooch this time," Kirk muttered with disgust and walked away.

Darth tilted his head and looked at Kirk, almost as if understanding the comment. Gil patted the dog reassuringly.

"Don't worry, buddy," Gil announced affectionately. "You're safe."

"He's never letting us near her again," Monroe remarked while frowning as he watched the couple by the ambulance.

"If only she hadn't gotten hurt--" Gil announced softly and shook his head while crouched alongside Darth. A frown crossed his face. "--again."

"Don't say anything in front of Zack," Ross suddenly warned and glared at the guys. "She took that hit for him. He's never going to forgive himself as it is."

"Where is Zack anyway?" Beck asked and looked around.

None of the others bothered looking.

"He disappeared the moment Holden showed up," Monroe replied while sighing. "I don't think he could face him after what happened to Jackie on his watch."

Bogart appeared interested in the comment. Although it sounded plausible, only Bogart knew that Zack was undoubtedly on a scavenger hunt for more weapons.

Over by the ambulance, the paramedic looked at Jackie's injury carefully taped together with thin strips of tape, mimicking stitches. The paramedic visually examined the injury then met Jackie's gaze.

"And the bullet was removed?" he asked.

Jackie nodded. The paramedic snorted a soft laugh while hiding his smile.

"That has to be the nicest home patch job I've seen in a long time," the paramedic announced. "I think we can just patch that up until you get to the hospital for stitches."

He placed a clean, thick pad on the wound and taped it in place. Jackie glanced at the paramedic as he finished his work and offered a tiny smile.

"Can I have a few minutes before we leave for the hospital?" she asked.

The paramedic nodded, collected his equipment, and headed toward one of the injured men handcuffed by the police car. Jackie inhaled deeply and looked at Holden as he joined her on the tailgate of the ambulance.

"I know you want to be mad at Ross and the guys," she informed him gently, "but I could have said no."

"I know," Holden replied and placed his arm around her shoulder, pulling her to his side.

"I understand if you don't want me doing anymore missions with them," she remarked and pulled away to meet his gaze, "but they're my father's team; his friends." She then hesitated and replied more softly, "They're my friends. I won't stop seeing them on a purely social basis. They're the only family I have." She hesitated and considered the comment. "At least that I know about."

"I know that too," Holden replied then inhaled deeply while staring into her eyes. He affectionately touched her face, offered a tiny smile, and indicated her injured leg. "Who removed the bullet and patched your wound?"

"Zack," she replied and managed a soft laugh. "He's had years of experience with meatball surgery in the field. Even on himself."

Holden sighed and gently took her hand, squeezing it. "I know how much the guys mean to you, Jackie," he informed her, "but you know how much you mean to me too, right?"

"Of course," Jackie replied. "That's why I'm choosing you over them. I don't want to ever lie to you again because they put me in that position."

He nodded with understanding. "I am glad to hear that," Holden replied then gently kissed her hand. He straightened and inhaled deeply with dread. "I guess the only middle ground here would be if I went along on those missions with you."

Jackie stared at Holden with surprise. She couldn't believe what she was hearing. "What?" she practically gasped.

"I know I'm not Ross's idea of a competent team member, but, hell, if Bogart can do it--"

She could barely contain her emotions and threw her arms around his neck, hugging him.

"Thank you, Holden," she gasped softly. "Thank you for giving me my family."

Jackie pulled back and kissed him passionately. He returned the kiss, almost reluctant to break it off. Holden pulled away and hid his smile.

"We should probably get you to the hospital," Holden announced gently.

"I can fly myself," Jackie replied. "Besides, someone has to take the helicopter back and someone has to fly Gil's plane." She grimaced slightly then muttered softly, "You know he's not getting his rental deposit back on that one."

"Should you really be flying?"

"We'll find out," she teased then smiled lovingly at him. "Will you be my co-pilot?"

"I always am."

Holden helped her to her feet. She leaned on him as they headed toward the guys. Ross jolted the guys with his elbow and indicated Jackie's telltale grin. The men laughed and relaxed, because they understood what that meant. Holden glanced at Jackie and cleverly raised his brows.

"Are there any other surprises you'd like to tell me about now that we're working on a clean slate?" Holden asked in a slightly stern tone.

Jackie tensed and stopped Holden halfway to the helicopter. She grimaced then attempted a smile.

"There is one small incident I should probably tell you about," she informed him gently.

"Does this have anything to do with the guy camping out in our house?"

She smiled weakly. "Oh, you met Othello," Jackie muttered softly. "No, but I'll probably need to explain that as well. This has to do with something that happened on one of our missions, but it's not a big deal."

His look turned tense as if not believing that it wasn't a big deal. "What is it?" he asked while attempting to sound casual but severely missed the mark.

"Well, a month ago, on our last mission," Jackie began then hesitated.

Holden's expression didn't improve. "You mean the last time you got shot?" he muttered.

"Yeah," she replied and grimaced. "It didn't exactly happen the way I said it did."

Holden eyed her with some surprise then squinted. "What *did* happen?"

She offered a timid smile. "When the guard got the slip on me, I took him down. Unfortunately, Bogart thought he was saving my life, and he accidentally shot me."

Holden's expression suddenly dropped. Jackie quickly touched his chest and attempted to smooth over the blow.

"In his defense, he would have shot the guy if I hadn't been taking him down myself," she announced quickly. "It was just inexperience on Bogart's behalf. I assure you, the guys haven't let him live it down."

Holden forced a smile, patted her hand, and nodded. "I understand," he announced gently.

"You do?" Jackie asked with surprise then let out a soft laugh. "That's such a relief."

"I'm going to punch him, but I totally understand."

✝

*I*t was late evening and the woods almost half a mile from the casino were nearly dark. Lilly casually leaned against the jeep fender and stared off into the woods while listening to the sounds of crickets and other creatures.

"Pretty quiet now, huh?" Lilly remarked.

"Yeah, but I suppose the police will be hanging out at the casino for days sorting out that mess," Betty replied from somewhere nearby.

Lexie and Kathy walked past Lilly by the jeep and approached the back.

"Think the cute guys won that battle?" Lexie asked, secretly hiding her smile. She was possibly revisiting her encounter with the brawny Kirk.

Betty approached the jeep fender not far from Lilly and watched her daughters.

"Who knows," Betty casually replied with a sigh. "I just wish we could have taken a few of those weapons from the back of that truck."

"Why didn't we?" Kathy asked from the rear of the jeep.

"Because, they may have noticed some were missing and then they'd come looking for us," Betty informed her daughter. "We don't need no feds poking into our business."

Kathy and Lexie carried a woman's body wrapped in a tarp from the back of the jeep and toward the freshly dug pit. The see-through tarp revealed blood smeared along the inside. Katrina's hideous high heels stuck out beyond the tarp. The girls dropped her into the pit without care. Betty approached the tractor with the attached frontend loader, climbed in, and started it. Kathy and Lexie joined Lilly by the jeep and watched as Betty filled in the pit.

"Seems a shame to fill in the pit with only one body," Lilly remarked to her sisters. "Why aren't we waiting until it's filled like the other?"

"Too many feds buzzing around," Kathy replied simply. "They may start snooping around out here."

"Besides," Lexie announced with a dreary sigh, "with the casino in the shape it was in, I doubt there'll be any more visitors for a long time."

Kathy frowned at the comment. "No more men with large wades of cash coming and going," she remarked and leaned her elbow on the jeep. "We'll need to find another way to earn money, I suppose."

Lilly frowned. "Well, that sucks."

Chapter Forty-three

$\mathcal{T}$wo days later. Not far from the old ghost town, the herd of nearly one hundred wild horses galloped across the open fields and toward the hilltop just before the abandoned ghost town. Six men on four wheelers chased the running horses for the hill. They screamed and yelled at the horses while sounding air horns to keep them running scared. The horses ran up the hill and disappeared on the other side. As the four wheelers approached the base of the hill, the sound of a cracking whip was heard. All six men immediately stopped their four wheelers and stared at the hillside.

"That can't be," one man cried out.

The horses returned over the top of the hill and ran back down, veering to the right to avoid the parked men on the four wheelers. They watched the running horses then looked back to the peak. Monique and Colleen stopped their horses on top of the hill. Colleen cracked her whip, allowing the last of the horses to run down the hill. Both girls made their horses rear up while giving the men below the middle finger. Monique cried out gleefully and sent her horse into a full gallop down the hill. Colleen cracked her whip and chased after her friend.

"Son-of-a-bitch," the first man shouted with anger. "Get those damned kids! I want those horses back!"

The six men on four wheelers chased after the girls on their horses just behind the racing herd. The horses ran up another hillside with the girls in hot pursuit and disappeared over the other side. As the men started up the hill, a helicopter suddenly appeared from the other side. Sal was positioned in the open side doorway. He fired rounds from his automatic weapon at the men on four wheelers. He laughed with glee while aiming mostly at the ground in front of their vehicles. The men turned their ATVs and raced back toward the ghost town. Sal stopped firing and motioned to his pilot. The helicopter turned and flew after the girls and the horses, escorting them back to their sanctuary.

The men on the four wheelers raced over the hill and headed into the ghost town where a makeshift coral and a livestock tractor-trailer awaited. All six men suddenly stopped their ATVs on the main road of the abandoned ghost town. Four men dressed in cowboy boots, hats, and leather duster coats stood in the middle of the street awaiting their arrival. They had cigars clenched in their teeth and six-shooters strapped to their hips and tied around their thighs. Ross grinned through the cigar pinched between his teeth.

"There's a new sheriff in town," Ross announced then glanced at Kirk, Beck, and Monroe standing in a line alongside him. "No one touches those horses or those girls."

All four men tossed their duster coats away from their hips to reveal the old western revolvers in holsters strapped to their legs. The six men on the four wheelers quickly did the math, apparently felt confident, and revealed their semiautomatics in shoulder holsters. There was an odd metallic clanging behind them. Three of the men uncertainly looked behind them. Bogart, dressed like Clint Eastwood with poncho and all, walked across the street behind them, his spurs clattering with each step. He held a shotgun over his shoulder and clenched a stubby cigar between his teeth. He grinned charmingly as Gil, Jackie, and Holden lined up alongside him, dressed the part of western gunslingers.

"I think your poaching days have just ended, boys," Ross informed the men.

All six men slowly raised their hands in the air, giving up. A loud explosion rocked the ghost town, startling everyone except Jackie and Ross. Ross rolled his eyes, groaned, and looked behind him at the torn apart inferno of what was once the tractor-trailer. Zack, dressed in his usual black commando gear, leaned against the porch support beam of the old saloon not far from the inferno and lit his cigar. Darth sat alongside him proudly wearing a blue bandanna tied around his neck. Zack saw the glares he received and gave them an innocent look.

"What?" Zack asked with surprise. "I was nowhere near that truck."

The End

Other books by Holly Copella!
Reviews left on Amazon are appreciated!

"The Battle for Andrea Marie"

A cruise ship attack turns six survivors into overnight celebrities after they take credit for the heroic act of a stowaway who died saving them.

The cruise is just what Jess needed--a bit of harmless fun far from her daily grind. But what begins as a relaxing vacation turns into a desperate fight for her life when terrorists take over the ship and start piling up bodies. Teaming up with a mysterious stowaway, Jess attempts to send out a distress call but knows they cannot wait for help to come. If she or the few remaining passengers have any hope for survival, Jess must act now. The papers dub it "The Battle for *Andrea Marie*," but to Jess it is the moment she fought side-by-side with her enigmatic Romeo, saving the ship--and losing him. She thinks the story ends there, but really, the nightmare is just beginning...

"Insanely Deadly"

When the dead return to life, it's up to an admiral's daughter and a mildly insane, former war hero to save their small town.

Jetta Cross, a Navy Admiral's daughter, is tasked with keeping her father's comrade, a former war hero turned town crazy, grounded in the real world. Capt. John Hunter is still fighting the war in his head, where imaginary dead people are part of his world. When a viral outbreak brings about a zombie uprising, Hunter is left to his own devices. He must resume his role as a one-man commando unit in order to destroy the ravenous undead. With Hunter still fighting his own inner demons as well as the undead, the townspeople fear their zombie neighbors may not be the only threat. Stranded at the island's luxurious resort with a handful of workers, Jetta is forced to live up to her father's reputation and take charge of the deteriorating situation at the hotel. She must wage her own war against the infected before the government declares her hometown a total loss.

"Deadly Institution"

A town recluse suspected of killing his wife teams up with a young woman in order to stop a killer.

After being accused of murdering his wife, Konrad Asher turns his back on the town that once adored him. Ten years later, he still holds his grudge and the title of the most feared man in town. With the reopening of the burned mental institution, where his wife had died, former employees are now murdered one-by-one, throwing suspicion back on Asher. A young local reporter, Jacey, is forced to reveal her long-time friendship with the infamous recluse in order to clear his name not only in the recent murders but to exonerate him in the death of his wife as well. Will Jacey's relationship with Asher invite the killer closer to her? Or is the killer already in her life?

"Screenplays: The Island Collection"
"Jungle Princess", "A.L.F. Resort", "Brighton Island"

Discover how romance and fun in the sun can be downright *chilling*!

"Jungle Princess" is a romantic/thriller that leaves a teenage girl stranded on an island with two male shipmates and a creature of "unknown" origin. She soon discovers the island is home to an abandoned prison with several prisoners roaming free. What really killed over one hundred prisoners? And is it still out there--?

"A.L.F. Resort" is a romantic/thriller set on an island resort with Artificial Life Forms as the main draw. At this resort, all your fantasies come true...until a malfunction removes safety inhibitors on the A.L.F.'s. Zombies, biker gangs, and mobsters run amuck, turning fantasies into nightmares. A young reporter gets more of a story than she anticipates, but will she survive long enough to write the story?

"Brighton Island" is a romantic/thriller set on a private island. When the owner's niece brings her psychic friend to the mansion, his presence awakens the spirits' tortured souls. As the psychic attempts to solve the old murders, the niece is confronted with the possibility that she's next to join the mansion ghosts. Stranded on the island with a crazed killer, her uncle wages his own war to save them. Will his "shock and awe" tactics actually save them or get them killed?

"Reaper of Souls"
A fantasy short story

A young woman must outwit an evil sorcerer in order to save her brother or become one of his minions forever.

Unwilling to believe her brother is dead, Reggie discovers an underhanded deal made with Kahn, a less than ethical sorcerer, who collects humans to serve as slaves in his kingdom. In order to rescue her brother from his horrible fate, she must complete his failed task or be forced to serve Kahn forever. After being transported to his world, Reggie realizes that even if she beats Kahn at his own game, she's at his mercy for him to uphold his end of the deal. All seems lost until Kahn's discontented, self-serving brother, Helsing, arrives. Can Reggie convince Helsing to help her? And at what cost?

"Death Displacement"

A grief-stricken man travels back in time to seek revenge on the woman who murdered his girlfriend but inadvertently falls in love with her.

Kane is about to marry the woman he loves. His life is perfect. A few weeks before the wedding, a vindictive woman from his girlfriend's past mysteriously arrives and kills her. He learns of a traumatic accident that happened five years earlier, which triggers Riley's hatred for his girlfriend. Distraught over his girlfriend's death, Kane uses an antique time machine to travel into the past in order to find and destroy the woman responsible. When he runs into Riley's younger self, he realizes she's not the monster she later becomes, and he can't bring himself to destroy her. With a little help from his oddball friend from the past, they formulate a plan to prevent the accident that sends Riley down her destructive path. Kane's plan backfires when he falls for the younger Riley. His new tortured existence is further complicated when future Riley, his girlfriend's killer, shows up with her own devious agenda that doesn't include him. Will he be able to stop the time ripple, which ultimately ends with his girlfriend's death? Or will future Riley take him out of the timeline forever--

"Dead Village"

After strange happenings isolate a small resort town from the rest of the world, nearly one hundred residents seek refuge at the closed hotel. Only eight survive the night. And that's just the beginning...

One day after the entire population of Fox Ridge Village disappears, a car wreck forces several unsuspecting crash victims to seek help at the closed summer hotel. Within the hotel, they discover the grisly aftermath of a brutal slaughter. Crash victims Vander and Devon, a reluctant clairvoyant, team up to solve the riddle of the "haunted hotel" and the mass hysteria plaguing the remaining survivors. By the time they discover the hotel's secret, they're already drawn into the hysteria. As the body count continues to climb, it's a race to isolate the source and bring everyone back to reality before they kill one another. Will Devon be able to communicate with the traumatized spirits before their fate becomes her own?

"Misfits, Inc."

A seemingly ordinary, young woman meets four misfits who claim she has given them supernatural powers.

While on a business trip to a remote island paradise, a bored secretary, Hailey, has her world turned upside down when her path collides with a psychic freak, Skyler. He attempts to convince her that they had met in his dreams, and she had chosen him as one of her four mystic warriors. After Skyler foresees a woman's death, they discover an unidentified creature has killed one of the guests. They are joined by a lounge pianist and a rich playboy, who also claim they had met her in their dreams. If Skyler's prophecies are genuine, the evil entity controlling the ravenous creatures needs to destroy Hailey to ensure its survival. Reluctantly accepting her fate, Hailey has to locate the last and most powerful of her chosen warriors, The Guardian. Their fate is in doubt when The Guardian turns out to be a self-absorbed, former cat burglar with a bad attitude. Can Hailey turn her company of misfits into an elite team of mystic warriors? Or will The Guardian's secret agenda destroy them all?

"Basement Dwellers"

A viral outbreak at a hospital leaves a mortician, sheriff, and coroner fighting for their lives against a horde of undead and the CDC.

After a massive car wreck leaves several survivors in critical condition at the local hospital, a surgeon uses experimental drugs on his critical patients and accidentally causes a zombie outbreak. When local mortician, Lexx, receives an infected corpse as her client, she becomes stranded in the hospital basement during CDC quarantine along with the local sheriff and the coroner. The infamous surgeon struggles to find a cure for his infectious blunder by using the other survivors as test subjects. Meanwhile, Lexx and the sheriff attempt to locate his missing sister, who's stranded somewhere in the battle zone that once was the emergency room. It's a race against time and the ravenous undead. Can they survive the undead before CDC sanitizes the hospital of all infection?

"Witness Protection"
Also available in audiobook!

After witnessing an execution, a resourceful young woman attempts to disappear while being pursued by a hitman and a handsome federal agent.

A helicopter pilot, Jackie Remus, reluctantly agrees to go on a date with one of her clients, but her date is unexpectedly cut short when she witnesses a man being murdered. After narrowly escaping with her life, she is placed into protective custody. When the safe house is breached, Jackie makes a daring escape from both the hired killers and the handsome FBI agent, who wants to return her to protective custody. With a little help from her sly and crafty friend, Monroe, Jackie is convinced she can disappear until the trial. While on her journey to meet with her friend, she solicits help from a few shady but lovable characters along the way. Although she manages to stay one-step ahead of the hired killers, the federal agent remains in hot pursuit. Will Jackie reach Monroe before she's captured by the FBI and returned to protective custody? Or will the hired killers silence her first?

"Town Darling"

After surviving a brutal attack that claims the lives of those she loves, a young woman seeks revenge on a corrupt town.

Going back home is never easy, but for Casey, it means returning to her corrupt hometown where she barely survived a brutal attack. Accompanied by two family friends, she seeks justice for the night that destroyed her life. Her physical scars are nothing compared to her emotional ones, forcing the local sheriff to believe that the town darling is back for revenge. As the conspiracy for her revenge appears to be leading up to the coveted town fair, the sheriff is determined to stop her from fulfilling her vengeful scheme...but guilt over his role on that fateful night continues to haunt him. Will his desperate need for Casey's forgiveness be his undoing? Or will Casey's desire for revenge destroy them both?

"Unconditional"

A young woman puts her life on hold to care for an unstable, highly skilled combat soldier, who believes someone is trying to kill him.

A botched military coup leaves a team of elite fighters injured with one clinging to life in a coma. When Harlan wakes from his coma, he's left with no memory of his past life. His commander's daughter, Indy, takes it upon herself to care for the fallen war hero. She's challenged with more than just his physical care as she combats with not only his memory loss but also his newly found desire for her. His infatuation with her becomes the least of her worries when he sinks back into his role of a combat soldier. Believing his life is in danger, his fighting skills surface, turning him into an unpredictable and dangerous man. Will his memory return to him before Indy is forced to commit him? Or will he finally find his nemesis, "the coyote", and possibly claim the life of an innocent person?

"Witness Protection 2"
The Return of Whiskey Tango Foxtrot

Believing she holds the clue to millions in missing laundered money, a young woman is placed into the protective care of a former Navy SEAL team.

Feeling sorry for her recently separated co-worker, Leeann invites Wiley to join her and her friends on their night out. Little does she know that finding her co-worker murdered is just the beginning of her nightmare. Leeann unknowingly holds the key to fifty million dollars in potentially laundered mob money. With hired killers pursuing her, the FBI places her into a different kind of protective custody. Former Navy SEAL team Whiskey Tango Foxtrot reunites to keep Leeann alive at their secret hideaway. What should be an easy assignment takes an unscheduled turn when secrets, lies, and betrayal threaten to derail their mission. Is the team prepared for a war on their own doorstep? Will Leeann's misguided trust endanger the lives of those sent to protect her?

"Deadly Institution 2"

When blackmail turns into murder, a young woman finds herself caught in the killer's crosshairs.

The small town of Stony Ridge is no stranger to scandal and persecution of the innocent. When a brutal killing shakes the town's prestigious country club, Jacey McMurray seeks help from a self-proclaimed vigilante, Konrad Asher. As her professional and personal worlds collide, Jacey fears the stress of the country club killings have finally taken their toll on Asher. Can a stressed out vigilante stop the killer before he strikes again?

Coming Soon!
"Awaken the Dead"

ABOUT THE AUTHOR

Holly Copella has been writing since the age of twelve when her frustration at a book's poor plot drove her to author her own story. Over the last decade, she's written a number of screenplays, some of which she's now adapting into novels. Her fascination with zombies and other darker material lends an edge to her writing, which tends to lean toward horror. As a fan of Agatha Christie, she appreciates the craft of a good plot and the importance of creating significant characters.

Hailing from Pennsylvania, Copella lives in the Endless Mountains on a farm with her rescue horses and other animals. In addition to writing and reading fiction, she enjoys riding horses and traveling to Las Vegas and Disney World.

www.ingramcontent.com/pod-product-compliance
Lightning Source LLC
Chambersburg PA
CBHW061131200626
46817CB00016B/798